VALLEY OF STARS

Niels Andersen

First Edition Design Publishing
Sarasota, Florida USA

Valley of Stars
Copyright ©2017 Niels Andersen

ISBN 978-1506-905-35-8 PRINT
ISBN 978-1506-905-36-5 EBOOK

LCCN 2017960689

November 2017

Published and Distributed by
First Edition Design Publishing, Inc.
P.O. Box 20217, Sarasota, FL 34276-3217
www.firsteditiondesignpublishing.com

ALL RIGHTS RESERVED. No part of this book publication may be reproduced, stored in a retrieval system, or transmitted in any form or by any means — electronic, mechanical, photo-copy, recording, or any other — except brief quotation in reviews, without the prior permission of the author or publisher.

This is a work of fiction. Names, characters, businesses, places, events and incidents are either the products of the author's imagination or used in a fictitious manner. Any resemblance to actual persons, living or dead, or actual events is purely coincidental.

Editor: Terrie Scott

To family and friends who have sacrificed so much to protect our freedoms and way of life at home and abroad. And to the thousands who work in our Intelligence agencies, Military, and Law Enforcement who put their lives on the line without fanfare. They are the true heroes who silently fight the marathon that is the war on terror, you deserve infinitely more respect than you get.

Acknowledgments

First, I want to thank my wife who patiently waited for me to finish this first book by asking, "isn't that book done yet?" each time I'd sit down for another rewrite. After quite some time, and a steep learning curve on how to be a better writer and story teller, I can now say... yes, it's done! Michael James, Chris Paige, and Terrie Scott who were gracious enough to open my eyes not only to the publishing process, but gave me some great advice to become a better author. A simple thank you doesn't seem to do justice to the immense impact you had on my writing.

Although this is a fictional story, the struggles by the people of Afghanistan is real. I'd like to thank the Afghan Embassy for helping to connect me with one of their countrymen to ensure I portrayed the lives of ordinary Afghans accurately and with respect. Especially to Hamid, I thoroughly enjoyed our conversations and hope to work with you again in the future. I pray that Afghanistan can find your "Qadir" who can inspire and unify, and bring peace to your troubled nation.

And finally, to the authors of Military/Political thrillers who inspired me like Tom Clancy, Vince Flynn, John LeCarré, and many others, I hope this story does the genre proud. It is a dangerous world we live in, and there are many people who work in complete anonymity to keep us safe. It is these men and women who not only work on the front lines of danger, but who support the tip of spear, who are the real heroes. Unseen and unheralded, I hope this story does justice to the tremendously difficult job you do every day.

Valley of Stars

N. Andersen

CHAPTER 1

Joint Patrol

There's been tension and instability all along the 1500-mile-long Durand Line that forms the disputed border between Afghanistan and Pakistan since the day it was drawn in 1896. Created by a treaty between the British Empire and the Afghan Amir, the Durand Line was an arbitrary barrier for political expediency to fix their respective spheres of influence. But it cut the Pashtun and Baloch tribal regions nearly in half. And like a river dam, pressure for tribal reunification began building as soon as it was drawn, driven today by the Pashtun dominated Taliban. It's a line that seemingly no one but the Afghan and American governments had an interest in protecting.

The area around Khost, in the central Kaitu River valley near the Pakistan border, is one of the most active for Taliban operations. This rib of the Hindu Kush Mountains between Afghanistan and Pakistan is dotted with small villages along its streams and rivers. Engorged with runoff from the melting snows of the high mountains, they feed a fertile patchwork of agriculture.

Cradled in the foothills of the majestic mountains to the north, far from the bustling city centers of Kabul and

Kandahar, the air is crisp and clean. The earthy smells of the countryside get carried on the gently swirling wind currents through the hills and valleys. The smoke and spices from a thousand cooking fires, the herbs and produce from the fields, and the ripening fruit in their groves form an aromatic kaleidoscope of the simple life on the Afghan frontier. But the picturesque serenity of the rugged frontier belies the danger hidden beneath its canvas of soaring landscapes, vibrant colors, and intoxicating smells.

It's a danger that creates a sense of dread that the serenity could rupture at any moment into a deadly fight for survival. It was that feeling of imminent danger that caused the allied patrol to move cautiously along the southeast bank of the Kaitu River about 20 miles east of Khost. This region had gone back and forth between allied and Taliban control for the past two years. Though the Taliban had some supporters in the area, the villagers around here just wanted to be left alone. It was this desire for independence that the commander of the ANA forces, Lieutenant Colonel Abdul Qadir, used for leverage.

With the U.S. drawdown, Qadir, Commander 2nd Battalion, 1st Brigade, 203rd Corps, had to work overtime to prepare his Afghan National Army troops to take over security from the Americans. When he wasn't training with his men, he was tirelessly working to build relations among the tribal and village elders in the region. Like the Anbar Awakening effort, the U.S. used to gain the trust of the Sunni tribes in Iraq, his efforts resulted in things being fairly quiet lately. But quiet is a relative term in the Afghan-Pakistan border region.

A calm, stoic, and religious man, Qadir conversed in the deliberate, indirect, almost circular way common in Afghanistan, very different from the direct manner of the Americans. It was a lyrical, noncommittal style, avoiding definitive statements so as not to offend, but always respectful. He had a knack for understanding people and how to appeal to their cultural sense of honor, loyalty, and religion, the bedrocks of Afghan culture. Qadir knew exactly when to use his authority and when to defer to the local elders. He not only listened to them but when he made a promise, he always kept it.

It wasn't just deference to the elders, but Qadir's way of weaving their common religion, traditions, and rich tribal history into everything he did, and said, to gain their trust and cooperation. He understood that every action he and his men took would be watched, analyzed, and judged against the backdrop of local norms not national. So, he demanded that his men adhere to the fundamental tenets of Islam in all interactions with friend or foe. None of this was lost on the villagers Qadir encountered. It solidified cooperation from village elders against the Taliban and had nearly shut down their supply lines through this part of Afghanistan.

Qadir was an imposing figure for an Afghan. At five foot ten and 180 pounds, he was taller than most Afghan men but had a powerful, muscular frame that was obvious under the digital camouflage of his uniform and body armor. With short brown hair, full beard, penetrating eyes, high cheekbones, and angular face, he emanated confidence and authority. He not only looked powerful, but sounded it too. In battle, his deep baritone voice thundered over the din of gunfire with clear, crisp commands. And unlike the indirect communication style he used in conversation, when the lives of his men were involved, Qadir was short and direct. His commands were issued with such authority that they were obeyed without hesitation.

Qadir had fought the Taliban for most of his life. He was a unique commander in the ANA, a Shia Muslim from the mountainous Hazarajat region who'd fought with the Northern Alliance during the civil war. The minority Shia Hazaras not only suffered from discrimination from the much larger Afghan tribes but from the 1400-year-old schism between the sects of Islam. The more radical Sunni elements believe Shia's to be apostates deserving only death. Yet here was Qadir, not only commanding respect from his Sunni men but absolute devotion.

His men trusted him, loved him, and would gladly die a thousand deaths if he commanded it. Quite an accomplishment, considering several under his command were former Taliban fighters, including his most trusted senior NCO. He had a charisma, not the boastful, gregarious preacher type, but a patient, quiet confidence with a deference to the common tenets of Islam and tradition that drew men to him.

Through Qadir's humility, dedication, actions, and words, he changed people's perceptions of both Islam and Afghanistan. He offered them a perspective they had never heard nor imagined, thereby turning enemies into friends, and friends into followers. It was this dedication to and from his men, Pashtun, Uzbek, Tajik, Turkomen, and Hazara alike that made him the only ANA officer who never had an Afghan soldier attack his American counterparts -- a green-on-blue incident, as the Americans called it. And within the ANA, his units came closest to matching the Americans in fighting skills, tenacity, and effectiveness.

The current mission was to check on several villages in a region where clashes with the Taliban were common. Today would take them to Zakar Khel, the last of the villages that straddled the river close to the border. The joint patrol had been out for several days, slowly making their way up the river. So far, they had not encountered any enemy resistance, but every man in the formation knew it could change in an instant.

The patrol had left Kazeh Kalay an hour earlier and was moving along a dirt and gravel road that was slightly more than a cart path on the east side of the river. Qadir was soaking up the warm mid-morning sunshine. The sights and sounds of the villagers working the groves of fruits, nuts, and vegetables, the children's aerial battles with their fighting kites and smells of the village lingered in his memory. He thought fondly of the odors of the kabobs, curry, and vegetables cooking. The smell of Cumin, Turmeric, Cardamom, Cloves, and Nutmeg, common in the milder seasoning of the Afghan cuisine over their Indian cousins, reminded him of his own home and childhood.

"Sergeant Hassam," Qadir called to his command sergeant.

Hassam jogged up next to his commander. He was about the same height but was wiry and muscular with a jet-black beard and brown eyes that looked like dark chocolate. "Yes sir," he acknowledged.

"This patrol's been quiet," Qadir said as he scanned the rolling hills rising from the river.

"Perhaps a little too quiet, sir," Hassam replied.

VALLEY OF STARS

"Agreed, that's what I think as well. Pass it along for everyone to pay attention to any detail that looks out of place. We're near the end and can't afford to have the men's minds somewhere else," Qadir ordered, knowing he was daydreaming only moments before.

It was easy for everyone in the patrol to get lost in the nostalgia of the countryside and forget about the danger. But while the Americans would spend a year here then go home, many of Qadir's men had been fighting most of their adult lives. The mind-numbing monotony of these patrols, broken only by the adrenaline rush of battle, meant that every soldier was in a constant state of heightened tension. A tension immediately felt by anyone who's ever had to constantly be on guard to react to an unexpected attack. After a kilometer and a half, the river bent northward as a ridge rose to their left in the shape of a fishhook.

Abruptly Qadir raised his fist over his head, "Halt," he ordered.

His voice echoed off the wall of the ridge rising to his left. Something was wrong; he could feel it before he saw it. Across the river, Qadir could see the fields of Kazeh Tala where two men from that village had knelt to pray facing the column of soldiers. The squad leaders immediately signaled each of their squads to take up defensive positions and await orders. The sudden stop caused the tension in the entire patrol to explode into anticipation. The resulting surge in adrenaline elevated the senses of everyone in the formation.

The American commander and his translator quickly moved up alongside Qadir, "What's the situation?" asked Major Watkins.

Major Douglas Booker Watkins, Operations Officer U.S. 2nd Battalion, 27th Infantry Regiment was an equally imposing figure. At six foot five and 250 pounds of muscle, he was a former tight end for the US Military Academy at West Point. Watkins came from a long line of decorated servicemen, from his great-grandfather who fought with the Harlem Hellfighter Negro brigade in World War I to his father in Vietnam. With two tours in the violent Anbar province of Iraq and three in Afghanistan, Watkins was the most experienced officer in theater as well as the most decorated. Having spent the past few months working closely with Qadir, the two had built a strong bond.

"No Kites, no field workers, two men praying on the river bank, wrong direction, wrong time," Qadir replied.

Qadir spoke three languages; his native Dari, Pashto, and English. He had learned English when he went to India for training at their officers' academy and enjoyed talking with Watkins about military history and tactics. But he wanted the translator at times like this when it was crucial to get the information right; men's lives were at stake, and there was no room for misunderstandings.

Watkins understood his meaning immediately; it was too quiet, and subtle details were out of place. He spent long hours in the theater of operations studying his enemy closely to better understand them and predict their actions. He knew the routine almost as well as a native. Islam requires prayer 5 times a day that are regimented at strict times, facing Mecca to the west, and a prayer rug. The morning prayers were already done, and it wasn't time for the next ones. Plus, the two men were praying to the North, away from Mecca, on dirt. They were being watched, and this was a warning.

* * *

Majeed saw the column come to a halt and take up defensive positions. From his location on top of the ridge, he could see both the approaching allied patrol along the river and Zakar Khel. Armed with an Iraqi Al-Kadesih sniper rifle, he could scan the terrain and provide fire support for the Taliban force in the village and the fields just outside of it.

His brothers in the village were depending on him for information on the movements of the approaching patrol. He didn't know what made the commander stop the column, but it caused him concern. The trap had been carefully set. The villagers had been rounded up when a Taliban spy reported that the coalition was going to check out Zakar Khel. Some of his fellow fighters would be hiding in the pomegranate groves outside the village walls while the rest would be inside. To draw in the unsuspecting allied patrol some village women would be forced to cook to make it appear normal, or their children would be executed.

"Movement from the rear," the spotter whispered.

VALLEY OF STARS

Just before his spotter spoke, Majeed had already noticed the movement of the American and another man coming up from the rear element to someone in the middle of the formation.

"I see them," replied Majeed.

He carefully watched the meeting between the three men and knew he had found both commanders and their interpreter. They pulled out some papers Majeed assumed was a map and spoke for several minutes. Focusing on the two men talking, he knew who his first target would be.

"Signal the village, the patrol is approaching," Majeed said with a satisfying smile.

He'd been with the Taliban for the past ten years and grown up not far from here, so he knew this area like the back of his hand. The coalition had been working hard to improve relations with the village elders for the past several months and had an ANA commander who was said to be extremely influential. If it was Allah's will, this would be that commander and Majeed would be the sword to strike him down.

Majeed saw the meeting break up and the American commander jog back to his formation. He huddled with his squad leaders giving orders and the ANA commander did the same with his lieutenants. Obviously, the American pig gave his lap dog instructions, and Majeed laughed at the thought of the ANA leading this mission. They had fought many battles with these joint patrols and it was usually the Americans who did the fighting, due to tentative or inept ANA troops.

But these ANA troops looked confident, not jittery like so many others; likely just false bravado of those who hadn't yet felt the sting of Taliban fighters. Majeed was sure his own commander had all possibilities covered. He didn't know all the details, he was the eyes, but he knew where everyone was located so he could support them with long range sniper fire if needed. And if this was that ANA commander he had heard about, he would be the battle's first casualty.

The American was giving hand signals as the rest of the formation started moving again. Majeed and his spotter started scanning the column to get an accurate count when the front of the column started yelling and motioning vigorously at something. Both men spun their focus toward the front of the column and spotted two men across the river who slowly turned to walk back to their village. The column was less than a kilometer from Zakar Khel, but before the two Taliban fighters could swing their scopes back to get a count of the enemy troops, they had moved to the base of the ridge and had begun to disappear around the hook in the river.

Chapter 2

Zakar Khel

The dirt road leading into Zakar Khel ran north from the point of the hooked ridge into the village. The village was located between the Kaitu River to the East and the ridge to the West. Just past the point of the ridgeline was a flat field where lush groves of mature pomegranate trees lined both sides of the narrow road all the way to the village entrance. Their striking orange-red blossoms against the dark green foliage looked like a sunset explosion in the warm mid-morning sun. The petals, used in a sweet tea mix, gave off a sweet aroma that enveloped the orchard and the village.

Pomegranates had become the chosen cash crop in the region due to the rich, fertile soil, and plentiful water from the mountains' winter runoff. While opium poppies were still grown in the province, the villagers of Zakar Khel sent their sweet, luscious red fruit to the juice factories in Kabul. The Pomegranates brought in 35% more revenue per acre than poppies, which gave the village inhabitants a relatively comfortable life. Revenues the Taliban were more than happy to tax in the areas under their control.

Zakar Khel was split into two opposing U-shaped compounds, with about 30 meters between open end sections forming a cross in the road at the village center. Rafiq Al-Youssef, the Taliban commander of this mission, saw the mirror flash signal from the over-watch team confirming the approach of the enemy patrol. He was quietly pleased with himself and praised Allah for the battle about to be waged. He had his men prepared, positioned both inside and outside the village. With the harvest still months away, the Taliban commander knew he had to position some of his men in the orchard to work the trees and draw in the unsuspecting allied patrol.

Satisfied he had planned for all contingencies, Rafiq knew it would be a defining battle for him, and the Taliban. The village had been a refuge for his men until a few months ago, when several supply patrols through this area failed to return. It wasn't so much that the villagers around here liked the Taliban, but they feared what would happen if they didn't cooperate. Though the Taliban had some supporters in this region, the villages around here were fiercely independent.

Rafiq's short, thin stature concealed his toughness. A long scar angled from just above his left eye down to his left ear lobe that made his eye droop slightly giving him a menacing look. After 10 years rising through the Taliban ranks, he was given command of his own troops two years ago. The commanders before Rafiq used torture and fear to keep the villagers along this supply route in line but those tactics made gathering supplies and money extremely difficult and dangerous.

So Rafiq tried to use a slightly less brutal approach in his dealings with the village elders which had shown progress until a few months ago. Something changed and the villagers had betrayed that kindness through their cooperation with the ANA, compromising this crucial supply route. He must remind them that collaborating with the infidel Americans was an insult to Islam. The movement's leaders needed this supply route to remain open so they could continue operations in the Kandahar region without interruption.

"Remember, we've trained well for this so just follow the plan. Allah's with us and your brothers are waiting for us in paradise," Rafiq said to his men along the walls.

The plan was meticulous and based on a battle his uncle fought in during the Russian occupation. His uncle was part of a Mujahedeen force that used the tactic over thirty years before in one of the later battles in that war. It was a devastating defeat for the Russians as nearly an entire Company of troops had been wiped out. His uncle was convinced that it ultimately caused them to abandon Afghanistan. Now a new enemy would feel the effectiveness of the tactic, and that weakling of a U.S. president would withdraw even sooner than planned, just as those pigs the Russians had.

Rafiq had the families of the village elders in a house in the back of the village. If the elders didn't do as he instructed, they would be executed. His men were in the orchard, some working but most positioned for attack. He had a sniper team on top of the hill providing over-watch and enemy movement information. The rest were inside the village compound behind the entrance walls and within several buildings. Rafiq knew that the ANA would be in the lead, in keeping with the Americans' feeble attempt to make it look like the Afghan government was in charge. The elders would go to the village entrance and welcome the troops into the village, and the trap would be sprung.

The sniper team would begin the battle by killing the ANA commander and, if lucky, the American commander as well. At the sound of the sniper shot, Rafiq's men in the orchard would catch the trailing Americans in a deadly crossfire, forcing the ANA troops to turn to face an enemy from behind. Most of these men would likely die, but that was Allah's will. Moments later his men inside the village would open fire, cutting down the front elements of ANA.

The less disciplined ANA would likely run, they usually did, but the surviving Americans would regroup quickly and attack methodically. Once the remaining Americans engaged, his surviving men in the orchard would fall back into the village. The Taliban troops along the walls would hit them with another volley and retreat, drawing them deeper into the village. As the Americans moved into the kill box just inside the village walls, Rafiq would complete the entrapment and kill the infidels.

He had no need for American prisoners, so they would be executed. If they caught any ANA, he would execute all the non-Pashtuns and try to turn the others. It would make the perfect video to recruit fighters and prove that the Americans can be defeated. He also would execute the chief's eldest son as punishment for cooperating with the Americans and the illegitimate government forces. This betrayal had to be dealt with firmly to make sure the villagers never make that mistake again.

Even if it were Allah's will that he and his men fail in their mission, he would kill as many of the enemy as possible, which would still be a victory for the Taliban. Rafiq did not believe it was his time to die, but just because they had Allah on their side, there was no sense in taking any chances. He had a few other surprises up his sleeve.

Rafiq smiled as he saw the ANA troops coming up the road first, just as he'd anticipated. They were moving slowly but deliberately, and it didn't appear that they suspected anything wrong. Ever since Majeed had alerted him of the oncoming patrol, he and his men had been flush with nervous anticipation as they prepared for battle. Rafiq watched the Taliban on the wall check and recheck their weapons, trying to stay calm. The men in the field had gotten as low to the ground as they could; the decoys in the fields kept glancing over their shoulders at the slowly moving enemy column.

"Steady everyone, let them come in," Rafiq repeated to calm the nerves of his men, urging them to be patient and bring the enemy into the trap.

He gave a hand signal to the leader of the men in the orchard to prepare, the battle was only minutes from starting. Rafiq said a prayer under his breath. Despite being a battle-hardened commander, even he could feel his heart nearly beating out of his chest with each approaching step the enemy took.

* * *

From his position above the village, Majeed scanned the scene unfolding below. The decoy men in the orchard looked nervous, but he hoped the oncoming patrol wouldn't notice. He fixed the positions of the Taliban in the orchard and the shooters at the walls. He began tracking the allied formation as they emerged from the protection of the hook in the ridgeline with the ANA in front, just as the commander predicted. Soon Rafiq would send out the elders to wave them in and assure them all was safe.

Majeed was upset with himself for not getting an accurate count of the enemy troops when they stopped on the west side of the hill. He had estimated at the time it was about a two or three platoon sized force, maybe 80-100 troopers split between Americans and ANA. He knew the Americans didn't trust the ANA to operate on their own, so always sent a larger force than needed, "just for support." The reality was that the Americans usually did most of the fighting in these "joint" patrols anyway.

The Americans would be behind the ANA, and it was up to Majeed to pick the right moment to initiate the attack. Knowing the Americans monitored the radios, he would start the operation by killing the ANA commander and then the American. Like the enemy says, "cut off the head of the snake." Majeed could feel the adrenaline starting to rise so he forced himself to slow his breathing and spoke a prayer to help calm himself. He smiled at the irony that the man who trained him to be a sniper was trained by the very same American pigs he was about to help kill.

As the ANA troops emerged Majeed started counting. Maybe 35-40, looked to be about four squads, but he wasn't exactly sure. This development caused a moment of confusion, it seemed like there were more when they stopped but it didn't change the plan. The ANA moved along the road between the groves of trees and Majeed started to get anxious with anticipation.

The Americans began to emerge from under the ridge, two squads. Something was wrong; now he knew there were fewer Americans, but he couldn't see them and hadn't seen any break off from the main force earlier. Majeed assumed that some of the American troops were being held in reserve out of sight from the village to elevate the status of this ANA commander. There wasn't time to go searching for them and satisfied with his own explanation for the reduced patrol strength, he shifted his sight through the scope of his rifle to find the two commanders. After he started the attack, it would be his job to hold off the trailing troops to allow his brothers to complete the ambush.

Majeed zeroed in on the ANA commander moving slowly in the center of the formation. He put his crosshairs on the

ANA commander's chest as his spotter whispered target distance and wind direction. The small piece of ribbon Majeed had set out in the orchard for wind reference danced in the slight breeze coming off the river. He expertly adjusted for Qadir's walking speed and the thermals coming off the ground from the sun that would affect the bullet's trajectory. The sniper moved his aim to the target's head, slowed his breathing and heart rate, and slowly fingered the trigger of his rifle.

* * *

Rafiq was proud of his plan. With Majeed holding the enemy from moving to the sides of the compound, and some well-placed IED's, he could funnel the enemy into the kill box. Once Majeed killed their commander, Rafiq estimated that the incoming ANA troops would panic and move recklessly toward the village after he detonated the mines. His men would then kill everything that moved.

The sound of two shots rang out across the pomegranate orchard before Rafiq could send out the elders. It surprised Rafiq and caused him to hesitate briefly trying to figure out why Majeed had started the action so soon. As the sound of the first shot echoed from the hill, Rafiq's men in the orchard popped out from their cover and began firing on the enemy patrol. He was annoyed but he didn't have time to get any answers, the battle was started and he had work to do.

"Fire!" Rafiq shouted to the Taliban on the wall.

A wall of flames erupted from the village as the roar of two dozen AK-47's rang out with their rapid-fire bullets going supersonic as they emerged from the barrels of the Taliban rifles. The red-orange tails from the rocket propelled grenades arced out like fingers of death with deafening explosions splintering pomegranate trees into thousands of high speed wooden daggers. Rafiq's men fired wildly, sweeping back and forth trying to lay down a deadly curtain of lead into the oncoming enemy. But the enemy was not responding as he anticipated.

As Rafiq's fighters emerged from the Pomegranate groves, they were cut down by the trailing Americans who'd somehow moved much faster than he predicted to counter the attack. And after the first volley from the village, the leading ANA element just seemed to vanish into the trees.

To Rafiq, the battle had an inauspicious start and forced his instincts to take over. He ordered his men to rake the fields with fire but just as he got the order out, the walls on either side of the entrance to the village exploded.

The dual blasts against the walls caused panic in Rafiq's men. Thousands of tiny, white hot shards of stone ripped through the ranks of the Taliban, instantly vaporizing three men and tearing apart five others. The acrid smoke of the explosive gas from the rockets, mixed with the odor of seared flesh, and the fine dust created from the disintegrating walls stung the eyes of the defenders. Combined with the dizzying concussion of the explosions, the screams of the wounded, and the roar of automatic weapons, the survivors struggled to return fire. The unexpected ferocity of the fight made even the most battle-hardened fighter fire in a wild panic along the walls. Praying that with Allah's help, the sheer volume of lead being fired would hit their enemy targets.

With his ears still ringing from the explosions, Rafiq ordered the IEDs detonated outside the wall. The improvised mines should focus the attacking force toward a frontal assault on his position. He had lost nearly 30 men killed or wounded in the opening salvo, not exactly how he planned it, but he still had another 40 in the village. Though the men in the field were likely lost anyway, the enemy countered against the city walls harder than he expected given the surprise attack, but he felt that his men had inflicted heavy casualties on the enemy just the same.

Rafiq could barely hear the radio transmission from Majeed's spotter, he was a good man but a bit excitable. The roar of the gunfire from both sides made him difficult to understand, but he reported that the ANA troops were hung up in the orchard, moving slower than anticipated, and the enemy had taken heavy losses. Rafiq ordered his men to fire one more volley and then fall back to their next positions. He figured as the direct fire from the village decreased, the enemy would move forward quicker thinking they had the Taliban on the run, straight into the kill box.

***

Staff Sergeant Edelman had to use every bit of his training to focus on his targets after the mad scramble to get into position. His lungs struggled to bring in oxygen and his muscles burned with the lactic acid from the strain of exertion to get here. Watkins had split off from the main force with two squads and a heavy weapons team when Qadir made his distraction at the river. They had looped around the northwest side of the ridge to come at the village from the west and hit it from the rear. Edelman had no idea why the commanders thought there was an ambush ahead, or what the enemy was planning, he had his orders. He'd been on enough of these patrols to know, they were right most of the time.

It was a tough climb. Going over a 200 foot rise without tipping the enemy was a big challenge. Even more so for Edelman who had to haul his 16-pound M110 sniper rifle, 10 pounds of ammunition, and the same 90-100 pounds of gear as the rest of the squad at a dead run uphill. His job was to neutralize the suspected Taliban sniper team and provide over-watch for the allied operation. He knew the rest of the patrol would have to slow down to give Watkins time to move. Edelman also knew if he failed, the whole operation was threatened, and a lot of good men would lose their lives today.

As an experienced shooter, Edelman figured the enemy sniper would be located where he could monitor the patrol along the river then again on the approach to Zakar Khel. He looked at the maps with Watkins and selected a perch where he could find and clear the enemy, then briefed his spotter and the interpreter. When the small attack group started their ascent, the three men had raced ahead to the chosen location.

The American sniper team was positioned above the village compound on a small rise along the spine of the ridge. After crawling to a small grouping of boulders that gave them cover, they scanned the ridge and found the Taliban shooter within a couple minutes, exactly where Edelman thought he would be. His spotter scanned the approach to the village, found the positions of the Taliban in the groves on either side of the road confirming the commanders' suspicions, and warned the column. It was uncanny how the commanders had predicted the tactic the enemy would use. The allied attackers would need to move fast once the first shots were taken.

Edelman's muscles were on fire, and his heart was pounding in a desperate race to get oxygen to them. Add to that the raging adrenaline from the anticipation of the oncoming battle, it would make even elite athletes shake. The slightest tremor in his hand could be the difference between success and failure which meant he had to use every calming technique learned from hours of strenuous training to slow his metabolism.

Edelman's spotter keyed his mic and radioed, "Ready, ready."

As Edelman lay in his firing position, he saw his target dialing corrections into his rifle and preparing to fire. He willed his heart to slow down and focused on his target. It was like the whole world disappeared except for Edelman and his scope. He took in a breath, ignoring the burning pain in his body, let it out slightly, and then holding it briefly, he gently pulled the trigger of his rifle between heartbeats. Three hundred meters away his target's head jerked to the side, and a spray of red exploded away from the shooter.

Just as the first shot was taken, Edelman's spotter keyed his mic and quickly radioed, "Go, go, go!"

Edelman chambered another round and took down the Taliban spotter as all hell broke loose in the orchard below. Two shots, two targets, and a good day any way you look at it he thought. But he didn't have time to savor the success as he and his small sniper team were up and moving to their over-watch position. The very same position as the two men he just killed.

From their watch position the American sniper team could monitor the deadly ballet being performed in the orchards below. The ANA and American troops were moving at almost the same time as the shots echoed across the orchard. The American squads quickly pivoted outward, moving into a slight backwards slanted formation in the fields on either side of the path. Just as the Taliban troops popped out of cover, the Americans opened fire on them almost before any of the enemy could get off a shot.

The trailing arm of the formation on each side quickly started moving toward the enemy, swinging like a door on a hinge, and caught the surviving enemy in a deathtrap of enfilading crossfire, raining death down their line. Edelman killed three more targets from his position, and within seconds the flanks of the formation were secured.

"Orchards clear, move, move, move," Edelman's spotter called on the encrypted radio, and the information was echoed to the ANA troops by the Translator as the two American formations swung forward and advanced at an all-out sprint toward the corners of the village.

The ANA troops moved swiftly into the groves on both sides of the road at the first "go" call on the radio. As the fire on the flanks erupted, Qadir shifted his men into an echelon formation with three staggered parallel rows of troops on either side of the road leading into town. A few of his men went down with the first volley from the walls of the village, but they maintained their formations and immediately returned fire. Edelman could see them moving forward very quickly, angling toward the outside corners of the compound and keeping in the groves for cover. Each squad laying down covering fire as another moved.

Each echelon force had a heavy weapons team who fired rocket propelled anti-tank weapons against the walls on both sides of the village entrance. The anti-tank missiles opened gaping holes as the heat and shockwave from the thunderous explosions could be felt by Edelman on the ridge. He knew that anyone on the other side was either dead or wished they were. The shock would stun the enemy, but not for long.

Edelman turned to the Interpreter, "Take that Taliban radio, call out faulty positions in an excited voice. We need to give our guys more time."

He hoped the adrenaline of the enemy would slow the recognition of the Interpreter's voice and give the allied forces a few precious moments' advantage. The anti-tank rounds seemed to cause a lot of confusion with the enemy and Edelman could see that Qadir's men were nearly at the walls when the Taliban commander detonated the IEDs behind them. Obviously, the enemy had expected the ANA to make a very different approach when they had initiated the ambush, but didn't seem to know that their eyes had been eliminated yet.

Edelman patted the Interpreter on the head, "Nice work Haj, I don't think they know where our guys are!"

Two more anti-tank rounds hit the walls, exploding them into a deadly eruption of stone missiles, expanding the huge breech holes. The Americans on either side had already passed the corners of the outside walls when the IEDs went off behind them and the second rockets hit the walls of the village. Fifty meters past the front corners of the compound, the two American elements stopped. Both flanks of ANA troops had moved away from the center road at a run but focused their fire at the walls either side of the entrance the village.

Edelman watched the ANA rifle squad and heavy weapons team move quickly along a cutout that was hidden from the view of the village, just below the ridgeline. The end of the cutout was in line with the opening between the compounds, and that's where the ANA M-249 Squad Automatic Weapon (SAW) team set up. From there they could swing right and left into the village through the gap between the two sections of the compound to support the attacking forces.

"Taliban falling back into the main section of the village, taking up positions in the buildings on either side of the road through the center of the compound. Roll outside in, SAW team in position," Edelman's spotter reported. The American sniper killed two more retreating Taliban fighters adding more kills to his day's work.

* * *

The sounds of battle reached Watkins as his force was about to emerge from the tributary coming down from the ridge. He and his troops only had a minute to catch their breath and steady their nerves. No matter their discipline and training, close quarters firefights are dangerous, messy, unpredictable affairs. The Taliban would often fire recklessly at anything that moved, sometimes even hitting their own fighters. But the rules of engagement were different for the Americans. The U.S. soldiers were more disciplined in returning fire as they tried hard to avoid hitting civilians. But they wouldn't risk the lives of their fellow soldiers regardless of the potential for collateral damage.

The rules of engagement would slow down the process of clearing the village. Even though everyone hated them, they were critical to maintain good relations with the locals. If

Qadir was right, then the Taliban will have disarmed all the men except their own so anyone with a weapon was to be neutralized. Watkins knew it was a risk, but given the sounds coming from the front of the village, it was justified.

Qadir radioed that the main attack force had opened some holes in the front wall and were positioned to enter the village as Watkins finally got to the back wall of the compound. Watkins reported that he was in position and Qadir ordered the final assault to begin. Watkins' men hit the back wall with anti-tank rounds and moved through the massive holes into the back of the compound without any resistance. Clearly the Taliban commander never expected an assault from the rear, catching the enemy totally by surprise.

Once inside the wall, Watkins heard the SAW from the ridgeline open fire on the houses on either side of the opening between the compounds. The fast staccato of its rounds exploding from its muzzle at one and a half times the speed of sound, roared like a hundred jackhammers. Its recoil pulsating through the body of the gunner, it was fired in short bursts to maintain control and accuracy, maximizing the effectiveness of its killing power.

The heavy machine gun was devastating from close range as the 5.56 mm rounds and high rate of fire could slice through the mud walls of the village houses. The energy of the impact on the walls of the houses made small holes on the outside, but burst into basketball sized craters on the inside, showering the defenders with a deadly blast of rock and metal fragments. If they hit a man, it could literally cut him in half, or blow off an arm or leg. Either way, the target was going to be out of action even if they survived.

The two rifle squads on either side of the center openings used the covering fire from the SAW team to enter the village and hit the houses in the back compound and protect Watkins entrance through the back wall. The squads would secure the middle of the village so the enemy had nowhere to move. But the enemy's confusion would last only so long. Once the fire teams engaged the main Taliban force from behind, it would draw some of their fighters away from the front wall, weakening its defense for Qadir's frontal assault. But the two squads would be vulnerable until then.

The teams reported taking heavy fire almost immediately. They had to dodge incoming RPG's with their distinctive whistle and smoke trail arching out behind them before erupting in a deafening cloud of fire, shrapnel, and smoke. After a few minutes of intense fighting, the two squads had secured defensive positions behind the main Taliban force and began engaging them with deadly accuracy.

Using the chaos caused by the multiple points of attack, Watkins' troops moved quickly to the largest house at the back of the compound. Through a side window they saw the families of the elders being held at gunpoint. The two Taliban fighters inside were initially stunned by the powerful blast from the rockets hitting the wall and seemed confused about the battle raging outside. Watkins gave a hand signal to the demolition team to breach the door.

The breach team stuck shaped charges at the hinges and lock, and blew the door inward. Two soldiers tossed in concussion grenades as the panicked Taliban fighters inside frantically tried to return fire. The blinding flash and thunderous clap hit the occupants of the house like a bolt of lightning. The resulting pressure wave pounded their ears and bodies, knocking the guards to the ground. The dizzying blast disoriented the guards long enough for two other soldiers to move quickly through the shattered doorway. They dropped to one knee and killed each Taliban with two rounds to the chest and one to the head. The families of the elders were now secured.

"Cobal this is Bulldog, back compound secure, anvil set, moving forward," Watkins radioed to Qadir to report the status at the back of the village.

The Taliban's escape route was now blocked. He would be the anvil and Qadir the hammer. Qadir's men would clear houses on both sides of the compound, pushing the enemy to the rear right into Watkins troops. The Taliban were boxed in with nowhere to move.

* * *

The Taliban were already pulling back when two more rockets hit the walls near the positions Rafiq's men had just left. Despite the rough start, he thought his plan was progressing though his losses were much heavier than expected. These ANA troops were better than others he had fought. Good thing Majeed had killed their commander.

Rafiq began repositioning the troops from the wall into their secondary fighting positions along the road through the village for the second phase of the trap. Suddenly explosions rocked the back of the compound and the distinct sound of a heavy machine gun fire erupted on Rafiq's flanks behind him. Fear gripped the Taliban fighters at the back of the village as their brothers who were poised to engage an enemy in front of them, were suddenly cut down from behind. Discipline among the fighters quickly broke down as men scrambled to find any kind of cover they could.

As Taliban spun around to engage an unseen enemy, they began shooting their rifles and RPG's indiscriminately in the directions of the incoming fire. Terrified fighters, desperately trying to escape what seemed like a death trap, fell after just a few steps. The shouts of their leaders attempting to maintain control, blinding flashes, flying shrapnel, dust, smoke, and the screams of the wounded engulfed the village in a cacophony of sounds, sights, and smells that overwhelmed the defending fighters.

Rafiq was paralyzed with confusion. He expected the assault to come from the front, but now there was fire coming in from all sides. Where had they come from? He hesitated, frantically trying to figure out where the most immediate threat was located. Finally, he ordered his fighters to fire at the entrance and the holes the enemy had made in the walls. He started screaming into the radio for Majeed to give him an update on the positions of the enemy...and was met with silence.

Rafiq's men were fighting an enemy they couldn't see and now had no idea where they were. He was blind and surrounded, the plan had failed. After a few moments of despair over his failure, Rafiq resigned himself to become a martyr. It was an odd feeling for him, everything became crystal clear even though he knew in the end, he was about to die. An odd calm came over him, and he was immediately flooded with confidence in his actions. He ordered his men to do a fighting withdrawal to a house in the center of the village. It was time for his last resort, praise Allah.

* * *

VALLEY OF STARS

The sudden attack coming from behind the Taliban gave Qadir the brief opening he needed to move his men into the village. As the gunfire toward his position subsided, his men launched grenades at the two closest houses and threw smoke canisters into the village. Soldiers moved through the openings in the walls while the heavy weapons squad raked the houses with covering fire. The large caliber rounds from the weapons shattered the doors and windows, turning them into hundreds of needle sharp lances ripping into the men using them for cover.

Although the enemy was clearly stunned by the attack from their rear, they recovered and started pounding the front of the village and the openings in the wall with gunfire. But they blindly fired their weapons instead of aiming, going through ammunition like water. Despite that, the defenders had the advantage of focusing on a small area where the ANA troops would have to move through. The ANA lost several men during the breach, but Qadir was proud of their execution of a near perfect attack.

He knew his men still had much to learn from the Americans, but they had overcome their fear and used the confidence built from months of mind-numbing drilling to prepare themselves for a battle like this. While many had been through skirmishes before, this was larger than any battle they had fought before. And for those who were once Taliban now following Qadir, it showed the effectiveness of the training and discipline he demanded.

Once inside, Qadir split his force and carefully moved to the outside houses on both sides of the village to clear from the outside in. They methodically moved from front to back, rolling up the Taliban fighters on both flanks. With the Americans holding the back of the village, the two fronts of the allied force slowly moved toward each other. Closing like the jaws of a vice, they crushed everything between them. The front compound was virtually cleared after about an hour of intense door to door fighting when the firing ceased from the Taliban now holed up in a few houses at the center of the village.

Qadir positioned his men surrounding the remaining enemy to ensure the Taliban's final surrender. Suddenly a woman came running out holding a young boy screaming for help, crying that he'd been shot and begging the soldiers not to shoot. The boy was crying and looking around.

"Halt," Qadir shouted, but she didn't.

She was 20 meters away, "Stop now!" he ordered again.

When she didn't stop, he shot her. The woman's head jerked backwards from the impact of the bullet spraying the boy's face with blood. Her body went limp, dropping the boy to the ground, then falling face first into the dirt. As she lay there in the center of the compound, the boy sat there stunned and crying. A moment later the house she had come from exploded with a thunderous roar.

Qadir's men rounded up the remaining Taliban prisoners who surrendered after the house with their commander exploded. They swiftly moved the boy away from the dead woman in the road as Qadir called for an explosives disposal team and cordoned off the area around her. The villagers were moved to the back compound away from potential danger when Watkins met up with Qadir. Pointing at the woman, Qadir knew the question Watkins was asking.

"She had a clenched fist holding the boy, and he was struggling with her. When we moved him, you could clearly see the detonator in her hand. She has an explosive vest on and had she gotten just five meters closer, she could have taken out dozens of my men," Qadir stated matter-of-factly.

"Then a good thing you took her down Colonel, seems you've created quite a few martyrs in paradise sir," replied Watkins.

"No Major, not martyrs, at least not for Islam. Many of these men are simply lost souls who have been deluded by leaders who twist the Prophet's words for their own power. Allah will have a special place for them, and it won't be paradise," answered Qadir coldly.

The enemy had lost over thirty-two dead, nineteen wounded, and fifteen POW; though the number of dead couldn't be completely determined as some of those in the house that exploded had little to no remains to be collected. Qadir had nine dead, ten wounded, and Watkins lost two dead and six wounded. As Qadir and Watkins met with the elders, they found out that three villagers had been killed but the boy whom Qadir saved, was the chief's son. Qadir had the ANA and Taliban dead brought to a large house that was relatively undamaged to prepare them in the Muslim tradition. Although they were the enemy, they were still brothers of Islam, and he knew that the villagers were watching every move he and his men made.

Watkins ordered the Americans to provide security until the support trucks arrived from Khost to remove the dead and prisoners. He understood from working with Qadir the past few months that this small act of deference was critical in building trust with the villagers and confidence that the ANA could provide security for them. Helicopters landed in the fields by the river outside of the village to transport the injured to the U.S. operating base for medical treatment.

Qadir knew that the villagers often resented both sides of the conflict because of the heavy hand each one used. Given the violence of the battle, he had tried to minimize the number of civilians caught in the cross-fire but would not allow his troops to take unnecessary risks. They were fortunate with the low number of civilians killed, mainly because the Taliban commander wanted to hold many of them as a group to force the elder's hand, and this gave him an opening.

Qadir apologized to the elders for the damage done to their village. He insisted on having his men remain to help the villagers clean up and make some temporary repairs. He pulled out a package of tea and offered it to the elders. He promised he would return with trucks and equipment to help them rebuild if they would honor him with their permission to do so. Asking permission of the elders cemented the impression that he deferred to their authority in their village, and it had the desired effect.

The village chief asked both he and Watkins to stay for tea, three times as is customary in Afghanistan. The meeting with the elders concluded, and Qadir left a platoon of ANA to provide security and continue helping the villagers recover from their ordeal. He, Watkins, and the interpreter shared a Humvee back to Khost, and talked about the battle.

Watkins had to ask, "How did you know what the enemy was planning in the village?"

Qadir replied, "During the Russian occupation my father was a leader of the Mujahedeen. I was just a boy but we needed everyone who was willing to fight, so one of my jobs was to gather intelligence as I didn't draw much attention. I got intel on a Russian patrol that was headed to a village in the area we were operating. He had several foreign fighters, mostly Pashtuns from Pakistan, fighting with him. It was rare for the Pashtuns to work with Hazaras, but he was a tenacious fighter and gained great respect. He devised a similar tactic that became a heroic story in my country from that time. When I saw the terrain and the two men across the river, it all came flooding back. It was an educated guess, but when your sniper team found theirs, it confirmed it for me.

"The Russian soldiers were mostly conscripts who didn't want to be there, and the Afghans who accompanied them were used more for their obedience than their skills. At just 12 years old, I was the sniper who took out their commander. Once he was gone, there was mass confusion. When my father's men hit them from the flank, the Russian Sergeant panicked and rushed the village, right into the kill box. It was a good day," Qadir said with a smile. Then turning to Watkins, "So I understand you will be leaving us soon."

Watkins was caught completely by surprise. He had been promoted to Lieutenant Colonel and was waiting his time to pin it on. He got orders just before leaving on this patrol.

"Why, yes I am. I have orders to take command of 1st Battalion, 3rd Brigade near Asadabad. Division called to tell me that when this patrol was complete, I was to be frocked, allowed to pin on the rank ahead of time, and leave as soon as possible. How did you know?" Watkins replied.

Qadir laughed, "They asked me how well you worked with ANA troops...I think they have their answer, no?"

* * *

The man in a grove of scrubby trees on a small rise across the river east of the village had a clear view of the battle. As he recorded the events unfolding in front of him, he provided narration of the battle preparations and the ongoing events. The details of the plan and its actual execution were critical for his leaders to evaluate tactics that worked, and those that didn't. When the battle turned against the defenders, he suggested ways to use certain events as propaganda regardless of actual events.

The man interspersed prayers to Allah with his description of the battle unfolding before him. Finally, after the fighting stopped, he suggested that they claim the allied patrol attacked the compound without provocation. That the villagers fought bravely, but were overwhelmed by the superior firepower of the Americans. Allah would rain death on those who did this horrible atrocity.

He sat there for hours documenting everything the allies did in the aftermath of the battle and focused on the ANA commander. When the afternoon sun was just a sliver over the ridge to the west, he climbed down from the tree and calmly walked across the border back to his safe house in Pakistan to edit and upload the video for transport.

CHAPTER 3

Lashkar-e-Jhangvi

"GILGIT, PAKISTAN (Reuters): Today a car bomb exploded at a Shia Muslim festival outside the mountain town of Gilgit, Pakistan, killing 35 and injuring 43. The bomb exploded near a series of tents serving food to families there to enjoy the festival. Almost a dozen children are among the dead. The violent extremist group, Lashkar-e-Jhangvi (LeJ), has announced on social media that 'their fighters have struck a great blow against apostates to the true faith.' The Pakistani government has pledged to track down the terrorists and bring them to justice."

The nondescript compound in Islamabad Pakistan looked like dozens of others along the street. Its tall stone walls enclosed a small courtyard that held back the bustling traffic along the road just outside, and a drab brown mud brick house. It was situated in an industrial area, near a slaughterhouse that produced a rancid smell from the discharge of waste into the nearby river and the boiling of animal fat at night. It was the perfect location to hide the smell from the manufacture of TATP, triacetone triperoxide, the explosive used in the Gilgit bombing. Although a relatively unstable compound nicknamed "the mother of

Satan," LeJ had perfected a manufacturing technique to make it safer to use.

Here in one of the several safe houses around Pakistan, Qureshi Farooq, the leader of LeJ, smiled at the execution of the blasphemous Shia. As head of the most feared Sunni Muslim extremist group in Pakistan, he found it insulting that Shia's would consider themselves Muslim at all. Like all who didn't follow the true faith, he believed they should be eliminated. While many focused solely on striking at America and the West, Farooq knew that the cleansing of Islam was just as important, if not more so.

The United States influence around the world had waned. Their President had shown weakness by running from the hard fights in Iraq and Afghanistan and grew weaker with his meager response to Caliphate operations in Syria. The movement's vision of finally removing these Shia from the heart of Islam, and the western infidels from the Middle East, was on the brink of reality.

The network of Muslim fundamentalist groups had grown well past the simple radicalism of Al Qaida who just wanted to strike at the Americans. Building on the successes of the Taliban in Pakistan and Afghanistan, along with their brothers in Syria and Iraq, the creation of a new Islamic Caliphate would finally unite Islam under Sharia law. The Americans still lumped them all together as Al Qaida, which was fine by Farooq. But the reality was Al Qaida was just a footnote in history.

"Look at this Sayeed," as Farooq turned his laptop toward his most trusted lieutenant. "The operation went perfectly. The Caliph will be very pleased, and the team leader should be rewarded for an excellent plan," Farooq said proudly. "So, is everything set up to get our friend's expert into the Valley?" he asked.

"Yes, we have selected our most trusted people, and Khan will shadow him. He'll be posing as a third-year university student but has already confirmed that the Valley should be a rich resource for us. The mules will be needed to move the heavy equipment but will be executed once they're no longer useful," replied Sayeed.

"A rich resource, yes, but we need our friends help to extract it so it can be useful. If they are as trustworthy as our leaders believe, then the cost of getting those resources from the mines is worth it to advance the cause. That is if they are trustworthy. So far, our friends have been very helpful, but I get the sense they withhold information from us. Might be just operational security, but I worry there are competing interests at work. Khan needs to be very careful," Farooq responded.

"True, but the General has done nearly everything we've asked and protected our assets masterfully without exposing that cooperation," stated Sayeed matter-of-factly.

"Yes, of course, you are correct Sayeed. I don't agree with much the Americans say or do, but I do agree with their saying, 'trust but verify.' Our people must always keep this in mind," replied Farooq. "So how are our plans proceeding with the next operation?" he asked.

"We've moved assets into Saudi Arabia and are awaiting confirmation of the readiness of our operative in place and timing. We don't yet have all the details, and our efforts have been complicated by the Saudi security services. Their commander is a distant cousin of the King, and he's very effective. However, despite a few setbacks, we should be ready when the time comes," stated Sayeed.

"I'll get some protection for them, leave it to me," replied Farooq.

Farooq was recruited to the cause during his Hajj to Mecca nearly 20 years before. He remembered fondly the feeling of walking in the footsteps of the Prophet and the rage he felt that the Americans were so close to the holy sites only a few years before. He had never met the movement leader, simply called the Caliph, he didn't even know who he was. The Caliph had to remain secret for his own protection until the Sunni world was consolidated.

But the man who recruited Farooq was extremely influential in the Kingdom and made clear that securing the holy sites was critical to the movement. He spent years rising through the ranks in the Saudi government and was a dedicated asset helping to undermine the Saudi's relations with the Americans. What the Americans didn't know was that their supposed friends in Saudi Arabia were about to fall, and fall fast.

The flame had been burning in the kingdom for years, the kindling ignited by the very family that ruled the country. In a desperate attempt to unify the nomadic tribes and assure their loyalty to the Kingdom, they introduced the fundamental interpretation of Islam known as Wahhabism. By creating a network of schools teaching the true faith, and claiming divine rights as protectors of the holy sites, they unwittingly created the mechanism for their own downfall. The King had no ancestral link to the Prophet, his family had defiled the holy sites for years. It was believed the Caliph was a direct descendant, it was only natural he should unify the Muslim world and sit on the throne of the holy lands.

The hot embers from that flame had finally ignited passions all over the world. The spread of the Arab spring from Algeria, Libya, and Egypt was more than just coincidence. Their allies in North Africa had been working for years to undermine the governments that the west believed to be stable. They simply created hundreds of small situations that forced the authoritarian strongmen in these countries to react predictably. The heavy-handed crackdowns built tension within their population spurred on by the movement's propaganda machine. The stronger the government response, the more sympathetic their cause.

Unfortunately, there were missteps along the way. Their brothers in Egypt tried to move too fast, and now there was a mess there which created problems for the longer-range plans against Israel. But Farooq and the other leaders within the movement were patient. Even the excessive brutality of the Caliphate fighters in Syria and Iraq served a purpose. It created the illusion that a strict adherence to Sharia was a moderation which would become the norm among the Sunni. Then the people would demand their governments fall into line once the cleansing of Islam had begun. And as long as the Americans saw Iran as the biggest threat, they were more than happy to provide all the military equipment needed for the coming fight, which was just a bonus.

"Get a message to Hamas, tell them we're sending them more rockets. We need to keep the Americans attention elsewhere. They think everything is going well in Afghanistan and their President is a fool to tell us exactly when and where they move. So, until we can secure the

Valley we need them to spend their efforts in that Palestinian cesspool and not here," stated Farooq bluntly.

The Palestinian puppets in Hamas were doing their job by keeping Israel focused on them. They masterfully used the killing of their own people to stir anger toward the Zionists around the world. Farooq had to laugh at the feeble American President who seemed to hate Israel as much as he did. Even going so far as to remain silent and let a UN resolution pass condemning Israel but saying nothing of the actions of the Palestinians.

It really was brilliant, Farooq thought. Deliberately place their weapons where the Zionists would do maximum damage to their women and children and show their dead bodies all over the lapdog western media. They loved to show dead bodies and never asked any questions. So predictable and yet so helpful. Makes the martyrdom of those devotees so much more satisfying to know their deaths were helping the cause. With Israel isolated and marginalized, no one paid attention to the movement's activities in the rest of the Arab world.

But that task was for others to pursue, his job was to secure Pakistan and build the network to join the Pashtun tribes and drive against the Shia from the east. The Iranians were showing their true intentions to destroy his Sunni brothers in both Syria and Iraq, and with their foolish work towards a nuclear weapon, Farooq had to laugh. In Pakistan, he already had the means and it was time to cut that Persian throat once and for all.

Pakistan's nuclear capability would make it easy to cut off the head of the Shia leadership when the time came. The "help" that Pakistan had given the Iranians to build their own nuclear capability ensured it would still be years before they figured out that the "help" was worthless. But only after his brothers had drained the Iranians of millions of dollars to acquire that garbage.

Farooq's first task was to bring many of his brothers in Pakistan together and communicated continually to get them to coordinate actions. Building that trust had been a challenge, but he was determined and had several leading Taliban clans and contacts in the Pakistan military and intelligence agencies finally beginning to covertly work together.

It was a monumental task to organize the widespread elements of their movement, but the task was made so much easier using the enemies' own tools against them. Social media, Twitter, online games, internet sites were invaluable to the network, not only for recruiting but for stirring the passions of the faithful to jihad. The mistake others made was to abandon these modern technical tools, as if it was Allah's will to live in caves.

His organization understood the power these tools gave them and learned to use them to bring more to the true faith, and become more active in the rise of the Caliphate. This power had brought recruits from all over the world to fight for the cause. It also brought them a much more advanced method of communication than Al Qaeda could have dreamed about. And Farooq was its master.

He created an elaborate communication system based on *Gods of Conquest*, a mass multi-player online war game. While the game allowed him to have some anonymity, it also provided the opportunity of using battle strategy in the game to conduct business. Farooq could give directions about targets and players but not specifics about how operations needed to be done. This way he kept the names of possible strike targets and the names of his network out of his written instructions. If one of the messages was lost, it gave no information about who, what, or when.

Another puzzle only his network understood.

"Well let's see what news we have today," he said as he turned to one of his computers.

Farooq had multiple computers for different uses to keep his information secure. The online game required its own laptop to keep it isolated in the event a foreign intelligence service located it and tried to hack it. No documents were stored there, its only purpose was to connect to the internet so if it did get hacked there was nothing of value to lose.

The computer had software that allowed Farooq to hide his identity and location by connecting to the internet through a series of zombie computers around the world. The software would leap around the globe with loopbacks until his laptop would connect from an IP address somewhere else in the world. After a couple minutes, his computer was connected through someone in Hong Kong.

The game was a simple, yet terribly complex communication channel all at the same time.

With game servers in nearly twenty countries, a dozen different "worlds" on each game server, and thousands of "alliance" groupings on each world, it was a massive blind playground. Even cells sharing the same world wouldn't know others were playing there. They assigned the distributed cell leaders specific servers and worlds to play with their cells. This way they kept the network secure as they operated independently without knowing what any other cell was doing.

Using the large grid layout of the world, player city names, and the game time setting, target and strike instructions were buried in the billions of messages used in these games every day. Farooq smiled. They didn't need code keys or complicated ciphers that could be broken; they simply gave their instructions in the open and used actual game play to cover their tracks. Even if one cell were uncovered, thousands of others would continue, and no one would ever know.

Farooq's current game name was *Wolfhunter 12*, and his alliance was *The Twelfth Kingdom*, which made him laugh. The names were veiled mockery of the Shiite belief in the Mahdi or Twelfth Imam. The Mahdi would come on Judgment Day to show them the true path...well, Judgment Day was coming to them; he and his followers would make sure of that. His network used names and avatars based on western players as most of the gamers came from the U.S. and Europe. It was sometimes a struggle. He had to make sure his "players" could speak English or at least mimic the European players' syntax. It was hard work, but the labor was worth it. And Farooq had some messages to send.

He logged into the game and looked at the in-game message from one of his cell leaders, code named *GameKing1990*. "Conquest of Khel city failed, got good intel about defense though. Will send reports to *Wellington* when he comes online at 23:00."

The message was about a real-world mission, and *Wellington* was their code for the cut out they would be using. Farooq frowned.

"Well, it appears the mission in Zakar Khel didn't go as planned. Hopefully, something of value was gained from it.

I'll collect the information from the courier after prayers. Sayeed, take these messages and let our contacts know that they will be delivered in the next 24 hours," instructed Farooq.

He knew that the NSA and CIA were desperately trying to find his network, but he was careful. He never used any of the keywords that these agencies looked for in the millions of electronic messages transmitted in the region every day. And with the reduction in human intelligence by the western nations due to cost cutting and a laughable belief that electronic collection gave them everything they needed, his network adapted. Add to that the mindless western press, who were so determined to destroy their own intelligence agencies, had proven extremely helpful for Farooq to learn the latest ways other cells had failed.

They gleefully reported their "anonymous" sources, and like a good jigsaw puzzle, he carefully put the pieces together and then changed tactics. And what the press didn't report, his friends in the ISI, Pakistan's secret intelligence service, passed to him from their contacts throughout the Muslim world. How foolish of the Americans to think that sharing intelligence with Saudi Arabia, Yemen, and Turkey wouldn't find its way to him. They had believers in all their intelligence agencies prepared to give their lives to advance the creation of the new Caliphate. But what worked today may not work tomorrow, so it took constant adjustment to stay ahead of the enemy.

Chapter 4

Trouble at Home

The Pentagon office suite of the Secretary of Defense looked out over the Jefferson Memorial and the Tidal Basin. Its sweeping vista of the Capital across the Potomac River, with the Lincoln Memorial to the left and the Washington Monument to the right, was one of the best views in all of DC. Especially in late spring when the Japanese cherry trees bloomed around the Tidal Basin, with their brilliant pink and red colors. But the serenity of that scene was in stark contrast to the hurried, and hectic activities inside the nations' military nerve center.

Secretary of Defense Madeline Coltrain strode through the outer office of her third-floor suite without a word and was met by her Chief of Staff, Victor Durchenko. Despite the pressures of running a department of more than 3 million military and civilian personnel, Madeline rarely showed emotion in public. She always maintained a calm, cool exterior but at times like this, beneath the surface she was a volcano about to erupt. And today her mood was as fiery as the scarlet red Armani pencil skirt suit that wrapped her lithe five foot nine frame.

After six years of working for the Secretary, her staff could read the subtle changes in her demeanor, especially after a meeting at the White House, and left her alone. It was a scene that had become all too familiar as the same arguments were repeated ad nauseam. Too many people inside Madeline's own party couldn't believe that an organization the size of DoD could run out of resources. But the strains of constant warfare and security tasking's around the world had depleted DoD's capability to levels not seen since the 70's. It made the meeting Madeline just left that much harder to swallow.

Durchenko was a political juggernaut who was feared by virtually everyone. Considered Madeline Coltrain's consigliere by her political enemies, his nickname within the Pentagon was "The Czar." Strict, demanding, connected, and ruthless, as a political operative he had few equals. Where Madeline used political finesse, Durchenko used a sledge hammer. And he looked like a mob boss with his salt and pepper hair always slicked back as the years of heavy smoking gave his face an ashen, almost leathery look. Combined with his tall, lanky, yet muscular frame, and constantly bloodshot dark brown eyes, he looked every bit the political angel of death.

The two entered Madeline's office, and Durchenko closed the door behind them. She slammed her briefing book on her desk, nearly knocking over an antique banker's lamp.

"Morons, absolute fucking morons! Why the hell does the President listen to that sniveling little prick," Madeline hissed as she could finally let loose.

"I heard you took a stroll past the White House press corps again, I'll bet that got some gums flapping. Figured it wasn't good news so came right over. Massey again Madam Secretary?" asked Durchenko as he took a seat.

"Of course, Massey. That shithead has convinced the President to draw down even deeper in Afghanistan," Madeline growled as she paced around like a caged tiger.

"Admiral Joffrey and I argued vehemently that it was a bad idea to take out so much military power. It will destabilize the whole damn region and let the Taliban regain a foothold, just like the Caliphate did in Iraq. We argued to reduce the visible footprint and minimize American casualties we should drawdown some heavy armor, and replace it with air cavalry and more airpower, against the wishes of General McAffey I might add," replied Madeline.

"We could have used air cav helicopters to move and support the ANA faster, and reduce the need for vulnerable convoys. But with the reduction of artillery fire bases in country, the trade-off was that our ground troops would need to rely more on air power for fire support. After all, you know how much Saldana loves his drones, so we figured he'd jump at the idea of precision airstrikes. While General McAffey argued strenuously that any draw down of heavy forces left him vulnerable, the Joint Chiefs felt it was a tradeoff they could live with," Madeline continued.

She knew full well the operational and psychological effectiveness of precision airstrikes from her time as an Army reserve officer during Desert Storm. She was an Intel officer with the support battalion in Dhaharan, Saudi Arabia that was hit by a Scud missile. She vividly remembered the nightly missile attacks, the sounds of the Patriot batteries engaging the incoming missiles, and the deafening explosion that took the lives of so many of her friends one night. But it was the movement along the infamous "Highway of Death," littered with the burnt bodies of Iraqi soldiers, that was indelibly etched in Madeline's memory. The pain and terror of men unable to escape the devastating attacks by coalition air forces, frozen forever in the death masks of their charred remains.

"But the President keeps listening to that asshole Massey. He driveled on about how 'the aerial bombings are damaging relations due to civilian casualties. That by reducing air power it would prove the U.S. was serious about fixing the problem.' The son of a bitch knows that those casualties are caused by the Taliban operating out of populated villages, and use the villagers as human shields.

"But that doesn't fit his narrative, so the Secretary of State's brilliant solution is to withdraw. He argued that 'the best way to eliminate the PR bludgeon of those casualties against the U.S. is to show that the ANA is up to the task of defending their own nation.' So now we must do a general draw down of all forces, especially heavy and air forces," Madeline said almost choking on the words.

"The ANA are able to defend the whole country? Really? In what fantasy world do these people live? Then again, this comes from a man whose only combat experience is doing shots and drugs in the strip bars of Boston's 'Combat Zone.' Jesus Christ Victor, this is Nixon's Vietnamization program all over again, but with even less of a chance of working! That son of a bitch," she hissed, her disdain for the Secretary of State on full display.

Her hatred for Massey was palpable and obvious. It was clear the only decision this President could make was no decision, and Massey had his ear. So, Secretary Coltrain had stormed out of the latest Oval Office meeting with the Chairman of the Joint Chiefs of Staff, Admiral Joffrey, in tow. She intentionally took a path past the White House press corps, her facial expression was more than enough to get the clattering started. Her patented terse smile and wave off of questions were sure to put chum in the water at the next White House briefing.

She had called an immediate meeting of the Joint Chiefs to discuss the situation and ordered the Chiefs back to the Pentagon. By the time she returned to the building, the Pentagon press corps was alerted to a possible fight brewing within the administration, in which Madeline took some pleasure. Every reporter feverishly began working their contacts inside the building in a desperate race to be first to get the story of what happened.

"I told you when we started Madam Secretary, Saldana packed his Cabinet with academic dickheads who tell him how wonderful and smart he is, but with no real-world experience. Present company accepted of course, and perhaps Commerce. It was destined to go in the shitter with morons like Massey blowing smoke up his ass," replied Durchenko wryly.

Commerce was a former CEO of a healthcare insurance company. Someone the President needed to twist arms and make the numbers for his signature economic agenda work. She was the only member of the administration with military experience. An Army Reserve officer during Desert Storm, she became one of the most respected senior analysts for the largest Defense consulting firm in the country after grad school. That led to appointments in the Defense Department under multiple administrations.

Her understanding of the global threat, and the strategies to counter them, were second to none. To Saldana's credit, he knew he needed a firm hand to control the military who would not be happy with his campaign rhetoric. But this also put her at odds with a President who acted like U.S. military strength was the problem, not the solution to the threats they faced.

To Madeline though, Saldana's Secretary of State Dr. Jonathan Massey was the chief dickhead. He was an academic from the John F. Kennedy School of Government at Harvard and had the President's ear. In her opinion, he owned the complete failure of U.S. foreign policy. One of Massey's first speeches was about American imperialistic treatment of other countries.

"Jonathan Massey couldn't put together a coherent idea if his life depended on it. His head is so far up the President's ass, if Saldana turns a corner too fast Massey's neck will break. 'Lead from behind' is that buffoon's brilliant strategy...what an absolute idiot," Madeline complained.

Massey was the first to suggest that the country needed to cede leadership to others. The "lead from behind" comment was his grand idea to show the world how benevolent America could be. As a former Army officer, Madeline knew leadership didn't work like that. In her experience, evil in the world only respected strength, and others were laughing at the weakness of the U.S. right now.

"These people are clowns, bumbling around like they can get things done just because they say so. It's like they've never had a history class in their lives," exclaimed Madeline! "We had it Victor, had it in our hands with Congress and the Presidency in our control. These fools deluded themselves into thinking it would last forever and they all just played political games. Jesus, look what they've done to the party," she said barely containing her frustration.

"That may well be true Madam Secretary, but it does work to our advantage. The more inept they look, the more you become the adult in the room. And given the information I've collected I assure you, you'll be the last one standing," answered Durchenko.

"Great Victor, I might be the last one standing, but I'll be standing on a shit pile of rubble. We started with so much hope and excitement, but it's just degenerated into one debacle after another. You'd think after he lost the House in the first mid-term Saldana would have pivoted back to the middle, but no, these jackasses just doubled down on stupid. They couldn't even win an election with bullshit economic numbers," said an exasperated Madeline.

Her party had lost the House during Saldana's first term when the opposition blasted the President's administration over "the ridiculously incompetent rollout" of the new health care law. The Secretary of Commerce had worked hard to make the drafters of the legislation understand the economic machinations required to get the various stakeholders onboard. He got most of what was needed into the law, but in the end, they changed several important elements, critical for its success. Her own party members in Congress had the President by the balls and squeezed every sweetheart deal, pork project, and outright bribery out of him to get the thing passed.

The obvious backroom deals, lack of bipartisanship, administrative deceit and incompetence (both real and perceived), had ensnared dozens of members of her party in a tar pit with no escape. The backlash was severe against those who had once not only supported that agenda, but actively argued for its passage. Even the more moderate members who had serious misgivings about what was in the legislation got their arms twisted off to support it, then got pummeled by their constituents at home.

Madeline was repulsed by how tone-deaf the party leaders were about what was happening in Middle America. The seemingly endless string of stories about incompetence, and the turmoil that followed, continued all the way into the next Presidential election. By all political measures, it should have resulted in Saldana's defeat, but didn't.

"Well he did win an election...," Durchenko began but the look that Madeline shot him stopped him in mid-sentence.

"Come on Victor, we both know how he did that. You'd think they'd have had the good sense to at least make it look good and get some more of our people votes. But that conceited shit running his campaign only thought of the President and everyone else be damned," Madeline said bitterly.

Although Saldana won a narrow victory for a second term, the President was embroiled in a new round of controversies surrounding the election. The guy at Commerce fudged the labor and economic data before the election to make the economy look better than it was, then severely revised the numbers downward after. Shortly after the election there were growing suspicions of ballot tampering in Ohio that had put the President over the top in the Electoral College.

"That arrogant son of a bitch hamstrung us with that shit. Hell, even our friends in the press couldn't cover it up for long. And you know that once the President was wounded, the wolves would attack. Then he compounds the problem by appearing unwilling to stop the waves of illegal immigrants pouring over the border, while our opponents beat us over the head with them," Madeline said with disdain.

Combined with the dramatic rise of the fanatical Caliphate vowing to take advantage of that human tsunami, it frightened even those who supported a more lenient immigration policy. Suddenly public opinion had once again turned against the President and all who advocated for him. It was out of fear, of course, but that fear was legitimate, and the President's political opponents pounced like lions to the kill.

By the second mid-term election, a record number of Congressmen and Senators from Madeline's party decided to retire as the economic malaise continued to crush their local economies. Virtually every member of her party running for office avoided being seen with the President, but for too many, it was a matter of too little, too late. It all created a perfect storm, and that tsunami swept the opposition party to win the Senate and control of both houses of Congress. It made Madeline furious that in less than 10 years, all the hope of what they could achieve had collapsed around them. The calamity of the past several years created huge schisms within the party.

"My god Victor, we've lost both houses of Congress, a dozen Governorships, dozens of State legislatures, and thousands of elected offices because of these fools. It's going to be a bloodbath in the next election cycle," Madeline said with a sigh.

" Madam Secretary, maybe it's time you stepped aside, for your own political skin," answered Durchenko.

So here she was, forced to consider her own political future. There would be questions about her role in several of these scandals, like the Algiers debacle, the faulty military agreement with Afghanistan, and the reduction of military capabilities that appeared politically motivated. She would need time to allow the public to forget their importance, even though she could blame the "imperial President" as some on the right were now calling Saldana. But to Madeline, she had to find a way to cleanse herself of the stench these constant scandals created. If only the President had listened to her, Algeria, the Egyptian train wreck, and the mess he made of relations in the Middle East and Afghanistan would have been different.

Madeline peered out the window. Across the Potomac the sun glistened off the Tidal Basin adding sparkles to the cherry blossoms, waving in the slight breeze. She thought it was so tranquil against the backdrop of the disaster President Saldana's political agenda had become which thrust her into almost impossible decisions. Madeline knew it was a self-inflicted wound.

The President was notoriously insulated by his closest advisors who controlled access to him with an iron fist. It was no secret there were only a few trusted people he listened to, and the Secretary of Defense wasn't one of them. All the scandals, incompetent appointees, and policy failures piled up on her party like concrete blocks, suffocating their message and dragging them further away from the center. With Massey pulling the strings, she had no doubt Saldana would make another foreign policy blunder. And while the condescending attitudes like those of that asshole were infuriating, it would make her revenge that much sweeter.

She shook her head, "No Victor, now's not the time. If I resigned now people would ask why now? Why didn't I speak up against the policies before? We must tread carefully and be patient. We need to continue laying the foundation first, these people will screw-the-pooch again and when they do, we'll be ready to drive the knife home," added Madeline.

She knew the political tradeoffs she'd have to make to reach her very lofty goals, but she had to be patient. The President made the famous statement that "elections mattered," then acted as if they didn't. The multiple scandals weakened him politically, and his response was to lash out.

There's nothing that turns people against their leaders faster than for them to think those leaders believe the law doesn't apply to them. True or not, she knew that perception was a reality for the American people, and if she made a quiet exit, she'd be painted with the same incompetent brush.

Instead, Madeline would make a triumphant exit, not as a scapegoat like so many of the President's mindless minions had done over the years, but as a martyr. His constant claim of "I didn't know" had only made him look like he was either lying or incompetent…she knew he was both. That would be her power stroke, and she just needed to wait for the right time."

Yes, you're right as always Madam Secretary. The President's allies in Congress will be the big challenge though, they control the fundraising plus the state and local party bosses," replied Durchenko.

"That's true, but right now the President is toxic to these people so we'll have the upper hand. We have to stay on message, we need to be seen as the answer and build up our friends while preparing to neutralize our enemies. All this grunt work should pay off soon," stated Madeline.

She and Victor had worked for months to lay her political foundation. The whispers, the subtle leaks of gaffes by those idiots at State, forcing the hand of the National Security Advisor to make the talk show rounds about Algeria, and her sudden NATO meeting when the president signed the Afghan Status of Forces agreement. All of it had created the undercurrent of discontent about her disagreements over policy.

All the time playing her part in which she used the same message of "faithfully executing the President's orders." Politically, Secretary Coltrain portrayed herself to be dutiful and loyal, even if she disagreed with the decisions. But the rumors kept building, and Madeline had no intention of letting them subside. Today's events only bolstered the view of a major battle between political titans.

"Time may not be on our side Madam Secretary, you have a bigger problem right now with the shit storm in the Middle East and Afghanistan. The Caliphate is making a mockery of the President's policies there, he's completely pissed off the Israelis, and with the not-so-secret talks with the Iranians our Arab friends wonder whose side we're on. To be honest, there's a lot of people in this building asking the very same question. Complaints are bubbling up that if we leave Afghanistan like we did Iraq, the same damn thing's going to happen there, and we're in even less of a position to do anything about it. Ma'am, the folks in the building, both permanent and political, aren't happy," advised Durchenko.

Madeline looked back out the window contemplating Victor's comments. After Saldana signed what the Pentagon viewed as a disastrous military agreement, he now wanted to dramatically accelerate the drawdown of forces in the Afghan theater. It would cause even bigger issues between the troops in the field and the administration.

"I know, I know," Madeline sighed as she considered her next move. "Okay, help General Palmer prepare a statement for the Pentagon press briefing. Say that the meeting discussed several regional issues and we had a frank discussion with the President about the options to meet the many challenges we face. That the President's guidance is clear, and the Defense Department will implement it to the fullest extent. I guarantee it will be addressed in the White House Press briefing so let them announce the drawdown first. Don't release our statement until they announce it. Delay our briefing if we have to, but it must come from the White House first," she ordered.

"I must admit Madam Secretary, I have to commend you on your performance. If things do go to shit, I think you'll be in good shape no matter how it plays out," answered Durchenko with a chuckle.

He marveled at the speed and ease at which Madeline could recognize political opportunity even in the darkest situations. With one clean stroke, she had laid the trap. Never admitting whether she agreed or disagreed, but able to shift the blame for failure or bask in its success, whatever the outcome. The tiger was never more dangerous than when it was cornered. These people who thought they could outmaneuver Madeline Coltrain would get their political throats ripped out and never see it coming. That made Durchenko smile.

Madeline's senior Executive Officer knocked on her door, "the Chiefs are ready for you Madam Secretary."

"Duty calls Madam Secretary. I'll get right on what we talked about," said Durchenko as he turned and followed Madeline out of her office.

It was a monumental task to get the data, charts, and people in position in the conference room called "The Tank." The individual service staffs dropped everything to prepare options for their respective Chiefs as work priorities changed in the blink of an eye. The Tank was in the bowels of the Pentagon and was the primary conference room specifically for the Joint Chiefs. Each of the Chiefs had their respective operations directors seated along the back row. It was the one place in the building where the three-star generals served the coffee, and they all came to attention as Madeline entered the room.

The Air Force Colonel in charge of the Tank had preloaded the briefing materials on the computers, prepositioned the Chiefs' documents at the conference table, brought in General McAffey on video conference, and then left. Only the SecDef, the Chiefs, and their operations directors would be allowed in this meeting. Madeline knew this was going to be a brutal discussion. There were no good options, and the Chiefs were going to have to come up with the best bad one.

The arguments went on for over an hour as the Generals went back and forth about options their staffs had come up with. As Madeline expected, none of them were good. Each option required a Hobson's choice, picking the least bad outcome from the available information. It seemed as if every pro had two or three cons. But as agreements fell into place, every person in the room had to face the reality that if the theater got a heavy push, casualties would be high.

The Chief of Staff of the Air Force pointed out that the secret air base near Ashgabat, Turkmenistan, code named Mary-4, was basically their only option for an operating base outside of Afghanistan. It was mainly used for logistics but was their lone choice to keep additional combat capability in theater. As a former Soviet air defense base, it had good facilities and would be able to support a large contingent of aircraft. The U.S. already had large E-8 Joint STARS airborne battle management and E-3 AWACS Airborne Air Control operating out of that location, but the base could handle the additional aircraft. Both the Iranians and Russians would get very nervous about U.S. combat aircraft so close to their borders, but that was a problem for State.

They could shift the F-16Cs of the 77th Fighter Squadron, and an element of F-16CJ Wild Weasel air defense suppression aircraft out of Bagram to Mary-4. They reinforce with F-22As of the 94th Fighter Squadron from Langley, leaving the A-10s of the 354th Fighter Squadron at Bagram. The slow A-10s would be close to the action and provide pure close air support.

The enhanced capability and low radar cross section of the F-22s would give them better air supremacy from a distance. And the multi-role capability of the F-16s allowed for flexibility as the threat developed. In addition, they would move AC-130 gunships to Mary-4 to provide cover for the special ops missions, but they would have a two to three hour flight time to the hot zones. This would allow the movement of two squadrons of combat aircraft out of Kabul without completely stripping the air support mission, but the remainder of Air Force combat capability would be removed.

Next was the Commandant of the Marine Corps and Chief of Naval Operations. They already had one squadron of AV-8 Harriers from the 3rd Marine Air Wing in Shindand Air Base in the western Herat province and would shift the second one out of Pakistan. As relations with Pakistan had soured over drone strikes in their territory, they had to move their combat aircraft out of Dalbandin in southern Pakistan.

The Navy would have to rely on FA-18 combat air patrols from the "Gipper," the aircraft carrier USS Ronald Reagan, in the Gulf of Oman south of Pakistan. The problem was that they had to fly over Pakistani territory to support operations. This gave them two squadrons of close air support plus the Super Cobra Helicopter gunships for the southern half of the country. The Navy would look at sending a second carrier, but it would take a couple weeks.

The Chief of Staff of the Army was in the toughest position. Not only would they have to withdraw some helicopter gunship units, but much of their heavy forces as well. He suggested moving the Army air mobile forces to Mary-4 and keeping a few more heavy assets in the field, thereby trading some airpower for additional ground forces. That way they could be out in the field while providing a less visible footprint in the cities. Then they could shift a squadron of Air Cavalry and gunships to Mary-4 to provide a quick reaction force for northern Afghanistan while leaving the rest in Bagram. That meant their whole force was drawing down to just over two brigades for the entire northern half of the country while the Marines had about the same force for the southern half.

General McAffey was furious, " Madam Secretary this is insane!" he shouted. "How the hell am I supposed to secure the entire Afghan area of operations with barely a division of soldiers and a wing of combat aircraft? The recent lull in Taliban ops is only temporary, and we've been lucky so far. But that's not going to last, and President Zazai is worried we're going to hang him out to dry and this will prove it to him!"

"General, it may well be insanity, but it's the best we can do. We're already operating well into the gray area of the President's orders by positioning so much combat power in Turkmenistan," Madeline said with a heavy sigh. "Okay gentlemen, let's get the ball rolling, and I'll brief the President." And with that, the meeting was over.

Madeline would have to call the CIA director to get more covert arms shipments to the Turkomen government and increase the "lease payments" for using their airbase to get approval from their leaders. A handful of aircraft and troops for the whole damn country and virtually no heavy weapons! Madeline shook her head as she made her way back to her office. What a joke this policy was. Removing more than half the air support, replacing artillery with helicopters, reducing armor, making their troops more vulnerable as if the Afghan Army was actually a fully capable fighting force.

At least using the Turkmenistan base allowed the President to announce his major withdrawal to the levels he had instructed. But he didn't exactly authorize so many combat units in that country. That would be a personal order from the Secretary of Defense that, if it blew up, wouldn't just be a serious blow to her career; it was unconstitutional. The President wouldn't be happy with that trade-off once he found out about it, but he couldn't risk an all-out revolt by the Joint Chiefs, and that was her trump card.

It gave Madeline some comfort that despite the President's careless decisions which could result in large scale U.S. casualties, at least she saved more combat power than Massey wanted. It would cause diplomatic issues with Russia and Iran, not that Madeline cared. They weren't friends anyway. But the Turkmenistan government would want assurances should things get dicey for them. Madeline was pleased with that; the President would jump at the chance at drawing down more forces, as SecState had demanded. Her shift to Turkmenistan would seriously push the boundary of the President's orders. But would create long meetings for that asshole Massey in Ashgabat, and that was priceless as far as Madeline was concerned.

Chapter 5

Welcome to Bagram

The hulking C-17 heavy transport landed at Bagram Air Base under a bright afternoon sun. Located about 30 miles north of Kabul on a fertile plateau in the foothills of the Hindu Kush Mountains, Bagram was the allies' main operating base for all of Afghanistan. The row upon row of permanent and temporary buildings extended for miles on either side of its long runway and aircraft parking ramps. A massive military city with a patchwork of facilities that housed the mountains of ordinance and equipment needed to prosecute the ongoing military operations. But to the thousands who work there, it was simply their home away from home.

As the C-17 taxied to its parking spot on the northeast side of the runway, it didn't take long for the dark grey paint scheme to heat the inside of the plane to something akin to a sauna. The soldiers inside were relieved when the crew finally opened the forward doors and the massive cargo door in the rear creating a mini wind tunnel. The sterile air of the seven hour flight from Ramstein Air Base in Germany was quickly replaced by the smell of jet and diesel exhaust from the busy air base. The soldiers of 1st

Battalion collected their gear, formed four lines, and began walking down the long cargo ramp to move to the in-processing center.

Staff Sergeant Shirin Kirkorian gathered her gear for her third tour in Afghanistan. The alternating waves of anxiety, anticipation, and exhilaration brought back memories that seemed like a lifetime ago. Years of training to suppress the emotions on the inside and show a calm, confidence on the outside, gave her the look of steely determination. A Texas born and raised girl of Iranian Orthodox Christian immigrants, she was often mistaken as Hispanic in the neighborhoods of her San Antonio home. Her dark brown eyes, ebony hair, high cheekbones and seemingly permanent tan, gave her a regal quality that accentuated her 5 foot 6 inch athletic frame.

But it was more than just the confidence she exuded when she walked, or her striking good looks that caused stares from other soldiers, it was the Ranger tab on her shoulder. While the shoulder tab caused double takes, the way she carried herself made people move out of her way. She moved with a cool, fluid, deadly resolve, the look of an Army Ranger.

The long trip to Afghanistan dulled Kirkorian's heartache of leaving her son with her parents once again. He'd been through this many times, more than she liked, but she knew he was in excellent hands and enjoyed living with his grandparents and Uncle Grigor. Her father and uncle owned a special tactics training center just outside of San Antonio, and what young boy didn't love the chance to shoot real guns. Plus, like his mother, he was very good at it. At least it gave Kirkorian comfort to know he was safe, and allowed her to focus on the mission at hand. So here she was in-theater again. It was time to get her game-face on.

Kirkorian was assigned to the 25th Infantry Division G2 Intelligence section and traveling solo. So, she got into line with a squad of soldiers from 3rd Platoon, A Company, 1st Battalion.

"Hey Sarge, mind if I tag along with your squad?" asked Kirkorian to the squad leader.

"Sure, no problem. Name's Tasker," he replied turning to face her.

"Kirkorian, thanks," she replied.

Tasker almost stopped dead in his tracks when he saw the Ranger tab on Kirkorian's shoulder.

"What's wrong Sarge, never seen a girl in uniform before?" Kirkorian laughed as she moved into line next to Tasker to exit the airplane.

Tasker cleared his throat, "well not one with a Ranger tab on her shoulder. Didn't know women could...they opened that up...to women I mean," he stuttered.

"Yah, well I'll tell you what, training was a fucking bitch. The physical tasks just about broke my ass in two. Good thing I can shoot, that may have been my saving grace," she replied.

Left unsaid was that Kirkorian was the first woman to ever complete Ranger school or the lengths she went to get there. She'd been in firefights and had seen men and women die in combat. Although some people still clung to the illusion that women in noncombat specialties weren't in combat, it hadn't been true since humans began fighting each other, and it certainly wasn't true today. So, despite the ban on women in combat specialties, she had volunteered for Ranger school every quarter, and got turned down each time.

She went so far as to write a letter to the Army Chief of Staff stating she would complete the course with her male counterparts and require no accommodation. When combat positions were opened to women, and whether it was the letter to the Chief or because the Secretary of Defense was a woman, Kirkorian got her wish. She was the first woman to pass the screening tests, and though she didn't ask for it, the one accommodation the Army insisted on was the haircut, giving her an ultra-short boy cut versus the shaved heads of the men. Everything else would be the same, and she wouldn't have had it any other way.

She wasn't an activist; if women wanted to fight, they should be allowed to fight but don't change the requirements to make it easy for them to do so. People's lives depended on the whole unit working as one, not the feelings of one member of that unit. But Kirkorian also recognized that men and women brought different capabilities to the battlefield and hoped that one day she might be in a position to show how to leverage those differences.

She remembered her first days at Ranger school, at the time it was the biggest challenge she would ever face. She knew everyone would be watching her, some desperately hoping she'd fail and others just the opposite. Her presence was met with both laughter and disgust from trainers and trainees. Kirkorian fondly remembered lining up in formation upon arrival at Fort Benning as one of the instructors, Master Sergeant Jericho, got up into her face.

"How the hell did you get here Soldier? I don't know what fucking genius thought it was a good idea to put a woman in Ranger school but don't expect mommy to come wipe your tears when you fail," Jericho said loud enough that everyone could hear.

Kirkorian had replied just as loudly, "I came by bus, Master Sergeant, and beat out 50 other soldiers to get here..." then added looking him square in the eye without any emotion at all, "...all of them men, Master Sergeant."

She had seen Jericho try to suppress a smile, then bellow to all the soldiers in her training unit, "I don't care who you beat out, beat up, beat off, or blew to get here. You get no special treatment, no favors, and I don't give a shit about your feelings. Look to your right and your left, chances are those soldiers will not be here at the end of training. You will be challenged mentally, physically, and emotionally. You will need to work as a team, anyone who thinks they can do this alone will be the first to go. Now move out!" he bellowed.

And so began days of gut wrenching physical, and mind numbing psychological challenges that at times, made Kirkorian want to collapse. But she managed to keep going. Though she made it through training, scoring records on several shooting challenges, the physical challenges were nearly her undoing. When Kirkorian was asked by the school commander how many women could do what she had done, she had to be honest and say maybe less than one in a thousand.

But she wouldn't change a thing. Rangers have to do things that normal soldiers can't, or won't do. It takes that mental and physical focus that only a very select few can maintain. It wasn't only the Rangers that believed that, her uncle had taught her that every time he took her hunting.

After a few moments to regain his composure, Tasker asked, "so how *did* you get through the physical shit?"

"Well, ten years of high level gymnastics and 20 hours of back labor with the birth of my son prepares a girl to tolerate a lot of pain!" Kirkorian replied with a chuckle. "But seriously, if not for some of my teammates, that high pain threshold, and being stubborn as a mule I might not have made it through."

"Son of a bitch. My wife only had 12 hours of labor and about broke my damn hands during contractions, and I thought she was a freaking hero for it. I can't imagine 20 hours, or back labor. What's that like?" Tasker asked innocently, then quickly regretted the question.

"Grab your balls and pull 'em up to your chest every four minutes…kind of feels like that," Kirkorian replied nearly dropping her pack laughing as she saw Tasker and some of the other soldiers within ear shot wince at her description.

"No worries Tasker, I'd go through it all again. In the end, I had a beautiful baby boy who's the love of my life," Kirkorian said.

"I'm sure he makes his daddy proud then, how old is he?" asked Tasker.

Kirkorian's smile vanished, "He's nine. His dad was killed in Iraq before he was born. An IED got him on an op in Anbar province. He was a Ranger too."

"Sorry Sarge," Tasker replied feeling embarrassed.

Kirkorian's face didn't show sadness, just a brief look of melancholy as she replayed the memories of her husband, "It's okay, you had no way of knowing. It was actually what drove me to enlist. Call it a little payback. The boy looks like his dad…but shoots like his mom," she said with a wink. And with that, the smile returned to her face.

Afghanistan had become a more dangerous place since the last time Kirkorian was deployed. Former Afghan President Khalizad had refused to sign a new military agreement which created a huge rift between the U.S. and Afghanistan. His inflammatory statements about civilian casualties attributed to international security forces defied reality. Every soldier in the country knew they were a result of Taliban indifference about putting civilians in the line of fire, using them as shields to prevent allied counter attacks. Finally, under pressure from many of his own elders, Khalizad signed a temporary extension until the new Afghan President took office. But the raw feelings remained.

Once Afghan President Zazai came to power, he signed a new security agreement with the United States and consolidated his power by purging members of the former regime. Not that his administration was any more or less corrupt, he needed to eliminate his competition and gain control of the military. But Zazai was a shrewd negotiator. He knew American President Saldana needed a foreign policy win after the debacle in Algeria.

The U.S. Ambassador there had been kidnapped, and the subsequent rescue attempt turned into an epic failure. Decisions by President Saldana failed to provide adequate fire support when the rescue went sideways. Kirkorian had read the intel on the rescue and was shocked at the incompetence of the State Department. They tried to recover the Ambassador themselves, even after they failed to protect him.

State refused military extraction believing that the kidnappers were low level criminals just out to get a ransom. The reality was that the Ambassador was captured by one of the most feared terrorist groups in North Africa. The State rescue team ran headlong into a force of well-armed fighters and had to be rescued themselves by the very military assets they refused. The propaganda value of the kidnapping, and the resulting failed rescue, emboldened Muslim extremist groups all over the world. In Afghanistan, it made the Taliban much more aggressive.

In the political fallout, President Saldana was quick to agree to terms that were a definite disadvantage for deployed U.S. forces. For the first time, an agreement put ANA commanders above U.S. commanders during joint operations. That agreement infuriated the U.S. military members in Afghanistan and along with the Algerian incident, became a huge problem during Saldana's reelection campaign. But through some political posturing, and some questionable actions during the election, he squeaked out a win for a second term.

When accusations of corruption started piling up against the administration, Saldana desperately tried to create positive news with an announcement for a new direction in the Afghan conflict. Just before Kirkorian left Germany, the President doubled down on exiting Afghanistan involvement and ordered an increased withdrawal from the country. The White House announced the numbers of troops and the timeline of the withdrawal, to the surprise and disgust of virtually every military member.

The President's spokesperson said it would make the U.S. footprint smaller in country as the ANA took a more active role. It would reduce American casualties while improving relations with the new Afghan government. To the soldiers in country like Kirkorian, it just made them feel exposed, vulnerable, and betrayed.

Intelligence assets were already spread thin in-theater and the drawdown put even more pressure on the overworked officers who had the language and regional knowledge to get information. As a woman, Kirkorian was an especially important asset. She could talk with the local women who wouldn't, or couldn't, speak to the men. As an enlisted soldier, she had the ability to work with the ANA officers without threatening their position. And she had a unique skill that none of the other intel assets in theater had. She not only spoke 10 languages, she could identify and speak multiple dialects of those languages as well.

So Kirkorian strode across the aircraft parking ramp to the in-processing center with her pack looking twice her size, and her M-4A1 carbine slung across her chest. The in-processing center was a semi-permanent building next to the airfield base operations center and was nothing more than trailers connected to each other. Just like every other military deployment throughout history, soldiers always seemed to be in a "hurry up and wait" mode. This was no different.

The in-processing center checked orders and assigned quarters. Some would be trailers, others tents, depending on how long the soldiers would be at Bagram before reporting to their unit or operating area. The newly arrived soldiers lined up at the processing center as the line extended out the door. Non-Commissioned Officers (NCOs) were already barking orders as the soldiers formed up into platoons and squads, while the NCO of the processing center called each squad for processing.

Kirkorian got in line with Tasker's unit as they dumped their packs on the ground and sat on them waiting for their turn to process. As always happens when soldiers are bored, they let the bullshit fly. Kirkorian had a good laugh at some of the newbies boasting on their first deployment to Afghanistan.

"So what deployment number is this for you Kirkorian?" asked Tasker.

"Third, you?" replied Kirkorian.

"Same here. Two in Iraq before that," answered Tasker.

"Jesus Tasker, these guys look like fucking babies," chuckled Kirkorian looking around at the young faces of Tasker's men.

Tasker laughed, "Only a couple are new, the others have been in the saddle before."

It was nice to relax before jumping into the meat grinder that was daily life in Afghanistan.

That is until she saw four Afghan soldiers standing near the outside corner of the processing center. The ANA soldiers were 20-30 yards from her group and about 15 yards from the door to the processing center. In an instant her senses and instincts were on high alert, she could feel something was out of place.

She slowly moved her hand to the grip of her M4 and shot a glance to Tasker. The sudden change in her demeanor made him stop talking and turn to where Kirkorian was looking. With a nod they both pulled their feet in, positioning themselves on the balls of their feet. It was the unspoken language of soldiers who've been through the grinder before as everything in their bodies began operating at maximum efficiency. She showed him two fingers with her right hand to indicate she had the two targets on the right.

Kirkorian and Tasker were moving before the Taliban infiltrators could get their rifles all the way up. The enemy started firing, and the distinctive double crack of the supersonic AK-47 rounds echoed off the buildings, hitting a squad just beginning to stand up to process. With a burst of fire Kirkorian took out one of the assailants and Tasker another. One of the infiltrators kept up his fire on the soldiers in line as the other walked his fire toward Tasker and Kirkorian while men dove for cover.

Kirkorian rolled to her right and with a second burst, walked her fire up the enemy's chest and took off the left side of his head. Tasker rolled to his left and put a burst into the last enemy as he was about to throw a grenade. The man fell backward, dropping the grenade which went off, showering the nearest squad with shrapnel.

It was all over in seconds, but there were four dead Taliban infiltrators and five dead Americans, with seven more severely injured. Tasker was immediately barking orders for his squad to set up a security perimeter as they had started moving when Tasker and Kirkorian jumped into firing position. Tasker's squad secured the area while the screams of the wounded and calls for medics rang out across the tarmac.

Kirkorian turned to Tasker and saw that he was bleeding. "Hey Tasker, hold up," as she pointed to his shoulder.

Adrenaline is a wonderful thing in battle. Not only does it enhance the senses of a soldier, it often masks pain until that rush begins to wear off.

"Son of a fucking bitch," Tasker exclaimed looking down, finally realizing he'd been hit.

Kirkorian called for a compression dressing and put it on Tasker's wound and pressed. "Goddammit, that burns," Tasker grunted.

"Looks like it just grazed you," replied Kirkorian holding pressure on the wound until a medic made it over to them after treating the most severely wounded.

The whole area was a frantic swirl of activity as people came running from all over the base. Medical teams with stretchers appeared as if from nowhere to carry off the men who were still alive as specialists from the base security forces and an intel team arrived to document the scene. A medic cleaned Tasker's wound, used dermal glue to seal it, and then put a clear adhesive bandage over it infused with antibiotics.

After the area was clear and it was determined there were no other infiltrators, Tasker and Kirkorian walked over to the dead Taliban who were now laid out in a line. The Division intel team was taking pictures and measurements to document the attack and collect information off the bodies. They were working to identify the four infiltrators and turned to the two Sergeants to get their first-hand account. Kirkorian and Tasker did a quick debrief with the team leader, and Kirkorian said she'd file a formal report when she got to the G2 section.

When they finished, Kirkorian looked down at the dead enemy and turned to Tasker, "Nice shooting, Sarge."

Tasker replied, "You too. Where the hell *did* you learn to shoot?"

Kirkorian looked at him with a slight smile, "My dad and Uncle run a special ops training center, and I've been shooting since I was old enough to hold a gun. My Uncle's a former sniper and taught me to shoot pretty much every gun in the inventory. Came in handy at Ranger school. My squad always wanted me on over-watch because I was a better shot than anyone else, made up for some of the physical limitations I had. So, how's the shoulder?"

"The Medic put on some super glue to close it up. Hurts like a son of a bitch but nothing to keep me out of action. So, I guess that *is* the real deal," as Tasker pointed to Kirkorian's Ranger tab. "You never told me, how'd you get into Ranger school? I thought spec ops was closed to women?" asked Tasker.

Kirkorian laughed, "Yah, it is. Don't know if it was because I was such a pain in the ass or because they thought I was bat-shit crazy. I pestered them constantly after my enlistment, even wrote the Chief of Staff basically begging for the chance. When they opened combat positions to women, I got orders to take the prescreening drills. I guess I was their guinea pig to see if women could stack up. My training sergeant told me on day one I'd get no help and no favors from anyone, I told him I didn't want any. I was always taught that the guidelines were the guidelines and you either measured up or you didn't. Guess I measured up," Kirkorian said with a sly smile.

"Hey, good news about that shoulder," stated Kirkorian as she turned and gathered up her gear to finish processing. "These babies are gonna need you to teach them how not to get shot!" Kirkorian said laughing. "HUA."

"And a comedian to boot! HUA Kirkorian," Tasker replied with a laugh as she walked away with a wave. Turning back to his squad he started barking orders, "alright meatheads, you just got shown up by a girl! Grab your asses and get moving. After processing, dump your gear and report to the firing range in one hour, we've got some work to do. Move out!"

After in-processing, Kirkorian tossed her gear in the trailer she'd be sharing with several other enlisted women, grabbed a bottle of water and headed over to the 25th ID Command Post as quickly as possible. She reported to the intel section to give her first person account of the green-on-blue incident earlier that day.

The intel team had found a torn piece of paper on one of the bodies, the one missing half of his head. It had already been scanned and sent to Central Command in Tampa Florida for translation when Kirkorian walked in. The assailant must have had instructions in his pocket at some point. It got caught on something as he pulled it out to destroy it, leaving this small piece behind.

As Kirkorian looked at the note, she mumbled, "Take the gold road to the Valley of Stars." She recognized immediately that it was Pashto common to the Afghan-Pakistan Pashtun tribal regions.

Lieutenant Colonel Angelo, the Division G2, walked over when Kirkorian entered and heard her comment. "Sergeant, I heard you had quite the reception. Glad to have you with us. I look forward to hearing your first-hand account. So, what do you think this means?"

Kirkorian came to attention and Angelo put her at ease, "Yes Sir, it's one way of getting over jet lag, though I don't recommend it. The words say, 'Take the gold road to the Valley of Stars.' Has anyone heard of the gold road or the Valley of Stars before?"

Another Sergeant started digging through some of the recent Intel from an area northeast of Kabul around Asadabad. He found a report from the week before and handed it Colonel Angelo.

"Colonel, we got a report from 2nd Brigade about a radio intercept that referenced some assets coming through the gold road but it went dead...they must have realized they were broadcasting over an unsecured freq and cut it off. 2nd Brigade looked at their maps and talked to some locals, but there's no gold road referenced and none of the locals indicated any knowledge of it," the Sergeant stated.

"OK, send it to CENTCOM and flag the 'gold road' and 'Valley of Stars' as watch words for other intel assets," ordered Colonel Angelo.

"Sir, permission to accompany the next unit heading to Asadabad to join up with 2nd Brigade?" asked Kirkorian. "If the Taliban are operating up there, someone is going to know something and they won't always tell our people straight out. Maybe I can work some of the villagers in the background for information. I haven't been in that area for nearly two years. Has anything changed up there?"

Angelo replied immediately, "Permission granted, 1st Battalion will be moving up to replace the 3rd next week after they get acclimated. They're seeing more infiltrations in the area, so the zone is getting hotter. I'll make sure you're free to accompany any units and patrols." That's when Angelo looked up and gave Kirkorian a little hand wave, "Sergeant, a word, my office," he ordered as he turned and headed to a door in the corner of the small intelligence center.

Angelo was the Division Director of Intelligence for the 25th Infantry Division. As he settled in behind his desk, he gestured for Kirkorian to take a seat. Pointing to the Ranger tab on her shoulder, "Well, I guess that explains the action earlier today. Sergeant I've been reading your file and have to say, I'm extremely impressed," as he opened up Kirkorian's personnel file. "PhD in Linguistics, fluent in at least 10 languages, Combat Infantryman Badge, Expert Marksman Badge, shooting records at Ranger school, first woman recommended for sniper school, Bronze Star, and you've spent more time outside the wire than virtually every other intel asset combined. Why aren't you an officer by now?" asked Angelo.

"Sir, it's simple, culturally I can be more effective as an enlisted soldier," Kirkorian replied. "The social structure here is that men are in positions of authority and women must defer to them. If I'm an officer, I hold a position of authority, and it will close off communication."

"Well I'm not complaining, I'm glad to have you here. I do like to understand what motivates my people though. So, tell me, why so insistent on Ranger school?" asked Angelo.

"Sir, my husband was a Ranger. He was killed in Iraq while I was in grad school, pregnant with our son. My son never had a chance to know his dad. Aside from wanting a bit of revenge, I knew my background was critically needed, so I joined up. Ranger school was for me, to know more about my husband and what he went through. He always said, 'if you want to be seen as the best, you have to be the best.' That's what drove me then, and still drives me now," Kirkorian answered proudly.

"Okay then, fair enough Sergeant. I'll contact 1st Battalion to let them know you're coming. They've got a new commander, Lieutenant Colonel Watkins. He's been in country a while and was recently working closely with the ANA down near Khost, report to him, you're dismissed," Angelo ordered.

"Yes Sir, thank you, I'll get right to work. Looks like I have a lot of catching up to do," replied Kirkorian standing and saluting as she turned and left the office.

CHAPTER 6

Keywords

The Southwest Asia section was one of the busiest in the CIA these days. The section's area of responsibility extended from Iran in the east, India in the west, and along the southern border of Russia to the north. It included all of the countries that are collectively called the 'Stans, including Afghanistan and Pakistan. Along with their CIA brethren in the Middle East and North African sections, they shared intel in real time. Together, they were the front line of the intelligence efforts to unravel the most dangerous Muslim extremist groups in the world.

At his workstation in the section's underground fusion center, Karim Rezek read through the latest intel reports coming from Afghanistan. The low hum of the air conditioning systems and bluish tint of the natural light LED lighting gave the section an eerie feel. Karim listened to his favorite alternative rock playlist on his iPod. Within the highly shielded walls, no electronic or radio signals could penetrate which meant no radio or streaming unclassified internet at his desk. So he had virtually every song he ever owned loaded onto the iPod because once he brought it into the center, it would never leave. Just one of the fun rules working at CIA Headquarters inside one of the most secure buildings on the planet.

As a senior analyst in his section, Karim had a reputation as one of the most accomplished analysts in the CIA. He was a third generation Lebanese American who spoke Arabic and Hebrew. Although he was raised Muslim, his mother was Catholic. He went to a Catholic private school, a Catholic Jesuit university, and prayers at the mosque. It certainly made for an entertaining household, especially over holidays. So here he was, the product of two of the three offshoots of the root of Abraham, a soldier in the oldest battle in human history.

Being Muslim inside the CIA was definitely interesting and Karim was accustomed to the enhanced screening he endured because of it. Maybe it was his mother's influence, or the combination of Muslim and Catholic discipline ingrained in him his whole life that gave him a deeper sense of authority than many of his generation. He easily rationalized the extra security for any Muslim, given the current state of threat. After all, it wasn't the 65-year-old Presbyterian grandmother who was trying to blow up an airplane. The threat was radical Islamism and the hate spewed by those who used his religion to manipulate people solely to gain power.

Karim was reading through the latest report about the green-on-blue incident at Bagram, and was impressed by the quick action of the soldiers. Someone had really good instincts that day. He read a little more and paused on the translation of the Pashto words, "Take the gold road to the Valley of Stars." The infiltrator had this written on a piece of paper, and the local intel referred to another radio intercept in the area of Asadabad about the "gold road." Karim remembered reading an NSA intercept from the Iraqi/Syrian border region that referred to the "gold road" in Arabic.

It was a satellite phone intercept from a Caliphate leader to someone in Pakistan and what made it odd was that it held no target information but talked about some kind of supplies through "the gold road." It was only mentioned once, and nobody had any reference to what or where that was. The current thought was that it was a passage through the mountains from Turkey to Iraq or Syria, but why would an infiltrator in Afghanistan have the same reference? Only three data points, brief and disparate mentions linking Iraq, Pakistan, and Afghanistan.

Gold, the common term here...Karim pulled his earbuds out, leaned into his workstation, and began a vigorous search of documents going back several months searching for the word gold in any context. Most analysts would simply search for the two words together, "gold" and "road" figuring it to be a descriptive term like the Silk Road trading routes of ancient times. Karim was sure it was but why use the term gold to describe it. He sensed there was more importance to this term than simply as a descriptor of a trade route.

Zack Gerlacher, section chief of the Southwest Asia section, noticed Karim suddenly very active at his computer. Gerlacher had seen him like this before. Once he got on the trail of a puzzle, he was in his own zone and focused like a laser. It was like a switch was thrown and he went from joking and affable to serious and thoughtful.

Gerlacher walked over to him, "Karim, what have you got?"

Karim paused for a moment, "Not sure, but something rang a bell in me about this gold road that's been referenced three times in three completely different contexts; Iraq, Afghanistan, and Pakistan. Just doesn't feel like a coincidence to me. I believe the key is the term gold and I'm running an intel search going back at least six months from those three countries."

Gerlacher was no longer surprised about the possible volume of data that search would return when it came to Karim. He could absorb information faster than anyone, and his mind became more efficient than a computer in cataloging it and tracing links between them.

"What can we do to help?" Gerlacher asked, knowing full well Karim could process things faster than the rest of the team put together.

"It's a long shot right now, just a feeling, but these are linked, and I just need to figure out why. Can we look at the word gold associated with any city names?" asked Karim. "If this is a supply route then maybe we can identify the cities referenced to it. But the concern is what changed? We know there are hundreds of smuggling routes. What makes this different? That's where the second bit of info comes in, the reference to the Valley of Stars indicates a known place somewhere between Pakistan and Iraq," he continued.

The border between Pakistan and Afghanistan was notoriously porous for smuggling relatively small levels of supplies along many routes through the mountains. Like the Vietnamese who carried war supplies along the Ho Chi Minh trail, the Taliban would kidnap villagers from the border regions and force them to manually carry contraband through the treacherous mountain passes. Along with guides that were paid but whose loyalty was guaranteed by holding their families, the Taliban smuggled men and equipment, mostly small arms, into Afghanistan and carried out poppies to produce opium. But this was something different.

Karim was the section's resident puzzle guru. He usually tore through the New York Times crossword puzzle, in pen, and had it done start to finish over lunch. He had an eidetic memory, some would call a photographic memory, with an uncanny ability to find links in random bits of information. It was this insight that caught the attention of the regional CIA recruiter, and Karim was recruited while he was just in his second year at Georgetown University. His cover was that he was as a market analyst intern for a major defense contractor, which was mostly accurate, as he could talk about conditions in virtually any country. And so he not only completed his Bachelor's degree, he finished a double Masters in International Relations and History in only five years.

His Master's thesis was on the use of faith and religion to gain and hold power throughout history. This made him a particularly crucial asset in understanding the thinking of the players in their area of responsibility. Karim's research had him study the Christian Bible, the Tanakh or Hebrew Bible, and of course the Koran. During his research, he identified a large number of similarities among the teachings of all three. The stories and prophecies contained in the holy texts were repeated, restated, and otherwise intertwined before they moved into their own paths of commentary for the faithful.

This gave Karim a much deeper understanding of the motivations of the various factions throughout the region and a recognition that their differences were embedded in all three religions. It had nothing to do with whether one faction or another would agree to live with the other; it was about control of the land of Abraham, the holiest land on earth. In essence, who was the rightful protector of the sacred lands that Abraham consecrated through his faith in God. It was this foundation of the historical tenets of Islam that the extremists had tapped into to bring believers to their cause.

Karim traced the biblical and historical accounts of early civilization, through the Christian and Islamic repression during the dark ages, to the current radicalization within Islam, and even the secular faith of the believers of communism. The language of manipulation, idolatry, and a belief that their leaders had some kind of divine knowledge well above ordinary people was the common thread across the ages and all human societies. Evil people use many ways to get followers to do evil things, but they all used the most powerful influencer of all, faith. This was exactly what was happening in the Muslim world today.

It wasn't that Islam had been radicalized in just the last few decades, there were radicals within Islam since the beginning. In the past, manipulation was strictly through the use of brute force to conquer and convert people. But today with modern communications, they could coordinate their actions and messages to target vulnerable people more effectively than any time in history. Even inside his own mosque, Karim heard rumblings against western ways, and some of the same garbage being spewed by those attracted to the Caliphate. But he knew the people talking were either just trying to promote themselves or were already under surveillance, usually both.

While he felt the majority of his fellow believers were angry that their religion had been hijacked for evil purposes, the fear of retaliation against any who openly spoke against these fanatics was real. Christianity was fractured into so many smaller factions who argued incessantly over this interpretation of the Bible or that one, none could act together. Islam, however, was more dogmatic. While it had its factions, more often it was a difference in the intensity of their beliefs than a difference in beliefs, except for the schism between the Sunni and Shia sects.

Those butchers in the Islamic Caliphate, Hamas in the Palestinian territories, and the Taliban in Afghanistan had proven that they were willing to ruthlessly enforce their brand of faith. Muslim, Christian, Sunni, Shia, or Coptic made no difference to them. If you didn't agree with them, you were marked for death.

Given the recent schizophrenia over American policy dealing with the Islamic world, there was little to no respect from the countries of the region toward the current administration. Both friend and foe saw the President's policies as weakness. Either because of, or in spite of, trying to accommodate even the most radical elements in the region, the radicals had gained momentum and penetrated senior positions throughout the Muslim countries. Pandora's Box had been opened, and the radicals were going to make it damn hard to put the contents back in.

Karim would be sleeping here tonight.

CHAPTER 7

Propaganda

Peshawar is a busy, noisy place. Narrow streets clogged with people, cars, and motorbikes that seem indifferent to any semblance of organized traffic flow. Sclerotic intersections where nothing should move, but does. While motorbikes buzz in and around cars in whatever small space opens, people jam the thin space next to buildings that serves as a walkway. Along with the stifling daytime temperatures that make the dusty, exhaust laden air thick and heavy, the constant screeching of car horns can be dizzying for anyone not accustomed to the city. But it's the perfect environment to lose someone tailing you, exactly the kind of place an experienced operative could hide in plain sight.

Farooq came out of prayers and turned north to the café just around the corner from the mosque, jostling through the crowd, skillfully dodging traffic encroaching on the walkways. As he sat down, the server came over to him to take his order, a sweet and frothy traditional Pakistani coffee made with cardamom and cinnamon simmered with milk, and Sohan Halwa, a traditional sweet brittle cookie. The server brought the coffee to Farooq and placed it on the table, skillfully palming a miniature USB drive under the lip of the saucer. Farooq picked up the napkin and spoon next to the saucer, effortlessly collecting the jump drive with them, calmly pocketed it, and turned to enjoy his mid-afternoon snack.

It was a hot day, and Farooq took his time walking back to the safe house. Not just to conserve energy but work his tradecraft. He completed several switchbacks to check if he was being followed. He stopped at several vendors along the way, conversing and looking at merchandise so that if he was being watched, they would have many false leads about where the pickup point was. Once he was sure he wasn't followed, he made his way to the safe house.

"Farooq, did you have any troubles with the pickup?" asked Sayeed as Farooq entered and shut the door behind him.

"No trouble at all, it was good to get out and move around. I saw some local police, but they were more interested in finding shade than pay attention to me," Farooq replied. "Alright, let's see what our man has sent us."

The two men sat down in front of one of the computers used to work offline as Farooq plugged in the USB drive. Farooq had several computers, some for internet access, some used only to upload to certain sites, and some only to work offline. He had to use physical barriers to keep as much information from the prying eyes of the NSA as possible. If one system was compromised, he only lost a fraction of the data he kept. In addition, he often used internet cafes and Wi-Fi hotspots to conduct business to prevent the NSA from locking onto a single IP address site. This computer was never connected to the internet but had high definition video editing software to manipulate the various videos used for propaganda. The videos he received from his network would be cleaned up, edited, and then saved for distribution.

Though some of his peers liked to decry the evils of modern advancements, Farooq relished them. The capabilities for advancing the Prophet's message to bring the world to the true faith were so much better than they had ever been before. It was how it was used and controlled, not the technology itself that was the problem.

And the fools in the west would suffer for their lack of control of them. This was one of those times, using technology to adapt reality to the message Farooq wanted to send to the world. The irony was that the United States president Woodrow Wilson was the one who first used the power of video to create propaganda and his underlings literally wrote the book on how to do it.

The USB drive contained a video file, and Farooq opened it to find the video of the Zakar Khel battle. The video came to life on the computer screen, a large high definition monitor that, combined with the digital recording, allowed Farooq to see every detail of the battle. The beginning of the tape was of the leader of the unit named Rafiq describing the operation and praising Allah. These parts were critical, and Farooq demanded that all ops he ran began the same way, with a description of what was going on, the desired outcomes, and why the target was selected. This was important to set the scene and the legitimacy of their actions according to Sharia law. So, no matter how the op turned out, they could claim success and get the proper propaganda effect out of them.

As Farooq watched Rafiq position his men for the ambush, he turned to Sayeed and said, "This is a well thought out plan with many contingencies built in. This commander should be commended for his actions. Others could learn a lot from this planning."

Farooq took notes as the video played, periodically stopping it to rewind and watch something in more detail. The videographer narrated the actions being seen that may, or may not have been actually occurring but guided the messaging Farooq wanted. He would add additional comments as voice-overs during editing before the video was released as directed by Farooq.

As Rafiq's men got into position, they signaled the videographer that the patrol was approaching. Farooq leaned into the screen when he saw the patrol come into view. He saw the ANA troops leading the patrol and saw the subtle movement in the middle of the formation of a man turning and giving a signal to the trailing elements. Farooq stopped the video and zoomed in to see the man's face.

"Is that the ANA commander?" Sayeed asked.

"Yes, and if this goes according to plan, the elders will go to the front entrance of the compound and wave the patrol in. That is the signal for the sniper to take out the commander and spring the trap," Farooq replied.

Just after the commander signaled, it was almost imperceptible, but he thought he saw the lead element of the patrol bring up their weapons. Suddenly he heard two shots, and the battle had begun.

Farooq stopped the video, "Did you see that?" he asked Sayeed.

"See what, I didn't see anything except the sniper started too early," replied Sayeed.

Farooq rewound the video, something was terribly wrong as the two men leaned into the monitor. He went back to the signal from the ANA commander and went frame by frame; the commander signaled, "There, right there, the lead element brought their weapons up. And look, the trailing Americans have already pivoted facing outward on either side of the road. The ANA and the Americans started moving, *before* the two shots!" Farooq exclaimed.

As they moved the video back and forth at the point of the two sniper shots, they could clearly see that a fraction of a second before the first shot, the patrol had begun their counter tactics.

Farooq stopped the video, "They knew Sayeed! This ambush was doomed from the start," he said staring at the frozen images on his screen.

"But how?" asked Sayeed dumbfounded, and he slumped back into his chair.

Farooq was not given to idle conspiracies, but it was obvious, the enemy knew what was happening and had devised a plan to counter it. All of the efforts toward operational security and yet somewhere along the line, it failed.

"We have a leak, my friend. We need to go through all of our communications to try and find out who," stated Farooq almost matter-of-factly.

The breakdown of operational security was critical and much more of a problem than the result of this one operation. He knew this was part of the ongoing game between the movement and the western powers who were desperate to stop them. It was the constant push-pull of adaptation to the actions of their adversary that forced them to change tactics and methods constantly to accomplish their goals. But that push-pull went both ways, so Farooq quickly made a note of the actions that needed to be taken.

He turned back to the video to watch the battle unfold and narrated the tactics used by the allies as Sayeed took notes. Clearly, the enemy had taken out Rafiq's spotter and sniper, but his actions didn't show it. Somehow Rafiq didn't know. Farooq watched the front walls explode as the Americans sprinted along the sides of the compound. He pointed out that the speed at which the enemy was moving had caught Rafiq completely off guard, so the detonation of the IEDs ended up being behind the fast moving force.

The video then jumped as machine gun fire and explosions rocked the center and rear of the compound. The enemy had split their force but where did they come from? Farooq didn't see them until they were already entering the village. He immediately recognized that the fighters were trapped in a deadly crossfire with nowhere to retreat.

"Genius. The allied commander split his force and maneuvered behind the village. Notice Sayeed, they blinded our commander by killing his sniper then surrounded him without tipping their hand. Our men were being cut down from all directions, and they had no idea how. This caused mass confusion, and our commander had no way to counter it. Our people had nowhere to run, allowing the enemy to methodically clear the village and kill or capture every one of our fighters. But look at the efficiency and discipline of the ANA force," mused Farooq with a hint of admiration.

Finally, they saw the house in the center, the woman with the young boy, the explosion, and her execution. Although not happy with what he had seen, Farooq was pleased that they had something they could use, and the videographer's narrative was very good. He rewound the woman's execution again and noticed it was the ANA commander who took the shot. Another coincidence that he knew she had a vest? Whoever this ANA commander was, he was dangerous and Farooq needed to find out who he was, and fast.

"This is not the ANA we have fought before Sayeed, they are different and so is their commander. Find out who this man is, now!" ordered Farooq.

Sayeed got on the phone and set up a meeting with another operative to begin plans to uncover the identity of the ANA commander. The last thing the movement needed was an effective Afghan military resistance. It was bad enough they had to deal with the western troops who they couldn't infiltrate, but an Afghan Army commander who can instill that much discipline into his troops generally means he also has their loyalty. And to Farooq, that was a very dangerous new twist to the deadly game they played.

After Sayeed left, Farooq spent the next few hours splicing various parts of the battle together. He started with the explosion of the front wall, then the shooting of the woman, then the explosion of the house, and ended with some of the house to house fighting. He took notes and wanted the narrator to describe the battle as an attack on the villagers by the Americans and their lapdog ANA servants. The Americans shot and killed the woman pleading for her life, then blew up the house and slaughtered the villagers who put up a fierce resistance to the attack. He was pleased with the footage, and despite the loss on the battlefield, the propaganda effect was actually better than he expected.

He saved it to another miniature USB drive and went to his internet computer to log into the *Gods of Conquest* game to send a message to the courier. He would send it to the videographer for completion and would upload it to several websites. A copy would be sent to Al Jazeera which would ensure its worldwide distribution. Within 72 hours, the Americans would be bombarded by questions about the massacre at Zakar Khel by his media plants.

Chapter 8

Blowback

Madeline jumped when her secure phone rang at 3 AM. It was General Jameson of the Defense Intelligence Agency's operations center.

"Coltrain," Madeline grumbled as she answered.

" Madam Secretary we have a problem. A new video has been posted on some radical sites, and Al Jazeera is reporting that there was an American-led massacre in Afghanistan. We're in contact with CIA and NSA to confirm its authenticity and try to break it down for any editing. We've also contacted General McAffey, and he's working to track down what operation this was for our side of the story. One of our techs is sure the video was doctored, but we're getting the metadata off the digital feed for physical proof. The situation room has been notified, and we're putting together what we know. Your briefing materials will be waiting for you in the ops center when you get to the Pentagon."

Madeline initially grunted her acknowledgment of a problem, but when General Jameson said, "American-led massacre" she was wide awake. "Shit, call the Chiefs and get General Palmer out of bed. This will be a public relations nightmare. And Admiral Corchoran of Legislative Affairs. Once we have more details, I'll need to brief the Senate and House Majority and Minority leaders. Tell the NMCC I'll be there in 30 minutes and find out if they've told the President yet."

"Yes, ma'am." replied Jameson, "Your car will be there in 10 minutes Madam Secretary."

Since taking her first job in DC, Madeline had become an expert at the five minute shower and makeup. She kept her hair short, so she could get it dry fast and since it was naturally straight, it saved her lots of time. Tonight, though she did what she could, brushed it out, and headed out the door. She had a whole prep team at the Pentagon if she needed to do any interviews. But in a room full of people in uniform during a crisis, it was about the decisions, not how she looked.

Madeline lived in a swank gated community in the Georgetown neighborhood of DC. With a 24 hour guard at the entrance, it was home to several top administration officials. Her own residence was a three-story Georgian Colonial surrounded by a four foot stone wall with a 3 foot wrought iron fence on top. It added an additional layer of security, which made her protective detail very happy.

Ten minutes after the phone call from Jameson, Madeline stepped out of her home and into the middle vehicle of the three car motorcade waiting to take her to the Pentagon. As Madeline climbed into the car, her military attaché already had her laptop loaded with the video, the Al Jazeera report, and the initial DIA assessment.

"Madam Secretary, CSAF and the CNO are already at the Pentagon. The Commandant and CSA are about 5-10 minutes out and should be there when we arrive," her aide reported.

Madeline fired up the video and after watching it, read the DIA assessment. The video had been clearly spliced. Although they were verifying the time codes, it was deliberately done to imply a premeditated attack. Of course, the other side would claim the NSA doctored it, but DIA had already reached out to the Saudis requesting they also verify the time codes.

The Secretary's security detail moved quickly through the streets of DC from her Georgetown residence with the lead car and trail car hopscotching at each major intersection. Choosing the Rock Creek Parkway route, they made the turn off the Arlington Memorial Bridge and radioed one minute out. The detail peeled off the exit onto South Washington and initiated the automated challenge and response system to drop the security barriers, so they never had to slow down going to the underground parking area. Madeline went straight to the NMCC, National Military Command Center, and into the briefing room.

The Joint Chiefs were already there along with Public Affairs and Legislative Affairs. General McAffey was going through the lead up to the Zakar Khel operation on a satellite video feed from Kabul into the conference room. The Generals came to attention when Madeline walked into the room. "Take your seats gentlemen, let's get to it."

"Ma'am, the after-action report covering the action at Zakar Khel is in front of you," began General McAffey. "The battle referenced in the video was at the tail end of an extended joint patrol two weeks ago. It included two platoons of ANA 2nd Battalion, 1st Brigade, 203rd Corps, led by Lieutenant Colonel Abdul Qadir, their Battalion Commander, and a platoon of the U.S. 2nd Battalion, 27th Infantry Regiment, 3rd Brigade Combat Team, 25th Infantry Division, led by Major DB Watkins, Operations Officer. The senior commanders were on patrol to work negotiations with the village leaders along the way to gain their trust and cooperation.

"Colonel Qadir is one the best commanders in the ANA, and has the best trained and most disciplined units. He led the operation, and our troops provided support. They had discussions with the elders of five different villages prior to the battle with very good success. If you look at Tab 1, this is the beginning of the description of the battle." General McAffey had the command center staff pull up the satellite imagery of the Zakar Khel area. They traced the battle from the position where the patrol stopped and split, through the flanking maneuver, the breech of the rear house rescuing the elders' families, to the final shot of the woman with the bomb vest, and the explosion of the house with the enemy fighters as seen in the video.

"Finally, Madam Secretary, it was Colonel Qadir who brought his own troops back to the village to help the villagers rebuild with a U.S. engineering unit providing heavy equipment. The final Tab contains the messages from the village elders describing how honored they were to be helped by the patrol and were especially impressed by the respect the U.S. troops gave them and the ANA troops immediately after the battle. The U.S. commander was highlighted by the elders for his compassion but also his strong deference to the leadership of Colonel Qadir."

"Okay, so the video was made at the battle. Have we determined where the person who shot the video was located?" asked Secretary Coltrain.

"Our best estimate, based on preliminary evaluation of the terrain features, would be in the area to the east of the village. They likely walked back to Pakistan just a half a click away Ma'am," replied Colonel Johnston, from the intelligence desk. "From there they could process the video and upload from any number of places. NSA is working to trace those upload locations, and CIA is working on the Al Jazeera link."

"General McAffey, have you spoken to your counterpart in the ANA?" asked Madeline.

"Yes, Madam Secretary, we have spoken, and he is briefing the Prime Minister from the same after-action report," replied McAffey.

"So, what's our game plan to contain this?" asked Madeline.

Major General Palmer, the SecDef's Director of Public Affairs spoke now. "Ma'am, normally we would clamp down and maintain complete control of the messaging. The Islamists will expect us to post a vigorous denial and then they will counter that we are the ones trying to manage the fallout. There is no doubt that this has been doctored as propaganda. But to the Muslim world, it will be used to discredit us even more. Even though we have confirmation from the Saudi's that the video is doctored, they have their own issues with Islamic radicalism. Their appearance to side with us could spark protests within their own country.

"The one thing they rely on is that our media will do all they can to use the story to discredit the military for their own sensationalism and therefore will run with the story 24/7. I propose we do something unexpected. We offer to fly the media to the village with no military handlers, including Al Jazeera. We use the Afghan commander to provide external security and have our own camera crew record the whole thing. We haul two satellite trucks in for a shared feed, which we will tap into and record all raw feeds. But we need to do this back channel because as soon as we let it be known, we give the enemy a chance to spoil our party," Palmer finished.

"So how would we do that?" asked Madeline.

"We ask each media outlet to identify one reporter and one cameraman for an undisclosed briefing and have them report to us. Make it a one-time offer but tell them nothing about what or where they will be taken. Tell them they have fifteen minutes to make up their mind and if they delay, they get locked out. Do it now, before the story gets too much traction, and the press won't be able to resist. They'd run over their mother to make this deadline. Once in our control, we fly them to the village," stated Palmer.

"That's a risky plan, General," responded Madeline. "Without controlling the message who knows what the press will come up with."

"Yes, Madam Secretary, but that's what we want. The fact that there could be competing stories puts doubt into the original video. By giving the media unfiltered access and a shared satellite link, the participants will have access to all of the raw feeds. So if anyone does try to spin it, the others will jump all over them. Having the ANA run point on security should satisfy the Afghan PM to ensure there's less chance of them trying to create blowback on us. It was, after all, a highly successful ANA led operation. That's where we direct the focus," responded Palmer.

"Well gentlemen, any comments?" asked Madeline.

Admiral Joffrey was the only one to speak for the Chiefs, "Madam Secretary, we're in agreement that the risks are worth the benefits. General McAffey will provide the logistics, and we'll have some of our own intelligence assets embedded in the group as interpreters."

"High risk, high reward, right? Then it's decided," declared the Secretary of Defense. "Contact the Situation Room and tell them I'm on my way to the White House to brief the President. Time to wake him up."

CHAPTER 9

Return to Zakar Khel

Sergeant Kirkorian watched the hulking C-17 land under a bright midday sun. It effortlessly glided to the parking area where she and the team from HQ would meet their guests. She was already in civilian clothes for her cover as a contract interpreter, and would accompany the press group to the site of the battle highlighted in the latest radical video.

The U.S. and Afghan governments had issued a joint statement decrying the video as being altered to show a misleading account of an important battle. As expected, the Muslim press replayed it over and over again and claimed it as fact. But Al Jazeera, the network who broke the story, held back its criticism due to the upcoming access to the battle site. Kirkorian suspected they had already verified the date codes at the urging of the Saudis, but they weren't overly friendly with the Kingdom.

It had been less than 24 hours between the Pentagon's offer to the press and the C-17 carrying the entourage landing at Bagram. The personnel from the 25th Infantry Division HQ had to move mountains to prepare for such a high profile mission with little upside, but the potential for massive downside if done poorly. They'd done a mad scramble to get DC the details of the op and coordinate the security assets for the visit to the village. Assets that would have to be pulled from other missions, but in the eyes of the Pentagon, this was the most important mission in theater right now.

As each news outlet accepted the Pentagon's offer, the Intel section was updated in real-time. Al Jazeera had replied to the offer immediately and was joined by the three mainstream American broadcast networks, Fox and CNN from the cable news organizations, IRIN of the UN Office for the Coordination of Humanitarian Affairs, Pajhwok Afghan News, Reuters, Associated Press, Agence France-Presse, and United Press International. There were some other smaller outlets who had a seat in the Pentagon press corps and the CIA also had a crew as part of the group, but Kirkorian wasn't sure which one. They were likely one of the more obscure news outlets.

"Ladies and gentlemen, welcome to Bagram Air Base, I am Major Blake and will be your point of contact during your visit," the senior public affairs officer began as the press gathered after exiting the airplane.

"You are being handed a package with a schedule of events, a summary of the after-action report, satellite imagery of the surrounding area of the battle, and a USB drive with images of the immediate aftermath of the battle. There will be a short press conference in the morning with the two commanders who led the operation at Zakar Khel, you'll then be airlifted by helicopter to the village. You will have free access to the villagers without any military handlers or interference, and the ANA unit in the video will provide security.

"These people here are contract translators and will accompany you on this junket. We have provided translators who not only speak your native languages but also English, Dari, and Pashtun," Blake stated as Kirkorian blended into the small group of contract translators.

"You will be escorted by Lieutenant Colonel Qadir, commander of the ANA unit who conducted the operation, and Lieutenant Colonel Watkins, commander of the U.S. forces supporting them. Colonel Qadir's battalion will provide physical security outside the village, and a small personal security detail will enter the village with you and the commanders to ensure maximum freedom for your visit. An Armed Forces Radio and Television Service crew positioned in Khost will accompany the ANA security force to Zakar Khel to provide a shared feed for the junket. They have two satellite trucks available for video and audio uplink for all news outlets," he continued.

The shared satellite feed was especially important as it ensured the Pentagon access to all of the raw feeds broadcast back to the respective media organizations. That way the Pentagon could prepare counter arguments for any news coming out of the junket before it could be aired.

"I know it's been a long trip, so from here you'll be escorted to your quarters. We're sorry that it is sparse, but it's the best we have to offer. You'll be in a group of trailers at the edge of the airfield and will be 8 people to a trailer. Once you're settled, we have food and drinks set up for you so you can relax before our trip to Zakar Khel. Ladies, please follow Sergeant Hopkins here and men follow Sergeant Jordan. They will take you to your assigned trailers and ensure you have everything you need to make you comfortable. Again, welcome to Bagram and we hope you have a safe and successful trip," Major Blake finished.

Although many field journalists were used to the inconveniences of working in the inhospitable environment of an active war zone, most of their guests weren't field reporters. To Kirkorian, that meant having to kowtow to the egos of a bunch of pampered elitists, but also made her cover easier to sell. Most of these people would only see things on the surface, but the field reporters, those would be the ones she had to watch for. They would know if something looked out of place.

Once the visitors were situated in their quarters, they were brought to the make-shift club for their impromptu mixer. This would ensure they were out of the way and kept under wraps until the press conference in the morning. Kirkorian mingled for a few minutes with the reporters at the informal meet and greet. This gave her the chance to converse with several of them to get a feel for who could be trouble.

Afterward, she headed over to the Division command post for the commanders' prep session. SecDef requested that the Afghan government have Colonel Qadir and some of his men meet at Bagram to provide immediate security for the junket. In addition, she ordered that Colonel Watkins join them and be available to the press. This was by far the biggest risk of the whole trip, and both military men would go through several hours of press prep.

* * *

DB Watkins' father had done countless interviews as a commanding General and had talked at length about how he dealt with questions from the press. Growing up, Watkins would help with his father's prep, and reveled in his ability to trip his father up. He was a relentless questioner who knew how to push his father's buttons, and usually it was his prep that got his dad through some pretty tough questioning. As the public affairs team moved through their preparation of the two commanders for the press conference, Watkins was active and aggressive. He huddled with the questioners several times to use different strategies against Qadir.

Qadir was a natural in front of a microphone, pausing ever so slightly after each question then calmly providing an answer, just enough but not too much. The prep team threw everything at him; inflammatory accusations of corruption and maltreatment of prisoners, opinions about Afghan leadership, even trying to interrupt his answers to throw him off game. Qadir handled everything calmly, coolly, and always maintained his stoic demeanor. The female translator who had arrived as their prep session was getting started provided translation when Qadir felt more comfortable answering in Dari. Both commanders marveled at her ability to shift from one language to another without hesitation.

Only once did Qadir slip up and it was when Watkins went after him about his being Shia and his enemies being Sunni Muslims. "Do you consider yourself an Imam over your men, Colonel Qadir?" asked Watkins.

Qadir froze, only momentarily but enough for the prep team to notice. He gave a slight smile and calmly replied, "No, I'm no Imam, just a leader of a group of very brave men who have grown to respect each other and the people of Afghanistan."

Watkins pressed, "What did you feel when you killed that Sunni woman?"

Qadir shifted his feet, uncomfortable with the line of questioning but he maintained a cool demeanor and answered, "I felt sorrow. We are taught that women should be revered and protected. It brings me great sadness to see anyone, especially a woman and possibly a mother, use herself as a weapon. Much worse that she would use a child as a human shield to carry out her evil intentions. She was a threat that had to be neutralized, as a soldier I had to set aside my concerns for this one woman and consider the safety of dozens of others, men, women, and children."

"Do you see this fight with the Taliban as a way to push back against those who desire the rise of a new Caliphate?" Watkins asked.

Qadir paused for a second and cleared his throat, "The fight with the Taliban is uniquely Afghan. It's about whether Afghans want the return of a theocracy that desires to control them by force and apply their own beliefs of Islamic faith. These brave men you see before you don't fight for someone claiming to be the next Caliph. They fight to protect their villages and families...."

Watkins interrupted Qadir with his next question, "Colonel, do you agree with Iran's intervention in Iraq, Syria, and Yemen on the side of the Shia against the Sunni?"

Qadir took a deep breath and replied, "There is no doubt that factions within Islam wish to continue a conflict that has raged for 1400 years, but our focus is our own country and our own people. It is up to our leaders to respond to events happening outside of our control."

Watkins smiled. He knew he put Qadir through the ringer and the slight sweat on Qadir's brow confirmed the intensity of the exchange even if others didn't quite understand. "I'm sorry to have made you uncomfortable, my friend. I intended no insult, but our press are not known for their sensitivity. I do believe they will try to get you to say something about the issues between Islam and the west, or between Shia and Sunni to support their own worldview. Plus, they love to get us 'grunts' to say something stupid they can club our leaders over the head with," he said.

"DB, how did you know that Shia and Sunni have very different views on what an Imam means?" asked Qadir quietly.

"Yes, sir, why did that question cause Colonel Qadir to stumble? I mean it was subtle and barely noticeable, but it was clear he was on the defensive after that," asked the Public Affairs staff officer running the prep.

"When I was in Iraq, I studied not only those we were fighting but why there was such a divide between the two sects so I could better understand the situation. It was critical in working with the Awakening groups and negotiating between them and the government officials. Once we understood the divides we had to cross, it was easier to find the common ground," Watkins began.

"As for the question, the Shia in Iraq felt insulted because the Sunni called those who led prayer Imams. To them, it minimized the importance of the role of the Imam in the Shia faith because they are considered the chosen ones of God and free from all sin. It's one of the many chasms in the rift between the sects and the Sunni's ability to trust the Shia run government. So, I knew that if I put Colonel Qadir on the defensive, it would make it easier to get him to say something he didn't intend. I'm impressed with your control my friend," replied Watkins turning back to Qadir.

"So you think these press people would risk insulting the government to twist the truth?" asked Qadir.

"I think they'd insult their grandmother if it meant they could get a better story. Most of them want to believe the garbage the enemy has put out about Zakar Khel. They already think we're the monsters and the truth doesn't tell as good a story," replied Watkins.

Qadir thought for a moment, "I see. Then I must pray on how best to deal with these people. Thank you, my friend... know your enemy, right?"

Watkins had to laugh out loud. Funny how military men everywhere had similar views of the press. They knew their importance but also the dangers of a free press.

Qadir turned to the interpreter and spoke to her in Dari, "Please forgive me for speaking directly to you young lady, but your Dari is excellent. Thank you for your assistance. May I ask your name?"

"Staff Sergeant Shirin Kirkorian, sir. It is an honor working with you on this mission. Please just call me Shirin during the trip with the reporters. As far as they know I'm a contract interpreter," she replied in perfect Hazaragi, the dialect from the Hazarajat region of Afghanistan, Qadir's homeland.

The surprise on Qadir's face was noticeable and confirmed why he was confused. Kirkorian was dressed in civilian clothes and wore a traditional hijab, the head-scarf that covers the head and chest of adult women in the presence of men outside of their immediate family. In addition, she stood behind the men and deferred to their authority.

"An American soldier, I would not have guessed. Your Dari is virtually perfect Sergeant, I must say I'm very impressed. I tried to place your dialect in a particular region of Afghanistan but couldn't. I've never met an American who spoke such perfect Dari," Qadir stated.

Initially, he thought she was Iranian because of the subtle intricacies of his Farsi based language. But she had this air of confidence, almost imperceptible, that his instincts as a soldier picked up...the eyes sweeping the room, her walk, not stooped and defeated but alert and ready. And though he saw no weapons on her, he was now certain she was armed.

"How did you know where I was from?" asked Qadir.

"Thank you for the compliment, Sir. I read your file before coming here, but I also heard the inflections in your voice. Your efforts with your men and your leadership is inspiring, and I'm humbled to be allowed to work with you," replied Kirkorian.

"Shirin, that's an Iranian name, isn't it? With the skill of your translation I could believe you were native to the region," said Qadir.

"My family is Orthodox Christian from northern Iran. My parents emigrated to the U.S. during the revolution. I've been speaking Farsi all of my life and Dari and Pashtun are derivatives of that so not a big stretch to vary the dialects. Plus, I have a PhD in linguistics, and I've studied all of the dialects of your country," explained Kirkorian.

"A doctorate? Why are you enlisted and not an officer?" asked Qadir.

"Sir, as an officer, your men would not talk to me. It could be insulting to them for a woman to have authority over a man. As an enlisted soldier, I fit better within the authority structure of your culture, and it allows me to be more effective," responded Kirkorian.

"You sacrifice much, Sergeant, I hope your commanders know just how valuable you are," said Qadir.

"Thank you, Sir, but then again I don't have to deal with all the crap either," replied Kirkorian with a chuckle. "Colonel, may I ask about your name? It's more associated with a Sunni name rather than Shia is it not?"

"Yes Sergeant, you are correct. I grew up during the Russian occupation and my father, as a leader of the Mujahedeen, gave me the name so I could blend in better to gather information. The Russians didn't care or understand, but their Afghan cohorts would have looked at me with suspicion if they knew I was Hazara. And who pays attention to a young boy running around. It's served me well over the years," he said with a smile and a twinkle in his eye.

"Ah, that makes perfect sense. Thank you, Sir. Seems we both have sacrificed to do what must be done," Kirkorian replied smiling.

Qadir turned to Watkins. "Colonel Watkins, you need to take very good care of this young woman. She may be your best weapon."

* * *

The next morning the press rallied in a hangar for the Q&A with Qadir and Watkins before jumping off for Zakar Khel. The constant drumbeat of helicopters coming and going, and the acrid smell of airplane exhaust permeated the air around them. Major Blake started the presser off by introducing Watkins and Qadir. He went through the details of the patrol leading up to the battle from the official after-action report handed out to the reporters the previous day. Kirkorian stood just behind Qadir throughout and provided translation. She wore sky blue baggy cotton pants called Panjabi, with the matching traditional long smock dress called Perahaan and a red headscarf common in Kabul, looking every bit a local.

"Colonel Watkins, Jeremy Perfeldt of NBC. Do you agree with President Saldana's drawdown of U.S. forces from Afghanistan?"

Watkins didn't hesitate, "As a soldier, we follow orders and it's not our place to agree or disagree. We see what's in front of us and take appropriate actions. We had a mission, we completed that mission successfully, but unfortunately, we lost some very brave men doing it, Afghan and American."

Jeremy pressed on, "Colonel, so many of the joint patrols end up with U.S. soldiers taking over the operation. Isn't it true the ANA isn't equipped to handle the Taliban on their own?"

Watkins' eyes took on a piercing, almost menacing look as he turned to respond to the reporter. "Sir, Colonel Qadir led this operation from start to finish, and his men performed as well as any soldiers I've had the honor to fight with. Do not dishonor the nine Afghan soldiers who lost their lives by implying they weren't skilled. The enemy tried to ambush us with a very large assault force, and when the shooting started, Colonel Qadir and all of his men executed their counter tactics perfectly. In addition, the care he took with the villagers and the prisoners was as impressive as his leadership in battle. I'm sure the villagers will tell you the same thing. Whatever has happened somewhere else, rest assured it didn't happen here."

"Colonel, Hassan Al-Ahmed of Al Jazeera. The video released by the Taliban paints a very different picture of what happened in Zakar Khel. Why did you blow up that house and shoot that innocent woman?"

Qadir tapped Watkins on the shoulder indicating he would answer the question and stepped to the microphone with Kirkorian behind him also with a microphone. "First of all, you already know the video was manipulated to show a false view of the actions in Zakar Khel. As the after-action report shows, the Taliban leaders had withdrawn to that house with the son of the senior village elder. The woman had a suicide vest and was using the boy as a distraction to get closer to our troops. When she didn't follow instructions, I neutralized her and rescued the boy. The Taliban acted cowardly, and against the teachings of Islam, by detonating the bomb in the house, sacrificing themselves."

"So, you are the one who shot the woman? How did you know she was a threat?" asked the reporter.

"Yes, it was my decision and mine alone. The woman had a clenched fist, and the boy was trying to pull away from her, indicating fear. After she was neutralized, she dropped the detonator. We secured the boy and called EOD."

"Colonel Qadir, Jaques Leroux, Agence France-Presse. Do you enjoy killing the Taliban?"

The question was so matter of fact that it caught even Watkins off guard, but Qadir sighed and looked down briefly before speaking. "No, I do not enjoy killing of any kind. These men are brothers in faith, misguided by evil men who use the Prophet to justify their lust for power. Sunni, Shia, Pashtun, Hazara, we are linked by our faith and our common history, different...but the same. I kill to protect the innocent, as the Koran demands. But when the killing is done, we pray, and honor those who are willing to stop their aggression. They deserve our forgiveness and help. Many have joined us to protect the villages of our country against their former leaders."

"Colonel Qadir, Erica Tabor, ABC News. Do you believe your troops can protect the people of Afghanistan, given the corruption inside your government and its confrontational stance toward U.S. policy in Afghanistan?"

"As to the question of our ability to protect our people, I'll leave that to the villagers of Zakar Khel to answer. We work closely with the international community who helped liberate us from the tyranny of the Taliban, and for many, there is still much to learn. As Colonel Watkins said, we are soldiers. We follow the orders of our leaders, we fight with what we have, and work with the Afghan elders to bring peace to our country," Qadir answered.

And with that, the public affairs officer ended the press conference and ushered the group to the helicopters. Torvath Dean, AP's top war correspondent, had held back during the short presser and positioned himself right behind the commanders as the group started moving. He was an Aussie who spent years covering all kinds of battlefields including the Afghan campaign embedded with several units at the height of the fighting.

Dean hadn't asked any questions at the presser. In his mind, they never got a straight answer from these guys except the pat, practiced answers the PA guys drill into them. He preferred to get into the field where the soldiers are comfortable and then ask his questions more privately. Years of working with military men taught him about their procedures, and he used that knowledge to maneuver himself into the same helicopter as Colonel Qadir.

The route to Zakar Khel had been swept both from the air and the ground prior to the arrival of the press corps. The two large CH-47D Chinook helicopters carrying the press were shadowed by attack helicopters, and unbeknownst to the press, an AC-130 Spectre gunship provided aerial coverage high above the group. U.S. Special Forces had taken up positions in the area around Zakar Khel to cover the landing zones. Qadir's men were already positioned defensively around the village, most out of sight, with a small protective force at the landing zone to meet the press and provide security inside the village during the visit. This allowed the press complete freedom inside the village and ensured they would not have any military interference.

Qadir was positioned at the rear ramp of the lead Chinook seated across from the reporter from the AP. Dean had seen all kinds of soldiers and studied Qadir carefully since Bagram. Qadir had an almost serene look on his face throughout the flight, a calm confidence rarely seen in soldiers. They had been in the air about 45 minutes when Dean saw Qadir look at his watch and noticed his demeanor change instantly. He sat more erect in his seat, his face became stern and resolute, and Dean saw him glance toward his command sergeant giving a slight nod. Dean understood right away that they were getting close to the LZ and it was game on.

The ramp of the massive helicopter was opening before the aircraft touched down. Qadir and this small contingent of soldiers were already on the move as the ramp hit the ground, deploying on both sides of the aircraft they set up in defensive positions. With a wave of his hand, Qadir commanded the reporters to exit and move quickly to the security of the vehicles that were at the LZ to meet them.

VALLEY OF STARS

For the less experienced reporters, the danger instantly became real as the soldiers set up their perimeter.

Many of the reporters found themselves complying immediately without realizing it. Dean knew this was partly for show, but he had also been on enough patrols to know that preparing for the unexpected was the difference between life and death in this place. It also told him much more about the man he was studying. Qadir and his men were extremely disciplined and executed better than any other ANA troops he had ever encountered.

As the group of reporters made their way to the vehicles, Dean held back a bit. The interpreter from the presser had silently glided up beside him and startled him by putting her hand on his back, "Is there a problem sir?" the interpreter asked.

"No, no problem" he replied.

"They won't move until you do, so perhaps you can move to the vehicles a little faster," the interpreter urged.

Qadir and his men formed up behind Dean and moved quickly, taking positions in each of the vehicles with reporters. Dean headed to the lead vehicle, guessing that was the one Qadir would ride in. He guessed wrong. Qadir headed to the middle one with the interpreter. Dean was just about to climb into the vehicle when he glanced back at the middle vehicle and saw the interpreter pause, just briefly, and scan around the vehicles. Dean's senses were suddenly heightened. This woman was not your normal interpreter. Either she had been in theater a long time or had training that makes one do things by instinct. He suspected the latter and made a mental note to find out.

The convoy of vehicles from the two helicopters joined up for the short trip to Zakar Khel. The vehicles moved up the road from the LZ by the river, only about 500 meters from the village. In each vehicle was a person pointing out geographic details contained in the after action-report of the battle. The walls of the village still showed the gaping holes from the missiles and pock marks of the bullets. The village elders met the convoy at the entrance and welcomed their visitors. They rushed over to Qadir as he stepped out of his vehicle, smiling, grasping his hand with both of theirs, and saying "As-salamu 'alaykum," "May peace be with you," then speaking softly but quickly.

Kirkorian and the other interpreters told the reporters that the elders were thanking Qadir for protecting them and asking if he would honor them by sharing some tea. Qadir responded to them and explained that the visitors were there to talk to them about the recent attack on their village. He went out of his way to ask the villagers to be open with the visitors. To answer their questions as best they could, and to be patient with the foreigners because they may not understand the village customs. He stated that the reporters are not there to deliberately dishonor them but if something happens, then please ask the interpreters to correct them, and if needed to call him.

At that point, Qadir turned to the reporters and through the interpreters, told them to please be respectful of the villagers. If they want to speak with the women, to please do so with one of the female interpreters as it is dishonorable for a man who is not related to speak with the women unless a male relative is present. He then assured everyone that respect given will be respect returned and that the soldiers will be on the outskirts of the village so that the reporters and villagers are free to speak without any interference.

Qadir turned to the leader of the village and asked if Colonel Watkins could join them for tea. While a bit of a breach in protocol, the elder immediately agreed with a big smile and hearty hand shake with Watkins.

Dean moved up next to Qadir and asked the elder, "Sir, if you would allow me to join you to ask you some questions?" Dean knew this wasn't the way to ask, but he needed to see Qadir with this man up close.

Once the interpreter relayed the reporter's request, the elder's smile vanished. But Qadir spoke up with a bit of a smile, "My friend meant no disrespect. He is here to understand what happened to you and your people. You would honor me to have him join us for tea as well."

As the interpreter spoke, Dean was astonished to have this military man vouch for him. He fully expected to be reprimanded by the elder or Qadir for such a blatant breach of respect, but he hadn't gotten where he was without taking chances. The elder nodded in approval but looked at Dean with suspicion.

The four men entered the elder's home, and he showed the men where to sit with the interpreter kneeling just behind the elder with Qadir to his right. The elder's wife brought out tea and food. Then, without speaking a word, quickly removed herself from the room with the children. Once the wife had left, the elder began talking to Qadir while the interpreter translated for Watkins and Dean.

"Colonel, we were excited to hear that you would be returning to our village. We praise Allah for you and your men, and are humbled by the care you have shown our village. And Colonel Watkins, we are honored by your return as well. Thank you for your kindness and respect, not all of our meetings with the foreign troops have gone so well, but you are the first Americans we met, and I hope they are all like you."

The military men made small talk with the elder asking about how his eldest son was recovering from the trauma of the woman who held him, praising the boy for his bravery and his fight that exposed her. They asked about the rebuilding of the village, and Qadir promised to send more help to repair the outer walls.

After a while, the elder finally turned to Dean. "You've been very quiet my friend. You said you had questions for me?" the interpreter translated.

"Tori Dean from the Associated Press, sir. After pushing my way to join you here, I felt it best to wait until you were ready. Clearly, you had some catching up to do with these gentlemen."

"Thank you, Mr. Dean, that was very kind of you. I owe my life and that of my family to these men, Allah be praised," stated the elder.

"Can you tell me what happened here, in your own words?" asked Dean.

"The Taliban came into our village and threatened us with death. We've had to deal with these devils for years, and they were punishing us for cooperating with the government. They beat several of our men in front of their families and held us at gunpoint to watch, wanting to know when the government troops would return."

"They forced my family and those of the other elders into a house at the back of the compound and ordered us to set the trap for the government troops or they would kill our children. They took all our guns and said that anyone who came out of their houses would be shot and their families executed. The other elders and I were the bait to bring these men into the trap, but they were smarter than the Taliban," the elder said with a smile.

"When the shooting started, we ran for cover, but some of our men were killed. The Taliban used our people as human shields, and it's only through Allah's will that these men were more skilled than our enemy. When the shooting stopped, I heard a woman screaming something and my son's voice struggling to get free. I was able to look out a window when I saw her shot and my son rescued." He put his hand on Qadir's. "I will forever be in this man's debt." The elder's eyes watered just a bit as he spoke the last bit and the emotion was not lost on the veteran reporter.

"How did the American troops treat you?" Dean asked.

"Colonel Watkins rescued our families and honored us after the battle by respecting our traditions. The Taliban promised to execute them if we betrayed their plans, or if the battle went against them. I believe they would have killed them anyway. They wanted to kill as many people as possible and blame the allied troops for the massacre. Colonel Watkins rescued them at the same time as Colonel Qadir entered the front of the village," replied the elder.

Dean looked at Watkins who understood the unspoken question and responded, "We circled around during the frontal assault and hit the rear house where they held the families. We breached the door and neutralized the Taliban inside. It's in the after-action report."

Dean pressed the elder a bit, "So you took out your anger on the prisoners for their threats against you?"

"No, Colonel Qadir protected them from our people. He wanted no retribution as much as we wanted to, and actually knelt and prayed with them before the trucks came to take them away," stated the elder.

"And the Americans?" asked Dean.

"Colonel Watkins' men collected the dead and placed them in one of our buildings carefully and with great respect. Then they stood guard as one of Colonel Qadir's men said prayers over them as is the Muslim tradition. I have never met any foreign troops who showed so much discipline and respect," responded the elder.

"So they treated them with kindness after the battle and after what the Taliban had done to your people?" asked Dean almost disbelieving what he was hearing.

"Not kindness, but respect. The Taliban are still dangerous men who follow brutal leaders. Men follow the lead of those who command them and that was the case on both sides. Many of the prisoners were shocked that here was the commander of their enemy, kneeling and leading them in prayer. Those that refused to pray with him were separated from the others and led away by Colonel Qadir's men and the two groups left in different trucks."

Dean looked at Qadir as the interpreter translated the elder's description of the interaction with the prisoners. Clearly this man was different. "Colonel Qadir, why did you pray with the prisoners?"

"They are brothers in faith led by people who use the Prophet to gain power for themselves. By showing respect and compassion through the link of our shared faith, I try and make them see a different path. Mr. Dean, perhaps you don't realize it but many of my men who now fight with us are former Taliban. They were manipulated, and I simply opened their eyes," replied Qadir matter-of-factly.

The shock on Dean's face was obvious to all sitting there and the elder chuckled a bit at his expense. There was little in this country that surprised this veteran journalist, but this did. It confirmed that Qadir was much more than just a competent Afghan Army commander, but someone Dean needed to keep on his radar as much as possible.

Qadir thanked the elder for his hospitality and suggested that their small group needed to check on the rest of the press group. It was clear the ANA had increased their patrols in the area and Colonel Watkins promised more help for the villagers to finish rebuilding. The two soldiers then presented the elder with some small gifts; Watkins, a container of tea and a package of dates from Kabul, and Qadir, a bag of loose tobacco, thanking him for honoring them with his hospitality.

The elder grasped each man's hand and put his other hand on his heart saying, "As-salamu 'alaikum." The officers replied "Wa 'alaikum as-salaam," "and peace be upon you." The elder then turned to the interpreter and extended his hand to her. She grasped his hand by the fingers and slightly bowed, as is the protocol, and the elder thanked the woman for her service to the group. Dean was a bit surprised by this, as Afghan men normally do not shake the hand of a woman. Clearly, the elder perceived she was no ordinary interpreter. Dean wasn't sure how, but there was something about her that was...different.

As the group walked from the elder's home, Dean and the interpreter followed the two commanders. Dean turned to the woman. "May I ask who you are?"

"Of course, you may ask," replied the interpreter but she stopped there.

Dean was again caught off guard as he expected her to continue. After a few awkward moments of silence, Dean asked, "I'm sorry, have I offended you?"

"No, Mr. Dean. You said you wanted to ask me who I am, so by all means, ask," replied the interpreter.

"I see, forgive me," said Dean. "Who are you? What's your name?"

"My name is Shirin. I'm a contract interpreter," replied Kirkorian.

"Where are you from?" continued Dean.

"I came down from Kabul, just like you," responded Kirkorian bluntly.

One of the things that frustrated Dean in this country was that people tended to talk in circles. They would answer the question, but often it only caused confusion and more questions. Getting answers from this woman was like taking two steps forward and one step back.

So Dean pressed a little harder. "What I meant was, where did you come from before Afghanistan?"

Kirkorian continued to look straight ahead while answering. "Where we are born and where we come from may be very different things, Mr. Dean. For instance, I suspect you were raised in the Canberra region of Australia but spent a great deal of time in Sydney. You also have a bit of New York influence in your voice. It was obvious, you have lived and worked in the U.S. So where do you consider yourself to be from?" responded Kirkorian.

Dean was stunned into silence and stopped dead in his tracks. "How the hell did you know that? Did you read a goddamn dossier on me before coming here?" demanded Dean indignantly, louder than he realized.

The whole group stopped, turned, and looked directly at him. Kirkorian looked at him with her eyes slightly narrowed, and her head tilted to the side. Before anyone else could speak, Kirkorian replied, "Mr. Dean, it is disrespectful to curse. I haven't read any dossier on you nor do I have any knowledge about one. You approached Colonel Qadir, not the other way around. I am a linguist. You can't hide the influences in your language. That's what makes me good at my job. It was simply an observation, nothing more, but your reaction confirms that I was correct."

Qadir and Watkins both glared at the reporter and Watkins shot back in a calm, yet menacing voice, "Mr. Dean, we had less than 24 hours' notice about this visit. Look how many of you from the press are here. Do you really think we had time to memorize everyone's background, or anything else before you arrived? Now I expect you to lower your voice and apologize to this young woman."

Dean suddenly realized that several of the village men were looking at him. Some soldiers had appeared as if out of nowhere, responding to a possible threat. A wave of embarrassment and fear flooded Dean's emotions. In a fraction of a second he went from the veteran reporter making his interviewee the nervous one, to the bumbling intern more nervous than the person he was questioning. "I...I'm very sorry for my outburst, Shirin. I meant no disrespect," Dean said looking like a whipped dog.

The group turned and continued walking, Dean striding to catch up to the two soldiers. Kirkorian smiled to herself. Everything she told him had been the truth in one form or another. She knew that it would shut down further questions about her from this reporter as the confusion, embarrassment, and frustration was written all over Dean's face.

The press visit was finally done, and the soldiers wanted to get the reporters out of there before sundown for their own protection. As they were gathering at the vehicles, Qadir was giving orders to his troops, and Dean had managed to regain his composure. He came up to Kirkorian for one last question. "Shirin, again I'm so sorry for earlier but may I ask you a couple of questions."

"By all means Mr. Dean," replied Kirkorian.

"Have you worked with Colonel Qadir long?" asked Dean.

"I met him yesterday, but his reputation precedes him," Kirkorian stated bluntly.

"What is your opinion of Colonel Qadir?" Dean asked.

"Colonel Watkins can tell you more, but in my interactions with these men Colonel Qadir is a unique man who changes attitudes and lives. I suspect the discussion with the village leaders brought you to the same conclusion," Kirkorian responded.

She waved her arm in a long arc across the village and the gathering soldiers. "Look around you. Here is a man from the minority Shiite Hazarat region of Afghanistan who stirs utter loyalty, devotion, and yes, love from virtually everyone he comes in contact with. Shia, Sunni, Pashtun, Tajik, Uzbek, Hazari, they follow him not just because of what he says, but by what he does. Ambitious but humble, deadly yet compassionate, driven but patient, feared and loved.

"In this part of the world, there is no one else like him. Yet if you ask him, it's not what he does, but what God does through him and the people he serves. That's the most impressive, he doesn't see them as serving him. He believes he should serve them," Kirkorian said.

"Now Mr. Dean, it's time for us to get moving back to the helicopters so please take your seat so Colonel Qadir can get us out of here," Kirkorian finished pointing to the vehicle they were standing next to, then turned and moved back to the command group.

Dean made notes as the group returned to Kabul. This was a man he had to know more about.

CHAPTER 10

Northwest Frontier

Positioned at the eastern end of the Kyber Pass, Peshawar, Pakistan was part of the Silk Road of ancient times and remains an important trade center for all of Central Asia. It was a hub of activity during the Soviet occupation of Afghanistan and provided a secure base of operations for the Mujahedeen resistance and U.S. CIA support. When the Taliban took power, it became the center of Pakistan's support for their government and allowed Pakistan to move military units to the borders with India. As some of the Pakistani Taliban got restive after the U.S. defeat of their brethren in Afghanistan, it became the center of responsibility to counter them in the tribal territories.

The problem for Pakistan was the historically deep ties between the military forces and Taliban chieftains in the area which created suspicions in the West about Pakistan's true intentions. They had a delicate balancing act to perform to prevent the area from exploding into another problem like Kashmir in the east. So when it suited them, Pakistan would run very visible operations in the tribal regions but with less than stellar results.

Peshawar itself was facing significant challenges now that the security situation had dramatically improved. Recently its explosive growth had strained its once pristine resources, as water and air pollution often became choking at certain times of the year.

But today there was a warm southern breeze that pushed the pungent smell of the smog north, away from the Pakistan Army XI Corps Headquarters compound. It allowed the commander to open the doors to the terrace off his office to enjoy the mild weather and a brilliant morning sunrise.

The XI Corps Headquarters complex covered about 50 acres on the southern tip of the city. Bordered by a tributary flood channel of the Kabul River and Hayatabad-Bare Road, it was a walled city within a city. The base contained everything from houses, office buildings, industrial areas, a school, and parade grounds. The Headquarters building itself was an ornate L shaped building, with a domed atrium at its apex, located at the north end of the compound. Housing the intelligence and command brain trust of the largest military district in Pakistan, the commander managed nearly 100,000 military and civilian personnel.

The current commander of XI Corps, Lieutenant General Muhamad Al-Zuq, seemed highly effective at getting results...or so the Pakistan leaders thought. Though he was known as a pious man, his sometimes brutal tactics caused concerns in Islamabad. But they seemed to have the desired effect and terrorist incidents had dramatically dropped in the area since his arrival. And in this dangerous game of strategic maneuvering, perception is reality. A perception of success the leaders of Pakistan were happy to bask in, no matter how it was accomplished.

General Al-Zuq sat with his second in command, Major General Ahmad Rabbani, at a small conference table laid out with tea and snack cakes. The XI Corps commander was a large man for his country. Six foot two with a broad muscular frame, he cut a very imposing figure. He was pleased with how things were moving along and was anxious to get the results of the intelligence mission he had initiated. But it took all of the control he learned over the years to wait patiently for his guest.

Rabbani took a long drag off his cigarette and blew a cloud of sweet, aromatic smoke that hung in the air and slowly wafted out the open terrace doors. "Congratulations on the very public executions of those animals who struck the children's school. It feels good to see all of the groundwork you've laid over the years finally bear fruit Sir."

"You know what they say Ahmad, 'the enemy of my enemy is my friend.' The tribal leaders kept their word and our agreement is working quite well," Al-Zuq chuckled.

Al-Zuq had worked hard over the years to reach out to the tribal leaders in the Northwest frontier. He had established contacts within the Afghan Taliban and those on the Pakistani side who weren't blinded by their own vengeance against Pakistan for their apparent alliance with the evil western powers. He also had his friends in the ISI, Pakistan's intelligence service, make contact with the LeJ who were working to bring a new Muslim Caliphate to the Islamic world. It was the delicate diplomatic leverage of showing them how each could accomplish their own goals by accomplishing their shared ones. The strategy had worked, and the groups quietly began to work together with Al-Zuq as the nexus of this power play.

Unfortunately, the recent mass shooting at the school for military families in Mardan, just northeast of Peshawar, was proof that not all factions were working with them. But even this was beneficial to the cause. A few phone calls to some of his contacts uncovered the group who executed the children at the school and guaranteed they would be hunted down. What the terrorist group didn't expect was that the Tribal areas weren't the safe havens they thought they would be.

Al-Zuq had them captured and personally witnessed their public execution by tribal leaders. He created the story that his forces had conducted an effective, widespread operation that tracked down and killed the terrorists in a heroic firefight. Then he worked the press for weeks afterward to maintain appearances that the tribal regions were completely lawless. As long as the world believed this, then he had complete autonomy to act. But the swift actions against the offshoot group sent the message that Al-Zuq wanted. There is no place to hide, and if you act against his wishes, you die. Not as a martyr with a place in paradise, but as an apostate.

"I think cooperation will be much more effective now. We're already seeing more of the groups falling into line, but there are still some outliers in the far north who are being stubborn. We will hold the line there while we confirm our suspicions with our guest. If this intelligence is compelling, it will completely change the dynamic in our struggle my good friend," Al-Zuq said with a smile.

"If so, then perhaps we can finally reclaim some of the territory rightfully belonging to us from those colonial British lapdogs in Afghanistan," replied Rabbani.

Bitterness over the 125-year-old Durand Line agreement was just as raw in these battle hardened soldiers as the dispute over the Kashmir province with India since the colonial partition in 1947. They considered that their brethren had been put on the wrong side of an arbitrary border, drawn by the unwitting colonial British. These random borders had sparked three wars with India and numerous cross border collisions with both India and Afghanistan ever since.

"That's true Ahmad, but it must be done carefully. If this information is as I think it is, our national leaders will turn a blind eye over how we take control of it, as long as they get a piece of it. Plus our benefactor is depending on this to provide long term financial support and political clout...for all of us," Al-Zuq replied as the steam swirled off his hot tea as he took a sip.

"Do you think the Americans will get in the way?" asked Rabbani.

Both men had fought the Afghans in multiple border clashes over the years, but were held back because of the presence of the Americans. It was infuriating to be bridled because they needed American weapons while their supposed allies actively worked against Pakistani interests. The Americans seemingly had no trouble violating Pakistani sovereignty with their constant drone attacks and the invasion of their country targeting the leader of Al-Qaida. That was worse than the drones because it gave the impression that the Americans could attack Pakistan with impunity any time they wanted.

"While they continue to have their accursed drones, their President has drawn down their forces to virtually nothing. My sources say they have confined themselves to protecting the major metropolitan areas and Helmand province, so are not as active in the area we are looking at. The good news is neither the Americans nor the Afghans have any idea about what is there, therefore no real reason to be much of a problem for us. But a wounded Eagle's talons are still dangerous if you get too close," Al-Zuq warned.

"The one positive from their operation to capture the leader of Al-Qaida in our country is that it reinforced my numerous demands for increased air defenses. The holes in our defenses on the western frontier got immediate attention and allowed us to move our own selected units back here."

General Al-Zuq made sure that he got the people he could trust and quietly manipulated the orders to place his people in the right places for when they were needed. The fact that the Afghans had established relations with the hated Indians made operations against them seem virtually assured and manipulation of orders easier. The western border wasn't as secure as Pakistan's leaders wanted so he easily took advantage of that fear to quietly make his moves.

"I pray the news is as you believe, then the work our brothers have done in that cesspool Syria will be well worth it. I just wish we didn't have to rely on those butchers in 'The Caliphate' to achieve our goals," stated Rabbani.

"'The Caliphate' fighters are just tools in the broader struggle my friend. Those fools believe their cruelty will bring acceptance and converts to Islam, but in reality they provide cover for the real movement. They have neither the money, the intelligence, nor the resources to build, never mind to protect a new nation state. But they are useful in diverting our enemy's attention and resources away from countering our broader plans. Plus, it helps us to gather information and move assets into position right under their nose," Al-Zuq answered.

What was left unsaid was that the more the Middle East needed Pakistani weapons and money, the more influence his country, and he, would have on truly consolidating the Sunni world. Al-Zuq may be a devoted soldier for the cause, but he also was an intensely ambitious one as well. The movement's leader was smart and savvy, but to Al-Zuq, the ancient proverb still rang true; "he who has the gold makes the rules." So he was determined to have control over whatever was found on this mission into Afghanistan.

Al-Zuq's Executive Officer knocked on the door, entered and saluted, "Sir, Dr. Balwani is here."

"Ah, send him in," Al-Zuq ordered.

Zahoor Balwani was a U.S. trained geologist with a PhD from CalTech. Al-Zuq and Rabbani stood as he entered. Balwani was a slight man. Clearly his trip through the mountains had taken a toll on him, but he was determined and loyal. The Taliban needed money for their war and had been bringing in small amounts of gold nuggets for over a year from a place they called the Valley of Stars. Small gold and silver deposits had been found for years in the mountainous region in Northeast Afghanistan. It was an extremely rugged area and treacherous to try and extract them. The Taliban often kidnapped young men from area villages as slave labor for the back breaking work and few of them survived.

"Dr. Balwani, please come in. Join us for some tea and rest for a spell, I'm eager to hear about your trip. This is my second in command, Major General Rabbani," Al-Zuq said as he waved the geologist to a seat at the conference table.

"Thank you, General. It will be good to get a hot shower and some sleep, but I have extremely exciting news. You were right. There is more there than the Taliban know," Balwani responded. The geologist sat down and launched into a technical explanation of the geological formations he found, most of which Al-Zuq didn't understand, but he let the scientist talk knowing he needed the emotional release.

"So, Doctor, you've talked about folds, faults, fractures, parallel striated veins, or whatever you called them and clearly it is all very important so I understand your excitement. But what's your estimate of the size of the deposit in terms that even an old soldier can understand?" asked Al-Zuq.

"General, it could be the largest deposit in the world of gold, silver, and rare earth metals!" replied Balwani excitedly.

"And what do the Taliban know of your discovery?" asked Al-Zuq.

"Nothing, since they asked you to help them look for oil, though I suspect you had something to do with that request. The fools see those barbarians in the Caliphate profiting from the oil in their captured territory and think there's more than poppies to fund their war without a thought to the difficulty in extracting it. I told them the geology of the area made it impossible for there to be oil deposits there."

"But it was difficult hiding the excitement of finding the ore deposits. There were a few times I had to hide some of the samples, as they had one of their University trained 'helpers' shadowing me. But he had only a cursory knowledge of geology, so I was able to cover my tracks with technical details he pretended to understand. It's hard to fathom how these people think that living in the 15th century is somehow better than today," Balwani said disgustedly.

General Al-Zuq sat quietly taking in all of the information the scientist provided. This was better news than he expected and provided the justification for Pakistan to reclaim their rightful territory. The accursed British and their arbitrary borders had been a thorn in the side of his country since the end of colonial rule. This would give Pakistan the natural resources they so desperately needed and Al-Zuq the power to divert them to whoever he wanted.

Balwani finished the conversation discussing the difficulties of extracting the precious metals and what they would need to do to retrieve the riches within the Valley of Stars.

"Thank you, Doctor, for this information, I share your excitement over this find. Remember this must remain an absolute secret, tell no one unless I authorize it. All will be lost if this information gets in the wrong hands. Do I make myself clear?" Al-Zuq said sternly and with a look that sent a shudder of fear through the geologist.

"Yes...yes General, absolutely," Balwani stuttered. At that the meeting was adjourned and Balwani shook hands with both generals and quickly left the room.

After Balwani left, Rabbani looked at Al-Zuq, "Shit that is even better news than you expected! At least it was better than I expected."

"We need to move quickly Ahmad, start our plan in motion. Time to get the pieces moving, go!" Al-Zuq ordered his second in command.

"Yes sir!" Rabbani replied standing, saluting, and leaving Al-Zuq's office quickly.

Once alone, Al-Zuq quickly made a call over an encrypted phone. He detailed the discovery and the challenges the scientist highlighted. The man on the other end of the line listened quietly and asked a few questions to clarify the potential size and how the scientist could determine that from the fragments he found.

Once he was satisfied with the result, "General, you have my permission to move forward with the next phase of the plan," the man ordered and hung up the phone.

This was what General Al-Zuq had been waiting for. He had spent months laying the groundwork and getting his most trusted people in place and now the time to execute was here. He had one more message that needed to be delivered, but not by phone.

CHAPTER 11

Coincidences

Karim settled into the plush leather chair in the corner of the coffee house near American University. He connected to the University wifi system and used a VPN tunnel to a server at his house. Then he connected through proxy servers in a dozen countries and logged into his favorite tool to relax, *Gods of Conquest*. His game name was *The Great Kazam*, a nickname given him by a colleague in his section.

He had spent the past week pouring over intercepts and intel reports from Syria to Pakistan and was frustrated. While he found bits and fragments of references about the gold road and Valley of Stars, he still didn't have enough to pinpoint them. NSA had assets to scoop up trillions of bits of data but needed to have a direction in which to look.

The fact that people believed they could snoop on every piece of electronics everywhere in the world all the time was a nice story, but it just wasn't realistic. He needed to find the link but had to think and couldn't think at his desk anymore. So Karim did what he usually did when he got stuck on a problem, he went to play a little mindless war game for entertainment.

He was a member of a very aggressive and active alliance, and his game mates believed he was a 16-year-old boy from Toronto. He played recklessly, like an over amped high school kid, to reinforce his online persona. After logging in, he got caught up on the results of the latest operation his team had run and looked at the planning for an upcoming one. He had some rebuilding to do on his attack forces after striking a player in the alliance, *The Twelfth Kingdom,* and conquering a few of his cities.

Half of the 40-member alliance would play in one operation, while the other half would rebuild, and they alternated, so their alliance was constantly on the attack. The current target was a player by the name of *Richard III* and all his cities were named after famous battles by the British. *Goran the Destroyer* was running this op and had divided the attackers into smaller teams focused on a couple cities each.

As he read through the battle reports, it looked like *Richard* was not a very experienced player as he didn't seem to make smart moves to protect a couple of his cities. Suddenly his cellphone lit up. It was Zack Gerlacher, his section chief.

"Karim, have you seen the news?" he asked.

"No, I was just grabbing a cup of coffee and relaxing for a bit. What's up?" he answered.

"I need you to get back here right now. A bomb just went off at Waterloo Station London," Gerlacher instructed.

"OK, I'll be there in fifteen," replied Karim.

He was about to close out of his game when he suddenly stopped. He took another look at the battle reports; there they were, the ones on *Richard*'s city of Waterloo. A large clearing attack occurred just before the conquest that had just landed. It was one of the primary targets for the team led by *Goran*.

He looked at the time of the attacks and noted that several of the in-game attacks had landed within the past few minutes, a coincidence perhaps, but his inner voice said there was no such thing. Karim had to get back to his workstation to see the result. He then looked at the players who were on the attack team with *Goran* and memorized their game names and battle reports. Were the two events connected? He was intrigued by the possibility, but he knew it would be another long day.

Karim made it back to his desk in just over fifteen minutes and was met by Gerlacher. Before he could get out any information on the attack, Karim asked, "What time did the attack occur?"

"17:30 GMT, hit during the afternoon rush hour, no casualty numbers yet but the London police have a mass response going on. It was a dual attack. A suicide bomber detonated in the concourse near the center #3 entrance and, as first responders arrived, they detonated a bomb inside a bus just opposite the entrance," replied Gerlacher.

"So the first bomb went off at 17:30, and the second went off about eight minutes later?" asked Karim.

"Yes, seven minutes later to be exact. It appears it was placed on a bus that arrived at the station just before the suicide bomber and then, as responders arrived, it detonated. How the hell did you know that?" asked Gerlacher.

"So, about 17:37 then," stated Karim to no one in particular.

"What's going on, Karim. How did you guess the timing?" pressed Gerlacher.

"I may have a connection, seems random but..." Karim trailed off in a thought.

"One thing I know about you Karim, is there's no such thing as random. You think you have a connection? What have you found and what assets do you need to confirm it?" demanded Gerlacher.

"I play this mass multi-player online war game, and there were some interesting coincidences today that I need to look at. I don't have a theory yet, just a feeling that this is linked. I need a worldwide list of terrorist attacks going back at least a year, an outside internet tunnel routed through European proxy servers, and two people to help plow through some data," replied Karim.

"Done, you can have James and Thompson. I'll have James set up Conference Room 3 for you. It will give you plenty of room to work. I think Thompson is a gamer as well," and Gerlacher was off barking orders.

Karim gathered up all of his background on the Golden Road and Valley of Stars and headed to Conference Room 3.

VALLEY OF STARS

Confident all of this was part of the same puzzle, he needed to start making connections. Hunting terrorists was a marathon, not a sprint, and Karim had been at it for years.

The CIA would gain ground, then the terrorists would learn from their mistakes and adapt. It was more than just Al-Qaida now but a wider network of organizations. On the surface, their link was the radicalization of Islam but there were several common themes. Karim had identified statements and activities that, by themselves, appeared random and coincidental, but taken together convinced him there was more coordination than publicly released.

"Hey Mo, how's it going?" asked Karim as he entered the conference room.

Dana "Mo" James was making connections to the computers embedded in the conference table and turned to see Karim enter the room. Mo was a bit of a computer savant. She was an accomplished hacker by age 15 who went by the nom de guerre "Mọ" which was "Ghost" in the Igbo language. A computer genius, she was the bane of the FBI for a few years until a guy in the FBI's cyber unit, with a PhD from MIT, finally caught her when she was still just 17.

A middle class black kid from California, her father was a workaholic for a software company in Silicon Valley and her mom a CPA for an accounting firm. During tax time she spent hours by herself and learned hacking to kill time. She thought it was funny to use an Igbo word from southeastern Nigeria that few knew and yet reflected her heritage. When she was caught, her criminal record was sealed and expunged after a CIA recruiter suggested that she could go to college for free if she used her talents to come work for them. So she officially worked for a cyber-security firm while completing her degree at Cal-Poly and was their unit's best IT specialist and cyber-snoop.

"Hey, KZ, putting together another puzzle I see!" replied Mo.

Karim's puzzle talents were notorious in the Southwest Asia section and Mo James gave him the nickname *The Great Kazam*, or KZ for short. It was a silly name, a joke about him having magical powers to make connections and master puzzles, but it stuck. It just seemed fitting that one person with an infamous nom de guerre would give someone else one as well.

"Ya, I just have all these pieces, but I don't know how they go together yet. Too many holes, that's why I need your help. We need to parse through a whole shitload of data."

"Well, we're not the NSA but you give me a target set of servers, and I'll get you whatever you need off of them," stated Mo confidently.

"Jake's coming as well, should be here anytime. How long before we're set to go?" asked Karim.

"Five minutes," she replied as she plugged patch cords into an isolation panel almost without looking.

The panel would route the external access through a series of data centers and zombie computers around the world making it virtually untraceable back to the CIA. The systems in the conference table had separate computers for internal and external source through the same monitor and the LED lighting in the outer bezel glowed either GREEN for external source or RED for internal depending on which one was selected.

Just as Mo finished firing up the computers, Jake Thompson strolled through the conference room door. "Hey, Mo, KZ, what we have cooking?"

Karim was already transferring files on the secure side and was putting them up on the big screen. "Hey, Jake, pull up a chair. We have a lot to do," replied Karim.

Jake Thompson was a junior analyst working on his Masters' thesis in International Relations at Georgetown. He came from a tough neighborhood in Kansas City and had worked his way through high school to help support his mom and four brothers and sisters.

"How's your Mom?" asked Mo as she finished the computer set ups and opened the secure tunnel to the outside world as Karim had asked.

"She's doing pretty well, glad she only has to work one job now," Jake chuckled. "My sister Tina got a full ride to Connecticut to play basketball, so that's a real load off her mind, and my wallet!"

Jake's parents divorced when he was 12. His dad was an abusive drunk, and Jake had beaten him with a bat defending his mom after another night of drinking. His father left the family that night when Jake told him to leave and never return. If he did, Jake would kill him.

His mom worked two jobs to provide for the family, but they always struggled to make ends meet. She was too proud to take welfare, and Jake felt responsible to help out as the oldest sibling. He did odd jobs for cash around the neighborhood and volunteered at the local food bank run by his church. In return, he was given food to take home. When he was old enough, he took a job at the corner market stocking shelves, but his mom insisted that he could only work if he maintained his grades, and if not, he had to quit. She'd find a way to make it.

He graduated with Honors and was one of only 36 students in the nation to get a perfect score on his ACT college entrance exam. From that came full scholarship offers; Duke, Stanford, and Georgetown. While he really didn't want to leave home, his mom insisted that the best way to help his family was to get the best education possible. So he came to Georgetown and was the only full scholarship student to also work, sending home whatever money he made, and like his mom insisted, maintaining his grades the whole time. After joining the CIA, he lived modestly and had helped put two of his siblings through college already.

"That's sweet, isn't she the youngest?" asked Mo.

"Yup, just one more to get through school and I can move my Mom here finally. She won't move until the last kid is out of school and supporting themselves. Tammy just graduated from the Naval Academy and got assigned to a destroyer, so that's exciting. It was fun being close enough to go to the graduation ceremony. They had SedDef as their commencement speaker. She's one smart cookie. All in all, things are going pretty well," Jake replied.

Mo finished making her final connections and sat down at the conference table, "Wow, tell her congrats for me."

"OK, so here's where we stand as of now. We got an intercept from 2nd ID after a green-on-blue incident that identified a 'gold road' as a possible supply route from Pakistan to Syria. In addition, there's only a couple of mentions of a 'Valley of Stars' that may be an important supply point along the road, but no other information yet. We've initiated a sweep on those keywords and only found a few references, but they come from different regions and different situations that on the surface seem disconnected," started Karim.

"Disconnected for everyone else you mean, KZ," interrupted Jake with a chuckle.

"Well, yes I guess, but as I've looked at the intel, there are too many coincidences for them not to be connected. Then today, I was online playing a wargame when the attacks on the train station in London occurred and they matched attacks in the game. I suspect the game is a communications conduit for Islamist factions coordinating their operations. Mo, pull up the folder GR001 on the secure system. I've put together all of the info I'm talking about. We need to go through it with some fresh eyes," Karim instructed.

The new information about a communications conduit made Jake and Mo sit up and look at each other. Finding how the enemy communicated was like hitting the motherlode in terrorist hunting. If they could break that code they could roll up entire networks, not one terrorist at a time making a single cut, but hack off an entire limb. Maybe even finding the head, now that would be something.

For the next hour, Karim explained the intel and the links he had already made. The team created a flow chart with actions, timelines, and possible cause and effect nodes where a specific action could be reasonably matched to a resulting action or attack. They began to organize the intel into tiles and known players graphically, which showed huge gaps in their information but also began to solidify other connections. Karim then finished with the latest coincidence in the online game.

Karim stood back and stared at the board for a minute, "Mo, we need to hack into the guts of the game and find out how it works. We need to gain access to its messaging and battle management coding without any footprints, so we can confirm more of these links and get a leg up on how deep this thing goes."

Mo looked at him with feigned disgust, "When has anyone been able to find my tracks?" she replied.

"Well, there was this one guy," chuckled Jake, who got a backhand to the shoulder from Mo in response.

"Jake, you and I have to cull through Zack's list of all the terror attacks of the past year. We need to cross reference the claims from the same group as the Waterloo Station bombing. Note the dates and times of the attacks and then search the game for attacks that match the terror attack in timing and/or city name. We can do that before Mo finishes her hack by accessing the game's stats site and looking at the stats for the players I've listed in the background. Mo, once you find a way in, can you set up a program to search the whole game site for these links? If I'm right, we'll find different groups that I suspect are different cells," directed Karim.

"I've written a new program that should scoop and sift all the data we need. I call it *GillNet*. Not as sophisticated as NSA's *Combine* system, but with specific targets and the limited databases of the game, it should be more than enough to handle it," replied Mo.

Combine was NSA's massive data vacuum that monitored virtually all internet traffic for certain keywords and algorithm strings used by the enemies of the U.S. Like a combine that harvests corn by ingesting the whole plant and separating the kernels from the chaff, *Combine* did that with data. It discarded the majority of innocuous bits and collected the suspicious ones for further analysis. Despite its capability to scoop up data, it all had to be targeted and analyzed. While it could flag suspicious strings, those had to be prioritized. Given the current administration's threat priorities of Syria, Iraq, Iran, and Ukraine, it was sucking up most of the intel assets to keep tabs on those situations.

Karim figured that between *Combine* and *GillNet*, they could sift through the trove of information funneled to the Southwest Asia section and loop the analysis from the Mid-East section through it now that they had some targets to look at. Jake created a player profile using the same game server, and world, as Karim to get access to both the in-game statistics but also the external third party game stats consolidator programs.

Mo started hacking the server to see the game code searching for the best point of entry for her attack. Every so often she would grunt, then a flurry of keystrokes, a pause then another flurry, and then the occasional exclamation of "got you" as she broke through the various firewalls. After about twenty minutes she stated that they were in and had the game server up on the big screen going line by line through the code.

"It took me a bit longer than I expected, but they had some fairly sophisticated encryption protocols at the server level, and I wanted to backtrack several times to ensure I hid my tracks. The game protocols are easily broken so we can get access to their messaging system without a problem, I just want to make sure they can't trace *GillNet* at the server level. Once we confirm that we can hide it in a message, you can send to whomever you want in the game, and it will lock onto their account and track everything they do," announced Mo.

"Mo, can you have it attach to every message the target sends so we can track them as well?" asked Karim.

"Yup, that's the way it works. Once it's in their account, it goes where they go and drops crumbs to be distributed everywhere their other targets send messages. We'll be able to read their mail and track every move," replied Mo.

"What about a key logger?" asked Jake.

"Yes, I can set that up inside *GillNet*, but we run the risk of their anti-malware software catching those and blowing the whole deal. Plus, you'd have thousands of false tracks that would just overwhelm the analysis. I suggest we track first then once we confirm some specific targets, I can work on hacking their accounts and inserting a key logger with an auto shut down feature when a malware scan begins. I'd have to bury it in the bios. More risk, but most malware checkers run quick scans that only look for changes in the operating system and not the bios," explained Mo.

"I agree with Mo," said Karim. "If they're using the game as a communications platform they're counting on the billions of messages throughout the game to cover their tracks by simple volume. Plus, they're likely to use separate computers for their data and game play. So, we need to be smart about how we go about this. If we target a few high interest players with the key logger, we might get lucky. If one makes a mistake and uses the wrong computer, we have them."

The three settled into hours of work. By the next morning, they had a list of a dozen players to look at and Jake managed to garner an invite to the alliance that had lost their city, Waterloo, the day before in the game. The first to get a message from *The Great Kazam* was *Goran the Destroyer*. He was the one who set up the op on Waterloo city so, if Karim was right, he would be a cell leader.

Chapter 12

Dominoes Falling

Farooq settled into a bedroom in one of his safe houses set up with his bank of computers. He had several located around Peshawar that he used at random. He never stayed in the same place more than two nights. Just one more lesson learned from the execution of Al-Qaida's leader. He didn't have communications blackouts though, that was one of the things the Americans noticed about the Al-Qaida compound before their attack. It was not normal in Pakistan to have a compound that large without phones or satellite communications. So Farooq made his look as normal as possible, hiding in plain sight and blending in.

The night was clear with a warm breeze coming from the southwest. Farooq had the windows open but had the gauze-like curtains drawn. They let the air in but hid his room from potential prying eyes. He had his television tuned to the BBC Worldwide channel and watched the news of the attack in London. Farooq smiled as information about the bombing of Waterloo Station came flooding in from news outlets across the world.

The attack was superbly run and all he had to do was to point to a target. He gave his cell leaders wide latitude to plan the attacks and they simply needed to ask for the proper supplies. He logged into *Gods of Conquest* from his internet computer to find a message from *Goran the Destroyer*.

"*Wolfhunter 12*, I thank you and your alliance for a good fight. Apologies for the conquest of Waterloo but this is a wargame, and it was a fun battle. I'm sure we'll meet on the battlefield again and who knows, maybe next time you'll be able to stop us...but I doubt it! LOL Cheers," *Goran* wrote.

Farooq marveled at the simplicity of his communications scheme and how well it worked. No one knew who the others in the network were or where they were located. They only knew that they got a target from their cell leader who planned the whole mission. They got supplies from dead drops, and those were abandoned if a member of the cell was taken or killed. Better to burn an op than to have their network rolled up by a foreign intelligence agency. Just one series of dead ends after another.

There was also a message from *Kubla Khan*. Farooq opened it and looked at it in puzzlement. The message said, "Finally got a successful report on 'Najma ki waadi City.' Mules proved stubborn but have been dealt with. Will need to replenish them. Do you want to meet at the Boar's Head for a beer and talk about next moves?"

Farooq frowned. This was not how things were done but it must be critically important to take such a high risk asking for a face-to-face meeting. *Khan* was one of his most trusted operatives in northern Afghanistan and was deadly efficient. His latest mission was to take an expert Pakistani geologist to the Valley of Stars and find out the value of its natural resources.

As usual, they used captured Afghan peasants to carry equipment through the dangerous mountain passes. Normally, they used them until they were physically and mentally broken. But this mission was special. With the presence of the Pakistani, *Khan* had to eliminate any chance that someone might talk about the foreigner. His plan was to execute them all once they came out of the mountains and it appears that was done.

Farooq's men had pulled small amounts of gold from the Valley of Stars for over a year, and he asked General Al-Zuq for help to find a scientist for him. He didn't fully trust the man, but the movement's leaders did. Plus, Al-Zuq had protected his fighters in the Northwest Frontier and provided valuable intel about activities on the Afghan side of the disputed border. So, Farooq used the excuse of trying to find oil, but *Khan* had already determined that was impossible so now they wanted the geologist to confirm what was there. With *Khan* posing as a third-year university student, Farooq had him watch the scientist and verify whether he could trust the Pakistani general.

He already had a report from the General thanking him for his assistance with getting the scientist in and out of the Valley for his investigation. Al-Zuq confirmed that there was no oil but said there were modest deposits of precious metals and rare earth metals in the valley and would commit Pakistani troops and equipment for a share of the commodities extracted. But there must have been much more to the story than *Khan* could explain in a message sent by courier.

Farooq replied, "Sure, how about tomorrow night at 6 after work?"

The protocol was that, whatever meeting time was specified, it would be 24 hours later. The Boar's Head was a code name for a tea house in the Northwest Frontier, so Farooq needed to travel. It would take him at least a full day to navigate his way into the tribal areas for the meeting. But he needed to make sure the meeting place was secured. He'd have his people do a complete security sweep before the meeting. Just then Farooq's lieutenant, Sayeed, knocked at his door and handed him a communique from a Caliphate leader.

"Farooq, he has confirmed that the commanding General of the Iranian Quds Brigade is leading the battle against the Caliphate in central Iraq. In addition, the 'Shiite Militia' are in fact Iranian Quds forces dressed as militiamen. The Iranians and Caliphate are now in a full scale war on the ground in Iraq and Syria. And the Russians have committed ground troops as well," Sayeed reported.

"And combined with those damnable Kurds who stopped the Caliphate's push eastward, this is not good news for the movement," Farooq added.

"How many times did we tell them it was a mistake to attack the Kurds head-on rather than play on their natural hatred of both the Shia in power in Baghdad and the Iranians? Had they used the Kurds' knowledge of fighting the Shia in Iraq and Iran, they could have made a Sunni link all the way across northern Iraq and Iran into the Helmand province of southern Afghanistan. But what's done is done," Farooq said with a bit of frustration.

Unfortunately, the Peshmerga proved to be much more capable fighters than the Iraqi Army. They stopped the Caliphate dead in their tracks. Worse, they now actively fight alongside the Americans and are closer to those animals than ever. But the Caliphate was making inroads to linking through Turkey with a more accommodating theocratic government solidifying its power there.

"Clearly the Iranians see the threat from the Caliphate and were eager to answer the call for help from that hapless dog in Baghdad. If only our Palestinian brothers would recognize that the Iranians are a much bigger threat than Israel and need to be eliminated. But they are blind in the hatred of the Jews," Sayeed replied.

"Quite true my friend. Once we eliminate the Shiites, the Jews can be dealt with later. Plus, now that the Iranians have backed the ouster of the government in Yemen, they are actively fighting a unified Sunni force there. Whether the Saudi's and the rest of those corrupt governments wanted it, they now are part of this war. A little earlier than expected but it was inevitable, and as you said, the Persians are the more important problem," answered Farooq.

Farooq knew it was time to hit the Iranians in their home territory. His own spies and the ISI had identified a secret nuclear site in Shush. They could hit it and blame the Israelis just in case the Iranians had figured out the help from Pakistan was worthless and found the answers on their own. And if they could throw suspicion on the Saudi's at the same time, all that much better. The Jewish Prime Minister had already declared they would do whatever was necessary to prevent them from getting a nuclear capability, and the only path was over Arab territory.

The secret facility in Shush was responsible for crafting the high explosive initiator for a nuclear weapon. The little known fact was that this was probably the most challenging part of the weapon as it required extreme levels of precision to start a fission reaction in the nuclear core. Not only the shape of the charge but the timing of the detonation. The slightest difference in pressure on the core would result in complete failure of the device.

It had taken Farooq nearly five years to get an operative in there, but he finally managed to accomplish it. It took another ten years for the operative to smuggle enough explosive material into it to cause a major setback to the Iranian program. It was time to activate him. Farooq turned back to the game and typed out another message to a player named *Hephaestion*. He was the leader of the Iranian cell, and Farooq had to laugh at the irony. His name was based on one of Alexander the Great's generals, the man who brought the Persian Empire to its knees.

"*Hephaestion*, we need to run an op on *King Xerxes* city of Susa. This needs to be an aggressive effort to try and pull their support away from attacks on our western cities. How long before your team can be ready? Resources being sent to Arandu for your attack units. Let me know what you need. *St Thomas* will provide you gold from Valley of Stars," Farooq typed. Susa was the ancient Persian name for the city of Shush, yet one more layer of irony Farooq was proud of.

That piece of business done, "Sayeed, notify my driver and security team. I need to leave for the Northern Territory immediately. *Khan* wants a face-to-face meeting," Farooq ordered.

"Yes sir," Sayeed replied and was off to give instructions to the men that would accompany Farooq.

Farooq had to take an indirect route to ensure he wasn't followed and make sure that if he was, he did his cover business along the way. He left instructions for his men at his safe house and packed his bags and laptop for the trip.

* * *

Ramin stumbled along the mountain path, he'd been walking for nearly 24 hours. Shot three times, and freezing at night, the 17-year-old pushed his body to the limit to survive. He knew he couldn't stop or he would die like the others left for dead near the border of Pakistan. Taken from his village a week ago, he was forced to carry heavy equipment through the mountains for the Taliban. He didn't know why but they seemed to be escorting a Pakistani who was definitely not used to the rugged terrain they had to travel.

He had some special equipment and anytime one of the captured laborers stumbled and their packs hit the ground, they were beaten and chastised. Ramin was bigger and stronger than most men his age, hauling feed and water for his father's animals and guiding them through the high mountain passes near his village. Every so often he would have to carry one of the goats on his shoulders back to the village so carrying the equipment was no big deal for him.

They had stopped in a high mountain valley where the man set up his equipment and spent a couple days there going this way and that. The laborers were given tasks like digging or moving some heavy thing on wheels across the ground and all of the rocks and dirt were scrutinized by the foreigner. After he was satisfied with whatever he was doing, they packed everything up and headed back down out of the mountains. Once they got to a small wooded area near the Pakistan border, they stopped for a rest, only it wasn't to rest.

Ramin became suspicious when the guards moved away from the laborers. They were never but a few feet away but now they had backed away with the laborers seated in a huddle in the middle. He was seated on some rocks and saw one of the guards grip his AK-47 stock a little tighter and just as they raised them, he started falling backwards and sideways toward a crevice in the rocks.

The guards sprayed bullets into the huddle of men and the head of the man next to Ramin virtually exploded. As he was falling, Ramin grabbed the man and pulled him on top of him, but not until he had been hit in the shoulder, arm, and side by bullets. He laid there and played dead, blood from the man on top of him mixing with his own, making his wounds look much worse than they were. The Taliban moved along and shot anyone who was moaning or suspected of being alive. Covered in blood, they passed Ramin by.

He lay there for perhaps an hour trying not to breathe, and listening for any possible movement. His wounds burned like fire and a thousand knives cutting into him, but he forced himself not to make a sound. Once he was sure the Taliban were gone, he started moving. He wasn't exactly sure where he was, but he understood the terrain and its dangers.

He knew he had to get to a river, and then he could find a village. He followed the small valley heading north and found a tributary. Following that he pushed forward for hours. While he moved he would drink from the mountain stream just to keep himself hydrated. Without it, the dry mountain air would kill him in mere hours with his blood loss.

The sunset created a long shadow across the valley as the stream began to open up into a larger river. Ramin was struggling to stay conscious, and he had to stop more frequently to rest. He had taken clothing off the dead to dress his wounds as best he could, and had added layers to keep warm. But it was taking all of his energy just to take a single step now. He thought of his father and his sister.

Their mother had passed away a year ago and as the only son, it was up to him to help his father tend to the animals and find a suitable husband for his sister. As he took one more step, he fell by some rocks on the side of the river, exhausted. He was dying and said a prayer to Allah, thanking him for his life and asking him to look after his family. Ramin looked up to see the shadow of a man. "Father, I'm sorry I failed you. May Allah have mercy." And with that Ramin slipped into darkness.

CHAPTER 13

Puzzle Pieces

Under the bluish glow of artificial light, Mo sat in the conference room that had become an ad hoc control center tracking the expansion of the net of potential targets. The low whir of the computers was only broken by the occasional mumble from one of the three analysts about something they were looking at. She was running *GillNet* on several players that *Goran the Destroyer* had contacted, as well as everyone those players had messaged. As expected, the net was gaining steam.

The program processed every message looking for any keywords the intelligence agencies were tracking. If any of the keywords were found, the message and sender were flagged for further investigation. *GillNet,* had already hit on several probable cell members that were separated and farmed out to the team for analysis. Once they identified a target, Mo would run a backtrace on their account to locate their physical location.

Some were easy and turned out to be nothing. Some went to proxy servers or were routed through numerous nodes in a deliberate attempt to hide their locations. These were the ones Mo focused on and all of their messages were downloaded and analyzed. Once deployed, *GillNet* proved to be tremendously efficient and the team had quickly built a database of suspected players.

Mo was scanning the messages flagged by *GillNet* when she suddenly sat up straight, "Karim, you need to see this." She quickly put up the message on the big screen for the team to see.

"*Wolfhunter 12*, is this the first message we've seen from him?" asked Karim.

"Yes" replied Mo, "but look at the reference to 'Valley of Stars'. It looks like another target."

"Have we scanned the game database for the city 'Valley of Stars,' Susa, and their owners?" asked Karim.

"Doing that now," replied Jake.

"If you find any players, send them a message and get them into *GillNet*. So *Wolfhunter*, giving orders are we...," Karim said letting his voice trail off.

Karim took in the whole message while Mo started looking for the city name of Susa in Iran and Jake looked in the war game. Karim read the message again and suddenly stood up, grabbed the phone, and punched the intercom button for the section chief.

"Zack, we need you in the conference room ASAP!" Karim called urgently then punching the phone off. "Jake pull up everything we have on Shush Iran, Mo put the map of eastern Iran on the big screen," Karim instructed.

Gerlacher strode into the room as Mo put up a map of Iran. Looking at the screen, he immediately knew this wasn't going to be good news. "What have you found, Karim?"

"Zack, I think we found another target. Jake is pulling the intel on it now, but I believe the target is Shush Iran. Mo, put up the reference messages. We're running a worm program that allows us to read messages of players in an online game called *Gods of Conquest*. One of the messages flagged the Waterloo attack, and another flagged our keyword search on 'gold' and 'Valley of Stars'. We believe there is an organization using the game to communicate and we've gathered several leads on cell members," Karim began.

"The trigger player we ID'd is *Goran the Destroyer,* and we might have found one of the organization's leaders, game name *Wolfhunter 12*. In this exchange, *Goran* references the attack on Waterloo. Soon after that, *Wolfhunter* messages another player, game name *Hephaestion*. The name is based on one of Alexander the Great's generals, and they want to run an op against *King Xerxes* city of Susa. Xerxes was the Persian king that Alexander the Great fought and ultimately conquered much of the ancient Persian Empire from. The city of Susa was the ancient name for the Iranian city of Shush. That's where I think the target is. Whoever this guy is, he has a great sense of irony and history," concluded Karim.

"What do we have on Shush?" demanded Gerlacher.

"Not much. There's a rumor of a classified military facility somewhere around there, but no specifics about exactly where, or what it is," replied Jake.

"Clearly they know something we don't. And what's this about resources to Arandu?" Gerlacher asked.

Mo jumped in. "I've tracked this to a village name on the border of Pakistan and Afghanistan. Add this to the mention of gold from the Valley of Stars, Karim thinks this is part of the gold road referenced in other intercepts."

"But, why Shush?" asked Gerlacher, thinking out loud.

"We've found some loose links between the Caliphate and the Taliban. Given they're talking about supplies from Pakistan, it must be in response to Iranian actions against the Caliphate, but only a guess. If true, then this is a major breakthrough in identifying the extent of the Caliphate network," said Karim.

"Hey, guys, we just got a flash message from 25th ID intel. Seems 2nd Battalion has recovered a young Afghan boy from an area about 50 miles north of Asadabad. A patrol found him on the side of a river covered in blood with multiple gunshot wounds and nearly dead. They evac'd him to Bagram for medical attention and had one of their intel people debrief him.

"He said he was captured by the Taliban about a week ago and, along with a dozen other men, was forced to carry equipment for a Pakistani man to a high mountain valley. They spent a day collecting rock samples and dragging around a machine that the intel group thinks was a ground penetrating radar. After they moved the equipment down the mountain, he said the Taliban executed all of the mules.

He played dead and walked for more than a day to where the patrol found him," said Jake.

"The kid described a geologist, and Pakistani you said," Karim said to no one in particular.

Mo pulled up another message that *Wolfhunter* got from *Kubla Khan*. "Look there!" she exclaimed. "This one references 'mules' being dealt with, that's what the kid said he was, and they executed them," noted Mo.

"Najma ki waadi is phonetic Arabic for Valley of Stars. This kid was in the Valley of Stars!" replied Karim.

"And the Army says he had a rock in his pocket that had a piece of gold in it," responded Jake.

Mo pulled up the third message from *Wolfhunter*. "In the third message, *Wolfhunter* instructs them to get gold from Valley of Stars..."

"They're looking for gold deposits there," interrupted Gerlacher.

"Looks like there's going to be a meeting, Mo we need to find out where this *Wolfhunter* is located," said Karim.

"Mo, pull out to show the entire region from Israel to Pakistan," demanded Gerlacher. Mo zoomed out and layered the country borders on the map.

"Now pull up the known locations of Caliphate, Al-Qaida, and Taliban strongholds and overlay this with our current intel."

With a few keystrokes, the map showed colors of the areas controlled by the terror groups and Mo inserted the general locations with red dots based on the latest intel.

"Now pull up the current positions of forces in Iran, Iraq, Saudi, Oman, UAE, Afghanistan, and Pakistan with the locations of the Golden Road references."

Red, green, blue, and gold dots began populating the maps.

"Shit" exclaimed Karim.

"Yah, I know" replied Gerlacher.

Mo and Jake looked at each other. "What's the issue?" asked Jake.

"We're looking at the possibility of World War III, and one that could go nuclear," Gerlacher stated matter-of-factly. "If the Caliphate and Taliban are working together with help from a nuclear capable Pakistan, we may have a full scale Sunni/Shia war coming. And if the Iranians are further along in their nuke program than we believe, both sides will have them. Given how willing they've both been to create martyrs, that's a really scary proposition."

"Look at the current locations of the Iranian, Pakistan, and Saudi military. They've all repositioned closer to their borders with each other. The Saudis along the Iraqi border, the coast of the Persian Gulf along with the Gulf states, and actively engaging Iranian-backed rebels in Yemen. Pakistan has shifted their western Corps along the Afghan and Iranian borders.

"With the actions of Iranian forces in Iraq and Syria against Caliphate troops along with their actions against the Sunni regime in Yemen, taken by themselves, are natural movements related to regional threats. But taken together they're encircling Iran. If they're going to pursue this, they'll need something more than oil to pay for it," explained Gerlacher.

Karim nodded. "If full scale war breaks out, the price of oil will skyrocket as production on both sides will be targeted. This will severely limit both sides ability to pay for a war. The Saudis are in the best position because their production facilities are farther inland and are heavily defended with our equipment. But Iran has missiles and spec ops that can disrupt them significantly. If the Iranians attack the Saudis, it'll no doubt pull us into the fight.

"If the Taliban pressure the Iranians from the east, then they'll need weapons from Pakistan to do it. The Pakistanis will be their proctor for purchasing equipment from the Russians and Chinese. So they're forced to find ways to finance it," added Karim.

"Right. To do that they'll need hard currency, and to get that they'll need access to the natural resource that can generate a lot of it," added Jake.

"Gold!" exclaimed Mo.

"The Valley of Stars," replied Karim nodding his head in agreement. "Zack, they believe that the Valley of Stars is a large gold deposit. We know there's gold in the mountains, but it's been extremely difficult to get at. Unfortunately, the USGS is short manned and has never done a full evaluation. To bring a Pakistani geologist in there covertly, it's pretty clear they expect cooperation from Pakistan to mine it. But why would they help the Taliban when they're supposedly fighting them on the Pakistan side?"

Gerlacher looked intently at the map. "They're going to help because they're going to take it for themselves. It wouldn't be the first time Pakistan has worked with the Taliban against Afghan interests."

The three analysts looked at him in surprise. "And risk a war with Afghanistan?" asked Jake.

"There are many in Pakistan who don't accept the Durand Line that forms the current internationally recognized border between the two countries. And the Afghan government is friendly with India, Pakistan's mortal enemy. Look at where the kid was located," Gerlacher answered pointing to the location on the map. "This is inside the disputed area, and there've been numerous cross border exchanges between Afghan and Pakistan forces in the same region. Remember, this was the area where Pakistan shelled ANA positions and the ANA responded, killing several on both sides."

"But what of the fight between the Caliphate and the other Sunni countries in the area?" asked Mo.

Karim fielded the question. "Zack's right. The situation's much more complex because of the Shiite/Sunni schism but also the acrimony between sects within the Sunnis like the Caliphate and Kurds, Egypt and the Muslim Brotherhood, and certainly Afghanistan and the Taliban. But current intel suggests the Sunni sides in the Middle East have already started pulling back from attacking each other. In Iraq and Syria, we're seeing much less Sunni sectarian infighting where the Caliphate is fighting mostly Shiite Militia. There are reports that Iranian Special Forces are on the ground actively fighting now. Our withdrawal from Iraq left a huge vacuum as we said it would, and now that scenario is playing out."

"And with Iranian influence in Iraq, Syria, and Yemen, growing, the Saudis and other relatively moderate Arab nations are feeling the threat. They know this is a fight for the heart and soul of Islam. It's the foundation of their very existence. So the fight between Sunni and Shia is taking on more importance, and the nationalist issues are taking a back seat right now," added Gerlacher.

VALLEY OF STARS

It was Jake's turn to ask a question. "But why would the Russians help Pakistan arm the Caliphate? Aren't they supplying arms to the Syrians and Iranians and fighting the Caliphate themselves?"

"The Russians are more than happy to provide weapons to both sides. As far as they're concerned, a shooting war in the Middle East that makes oil and gas prices skyrocket helps their economy through weapons and energy sales. Killing off a few million Muslims won't matter to them. It even helps them with their own Muslim problem in Chechnya by drawing fighters out of there into the killing fields of the Middle East. Plus, it takes the focus off what Russia's doing in Eastern Europe, and gives them a reason to expand their sphere of influence back into the 'Stans' on their southern border," responded Gerlacher highlighting the countries bordering Afghanistan.

"So, how do we keep the dominoes from falling?" asked Mo.

"Right now all we have is rampant speculation but logical actions we think may happen. Karim, package this up, we need to brief the Director right away. But to answer your question, Mo, we need to stop the money. That means finding the Valley of Stars and preventing the enemy from getting their hands on what's there," replied Gerlacher. With that, Karim quickly drafted a presentation and gathered what documentation they had and headed to the Director of the CIA's office with Gerlacher.

Chapter 14

Move / Counter-move

General McAffey sat in the Afghan President's ornate office inside the Presidential palace. The polished red marble columns matched the floor to ceiling fireplace façade and inlay table top of the small round table the three men sat around. President Zazai sat on an antique blue satin Queen Anne sofa across from the fireplace flanked by McAffey and the Afghan Chief of Staff, General Mahmoud, in the matching chairs.

The sweet smell of cardamom and sugar permeated the room as servers poured the traditional creamy spiced Afghan tea into the elaborately decorated teacups for the three power-brokers. President Zazai often used ceramics from local artisans with his guests and this set was from northern Kabul with their traditional turquoise and bright colored patterns. The servers then left a bowl of Asabia el Aroos, a sweet and slender crisp filo pastry similar to baklava filled with sweetened nuts known as Brides Fingers.

Once alone, the two commanders briefed Zazai on the suspicions of the intel community about the Valley of Stars, the movements of Pakistan troops, and the disposition of known Taliban forces.

Zazai looked at his top general, General Mahmoud, "well General, what about the status of our own forces?"

Zazai had been working to replace ineffective commanders, but the process was slow. There were some units that were very effective and others with very questionable loyalty. This crisis demanded only the most loyal troops.

"Sir, due to the possibility of a strong incursion in the north, we should move units that have worked best with U.S. troops to the suspected hot zone. Shift our most loyal units to the Pakistan border area in the south, and those of questionable loyalty to the border with Iran," the President's military chief advised.

"Mr. President, I believe General Mahmoud's reasoning is sound. If Pakistan is going to make a move, it will likely be in the area where the boy was found. Having troops who are comfortable with joint operations is the best option and will require a high degree of coordination due to the rugged terrain. The southern border is still a threat, but we have units in place and flatter territory where armor and air support can be more effective on troops in the open," McAffey added.

"The Iranian border area is still dangerous due to being deep in the Helmand province. The majority Sunni fighters of the ANA will be a more natural guard against Iran trying to take advantage of the situation. Despite the violent differences between the tribes and the dominant Taliban region of the south, there is no love for the Iranians there," Mahmoud stated.

"Mr. President, we believe we're close to identifying the location of the Valley of Stars, and when we do, we can get experts in there to confirm our suspicions. If confirmed, we'll need our best fighters to protect it. Lieutenant Colonel DB Watkins, 1st Battalion, 3rd Brigade in the north has worked closely with a battalion from 203rd Corps led by Lieutenant Colonel Abdul Qadir, 2nd Battalion, 1st Brigade.

"If you remember the action at Zakar Khel, the two worked extremely well together and handled the press exposure better than expected. I feel that we couldn't have two units more effective than those and recommend we move 2nd Battalion north to join up with the 1st near Asadabad and have them operate jointly. The commanders know each other, trust each other, and we'll need that cooperation if the real thrust is in the north," stated General McAffey.

General Mahmoud spoke next. "Sir, if we move 2nd Battalion north, we leave 3rd Battalion in Khost. Their commander was a protégé of Colonel Qadir, and has made upgrades and improvements in skill and discipline very fast. We moved some of 2nd Battalion's NCOs with him, and they've dramatically improved the Battalion's performance level. Not to the level of 2nd Battalion, but enough to gain the trust of the U.S. commander in the area."

"We would then move 201st Corps east from Kabul to Jalalabad and shift 2nd Brigade, 209th Corps from Kunduz to Mahmude Raqi. That will keep them out of the population areas but within 100 miles of the border and in position to quickly move up to reinforce north or south. The 2-209 is made up of a majority Tajik troops, so their loyalty is much better against the Taliban," Mahmoud suggested.

"Sir, we will have helicopters at Bagram ready to transport quick reaction troops, with a special ops unit on standby at all times. Moving the 201st from Kabul east puts a blocking force along the border to respond in any direction, and guards the main routes into the capital. By shifting the U.S. 3rd Battalion, 3rd Brigade to Kotkai Kalai, and the 3-1 to Peer Kalai, all roads to Gardez are blocked. The remainder of the 203rd Corps in Gardez are then able to respond to any incursions in their zone," added McAffey.

"Mr. President, please understand that these moves are based on speculation. But our intelligence assets believe that the presence of the Pakistani expert actively helping the Taliban, along with the latest activity of the Pakistan Army movements on their side of the border, seems to support their opinion. At best, we are in a better position to respond to an aggressive action by either Pakistan or the Taliban along the border. At worst, we have a chance to exercise working more closely together," stated General McAffey.

"If nothing happens, we will announce the movements as a joint training exercise and return to normal operations," added General Mahmoud.

VALLEY OF STARS

President Zazai clasped his hands in front of him and thought for a moment. "Execute the orders, General. Let us pray the intel is wrong, but prepare we must," he ordered.

* * *

Madeline sat quietly, listening to the intel brief from the joint intelligence analysts to the President and his senior national security team. CIA confirmed that Pakistan had moved nearly a division strong force toward the border with Afghanistan in the northern territories, lending credence to the theory of their intentions. When they had finished, it was her turn.

"The 25th Infantry Division is working to get the Afghan boy who brought them the information about the Valley of Stars healthy enough to lead a team to its location. According to General McAffey, the Afghan military is getting nervous. If we are to stop a large push from Pakistan, he recommends moving a heavy brigade back into Afghanistan immediately to give Pakistan something else to worry about. The Joint Chiefs agree Mr. President," she stated.

Secretary Massey pounded on the table, "Diplomatic measures must be taken before any military units are moved back into Afghanistan. Relations with the new government are too tenuous and delicate right now. Moving additional forces into the country could undermine President Zazai and all the progress we've made at reducing our exposure to their people," he insisted.

"Jonathan, your analysis is pure bullshit. It's President Zazai who has specifically expressed concern about increased cross-border incursions by regular Pakistani troops all along the Durand line. He's already trying to shuffle his military units as fast as possible to cover possible attack points, but he doesn't have the reliable manpower or firepower," Madeline countered.

"Zazai is actually trying to identify their most effective field commanders and units as we speak. He's actively replacing those who used political connections to get their commands. Clearly, he's concerned about the corruption under former President Khalizad, as the units most loyal to him were the ones with the most green-on-blue incidents. And Jonathan, for your strategy of Afghans taking more responsibility for security, we need to do what the new president needs to make that transition happen. Zazai knows they need to take a step backward for them to take two steps forward," Madeline demanded.

Massey raised his voice and shot back, "Dammit Madeline, more heavy troops will only antagonize the tribal regions and further destabilize them. Not only will we lose the support of the Afghan populace, Zazai will too."

Madeline then looked at Massey and got that icy glare in her eyes that her staff knew all too well. The one that made it clear she was about to cut your head off and impale it on a stake for all to see. Rather than having a volcanic temper, when the Secretary of Defense was about to strike, her voice got quiet and forced the antagonist to lean in as they got sliced and diced by her.

"Secretary Massey, isn't that so convenient. You completely ignore the fact that the Loya Jirga, voted overwhelmingly to have Khalizad keep U.S. troops with a new forces agreement. If we follow your advice and Pakistan attacks with any force whatsoever, American losses will be steep. They are battle hardened from their constant troubles with India and are extremely well trained and equipped.

"Make no mistake, this is not the JV squad! If we don't move the proper forces, we leave our people exposed with little defense and no backup. Their blood will be on your hands...and on yours, Mr. President, and there will be no hiding it. No amount of spin will be able to cover up the hundreds of body bags coming home, and they'll be laid at your feet," stated Madeline coldly.

The Secretary of State virtually blew up as he came out of his chair, shaking his finger at Madeline and yelling, "That comment is bullshit, and so full of hyperbole as to be ridiculous. We have more than enough force in the area to defeat the Pakistanis..."

"A country with nuclear weapons," interrupted Madeline calmly.

Massey was nearly apoplectic by now, "Fuck you! You highlight the worst case scenario as if it was fact. If anything does happen, we will have enough warning to move troops if necessary."

"Really? Move troops from where? Under your advice, we've pulled more than two thirds of them out of theater and it'll take weeks to move them back. That's a shitload of warning you're counting on," Madeline replied sternly.

As the back and forth got nastier Madeline remained calm, her demeanor made Massey even angrier.

Finally, President Saldana put up a hand. "Enough! Everyone stop talking. Thank you both, I think I have enough information. I have to think about what to do and I'll let you know my decision shortly."

And with that, the President ended the meeting. Madeline knew Massey would hang back and talk to Saldana alone and this would likely not go her way. She had to do some damage control at the Pentagon.

* * *

Kirkorian had moved out of Bagram with 1st Battalion and their new commander after the press junket to Zakar Khel. She'd been in the field for the past two weeks with the American patrol moving along the Kunar River north from Asadabad. Their mission was to talk with villagers about the missing men who hauled the equipment in and out of the Valley of Stars and find the massacre site.

Kirkorian had debriefed the teenage boy found by the earlier patrol after medics stabilized him. She flew back to Bagram with him for further questioning while doctors treated him. She'd been extremely patient with the boy. She would talk with him a couple hours a day as he got stronger and stronger, and was able to use his understanding of terrain and sun angles to get a fairly detailed description of direction and distance.

She was able to narrow the location the boy described by the terrain features. Then backtracked from where he was found to the general area of the execution site of the men used as mules.

Now she was back with a patrol in the area talking with local villagers, trying to find this valley the boy described. They had found the execution site nearly a week ago, and after collecting the dead, they retraced their route with the bodies to bring them home to their families. They had located several villages where men and boys had been kidnapped by the Taliban, and returned the bodies to their families.

Kirkorian ensured the bodies were treated within the Muslim traditions and briefed the patrol leaders on the correct way to address the village elders. Each time they'd describe the valley to the villagers, and would inquire about knowledge of any mountain valleys fitting the wounded boy's description. They were now in a small village called Sosha to repatriate the last of the Afghan dead. The patrol was gearing up to head back to base camp when a young woman approached Kirkorian.

"Sergeant, thank you for bringing my brother home. My father deeply appreciates the care you showed him. My brother was his last son, and my father is very angry with the Taliban. With the loss of my brothers, I have tried to help tend to our animals. There is a high mountain valley that is much hidden where I sometimes take them to graze. It sounds like what you describe. Perhaps it is the one you're looking for? I will ask my father if I can guide you to it. Please come back in three days after our mourning period for my brother," said the girl.

"Thank you. Do you want me to speak with him before I leave?" asked Kirkorian.

"No, he is too overwhelmed with grief. I promise I will talk to him when the time is right," the girl replied.

"Again, thank you. What is your name little sister?" Kirkorian asked.

"Delara. Remember, come back in three days," the girl replied.

"Delara, a beautiful name for such a brave young woman. My name is Shirin. I assure you we will return. Thank you, Delara," answered Kirkorian.

Kirkorian said the traditional Afghan goodbye as Delara turned and went back to her father. Kirkorian met up with the patrol leader, and together they spoke with the village elder. They thanked him for the hospitality of his people, and gave their condolences for the loss of their brothers. With that, the team left and returned to base camp where she made an immediate after action report.

* * *

Farooq dabbed the sweat from his forehead caused by the sweltering heat as he sat in a safe house just outside of Peshawar contemplating his recent meeting with *Khan* less than 24 hours ago. *Khan* was a marvel at details, and related everything he did and saw during the expedition to the Valley of Stars. It was clear that the Pakistani expert had found much more than he let on and *Khan* was sure the deposit was much larger than was officially reported. He observed the rock formations, and the excitement in the man, barely noticeable to the untrained eye but clear to *Khan* as an intelligence asset.

Immediately after meeting with *Khan*, Farooq contacted Al-Zuq for a face-to-face. While it was a serious risk, it was dangerous to be seen in the open with contacts, this situation was much too important to be left to messages. So Farooq had quickly arranged to meet with Al-Zuq at the safe house near the General's headquarters. But Farooq had a dilemma. He needed the Pakistanis but wouldn't bow down to their control. This find was to fund their worldwide Caliphate, not to enrich corrupt officials in Pakistan.

Farooq's head of security knocked on the door, "They're here."

The first person through the door was Al-Zuq's security officer. He did a complete electronic sweep of the small one room house and then checked Farooq for weapons. When done, he went to the door and motioned the all clear. General Al-Zuq strode confidently through the doorway and shook hands with Farooq. Al-Zuq's aide followed him into the house and started a pot of tea while the two leaders exchanged traditional greetings.

Farooq thought Al-Zuq was an imposing man. Tall, with a muscular barrel chest and dressed in battle fatigues, he was not at all like so many other Generals. Too often they were politically connected and were soft from the trappings of power. This man was clearly made for combat. Despite his help with Farooq's brothers, the tribal regions of the Northwest Territories were still a very dangerous place for the Pakistani military, especially this man.

Farooq began the conversation. "General, thank you for your help with the geologist confirming our suspicions. We really didn't expect oil there, as I told my contacts in the Caliphate, but they had so much success selling the captured Iraqi oil on the black market that they want to find it everywhere. I hope my men made his trip as comfortable as they could."

"It was my pleasure, my friend. I'm just glad the result was satisfactory for you. But I wonder, what was so important to take such a risk to meet face-to-face? Forgive me for being blunt, but you could have offered your appreciation through our normal communication channel. You wouldn't have asked for this meeting unless there was a very serious issue to discuss," replied Al-Zuq quizzically.

"As you know, we have built a fair amount of trust these past years, and your strong leadership has been one reason why. With the Iranians now actively fighting us in Iraq and supporting those pigs in Syria, and the Afghan government working with the Americans and Indians, we have some common enemies my friend. We know you worked both sides of the Iraq-Iran conflict in the 80's and have helped the Iranians with their nuclear research, so forgive our concern," began Farooq.

"Don't you trust me, Farooq?" asked Al-Zuq as his aide placed tea in front of both men.

"I trust you as much as you trust me, General. Did you not have your security sweep here before you entered? Of course, just as I had you followed here and made sure there were no special troops shadowing you to threaten me."

Al-Zuq laughed and slapped the table. "Seems we are both very cautious men. I see your point. But certainly something has caused this concern you state. What is it?"

"As the Americans once said, General, 'trust but verify,' so we needed confirmation of our suspicions of the resources in the Valley of Stars. Do you think your geologist was the only expert in the valley? We know your geologist under-stated what was there, no?" Farooq asked.

Al-Zuq took a long sip of tea as he contemplated his reply. He looked up at Farooq. "He gave me ranges of what he thought was there. When asked, he suggested a more conservative estimate would be better until a proper analysis could be completed. We may have underestimated some." And that was the admission Farooq was looking for, a deliberate understatement.

"General, we both know that the resources in that valley are much more plentiful and very important to our mutual interests. We prefer to work with brothers who share our beliefs to take advantage of those resources. Certainly, it would be beneficial to use those resources to achieve both our goals, yes?" asked Farooq.

Again Al-Zuq took a long sip of tea before speaking. "Of course, Farooq, we have always expected as much, but we risk much as well. Helping you secure the Valley of Stars could ignite a major conflict with not only the Afghan government but directly with the Americans. While that may be fine for the Taliban, we have the Indians to worry about. Opening a two front war would not get you what you want and would shift our resources to defend our eastern borders. A fair payment for that risk is what we seek."

"Yes, General, it is a risk but one that's lessened now that there's only a token American presence. They are mostly locked on their bases because their President pisses his pants over even the possibility of 'civilian casualties.' That leaves the ANA who are barely considered fighters," began Farooq.

"But they've stopped your people very effectively these past months along the border," interrupted Al-Zuq.

"I admit that some ANA units are more effective than most. But if we mount a major offensive in the south, it will draw their best units to that fight along with the Americans while limiting their forces further north near the Valley," answered Farooq.

"But it still means a risk if we reclaim the territory around the valley. It will bring international ridicule. So what do you offer for payment, my friend?" asked Al-Zuq as the real reason for this meeting was now clear. And so the negotiations had begun.

"Yes, there will be difficulties from the west, and especially the Indians, but the gold from the valley will enrich your country through the purchase of weapons for our fight," replied Farooq.

"Ah, my friend, but it will make it more difficult to get so many things my country needs. There will certainly be sanctions, and our back channels will be severely tested. So, forty percent of what is mined should go to us, and we'll provide the weapons and security," countered Al-Zuq.

"That is a steep price, General, considering we must do all the work in an area that is exceptionally hard to access. Ten percent, and we purchase the weapons and pay for security as we need it. We have fighters too," responded Farooq.

"It will take you years, my friend, to gain the expertise to recover the resources from that mountain. Thirty-five percent of what's recovered, and Pakistan will get the contract to provide the equipment and materials to extract and refine the resources," stated Al-Zuq.

"But we can get a company to help us mine it, General, though having our trusted brothers' help would be very good for both of us. So we accept your weapons and help with security, and agree to the equipment, but twenty percent of the resources," countered Farooq.

"Acquiring oil will become a problem so we will need the precious metals to buy the oil and weapons for you. Thirty percent and we agree to the rest," stated Al-Zuq.

"Then it is agreed, General," answered Farooq. The two men shook hands, and the deal was done.

"Now, we must plan for the operation to secure the valley," declared Al-Zuq.

Chapter 15

Political Chess

Mo read through messages as *GillNet* spit them out, rubbed her tired eyes, and took a swig of coffee. Like so many terrorist hunts she had worked on they all followed a similar script, a rush of activity, then mind numbing monotony waiting for something to happen. The *GillNet* program tracked keywords and provided statistics on the volume of messages from each user identified in the network as well as those of the recipients. While many of the suspected leaders were good at hiding their tracks, others only had minimal security.

They had traced dozens of players to locations in Germany, France, Syria, Iraq, Turkey, Pakistan, and Afghanistan. Despite having to work through some proxy server hopping, they were all plotted on the map. At least a dozen were located in Pakistan and Afghanistan, so Mo focused her hacking skills on them. It started slowly, a mass mail to a number of players, then accelerated into a cascade of messages.

She picked up the phone and rang Karim. "KZ, something's going on. You might want to come over and check it out."

Karim was there in less than a minute. "What've you got Mo?"

"Looks like a warning order went out and suddenly the board lit up with follow-on messages. Some are cover messages to the players in the game, but then they sent out individual messages to others," she replied.

"Okay, can you put the stats up on the big screen with their locations?" asked Karim.

"Done," she said.

They looked at the locations of the players. Several were in the Helmand province, Khost, and Kabul in Afghanistan; and Abbottabad, Peshawar, and Chitral on the Pakistan side.

"Karim, look at these messages here," as Mo highlighted a few of the messages that had time inferences. "Something big is going to happen within the next week. Not sure where, but given the locations of some of the most vocal players, looks like a major coordinated effort in Afghanistan," said Mo.

Karim pulled up the latest analysis on message traffic from NSA. "No reports of increased chatter from NSA yet. Maybe we got the first sniff," he replied.

He then pulled up the latest intel reports from DoD and saw the last messages about the Valley of Stars. 25th ID appeared to be getting close with their lead from the village on its location. They were already planning a patrol in a couple days to return and get a guide to lead them to the suspected location.

Karim punched the intercom and called Gerlacher. Moments later he strode in with Jake. "What do we have?"

"*GillNet* is showing a considerable spike in traffic in the Pakistan/Afghan area. We think a major operation is about to start within the next week," stated Karim.

"Alright, time to get us some help. Jake initiate Joint Protocol 4 and start gathering the assets we need. We already have the system set up. Mo, I need you to hack the top 3 suspected players. Time to see what they're doing and get whatever we can. I'll contact the Director and DNI and request activation of the intel fusion center. Karim, you and I need to head over to DIA right now and start coordinating with DoD to get them plugged into *GillNet*. Mo, make sure we have ports setup for them to get the data real time. Let's move people, the clock's ticking," ordered Gerlacher.

And with that, Gerlacher moved quickly back to his office and made the appropriate calls. Within five minutes, he and Karim were out the door headed for Bolling Air Force Base and the Defense Intelligence Agency.

* * *

Madeline was just finishing her morning coffee and reading the Early Bird news stories when her secure phone rang. It was David Anderson, Director of the CIA. "Morning, Madeline, sorry to interrupt your morning but the unit working Afghanistan has activated Joint Protocol 4. Looks like a large scale operation is ginning up there. My section chief and his lead analyst are on their way to DIA to plug you in. We'll have a joint briefing on their findings in twenty minutes."

"Where'd the intel come from, David?" asked Madeline.

"They've been running a worm program on a suspected communications channel, and they say the traffic has just lit up in the past couple hours. Add that to your people getting close to this Valley of Stars we've been talking about, and this could mean a major push in the Afghan/Pakistan border region. We've got NSA working on more specific targets to ID chatter and expect we'll hear more from them in the briefing. Gotta run. More calls to make Madam Secretary." replied the CIA Director. And with that, the line went dead.

Madeline called her Executive Officer. "Joe, call the Chiefs, tell them we're meeting in the NMCC in 10 minutes."

With that Madeline secured her office and headed to the National Military Command Center deep in the Pentagon. With the activation of Joint Protocol 4 from the Southwest Asia section, the region's alert level went to Threat Level 4, impending threat. All of the national security assets from Egypt to India went on alert and started real time fusion of information through the agency with the responsibility to respond, in this case, DIA. Intelligence experts from multiple agencies were already en route to the Joint Intelligence Center, and operations were being coordinated through the NMCC.

"Good morning gentlemen. Please be seated," began Madeline. "Admiral, what do we know?"

"Madam Secretary, as you know tensions have been mounting in the Afghan/Pakistan border region with multiple incursions the past few months. Most have been small, more probing and harassment attacks than full scale operations. But since the incident at Zakar Khel, it's been pretty quiet. On the other hand, there's been a significant increase in the Caliphate's operations in Iraq and Syria with their push to take the critical oil fields in south central Iraq and the western push to Ramadi.

"Combined with the President's latest concessions to the Iranians and the agreement in principle, this has made the Saudis, Egyptians, Jordanians, Kuwaitis, and other Sunni Arab states in the region very nervous. What was once just a radical form of Islam making noise has now escalated to a proxy war between the Sunni and Shia sects of Islam, with us in the middle. Add to that the increasing intelligence that the Taliban, who share the Caliphate's views and appear to be actively working with them, and main players in Pakistan becoming more radicalized, the sectarian tensions may be near the boiling point.

"The Afghan/Pakistan relationship is of particular concern because of the possibility of a fight over natural resources, specifically precious metals that could fund the Caliphate and Taliban movements. Given recent satellite imagery showing movement of regular Pakistan Army units out of their barracks and into positions towards the border, the picture becomes very worrisome. When contacted through back channels about their movement of troops, they told us they were about to start an operation in the tribal areas and these were simply defensive movements. If these elements are supporting the Taliban rather than fighting them, it's a different story," stated Admiral Joffrey.

"General McAffey, what would you need if we were to assume the worst?" asked Madeline.

"Madam Secretary, more heavy guns and troops. If it's Taliban only, then beefing up our air assets in Mary-4 and Bagram, and more special ops troops, is the best option for a major op from them. They have mostly light weapons, but it will take more urban warfare tactics to deal with them. In the two main border areas near Kabul and Khost, we and the ANA have already begun redeployment of troops that can handle this type of action.

"The ANA is shifting their best, most loyal units to the areas of greatest threat and President Zazai doesn't trust, or like, the Pakistanis one bit. If we're fighting Pakistan regulars, I need at least two more Brigades in the north and another in the south with 24/7 JSTARS, Rivet Joint, AWACS, and cap assets. I won't sugar coat it, Ma'am, it'll be bloody with what we have in theater right now," answered General McAffey.

"Holy shit, General. You know the President is already trying to decide between more of a drawdown or just holding what we have. And now you're asking for more? General Jameson, please walk us through all the intel we have right now," ordered Madeline.

For the next hour, DIA carefully walked through everything they had collected and analyzed, created a timeline leading up to the activation of the Level 4 protocol. While the direct link between the Pakistan Army, the Taliban, and the Caliphate was highly circumstantial, there were too many small things to be a coincidence. Finally, Madeline brought the conversation back to military moves they could make now in case this thing blew up.

"OK, gentlemen, so we don't have a lot of options. General Vickers, get those B-2s moving to Diego Garcia right now and have your people come up with some joint exercise name we can use as a cover. We might need to ask for overflight authorization from India, so we need to work that in the background immediately.

"It's a Hobson's choice, I know. Either overfly Pakistan and risk a direct military conflict with them, or overfly India and risk igniting another regional war between India and Pakistan, two nuclear powers. If the shooting starts, overflying Pakistan is shortest and if we're engaging Pakistan regulars, it'll scare the shit out of them, so that's our first choice.

"The Gipper's aircraft are more problematic because they too will have to overfly Pakistan. They will have to provide air support in the event of Pakistan Air Force operations against Afghanistan in the south and will threaten the port facilities in the Indian Ocean. Less than what we want but what we can do. We shift a Marine recon unit to Khandahar, an Army Ranger unit to Kabul, and a Seal Team to Bagram for immediate action. And let's get some more Combat Control teams in the field with the 25th ID.

"Lastly, get additional AWACS, JSTARS, and RIVET JOINT aircraft in position at Mary-4 and spin them up for 24-hour ops for the next couple weeks. General McAffey, I'll ask to move a heavy battalion from Turkey back in but it's a long shot. Let's reconvene this afternoon at five DC time, that's eight hours from now, and hopefully, I'll have some decisions from the President by then," instructed Madeline.

With that, she called the President to inform him she was on her way over, then contacted the Senate and House leadership to let them know to be prepared for a situation briefing after lunch. Twenty minutes later Madeline and Admiral Joffrey entered the Oval Office. Secretary Massey and Director Anderson were already there.

"Gee, Jonathan, do you have a room here or what?" Madeline remarked.

The CIA Director had to muffle a laugh at the dig toward the Secretary of State. Everyone knew the top two cabinet members hated each other, but neither had the power to remove the other. Massey had the President's ear, but Madeline had the Joint Chiefs. DC's version of the immovable object and the unstoppable force.

"Nice to see you too, Madeline," replied Massey snidely.

Massey believed that the way to utilize power was to leverage and manipulate the powerful. The age old tale of playing puppet master behind the scenes without taking responsibility, or suffering the consequences, for the decisions. Madeline understood that you don't try to move the immovable object by pushing on it harder, you had to go around it, over it, or break through it.

To Madeline, the real power wasn't necessarily from the top, but manipulating the individuals who had to interpret and implement the decisions underneath. She spent a lot of time working with the "underlings," gaining their trust and respect. Expertly asking them how the rules can be used to get what she wanted, and rewarding the people who got her there. Because of that, she didn't need to overtly push the President one way or another, but rather she interpreted the directives and changed the narrative to her benefit.

"Please, everyone, let's have a seat. Madeline, Jonathan and David have been bringing me up to speed on the situation and the activation of the Level 4 protocols. To be honest, it does seem to be a bit of an over-reaction to me," began the President. "We're operating on some very tenuous intel with an unproven communications link and a coincidental comment on a real world terrorist attack."

Madeline looked directly at Massey who sat there with the smirk of a Cheshire cat. Though the President's mouth was moving, she swore she could see Massey's hand up his ass, moving his lips like a ventriloquist dummy.

"I'm not sure there's as much of a threat as you do," finished the President.

"Interesting you've come to that decision without even hearing the military intelligence on this, Mr. President," replied Madeline.

"David gave me the run down, I think I have a pretty good picture. This really does seem more like the Taliban's normal activity ahead of one of their operations. Jonathan assures me the Afghans are confident they can handle this problem on their own and would give a huge boost to the image of the ANA within the country for providing security," responded the President.

"Is that the Secretary of State's opinion or President Zazai's, because that's exactly the opposite of the conversation General McAffey had with him yesterday. President Zazai asked us to keep troops in his country to allow him time to build trust in the ANA. President Zazai is concerned about the vacuum our forces have left in his country allowing the Taliban more freedom to operate. President Zazai believes there is an imminent threat to his nation and has requested more troops return to help him meet that threat," said Madeline.

"Based on our intel," interrupted Massey.

"Mr. President, I agree with the Secretary of Defense on this, there is a specific threat," added Director Anderson.

"Based on an unsubstantiated theory, pulled from an obsequious fascination with communications in an online war game and hearsay, without probative evidence," interjected the President.

Madeline was furious but remained calm on the outside. She knew that once the President started talking like an academic trying to prove he was smarter than everyone else, he stopped listening. She knew then and there, nothing she, or the Director, could say was going to change whatever decision he'd made.

"Bring me something concrete, some specific quote that says X is going to happen at this time and place, otherwise our forces will remain on their bases and only support the ANA if things get out of hand," ordered the President.

"Mr. President, intelligence doesn't work that way. We take seemingly random bits of information and weave a picture from what we observe, then fill in other areas based on our understanding of how the enemy operates. They are smart, not stupid. They learn from their mistakes and find other ways to get things done. This new communications method is still being mined to find that smoking gun you desperately want, but by the time we get it, they will already have adapted and moved on. I believe our best analysts who've been working this. Can I be 100% sure that things will happen the way they think? No, no one can. But I've seen their success in the past and past performance is critical in this type of work," stated the CIA Director.

"David, you make a fine argument for the intel, but there's very little actionable material here. I'm not going to authorize spending hundreds of millions of dollars on shifting troops, and risk the delicate balance we've worked so hard to build, to make that bet. I'm confident whatever risk we face, we have sufficient force to meet it. Get me information on this Valley of Stars and find out if it is as rich in resources as you seem to think. If it is, then we'll help the Afghans secure it and mine it. Otherwise, my decision stands. I will not expose our troops in the open and risk further casualties on our part, or the civilian Afghan population."

And with that, the President stood up and adjourned the meeting. As Madeline stood, Secretary Massey stayed seated, smiled at her and gave a condescending wave goodbye as she and the Chairman of the Joint Chiefs left the Oval Office.

The car was silent as they drove back to the Pentagon. As they pulled into the underground garage, Madeline turned to Admiral Joffrey, "Admiral, I'd appreciate it if you said nothing of the meeting with the President to anyone, and I do mean anyone. I need to think a bit on what our next moves will be."

"Yes, Madam Secretary. Do you still want the meeting at 17:00?" asked Admiral Joffrey.

"Let's move it up if we can. I'll have General Jameson brief the House and Senate leadership on the intel only and tell them we're working on an appropriate response," replied Madeline.

CIA was on her side, but Director Anderson wouldn't fall on his sword over this. Just easier to let the President blame faulty intel for his stupidity rather than let everyone know the intel was right and his decisions were horrible. For Anderson, it was a win-win. The enemy thinks his people are ignorant morons and he can lobby for more money to improve his intel capability with Congress.

The White House, State Department, and Pentagon press pools were buzzing at the unscheduled meeting that just occurred. SecState showed up at the White House with the Director of the CIA, followed by the SecDef with the Chairman of the Joint Chiefs 20 minutes later, and nobody was saying a word. The press was desperate to find out any information and were madly trying to mine their contacts in the respective agencies. But none of them were talking. All they had to go on was a meeting, and so they quickly started pummeling the agencies' media offices for information and clarification.

Madeline called General Palmer, head of the Pentagon Public Affairs, to her office. She described the meeting in general terms as a strategy meeting and said there was strong disagreement between her and SecState over how to proceed. The President took SecState's advice, and they needed to wait for those two to respond first. She ordered him not to respond to any press inquiries about the White House meeting, and she would call him to coordinate her response. After he left, she picked up her cell phone and called the personal cell phone number of John Griselle, the internet mogul who bought the prestigious Washington Tribune newspaper.

The Trib was one of the oldest and most influential papers in the U.S., if not the world. They had a stable of political and investigative reporters that were plugged into the national political scene like no other media outlet. Founded in the 1800's by a liberal Congressman, the paper always had a leftward tilt but did try to stay somewhat near the center. Though it struggled to remain relevant in a new media world, it was no surprise that an internet billionaire purchased it. And Madeline had shared a table with Griselle at the National Press Club dinner the year before, talking politics for several hours. "Hello, John, it's Madeline Coltrain, I need a favor...."

Two hours later Madeline was back in the NMCC conference room with the Joint Chiefs, watching the State Department's spokeswoman give her afternoon briefing. The White House had put out a press release saying the President had called a meeting that morning to discuss a variety of topics about the response to the framework agreement with the Iranians and the actions to be taken in the continued drawdown of U.S. forces in Afghanistan. Pure bullshit, but they had to say something that made sense.

Madeline was more interested in the statement that would be made by State. If she were right, Massey wouldn't be able to contain himself to take credit for influencing the President's decision. As the spokeswoman finished her briefing and opened up for questions, Madeline got her wish. The first question went to the New York Times reporter, an obviously planted question about how the meeting went, specifically about the situation in Afghanistan.

The spokeswoman gleefully answered. "The meeting was a great success. As you know, the Secretary has urged increased dialogue with the Iranians as a way to get them to give up their nuclear ambitions. We believe much progress has been made, though the details of the reporting on that progress have been erroneous. As for Afghanistan, Secretary Massey has always supported the President's desire for Afghans to take responsibility for the security of their own people.

"As the action in Zakar Khel proved, the ANA is more than capable of dealing with the Taliban and the threats to their nation. As a result, he advised the President that the ANA should continue to be more visible in dealing with security with our troops serving more as advisors, and act as a reserve to help when needed."

Madeline smiled and thought to herself, "check."

The second question went to Terence O'Malley, the Washington Tribune reporter who covers the State Department. "Did everyone in the meeting agree with this course of action?"

The spokeswoman was almost too eager to answer this one. "Of course, there was complete agreement by everyone in the meeting. The results of the past several months speak for themselves. It shows that the Secretary's approach is showing great success."

Madeline let out a long breath, "and mate." Massey's talking head didn't even realize she'd just buried her boss. It was his approach, not the President's.

"Sources have reported that there was angry disagreement from the Pentagon and that Secretary Coltrain stormed out of the meeting. Can you comment on that?" pressed the reporter. The storming out of the meeting wasn't true, but it made for great news and reinforced the Washington press corps' suspicion of the discord between Defense and State.

The spokeswoman stumbled just a little in her answer, just enough to lend credence to the report. "Ah, well, as you know, there's always a vigorous discussion to ensure the President gets all of the pertinent information to make a decision but everyone left the room supporting the course of action."

The spokeswoman then shifted to another reporter from NBC who would be more supportive of the narrative she was trying to put forward. Unfortunately, there was blood in the water, and this was more chum in the battle between two liberal giants in the administration. The sharks would get their bites in from both sides.

"Okay, shut that drivel off," commanded Madeline. "Gentlemen, the meeting with the President didn't go well. He insists that the intel is wrong and that there is no bigger threat despite the Afghans' specific request to beef up our forces. SecState has convinced him that the ANA can handle whatever that chatter was about, despite our pleas to the contrary. The President has ordered us to provide advisory assistance only and has restricted our troops to their bases to let the ANA be more visible in protecting the Afghan people."

The Chiefs nearly came out of their chairs in protest at that, but Madeline held up her hand for silence and continued. "Gentlemen, gentlemen, I'm in complete agreement with you. It's insanity, but that is what we have been instructed to do. Now I know how General Longstreet felt at Gettysburg."

Her reference wasn't lost on any of the military leaders in that room. General Longstreet was Robert E. Lee's top general in the Civil War who argued with Lee against fighting at Gettysburg because the Union had the high ground and the upper hand. He argued that the Army of Northern Virginia should have moved and fought where they had better positions. Lee refused, either because of his own ego or a misplaced belief that his troops could do the impossible.

51,000 troops from both sides were killed, wounded, or captured in that battle. Lee's army was decimated, never able to mount an offensive campaign again. It was a turning point, and now Madeline believed that whatever operation the enemy was planning was very likely just as important.

Madeline continued, "We have limited options, but the President also said that he wanted us to find the Valley of Stars and get him the confirmation he needed. He did not specify 'how' we should go about doing that, isn't that right Admiral Joffrey?"

"That's correct, Madam Secretary, he most certainly did not," replied the CJCS.

"We know our people are much more effective in the field and on the move than sitting waiting for the enemy to lob mortars and rockets on our heads. General McAffey, who can we get into the field right now?" asked Madeline.

"Madam Secretary, I've already coordinated with President Zazai to have the 1st Battalion, 3rd Brigade in the north meet up with the ANA 2nd Battalion, 1st Brigade, 203rd Corps near Asadabad. The two commanders worked together before at Zakar Khel and are the most capable commanders in theater right now. We have the ANA 3rd Battalion in Khost, led by a protégé of Col Qadir, we're moving their 201st Corps east from Kabul to Jalalabad, and the 2nd Brigade, 209th Corps from Kunduz to Mahmude Raqi. I'm shifting the U.S. 3-3 to Kotkai Kalai, and the ANA 3-1 to Peer Kalai, then all roads to Gardez will be covered. The remainder of the 203rd Corps in Gardez will be in reserve to react north or south," added McAffey.

"We're sending you some special ops troops, General. Unfortunately, the Marines in Helmand province will be at a disadvantage because the valley is in the north. But he did say we could 'advise' the ANA so get as many Marines in the field 'advising' as we can without making it too obvious. We might need to use our bases as bait. They won't like it but if the shooting starts then all bets are off, and we take whatever maneuver is necessary to give us the advantage," informed Madeline.

"General Vickers, we need to get those B-2's moving in the next 24 hours. Get a C-17 over there to airlift extra crews to Diego so we can start operations as soon as possible. Have the Wing Commander get with the families. With a short notice deployment there will be whispers of something going on that's not an exercise. We need them to stay quiet," ordered Madeline to the Air Force Chief of Staff.

After another hour of working through the strategy and movements, the orders were given, written up, signed and executed. The machinations of war were once again moving for U.S. forces. Madeline huddled with General Palmer, the Pentagon spokesman, to craft their statement.

An hour later he was giving the Pentagon's press conference. "As reported earlier, we are executing the President's plan in Afghanistan in full coordination with the Afghan government. Diplomatic efforts are ongoing as Afghan forces continue to assume greater responsibility over their country's security with the drawdown of U.S. forces. The State Department has assured the President that the political situation in that country is stable and that the government has been effective in countering the Taliban threat. As such we've been given new operating instructions that ensure we are providing the best military advice possible and have restricted our movements to provide support and reinforcement if needed.

"The situation in the Middle East is more fragile though, and we are watching events unfold there very closely. We've moved some units back into Iraq as advisors and support, to help the Kurds and Iraqi government forces against the Caliphate fighters. As the nuclear negotiations with the Iranians continue, the challenges in completing them are compounded by the proxy fights between Sunni and Shia militants in the region. We are prepared to act if directed and offered options to the President this morning. Finally, we have initiated a long delayed exercise in the

Pacific, and Indian oceans called Agilent Sword, to enhance the coordination between Air Force and Naval forces. Okay, let's open it up for questions," finished General Palmer.

The comment about the morning's meeting was a delicate stretching of the truth, as was the exercise. But they gave cover for any troop movements as a response to events in the Middle East and diverted attention from Afghanistan.

The first question was from the Washington Tribune's Pentagon reporter. "General, earlier today the State Department's spokeswoman characterized this morning's meeting as everyone in complete agreement. From your statement, that may have been a generous characterization. Did the SecDef agree with the course of action?"

"Jeremy, the SecDef strives to give the President the best possible advice and they did say there was a vigorous discussion. The President has made his decisions based on the advice given by his top advisors, and we will dutifully execute those decisions," replied Palmer.

"General, there are reports that Secretary Coltrain stormed out of the Oval Office, not the picture of complete agreement. Can you confirm those events?" asked the reporter from CNN. The rest of the press had taken the bait.

"Charlotte, I can safely say I've never seen the Secretary storm out of any meeting," Palmer said with a chuckle. "Everyone knows as a veteran herself she's a staunch defender of the troops in the field and is passionate about her opinions. She knows that the best decisions come from listening to multiple voices, not just one. And as a former soldier, she will follow the lawful orders of the Commander-in-Chief and execute them to the best of her ability to ensure a successful mission."

Madeline sat in her office watching the press conference and smiling to herself. Palmer was a maestro, he never really answered directly and gave just enough latitude to others to hang themselves. But he skillfully inserted the knife into the belly of that bastard at State and hung any failure squarely on his shoulders while any success would go to her for the "execution" of a flawed strategy.

The smoke had become a roaring fire, and the press would now go after every word. This was what they lived for in Washington DC, power struggles, political intrigue, ah yes, what a city!

Chapter 16

Finding the Valley of Stars

Given the high level of Taliban activity in the area where the suspected Valley of Stars was located, the theater commander had ordered a reconnaissance in force. This area of the Hindu Kush Mountains had peaks 13-15,000 feet high, and the suspected location of the Valley of Stars would be around 7-8,000 feet. It would make the terrain some of the most difficult and challenging in Afghanistan and severely limit the use of heavy vehicles. That meant most of the infantry would be walking with armored MaxxPro Mine Resistant Ambush Protected vehicles, or MRAPs as the troops called them, running point and HUMVEEs for support.

The mission fell to Qadir and Watkins. The current patrol had three companies from Qadir's 2nd Battalion and two from Watkins 1st Battalion with Qadir as the overall commander of the joint force. They would be responsible for probing the high mountain passes for the Valley of Stars. The remainder of the joint force was positioned in Asmar along the Kunar River, just north of Asadabad under the command of Major Andreesen, the 1st Battalion's XO. Andreesen would move up the Kunar River protecting Qadir and Watkins' right flank and to find the location of the lowlands approach to the Valley.

"How are you feeling Ramin?" Kirkorian asked the young Afghan survivor.

"I am well, the side is sore, but healing and the shoulder gets stiff. But if you find this valley you are looking for hopefully I can return to my father," Ramin replied.

"Let me know if you need to rest. We have a long, hard trip ahead of us and you are still recovering," answered Kirkorian.

"Thank you, but if these brave soldiers are expected to lay down their lives for me, I will endure whatever they do. If they walk then I will walk, and if they fight then I will fight," responded Ramin proudly as Kirkorian nodded in acknowledgment.

"Sergeant, what did he say?" Watkins asked Kirkorian as he walked alongside of her and Ramin. After she translated the short conversation, Watkins shook his head in amazement, "that's one tough kid. Not sure I'd be so quick to get into the field a month after taking three AK-47 rounds and nearly bleeding to death," he continued.

"Teenagers, they think they're indestructible. Guess it's nice to have the restorative powers he has while still growing," replied Kirkorian laughing.

Three and a half weeks after being found, Ramin had finally left the hospital. His extended stay in the hospital helped speed up his recovery but also ensured that his presence could be kept secret and under American control. He was extremely fortunate that two of the gunshot wounds were through-and-through, one in the shoulder and the other in his side. The one in his side nicked his liver that required arthroscopic surgery, and he had a bullet removed from his arm.

Although still not completely healed, he wanted to help the Americans find the location of the Valley of Stars, so he could go home. Since the Taliban had tried to execute him, the Americans felt it safest for him to stay dead until the Valley could be secured. Ramin knew it would be painful for him to walk back into the rugged mountains, but nothing like the pain he had walking out of them weeks before.

The joint patrol stopped at the village called Sosha, north-northeast of Asmar along the Kunar river, where two nearly parallel mountain passes and their tributaries met the river. Sosha was the mountain village of the young woman who volunteered to help, so the two commanders went to speak with the village elders. The patrol set up a defensive perimeter outside the village while the commanders and a small contingent entered.

As the soldiers approached the small group of village leaders, Watkins removed his gloves and extended his hand to the village chief. "As-salamu 'alaikum."

"Wa alaikum as-salaam," replied the chief, shaking his hand and then placing his right hand over his heart to indicate his respect. "We wish to thank you again for returning our son to us," he said as Kirkorian translated.

"It was an honor, sir. Too many fathers, brothers, and sons have been lost in this struggle," replied Watkins. Watkins proceeded to introduce Qadir to the elder and greetings were exchanged.

"Come, let us have tea and talk," concluded the chief as he escorted the party to his house.

The commanders questioned the elder about Taliban activity in the area. They confirmed it had recently increased and that several villagers who trade with others along the river had some dangerous encounters the past several days. As the elders pointed out areas on the map where encounters had taken place, there was a clear pattern of activity around Barikot near the Pakistan town of Arandu. Qadir and Watkins gave a knowing glance at each other; it was the exact place that Intel said had an increase in Pakistan regular army activity. The likelihood of cooperation between them and the Taliban was now very real.

The meeting was finishing up when Watkins asked about the young girl, named Delara, from their previous visit who offered to lead them to a valley that fit their description of the Valley of Stars. The chief called for Delara and her father. When they arrived, Delara stayed outside while the man spoke with the elders and the commanders. Watkins welcomed him and asked him to join them for tea.

"Sir, it was an honor to return your son to you. I just wish we could have met on a more joyful occasion. I have two daughters and a son myself. I know I would want vengeance on those who did this, though my faith says otherwise," stated Watkins solemnly as Kirkorian translated.

"Thank you. I know what has happened is Allah's will, but like you, I want to see the people who did this punished," replied the man with a glint of anger in his eyes.

"There is something the Taliban and those who killed your son believe is very important here, important enough to kill dozens of your people to keep it a secret. When we were last here, your daughter spoke with this woman," Watkins began, pointing to Kirkorian.

"She suggested that she could lead us to a place like the one we described. We have a young man who survived the massacre that took your son who can confirm if it is the place. But he is being hunted by the Taliban so we must be careful. If there's another way to this valley without having to take the boy through very hostile territory, we would like to find it. Would you allow your daughter to show us to this Valley?" asked Watkins.

The man looked at his chief, then at Watkins and Qadir. "You say a boy survived the attack that took my son, and he is here with you? May I meet him?" asked the man.

Qadir immediately called for one of his men to fetch the boy. Ramin entered the house and looked nervously at the men seated.

"Sir, this is the young man who survived the Taliban massacre, his name is Ramin. Ramin, this man's son was with you in the group of men who were executed by the Taliban. He would like to ask you some questions," Qadir explained.

"I will answer if I can," replied Ramin.

The man stood and studied Ramin for a moment. Despite his injuries and time in the hospital, Ramin was still larger than the man and maintained his muscular features.

"Did you get to know my son? His name was Hakim, and he was a little shorter than you but very muscular. He had a scar over his right eye," Delara's father asked.

"Unfortunately, the Taliban prevented us from talking to each other much, so we never knew any of the other men. But I remember your son. He was a good, strong man. He was proud, not one of the others who cowered to the Taliban, but one who could have been very dangerous had they not kept such a close watch on us. I only survived due to Allah's will. I was able to start moving just before the shooting started and though I was wounded, the Taliban passed by me as they moved among us and killed any survivors," Ramin explained.

Over the next half hour, the man listened intently to the boy's story of his capture, the trek to the valley, the massacre, and his eventual recovery. With a sorrowful smile, the man thanked Ramin and shook his hand, praising Allah for watching over him. He then turned to the commanders.

"My daughter is the only child I have left. It would be too much for me to lose her," replied the man.

This time Qadir spoke to him. "Your son was a brave and honorable man, like his father. It is clear that your daughter is just as courageous."

Watkins added, "Sir, I give you my word that I consider her as my own daughter and will protect her with my life. This woman here," again pointing to Kirkorian, "is a lioness, fierce and deadly protective. She will not leave your daughter's side and will kill anyone who tries to hurt her."

Qadir added, "Sir, I assure you that my men and I will guard her like the precious jewel she is. If any harm comes to your daughter, that will mean we are all dead."

The man looked both commanders in the eye and nodded his agreement. He called for Delara and told her she had his permission to go with the patrol.

Kirkorian grabbed her hand and gave it a little squeeze. "Hello again Delara, I told you we would return. Don't worry, you are safe with me," stated Kirkorian.

And with that, both commanders offered their hand to the man and the village chief. Kirkorian and the girl followed her father back to their home to collect some things for the journey. Delara gathered her belongings and said goodbye to her father.

As the two women were about to leave, the man turned to Kirkorian. "Zmarei, please bring her home to me," as he extended his hand to her.

The gravity of this gesture wasn't lost on Kirkorian. It's rare for an Afghan man to address a woman who is not related and offer to shake hands with her. Addressing Kirkorian as Zmarei, Pashto for lioness, showed his trust and respect for her.

Kirkorian grasped the man's hand and bowed her head slightly. "Father, it is my honor to be my sister's guardian. I will bring her home," reinforcing that the girl, and the man, were considered her family now. The women headed over to where the patrol was preparing to move out.

Delara put her arm in Kirkorian's and gave her a little hug, "Zmarei, I've never had a sister before. I'm glad it's you."

Kirkorian had to laugh; seems she now had an Afghan name.

Watkins radioed the reserve force in Asmar and ordered them to move up to Sao where the next major tributary fed the river. If clear, the reserve force would probe further up the river keeping a blocking force at Sao to guard any approach from the southeast. It was unlikely that the Taliban would come through that pass as it rose to a high mountain ridgeline that extended to over 11,000 feet of rugged mountain peaks along the Pakistan border. But in Watkins' experience, the approach least expected was usually the most successful. Orders given, the main force moved out to the north following a dry stream bed that meandered through a valley with modestly rising walls for the first couple miles, then got significantly steeper as they moved forward.

The column was led by a couple of MRAPs with Watkins, Kirkorian, Ramin, and Delara in a Humvee about 100 yards behind. As the column came upon smaller canyons that moved off from the main route, it would stop as a squad moved up to clear and secure, then they'd move forward again. This hopscotch approach was slow going, but both Watkins and Qadir knew that caution was the best strategy.

They knew the patrol could move faster by moving slower. An odd thing that most people couldn't understand, but to the two battle hardened commanders, a prudent lesson learned with the lives of good men and women. They'd moved four miles and 2,000 feet of elevation in three hours when they encountered a Y in the valley. Delara told the commanders that the split to the right went to a deep valley shaped like a walnut tree leaf, but ended in a dead-end with an extremely steep ridgeline surrounding the end of the valley.

The description didn't quite match the one Ramin described, but it was large enough to check out anyway. Watkins led a platoon up into the valley with Kirkorian, Delara, and Ramin to verify whether it was the Valley of Stars. As they moved deeper into the valley, Delara narrated stories of bringing the family's animals up there to graze and, as the weather got warmer, she would move them farther up the dry stream bed that the column was following to look for good grazing land.

The terrain in the bottom of the valleys and canyons was extremely fertile from the winter runoff coming down the ridgelines each year feeding a carpet of brown-green grasslands. Ramin added that he too would go into the mountain passes to graze his family's animals. Kirkorian smiled to herself as she watched the teenagers take side glances at each other as they walked. After an hour, the valley had been investigated and determined that it was not the one they were looking for, so the patrol continued up the main valley.

Another three hours of hopscotching got them almost five miles and 1,000 feet more elevation, but with the grade leveling out a bit, they were able to make better time. The column came to a broad curve in the dry stream bed turning east, and Delara told them to stop. She pointed to a narrow path continuing north, virtually imperceptible if you didn't know it was there.

It was especially hard to see due to the fading light of the day and the shadows of the mountains above them covering the terrain. With the waning daylight and the rugged, unknown terrain, the commanders decided to stop for the night in the small canyon they had just passed and cleared. It gave them good security, was large enough for the entire force to get out of the main stream bed, and was elevated, giving them a very good defensive position. The commanders posted sentries, which would be swapped out every two hours, so everyone could get some food and sleep.

The Americans took first watch to allow the ANA troops time to conduct their evening prayers and eat, Watkins insisted. The trust, respect, and understanding between the two commanders was clear to every soldier and was emulated throughout the ranks. It wasn't patronizing or done to be politically correct. Both men understood the power of maintaining the health and welfare of their troops; physically, spiritually, and emotionally. They both seemed to know exactly when to make a small sacrifice for the other to ensure the integrity of the mission. That sense of shared purpose and shared sacrifice which had enabled small armies to defeat larger ones for millennia was imbued in these soldiers, American and Afghan.

As morning broke, the encampment was already buzzing with activity to prepare to move out. Commanders got their intel briefs, gave orders to the officers, who gave orders to the senior enlisted non-commissioned officers, who then gave orders to their troops. Soldiers grumbled about this and that as they stowed gear, checked weapons, ate a little chow and got that last smoke before mounting up for the next leg of the trip.

"Hey Kirkorian, what's for breakfast," Tasker called as he bounded over to where Kirkorian was sitting with Ramin and Sergeant Hassam, Qadir's Command Sergeant.

"Bacon and Cheese omelet, want some?" laughed Kirkorian as she used the chemical heating package for her MRE, meal ready to eat.

"Very funny, you mock me now! You know my kind don't eat pork. These damn MRE breakfasts always have ham, sausage, or bacon in them. Took me ten minutes to find just an egg and cheese biscuit sandwich in the pack," Tasker replied chuckling as he ribbed Kirkorian. "Hey, trade for your granola bars."

"You don't eat pork, are you Muslim?" asked Hassam innocently.

"Jewish, and Kirkorian loves to rub it in my face by cooking that bacon that smells so damn good! The names Tasker," Tasker said reaching out his hand to Hassam.

"Hassam, Colonel Qadir's Command Sergeant," Hassam replied.

"Glad to meet you. May I ask, where did you learn English?" asked Tasker.

"You can thank the American CIA," Hassam replied. He was one of a few ANA soldiers who spoke relatively decent English. "They taught me as a young boy near the end of the Russian occupation to spy for them. After they left, I was with the Taliban as an interpreter," Hassam said matter-of-factly.

"You were Taliban? How'd you get here?" asked Tasker, nearly choking on his coffee.

Hassam looked at Kirkorian, and the two started laughing, "Colonel Qadir. I had already grown concerned about the tactics the Taliban used and how they justified it with religious edicts that were different than those I learned as a boy. I was captured by Colonel Qadir many years ago after a battle, and he opened my eyes as to what it meant to be a Muslim, and an Afghan," answered Hassam.

"I've never met a man like him before. I will lay down my life for him, as will every Afghan soldier on this patrol. And you should know Tasker, many in our unit are former Taliban fighters," Hassam said with a twinkle in his eye to the clearly surprised Tasker.

"Holy shit, Kirkorian did you know this?" Tasker asked.

Kirkorian started laughing, "Yah I did Sarge. And just so you know, Qadir's never had a green-on-blue incident...ever!"

"Son of a bitch, now that is impressive. Well glad to work with you Hassam, guess you have a lot of insights on how these guys fight, would love to pick your brain when we get more time," Tasker replied. "So back to the real important shit...food. Hassam if you have any of that mutton jerky, I'll trade some coffee for it," Tasker declared.

"Jesus, don't you ever stop horse-trading, Tasker?" Kirkorian mocked.

"I'll keep my own food my friend, a little jerky and some dates we picked up in Sosha when we stopped, is good. But I'll keep that in mind for later," answered Hassam laughing.

After a few minutes Watkins walked up, "alright, mount up," he ordered.

And with that Kirkorian took one last pull of her coffee and tossed the rest. It's a testament to the efficiency of more than 700 soldiers that within an hour the formation was once again moving north, taking the trail Delara pointed out. The nearly invisible path wound through a small canyon with steep sides perhaps only 50 feet wide, forcing the formation into a single file. After about a quarter of a mile, it opened up again into another rocky creek bed, not as large as the main one they had been traveling from Sosha, but still made for a slightly easier route.

The sides of the valley were not as steep as before, and there were fewer canyons for the force to check out. After several hours, and about five miles of winding marching, the valley took another Y. The main creek angled off to the east, and a very small canyon moved to the north and looked like it dead ended. Delara told the formation to stop and directed them up the small canyon. Qadir ordered a platoon to escort the command group with the teenagers into the canyon. As they approached the back of the canyon, there were two large, nearly vertical crevices angling off in both directions.

The crevices were fractures in the vertical rock. Each was only 20 feet wide and would be a tight squeeze for their MRAPs to move through, barely giving room to maneuver if one got stuck. They looped around in a horseshoe shape that opened up on the other side of the wall behind several large boulders the size of two-story houses. The valley was shaped like an arrowhead with the boulder formation forming the base. At nearly 8,000 feet of elevation, the valley was almost completely enclosed. It was about a kilometer wide at its widest point, and one and a half to two kilometers long with the walls sweeping up to nearly 10,000 feet around them.

Delara led half of the platoon through one side of the horseshoe, and the other half went through the other side. As the group emerged from behind the boulders, Ramin looked around and put his hand on Kirkorian's shoulder. "Zmarei, this is the place."

"Are you sure?" asked Kirkorian.

"Yes, at the other end of this valley is a cut through that high pass," Ramin replied, pointing to the point of the arrowhead at the northeast end of the basin.

The Valley was located at the treeline and had bundles of stunted, twisted trees that were nothing more than tall bushes lining the walls near its base. The walls of the basin had several fractures and fissures from the geologic forces that created the Hindu Kush Mountains. The floor of the valley was littered with gravel washed down from the ridgelines into the basin from a millennium of erosion and earthquakes that had dislodged the aggregate. As they looked across the valley, it literally sparkled all around them, glittering in the sunlight. Watkins picked up some of the gravel and could see streaks of gold running through them. So, the intel was right, this could be a treasure trove of resources.

Kirkorian told Watkins what Ramin had said, and he immediately issued orders to secure the valley. He sent two squads racing across the basin to the point of the arrowhead to secure the pass Ramin indicated would be there. The rest of the patrol would spread out and check the walls and ridgelines then document the area in pictures and laser measurements to relay back to headquarters. Kirkorian moved to the communications HUMVEE and sent a flash message. The Valley of Stars had been found.

CHAPTER 17

It Begins

Karim and Jake were alternating 12-hour shifts at the joint intelligence center set up in DIA headquarters. Deep in the bowels of the nondescript concrete building on a military base southeast of DC, they had a direct link to Mo's data from *GillNet* and were in constant contact. Karim was pouring over a mind-numbing volume of intel data coming in from a variety of sources when his direct line with Mo rang.

"KZ, pull up the latest messages from *GillNet* right now! Several execute orders just went out throughout Afghanistan and Pakistan. We must have missed something in our intercepts, or this was a plan started before we cast our net," insisted Mo.

Karim did what Mo asked and saw that it started with their target *Wolfhunter*, then cascaded through players traced back to Pakistan and Afghanistan.

"Mo, this is too widespread to be just an isolated terror strike. We haven't seen this much chatter since the Caliphate moved on northern Iraq," Karim replied.

"I know. Zack called the DDI right away. There is no timing but seems all of the messages are urgent so how long do you think we have?" asked Mo.

"Given the speed at which the message was spread, I'd say less than 24 hours, but we have no idea where they plan to hit except that it's likely in the Afghan region," stated Karim.

"Well, looks like we don't have much time then. We need to go over all the *GillNet* messages for the past few days," replied Mo.

"Okay, I'll get some help from this side. We need to work fast but smart and divide up the messages," responded Karim.

Between the Joint Intel center and the CIA Southwest Asia locations, they had six people pouring over the massive amount of *GillNet* messages. Pulling things that were suspicious and running search strings for other references across the game and other intel sources for the next several hours. One of the military analysts tapped Karim on the shoulder.

"I may have something. I was searching for any messages referencing that village, Arandu, that we think is a supply depot. I found this one confirming to wait for the 'go' signal from Chitral and move from Arandu. I think this guy screwed up and used the actual names rather than their code names. Another player scolded him to keep operational security. It doesn't say what the signal is or where they are going, but this is the second mention of Arandu as either a supply route or a jump-off point for their fighters. I traced Chitral, and it's about 45 miles north of Arandu in the tribal region of Pakistan," the analyst stated.

"Okay, thanks. Mo, pull up everything we have on Chitral," ordered Karim. The latest intel came up on all the screens from CIA, which wasn't much. The DIA analyst overlaid their intel with maps indicating locations.

"Sergeant, can you pull up any satellite imagery we have for the area?" Karim asked.

The overhead screens came alive with satellite feeds and DIA's aggregation of known Taliban and Pakistan army locations in the area. "This is a few days ago. We'll have a bird over the area in 10 minutes, and we can get a new picture," stated the analyst.

VALLEY OF STARS

"Can we get a live picture?" asked Karim.

"You bet," was the reply.

Minutes later the video picture flashed on the screen as the satellite approached Afghanistan. The analysts had already programmed the computer to overlay friendly forces with green and blue dots on the video feed from last reported positions. They zeroed in on the target area along the Afghan/Pakistan border.

"Look here, who are the allied forces in that region? How far away are they from Chitral?" demanded Karim.

Suddenly lines showed up on the map with coordinates, direction, and distance. "Reportedly a joint patrol, 50 miles almost due west," was the reply.

"Find out what they're doing there," ordered Karim.

Arandu was the first checkpoint to come into focus, and the analyst zoomed in. The room went silent as the images flashed before them. The Sergeant spoke first. "Shit that looks to be at least a Regiment, maybe a full Brigade of troops and vehicles."

They panned up to Chitral, and this time it was Karim's turn. "Son of a bitch, that's another Brigade. We might have a whole damn division within a few miles of the border. Dammit, find out who those friendlies are now!" demanded Karim.

The video was downloaded, and the military analysts grabbed the screenshots and raced to identify the structure of the Pakistani military force, and which units they might be. The team had to fight the urge to fire off urgent warnings as they still didn't have a clear enough picture of what all this meant. But nuggets of intel began trickling in that, to Karim, confirmed this was not going to be pretty.

The friendlies were identified as elements of a U.S. battalion from the 25th ID and an Afghan Battalion on a reconnaissance in force to find the Valley of Stars. If they were close to that valley, and it was as important as Karim thought, this was plenty of force to overwhelm the allies there and take it. Most of the pieces of the puzzle were on the board, and to a puzzle master like Karim, he could see how each curve, loop, and notch went together. Combined with a few unsubstantiated reports of large numbers of Taliban in the area near Arandu, he moved the pieces around the board in his mind.

Like a chess master looking several moves ahead, Karim created a mental picture of what the enemy was going to do before they did it. When the flash message from 1st Battalion came into the fusion center confirming the location of the Valley of Stars a few hours later, he knew the first moves of the game had already been made. Karim was certain this would be a move to take the valley, but Zack said the powers that be needed more concrete proof.

"Shit," thought Karim, "how much more proof did they need? Dead Americans?"

The intercepts talked about a "go" signal to start operations, but what that signal would be no one knew. What he did know was that once that signal was given, the troops in the Valley would need a whole lot of reinforcement.

* * *

The patrol made their way to the eastern end of the Valley of Stars and found the high pass that Ramin said was the entrance to the valley used by the Taliban. The two commanders decided that the route into the valley from the east needed to be scouted. The boy would guide them down to the location of the execution and possibly give them a chance to talk to villagers near the border. This would be dangerous. The border areas were hot zones so it was decided the ANA troops would conduct this recon with a squad of U.S. troops to escort Kirkorian and the two Afghan teenagers. Delara wanted to go with the group, mostly because she wanted to stay with Ramin, and she was a mountain girl with a teenager's curiosity. Kirkorian tried to convince her to stay in the valley, but Delara reminded her of the promise to stay together at all times.

Just before the soldiers were about to move out of the valley, Qadir approached Kirkorian and the teenagers. "Sergeant, do you think it wise to bring this child on this mission?"

Before Kirkorian could answer, Delara straightened her back and answered, "Colonel, I'm not a child, and Zmarei is my sister, I'll never leave her side."

Suddenly embarrassed by her uncharacteristic breach of cultural norms, Delara looked down and apologized to Qadir for her outburst and moved slightly behind Kirkorian.

Qadir chuckled. "Well, seems you've made quite an impression on this...young woman, Sergeant. Stay with me at the center of the formation. The boy will go with Sergeant Hassam," ordered Qadir. Kirkorian confirmed the order and started gathering her pack for the next trek.

Suddenly she heard a familiar voice. "Hey Kirkorian, looks like we're babysitting you again this trip."

Kirkorian spun around and replied, "I think you got that ass backward Tasker. Seems I need to babysit you guys." The two laughed, "Have you taught those puppies how to shoot, or better yet, how not to get shot?" Kirkorian ribbed.

"Ah hell, I'm still a better shot one handed than most of these jokers," chuckled Tasker. "It's all good, the newbies are learning fast, and someone's got to keep you in check. You know how you Rangers like to go rogue on us regular grunts!" he shot back with a laugh. "In all seriousness, what do you know about these ANA guys?" asked Tasker.

"Probably the best the ANA has. Colonel Qadir led this group at Zakar Khel, some of the best fighting we've ever seen in country," replied Kirkorian.

"That's good to know. I didn't really want to get hung out to dry on this mission if we run into trouble. Either way, it's nothing to keep me out of this shit storm, just wanting to know how big a shit storm it could be," said Tasker.

"Trust me, after reading the after action report and talking with the villagers in Zakar Khel, these are not the guys you want to fight if you're the Taliban. Colonel Watkins led our guys in the same battle, and these two commanders think like one. They're the tightest operators I've ever seen," answered Kirkorian.

Finally, the order to move out was given. The troop moved through the narrow pass and started down the winding gulley. It was an extremely steep grade, making it challenging to maintain footing and made the heavy MRAP's move slow. The thin air at this altitude took its toll on the soldiers' stamina. After 500 meters it opened up into a narrow valley with a more manageable grade and steep ridgelines on both sides.

They were quickly losing daylight as the shadows from the ridges reached across the valley like dark fingers engulfing the patrol. Qadir had the formation slow as they approached some small canyons splitting off from the main valley like fish bones. Suddenly he ordered the group to stop as he scanned the ridgelines. He sent squads into each canyon to check them out, and another forward to stand point. The rest of the patrol fanned out on both sides of the valley.

As the soldiers were settling down, Kirkorian saw Ramin and Sergeant Hassam walking their way when Delara tugged on her arm. "Zmarei, I need to pee."

Kirkorian looked around and saw a group of rocks near a grove of trees about fifty yards up the valley wall just forward of where they were. "OK, we'll go up there for some privacy. Give me a minute," replied Kirkorian. "Hey, Tasker, going up to those rocks up there so the girl can relieve herself," she called.

Kirkorian and Delara started up the hill as Ramin and Hassam walked up, and the two teenagers exchanged shy smiles as they passed each other. The rock formation was fully covered in the dark shadows of the rapidly setting sun. As she waited for Delara, Kirkorian thought that she hadn't had a drink of water in over an hour and needed to stay hydrated in this dry high mountain air. She scanned the ridgelines, and when Delara came around from behind a rock, they started back to the patrol. The rock formation was a group of very large boulders and, as the two women turned the corner from behind one of them, they came face to face with five Taliban fighters. Kirkorian recognized the situation moments before the Taliban, dropped to one knee and got off a burst of fire, raking from left to right as she swung her M4 around from her chest.

Delara screamed as the gunfire erupted. Kirkorian hit two of the Taliban before two others rushed her. She reflexively brought her weapon up to block a strike from the attacking Taliban and was rolling backward when the two fighters hit her. Kirkorian managed to get one leg up in the abdomen of an attacker as they hit her and she used his momentum to launch him head over heels. The three soldiers tumbled down the hill in a ball of thrashing arms and legs with rifles and equipment spilling out of the furball as they tumbled. With one attacker stunned, Kirkorian focused on the other and got a few punches in while taking a heavy strike to the side of her head. As they struggled, she managed to get her hand to her boot knife and drove it up from the bottom of the attacker's sternum so hard that her hand compressed the soft tissue below his ribcage and into his heart killing him almost instantly.

While Kirkorian was fighting with her two attackers, the last Taliban rushed Delara knocking her to the ground. The young girl struggled mightily hitting, kicking, and biting her attacker. As Kirkorian was rolling the dead Taliban off her to engage the one she had kicked, she saw something flash by her peripheral vision. The Taliban fighter in front of her had recovered his AK-47 and was raising it toward her. Suddenly the fighter's chest exploded into a red mist as he took a rifle blast from behind. As he fell, Kirkorian saw Sergeant Hassam behind him, panting with the slight wisp of smoke coming from the barrel of his rifle.

Ramin leapt at the Taliban struggling with Delara and drove his hands down on top of the attacker's shoulders in two powerful blows shattering his collarbones. As the attacker fell, the young man grabbed him around the neck, picked him up by his head over his back like a sack of potatoes, then dropped quickly to one knee snapping the Taliban's neck and killing him instantly.

Tasker, Qadir, and several other patrol members rushed up the hill and spread out in a defensive formation around the women and the attackers. One of the men Kirkorian shot was still alive, and the soldiers secured him for questioning. She was covered in blood, some bruises were forming on her face, and the sleeve of her uniform was torn, but otherwise, she was alright. Delara had her arms wrapped around Ramin's neck, sobbing into his shoulder as the young man's muscular arms carried her down to where the others were. She wouldn't let go of him.

"Zmarei, are you hurt?" asked Sergeant Hassam using the nickname given her by Delara.

"I'm good. A little beat up but nothing fatal," replied Kirkorian.

"Kirkorian, you okay?" asked Tasker panting heavily as he came rushing up behind Hassam.

"Yah, they were as surprised as we were, gave me a little time to get the jump on them," responded Kirkorian.

"Holy shit, that kid is fast. He was off like a rocket at the first sound of gunfire, and without a weapon at that. Hassam was right behind him, but the kid pulled away from us, going uphill. What the hell happened up here?" asked Tasker trying to catch his breath.

"The girl had to pee. We ran into these guys as we were headed back to the patrol. Got a few shots off before these two hit me and the other grabbed Delara. Got one off me, managed to kill the other when Hassam took the live one out. Guess Ramin took out the one that grabbed the girl. She hasn't let go of him yet," replied Kirkorian.

Tasker looked over at the dead Taliban fighter Ramin killed. "Son of a bitch, the kid, snapped him like a twig. Remind me not to piss him off!"

"Your Colonel was right, you are a Zmarei, the name fits you," Hassam said as he came over and offered Kirkorian a hand up.

"Thank you, Hassam, just trying to stay alive. I hear we have a live one?" replied Kirkorian.

"Yes, but he won't last long. Medic says he won't survive so we need to question him quickly," answered Hassam. "Ramin, do you know how to use one of these?" asked Hassam as he picked up one of the Taliban's AK-47's.

"Yes, sir, I carry one when taking the herd to the mountain pastures for protection," answered Ramin.

Hassam walked over and hung it off his shoulder. "Next time you go running toward gunfire you better have one of these then," as he slapped the young man on the back and turned to head down the hill.

Kirkorian walked over to Ramin and Delara who was now standing but still holding tightly to Ramin's arm. "Delara are you hurt?" asked Kirkorian.

"No, Zmarei, just a little bruised," replied Delara looking at Ramin and grasping his arm just a little tighter.

"It's okay, Zmarei, she's safe," Ramin answered as he looked down at the girl on his arm, "I promise no harm will come to her as long as I'm alive."

Kirkorian smiled as she patted him on the arm then reached over and gave Delara a big hug. "I promised your father I'd bring you home safe little sister. Seems you have more than one protector now," Kirkorian said with a smile. Delara's face lit up with joy as she leaned into Ramin's shoulder. The outward show of affection between the two young people went against a thousand years of Afghan culture. It was forbidden for a non-family male to touch a

VALLEY OF STARS

female but the emotion of the events overtook the cultural norms, and nothing would keep Ramin from Delara's side.

As they made their way down the hill to the valley floor again, Kirkorian saw Qadir kneeling beside the mortally wounded Taliban fighter, praying. She started walking over to them when Hassam stopped her.

"Zmarei, wait," Hassam said as he put his hand up. "Let Colonel Qadir handle this. This is his specialty, he always knows exactly how to speak with these men to get the information we need."

After about thirty minutes, Qadir put his hand on the head of the now dead Taliban and said another prayer. He directed that the five bodies be taken back to the Valley of Stars and called the Platoon commanders to meet for a briefing.

Turning to Kirkorian, "Zmarei, contact Colonel Watkins in the valley. The enemy is in force just over the river at the base of this approach to the Valley of Stars. This group was an advance scout for an operation to the Valley of Stars, but others are coming soon. He also said there were Pakistan Army troops in Arandu, a lot of them, but they left the Taliban fighters alone."

Kirkorian turned to the two teenagers, "Ramin, Delara, go with these soldiers back to the valley now! Ramin, take as much of the ammunition as you two can carry off of the dead Taliban," she ordered, and this time the tone of her voice made clear she was in no mood for an argument.

Delara began to protest, but Ramin put his hand up stopping her in mid-sentence, "Zmarei, we will go. I meant what I said, I'll keep her safe."

And with that, Delara rushed over and gave Kirkorian a big hug as tears began trickling down her face. "Be careful Zmarei, don't forget your promise," Delara said as her voice trembled with the recognition of the danger they now faced.

"Be strong little sister," Kirkorian whispered in Delara's ear, "I always keep my promises."

Kirkorian shot an acknowledging nod to Ramin, the silent confirmation that a promise made must be a promise kept. The boy stood straight, showing every inch of his height and had that steely determination in his face that Kirkorian recognized immediately. He was every bit the strong, powerful young man who would protect the woman he loved, or die trying.

Delara turned, wiping the tears from her face, and picked up an AK-47 from the dead Taliban. She slung it over her shoulder, hanging it in front like she saw Kirkorian do with her M4, and pulled on a pack stuffed with whatever they could scavenge from the dead fighters. The change in the girl's demeanor was just as stark. Delara was no longer the giggling, playful little girl, who had left her village a couple days before. She looked proud, with an air of confidence rarely seen in Afghan women.

The squad of soldiers carrying the dead back to the valley moved out with the two teenagers.

* * *

The truck pulled up to the fence only ten yards from the western wall of the Pakistan Army barracks in Chitral as the sun was setting. The day's final call to prayer was bellowing over the mosque loudspeakers as the driver of the truck calmly got out and walked away. Around a corner near a coffee shop, he got into a car and drove to a mosque for prayer.

Ten minutes into evening prayer, the sound of a massive explosion ripped through the small city shaking buildings throughout. The wall of the barracks evaporated and the place where the truck once stood now contained an oblong crater. The bomb had been built to be directional with the vast majority of the blast directed toward the barracks building and creating minor damage to the building across the street. Much of that damage was from the shock wave of the blast and the shrapnel from the disintegrating barracks walls.

Seventy-Five Pakistani soldiers were killed instantly with another 50 severely injured. The sound of ambulances rang out within minutes, and the Army started pulling out bodies and blaming the Taliban for the blast. Within the hour, the blast was news worldwide with the commander of the Army for the Northwest Territories vowing to hunt down those responsible, no matter where they went. Mobilization orders went out to all forces in the territories, and by midnight Pakistani forces all along the Afghan border were on alert, and on the move.

Chapter 18

Chaos

"We have breaking news, this just in, there has been a major terrorist attack in Chitral Pakistan. A car bomb was detonated next to a Pakistan Army barracks, the death toll is currently at 60 soldiers and climbing with dozens still reported missing. Let's go to Casey Sorrenti, in Islamabad, Casey what can you tell us?" asked the cable news anchor breathlessly.

The joint intel center fell silent as the story of the terrorist attack was reported by the worldwide news organizations being monitored by the intelligence personnel. Karim stared at a wall of televisions as the images of fire, and rubble from the destructive power of the blast played across the screen. The news networks dutifully replayed the video of dozens of dead bodies being pulled from the shattered remains of the Army barracks. It's a testament to the interlinked communications age that an event in a remote city in Pakistan was the lead story around the world within a matter of hours.

The reporter interviewed the Pakistani commanding General who immediately blamed the Taliban for the attack. He proclaimed he would track down the perpetrators wherever they were and get his nation's revenge on them and whoever helped them. Karim had spent hours poring over intel reports trying to find that link that would complete the picture they were trying to build. The flash message from the allied patrol in the valley of the encounter with the Taliban scouts and the recent terrorist attack were linked, he knew it. This attack must be the signal that earlier messages referenced, but signaling what?

Suddenly, on the other side of the intel center, there was a rush of activity as the message boards started lighting up across Afghanistan. Reports of Taliban attacks started sweeping across Helmand province in the south and border area in the north near the Northwest Territories of Pakistan from Afghan police stations and ANA outposts. Then the Marines reported major attacks occurring at their bases and the Army began getting hit in Kabul and Bagram. It seemed as if the whole country exploded at the same time.

As the chaos erupted in the intel center, Karim suddenly realized what was happening. This was the justification for Pakistan to go after the Valley of Stars. He ran over to the Air Force General who was the shift commander for the Joint Intel Center. "General, I need to talk to you for a minute."

"Son, not now. We've got a hundred attacks we're trying to weed through so our folks in theater can understand what's going on," responded the General.

"Sir, I know, that's what I need to talk to you about. They're diversions," urged Karim.

"Diversions? If they're diversions, then they're pretty goddamn good ones. Diversions for what?" demanded the General.

"They're cover for Pakistan to invade. Think of it as the Taliban equivalent of the Tet Offensive during Vietnam, only this time it's Pakistan not North Vietnam planning to take advantage of it," declared Karim.

"I know that was the theory up to now, but actions on the ground don't seem to support that son. All of these are Taliban attacks, and the Taliban just hit the Pakistani army, so I seriously doubt that Pakistan wants to help the Taliban. Right now, we have no reason to believe they're preparing to invade Afghanistan," the General replied indignantly.

"Sir, we know someone in Pakistan helped the Taliban find a potential treasure trove of natural resources in the valley that 25th ID just found. We also know that Pakistan has nearly a division of troops less than 50 miles from that valley. The allied troops in the approach to that valley encountered a Taliban scouting force, and one of their fighters who briefly survived that engagement suggested a larger one to follow. Sir, just like Putin engineered a crisis in Ukraine to take the Crimea, someone in the Pakistan government has created the perfect storm to justify entering Afghanistan. If I'm right, the next thing you'll see is a claim that Afghanistan helped the Taliban somehow in the attack," argued Karim.

"I'm not entirely convinced, and we have to brief the Chiefs and SecDef within the hour. Put together your intel and get ready to make your case, but right now, we have to react to what's happening on the ground," replied the General.

"Yes, sir," was Karim's response as he rushed back to his desk and called Mo.

Jake came rolling into the intel center when he saw the news of the terrorist attack in Pakistan. Karim was on a video conference with Mo and Gerlacher. "Hey guys, what's up?" asked Jake.

"All hell's broken loose. Think Tet offensive, and you'll get the picture. Pull up a chair," replied Karim.

"Holy shit," answered Jake as he threw his gear in a corner.

Karim quickly brought him up to speed with the latest events. He told him the team was trying to find a concrete link between the Taliban and Pakistan military. Jake pulled out the notes he'd made from his previous shift and dug through some of the *GillNet* messages he was reviewing the day before. He quickly found what he was looking for.

"Guys, I found a message between *Wolfhunter* and a player named *Seleucus I*. It says that the trigger is set and he wants to confirm his forces are ready to move. But I think he makes a mistake and calls him 'General' when he asks if he will declare the justification for the actions," stated Jake.

"Did *Seleucus* respond?" asked Karim immediately.

Jake nodded his head, "he just replied with a simple 'Yes' and that was all."

"Mo, I need you to trace where this message was sent from as fast as you can," ordered Karim.

After what seemed an agonizing few minutes, Mo replied, "Pakistan. But it's weird. NSA shows the IP address to be associated with the Pakistan Army, though it came through a civilian internet provider in Peshawar."

Karim's mind was racing. Seleucus I Nicator was the founder of the Seleucid Empire encompassing modern Afghanistan, Iran, Iraq, Syria, and Lebanon, with parts of Turkey, Armenia, Turkmenistan, Uzbekistan, and Tajikistan. These guys had a flair for irony and history. Seleucus was a General and close friend of Alexander the Great. A General and the message specifically called him "General" and suggested he would be announcing the justification.

Karim spun around quickly, "Sergeant rewind the news reporting of the attack on the Pakistani Barracks," he instructed.

The report came to the Pakistani General who was vowing to chase the perpetrators wherever they would go. "Stop!" shouted Karim. "Who is this guy?" he demanded.

The operator rewound the video to the beginning of the General's comments, and the tag under his image identified him as Lieutenant General Muhamad Al-Zuq, Commander XI Corps, Pakistan Army.

"Got him!" announced Karim. "People, meet *Seleucus I*. Zack, we need to put this all together to brief the SecDef and Chiefs in about 15 minutes. Can I have them conference you in?"

"Yes, I need to brief the Director right now. He needs to be in on this as well," replied Gerlacher, recognizing immediately what Karim had found.

Twenty minutes later the SecDef, Joint Chiefs, Director of National Intelligence, CIA Director, and NSA Director were all on the video conference for the current military situation and intel. General McAffey presented the situation on the ground with the ongoing attacks. JSTARS, the aerial ground control aircraft, and AWACS were airborne, providing coverage. A Combat Air Patrol was established should the Pakistani Air Force decide to make a move. Marine AV-8s, Air Force F-16s, A-10s, and Army Helicopter gunships were providing close air support. But the air assets were stretched thin with so many requests for fire support.

SecDef asked about the Marines and Army restricted to their bases, and was told they were taking heavy mortar fire supported by heavy weapons and RPGs. Casualties were modest on the allied side, heavier on the Taliban side.

When he finished his assessment, Madeline looked around at the Generals and said, "General, get your forces moving. You have permission to make whatever moves necessary to meet this threat. I don't want another Beirut on our hands because we were sitting with our thumb up our ass for political reasons."

Now it was Intel's turn to try and explain what was happening and what might be coming. Karim laid out their theory and used the *GillNet* intercepts to support their hypothesis. NSA provided some supporting electronic intercepts that pointed at some coordination between Taliban cells, Caliphate, and a few elements within the ISI, Pakistan's intelligence service. They described the search for the Valley of Stars, its recent discovery, and the positioning of forces in the area. General McAffey described the repositioning of ANA forces based on the earlier warning and the current known Pakistani order of battle in the region.

"General, what about those units that found the Valley of Stars?" Madeline asked.

"Ma'am, it's a battalion sized force made up of three companies of ANA and two of ours. The two commanders are the ones that did the op at Zakar Khel. General Mahmoud says that unit is the best in the ANA and, given the action reports I've had on both commanders, they're the best in theater. We got lucky," replied General McAffey.

"Well, so far that's the only good news we've had. Okay, if this valley is so damned important that Pakistan would risk an invasion then we have to protect it, no matter what. General, tell them to hold it at all costs, and we need to look at what help we can get moving their way. Prioritize your needs, and we'll be ready to move on your request," ordered Madeline. "Gentlemen, that's all we can do for now. General McAffey, hopefully, the moves you've made with General Mahmoud will be enough, if not, then God help us.

There are limits to how far we can stretch the President's orders."

As the meeting was about to adjourn, General Jameson interrupted. "Madam Secretary, we all need to hear this."

He had the news reports brought up on the screens. The reporter based in Pakistan following the developments in the Chitral bombing was reporting breaking news.

"Lieutenant General Muhamad Al-Zuq, Commander XI Corps, Pakistan Army forces in Pakistan's Northwest Territories just finished a press conference on the recent terror attack on their Army barracks in Chatral. He stated that Pakistan had tracked the terrorists into the disputed border area controlled by Afghanistan, but the Afghan National Army has blocked Pakistan from apprehending them. Pakistan has demanded that their forces be allowed to move into the border area to find the perpetrators and bring them to justice. Also, the General implied the terrorists may have had assistance from elements inside the Afghan government to ensure the Northwestern Territories remain restive and keep Pakistan from encroaching on the disputed Durand Line that forms the current border.

"He declared that if Afghanistan refuses to allow Pakistan to kill or capture the terrorists, Pakistan will conduct operations independently no matter where the terrorists are located. Shortly after his press conference, hundreds of demonstrators poured into the streets here with angry chants of 'blood for blood' and signs urging Pakistan to invade. Needless to say, this has escalated tensions to their highest levels since the U.S. invasion to dislodge Al Qaeda and remove the Taliban from power. This is Casey Sorrenti reporting from Islamabad," the reporter finished.

The General in charge of the intel center turned and gave a look of understanding at Karim and nodded his head in acknowledgment. Karim was right.

* * *

Qadir had the patrol on the move. He ordered Alpha Company to take the left flank, Bravo Company the right, with Charlie Company in the middle. The two wings would move in a forward angled line from the center so that the whole formation was a flat bottomed V across the valley. By now the valley was blanketed in pitch black darkness as a thousand stars twinkled in the crisp, clear mountain air. The moon hadn't come up yet, so Qadir ordered the formation to halt and dig in for the night with no fires. He relayed their position to Watkins back in the Valley of Stars, and included several of the terrain features that would be advantageous should his patrol have to pull back.

The two commanders decided on the narrows just at the entrance to the Valley of Stars as their last stand location, and Watkins quickly got his troops working on preparing defensive fortifications. He then moved one of his platoons with MRAPs to a position approximately one kilometer behind Qadir to provide fire support if needed. Given the intel they just received, it looked like it was more of a when not if.

Just before dawn, during that period of charcoal grey skies that precedes the glow of the coming sunrise, Qadir had his troops on the move again.

"Alpha Seven Delta and Kilo Five Five, send a squad and scout ahead. Tell them to stay in the shadows of the rocks and report contact with any enemy formations. Everyone else, move out slowly," Qadir ordered his two companies on the wings.

As the scouts raced ahead, the rest of the patrol began to move. The cold mountain air was almost stinging, especially after a few hours of rest with no fires to heat the men overnight. The ANA troops moved nervously, anticipating the engagement everyone believed was coming. Despite the cold, many were already sweating from the rush of adrenaline that comes with the expectation of the deadly dance about to occur.

The anticipation of the battle was almost worse than the actual fighting as men had time to think of all the bad things that could happen. Once the fighting started, it was moving on instinct, training, and the will to stay alive that guided their actions, not the "what-ifs" of the unknown. Battle was a known; kill or be killed, move to cover, fire for effect. If a soldier had to think he wasn't proactive and likely going to die.

The ANA formation moved down the valley carefully and deliberately for over two hours. The sun peeked over the tall mountains casting a kaleidoscope of shadow and light throughout the valley. The shadows behind Qadir and the ANA patrol were receding faster now that sunrise had arrived and the commander knew they would be in sunlight before the enemy. But they were still in the shadows when the lead squads reported large numbers of Taliban headed up the main valley. Qadir ordered a full stop to take cover and let the Taliban come. The scouts reported several hundred fighters in two long parallel lines moving toward the center of the ANA formation.

"Hold fire, hold fire. Draw them in," Qadir ordered.

The leading elements of Taliban were casually walking and talking among themselves. At 25 meters, Qadir stood up, raised his rifle and yelled, "Fire."

The sudden eruption of gunfire in front of the Taliban column sliced through their leading ranks cutting down dozens of Taliban fighters, men falling like dominos. The enemy column faltered and immediately fell back, searching for any cover they could find. Once the column took fire, the trailing elements of Taliban rushed forward, moving up the ridgelines to try and flank the blocking force in the valley.

The two wings of Qadir's formation opened up with a devastating crossfire and drove the enemy back down to the valley floor. The Taliban commander quickly regained control of his troops and returned fire. But the less disciplined Taliban fighters fired their weapons wildly, and many were killed by the more aimed and concentrated fire of Qadir's soldiers. With heavy gunfire coming from three directions, the enemy was forced to withdraw from the deadly barrage. After a furious battle lasting a bit more than twenty minutes, the Taliban retreated with over a hundred fighters either dead or wounded.

It had been nearly 30 minutes since the engagement with the Taliban when Qadir heard the unmistakable echoes of heavy tracks rolling up the valley. He knew the armor could only mean the arrival of Pakistani regular army forces. It made this fight much more dangerous.

"Fallback, staggered withdrawal 200 meters, move," radioed Qadir urgently to his patrol.

The forward squads began withdrawing immediately, and each successive squad in the V covered the move of the one in front of them. Just as the first eight squads moved, there was a thunderous roar of incoming heavy armor fire with shells hitting near the spots the leading squads had just left. These were from Pakistani Al-Khalid main battle tanks and some of their tracked artillery. Qadir immediately ordered a swift withdrawal of the remaining force and reported the artillery fire to Watkins as it began pounding the positions they had just left.

Qadir's troops escaped with minor casualties and only one killed, but he knew the element of surprise was no longer on his side. While his men had been in many battles before, the Taliban relied on mortars, RPG's, and recoilless rifles as their heavy weapons. But most of the ANA had never fought against an enemy with modern tanks and artillery, and the impact of the 125mm shells shook the ground and reverberated off the valley walls like rolling thunder. As the fire coming from the enemy armor was walked back toward their new positions, he knew the infantry would be right behind it.

"Sergeant, call it in, see if we can get some air support in here," Qadir ordered.

"Lighthouse, Lighthouse, X-Ray One One, engaging a large infantry force, Battalion strength or larger supported by armor and mechanized infantry, and taking heavy fire. Request close air support," the American squad radioman called to the orbiting AWACS.

"X-Ray One One, Lighthouse, roger. Be advised all assets currently engaged, but we'll get you something just as soon as we can," the AWACS controller replied.

"Sir, looks like it could be a while. All CAS is tied up, but they'll get us whatever they can," the radioman reported.

"Alpha Seven Delta and Kilo Five Five, get over-watch on the ridge now," Qadir radioed to his companies on the wings.

The ANA snipers raced to the top of both sides of the valley to get eyes on the enemy movement in this deadly game of cat and mouse. The enemy was positioned southeast of the allied force with the sun behind them. The sniper teams reported Taliban and Pakistan infantry supported by armored vehicles slowly moving forward, pressing Qadir and his troops. The ANA responded with mortars and anti-armor missiles that arced across the valley, slowing the advance of the enemy columns. Their rockets traced an eerie red-yellow glow against the shadowed walls of the valley, cloaked in the grey veil ahead of the rising sun.

Qadir moved along his lines to bolster his men fighting a modern military force for their first time. As a young boy during the Russian occupation, he had been through many ferocious battles at his father's side. The Russians were notorious for using bombs, tanks, artillery, and helicopter gunships indiscriminately with no regard for human life. To the ANA soldiers, the more intense and chaotic the fight, the more Qadir became like the mountains of his childhood; strong, cool, and larger than life. He spoke with such authority that his men complied without hesitation and gained courage and confidence from his strength.

The battle raged for over an hour. Qadir's forces would hit the enemy and then move to lessen their losses, slowly trading ground for enemy casualties. The Pakistani's would push, the ANA would counter, and this process repeated itself over and over. The American MRAP's would move up to provide covering fire for the infantry to move back then would pull back when the Pak armor would start ranging their guns on them. It was an agonizingly slow crawl up the valley for the Pak troops, but they made steady progress and Qadir was taking casualties he could ill afford. He knew his fighting retreat would have to accelerate due to simple numbers.

The snipers on the ridges were directing fires, targeting the high value commanders of the oncoming enemy, and reporting enemy positions so their own units could fall back before their locations were compromised. Although the sun was now high in the sky, the team on the northern ridgeline were looking in its direction and got careless. A Pakistani sniper caught a flash reflection off of the ANA sniper's scope exposing his position. In the blink of an eye, the ANA sniper and his spotter were dead. A-Company was in trouble, their eyes were dead, and now the enemy sniper had them pinned down, unable to withdraw. Six men were quickly killed or wounded as mortars, and armor rounds began falling all around them.

"X-Ray One One, Alpha Seven Delta, over-watch dead and taking heavy fire. We're pinned down and blind," called the A-Company Commander over the radio in extreme panic. With Alpha Company hung up, Qadir couldn't move and leave them behind, and the entire formation started taking increasing fire from both infantry and artillery.

"X-Ray One One, Victor Six One, we'll take it," radioed Kirkorian.

Kirkorian slipped off her pack and pulled out a Remington Defense Concealable Sniper Rifle (CSR) and had it together in less than thirty seconds. It was similar to the Mk13 rifle her uncle taught her to shoot as a young girl growing up but had more range with its .308 Magnum rounds. She threw a pair of ranging binoculars to Tasker and told him to spot for her, and the two rushed up the northern ridge. Using the reports of where the ANA troops had been hit, she scanned the ridge and selected a conceal position.

"Tasker, scan along the southeast ridgeline about two thirds of the way up the valley wall. Look in the craggy rocks," Kirkorian thought for a second, "between 1000 and 1400 meters."

Kirkorian began searching with her scope in a standard search pattern from left to right while Tasker searched right to left. The noise around Kirkorian and Tasker was deafening as rounds began hitting closer to their position. The scope on the CSR was a covered coated lens that minimized reflections and had a laser range finder.

"Got him, 1300 meters out," Tasker suddenly announced.

The scope was linked wirelessly to the binoculars so that it gave small arrows indicating where the binoculars were pointing and vice versa so both sniper and spotter could quickly sight on the same spot. Kirkorian slewed the rifle to the location Tasker had spotted. She looked around for cues for wind direction and saw thermals rising off the rocks where the sun's heat touched them.

Going from sunlight to shadow was a very difficult shot with the wind swirling along the path the bullet would take across the valley. The enemy sniper was located on the southernmost ridge behind a group of rocks. Kirkorian saw him move ever so slightly and take another shot, then located his spotter as well. She loaded a round and slowed her heart rate and breathing as she ranged the enemy and dialed corrections into the rifle. Taking a shallow breath and letting halfway out she squeezed the trigger slowly but firmly.

The rifle jumped as the .308 Magnum round left the barrel. She could see the shockwave of the bullet moving through the air. A second later the bullet entered the top of the sniper's head, exploding the back of his skull and smashing through his back. The spotter was still giving range instructions when he lifted up and turned his head to see his partner dead, a second round hit him just under his chin, ripping through his chest, killing him instantly. Tasker patted Kirkorian's head. Two shots and two kills at 1300 meters!

"X-Ray One One, Victor Six One, enemy sniper neutralized," radioed Kirkorian.

"Alpha Seven Delta, X-Ray One One, covering fire coming your way, now move!" Qadir ordered.

The sniper taken care of, Qadir shifted mortar fire to cover the withdrawal of A-Company as they carried their dead and wounded. Tasker and Kirkorian ran back to the squad of Americans near Qadir as the din of battle increased to a deafening pitch. Just then, the volume of incoming fire started to die down, and Qadir heard the unmistakable whistle of incoming heavy artillery.

"Pull back, 200 meters now!" Qadir radioed to his entire force.

A few 155mm heavy artillery shells landed just short of the lines Qadir's men had left. The heavy artillery shells shook the ground like mini-earthquakes as they hit. The concussion from their explosions rippled through the bodies of the soldiers like a heavyweight boxer hitting them, knocking some of Qadir's retreating men to the ground. As the ANA soldiers desperately scrambled to move, Qadir knew the real devastation would hit in a matter of moments. The whistles of multiple incoming shells caused the ANA patrol to dive for cover as the artillery barrage made the floor of the valley erupt into a wall of dirt, rock, and fire. The deafening explosions rocked the allied troops as the shells moved back toward their lines.

"Sergeant, get some air support in here now before that artillery walks us all the way back to the narrows!" commanded Qadir.

"Lighthouse, Lighthouse, X-Ray One One, we have incoming 155 mike-mike and taking heavy fire. Require immediate close air support," the squad radioman called to the orbiting AWACS excitedly.

Kirkorian grabbed the binoculars and started shouting grid coordinates to the American and ANA radiomen. They relayed them to the airborne battle controller and ANA mortar teams to pinpoint the positions of the enemy.

* * *

The first call about heavy armor in the valley hitting Qadir's troops lit up the battle board for General McAffey as it announced a major battle now occurring between allied and regular Pakistani forces.

"Get some more A-10's and Apache's airborne now, launch air refueling and additional CAP assets from Mary-4 and tell them to punch it, and move an MC-12 over there to help Lighthouse," ordered McAffey.

Airborne intel assets were stretched thin to the extreme. The JSTARS ground battle aircraft had just arrived on station to help the Marines in the south coordinate their ops against the Taliban hitting their positions in Helmand province. But if the northern engagement was against Pakistan regulars, this was an extremely dangerous situation, and General McAffey had damn few options. The MC-12W, a modified Beechcraft King Air, would give them some limited signals intelligence and video surveillance. It wasn't much but it was what McAffey had available and so was sent to where Qadir was engaged.

"Get a Global Hawk and an armed Avenger to that area as soon as we can, we're fucking blind up there. When will that satellite be overhead?" McAffey demanded.

"Five minutes for live picture sir," answered the Intel Officer.

In battle, time is measured by a series of bursts of action, movement, and preparation for the next burst of action. Minutes can feel like hours and hours go by like minutes as all sense of actual time is lost. It seemed like forever to McAffey. The satellite picture slowly came to life on the screens in the theater operations center and the joint intelligence center simultaneously. He leaned in as the cameras began focusing on the area surrounding Arandu.

McAffey instantly recognized the mass of troops and machines streaming across the two bridges spanning the Kunar River and winding into two valleys just on the western riverbank. Also, it showed another stream of troops and vehicles moving south along the eastern riverbank of the Kunar. There were audible gasps from several members of the operations center as the reality of the situation hit the ops staff regardless of their experience. This was a full-scale invasion.

McAffey immediately started barking orders. "Move the 2nd Brigade, 209th Corps from Mahmude Raqi to intercept the breach from the northwest and drive down those two valleys that run into the Kunar to flank the enemy from the north. Move a brigade of the 201st Corps north to provide blocking and reinforcement. Move the remainder of 25th ID to Asadabad. I want air recon along the Kunar from the south to see how far down their forces have pushed. Tell 1st Battalion to move their ass and secure that southern bridge at Naray. And link General Mahmoud's command center into our feeds. Ladies and gentlemen, there will be a lot of information flowing in, let's work the problems and communicate."

"Gerry, if we take those bridges out, we trap them on the Pak side of the river, right?" McAffey asked the Air Force Component Commander, Major General Gerald Holt.

Holt looked at the border lines and current forces.

"Yes, sir, that would slow them down. The question sir, is do we hit them on their side of the bridge? They're going to have air defense systems, probably FM-80's protecting their crossing assuming that's the XI Corps. That will be a direct attack on Pakistan soil," replied Holt.

"Shit no, we have to call the Pentagon for clarification, but our orders are only if our forces are directly engaged. Technically it's between the Afghans and Pakistanis, so right now we must be pure defensive on the Afghan side of the border until something changes. So get some close air support in the valley right away to slow their advance. We have to assume they have FM-80's with them as well. Can we do it without Weasels?" asked McAffey.

"Can do, Sir. We have the A-10s follow this valley up to the location of 2nd Battalion in the Valley of Stars to give them cover and surprise those troops pressing up from Arandu. Looks like they were expecting us to come from the south and not the valley," answered General Holt.

VALLEY OF STARS

"Sir, Lighthouse has pulled some A-10's off of another mission southwest of Kabul and sent them to support 2nd Battalion in the valley, should be time on target in 50 minutes," stated the Air Operations Officer.

"Okay, launch Rivet Joint and get the Wild Weasels spun up and ready to go, we need to get our recon and surface-to-air countermeasures airborne. Scramble the F-16s for air-to-ground and get the air assault assets moving out of Mary-4. Tell 1st Battalion armed recon coming their way," ordered McAffey. And so the race was on to the Naray Bridge.

* * *

The order to scramble the 4th Battalion, 227th Aviation Regiment, E Company out of Bagram was given, and the aircrews raced to their gunships. The 4-227th 'Guns Attack' Battalion had its roots as the first armed helicopter unit, and the Echo Company 'Equalizers' were the closest attack squadron to the Kunar River valley. Flying their AH-64D Apache Longbow aircraft the mission was armed recon, their specialty, and the crew's adrenaline started the moment the go order was received.

They'd been on many of these missions during their year in country, and even though it was fairly routine, it was still dangerous. The Taliban was known to have some shoulder launched surface to air systems, but most were the old Russian knock-offs built in Pakistan. They weren't very accurate but could be bad news if the Taliban got lucky. Pakistan had tried to copy the Stingers that were so effective during the Soviet occupation of Afghanistan. But those weren't very reliable either. However, they did have a bigger warhead and could bring down a helicopter if they got a hit.

The flight leader was Captain 'Scorpion' DeWitt and his copilot and weapons officer, Chief Warrant Officer 'Scooter' Mansfield. Their reconnaissance run would take them along the Kunar River valley out of Asmar and would loop north to the suspected entrance to the valley. The ops briefing said the ANA was engaged with the Taliban across the river from Arandu. There were reports of Pak troops crossing the border, but with the chaos of all the Taliban attacks around the country, their orders didn't include a whole lot of information. So the flight of four attack helicopters lifted off and headed east.

It took the Apache flight less than an hour to reach the joint patrol led by 1st Battalion's XO, Major Andreesen, moving along the Kunar River. The Apache flight paused to establish contact with Andreesen's formation and then proceeded ahead, scouting the river valley from an altitude of about 200 feet as they went. Suddenly, the radar early warning indicator lit up.

"Scorpion, we've got an L-Band long range radar up ahead. We're below it but time to get everyone's head on a swivel," reported Scooter.

"Okay Cobalt flight, keep your eyes open, and be ready," Scorpion radioed to his flight.

The formation passed over a bridge about a kilometer north of Naray. Another kilometer north of that, as the river swept around a bend to the east, the formation came around a steep cliff, and their radar warning indicators lit up like a Christmas tree.

"Shit, E/F-band radars just lit us up. J-band has us locked!" called Scooter excitedly.

"Two missile tracks, one o'clock, popping flares and chaff," Scorpion called as he violently threw the helicopter in a maneuver to avoid the surface-to-air missiles roaring up at him.

The rest of the aircraft in the formation were doing the same evasive maneuvers while their weapons officers struggled to get a fix on the missile launch site. Scorpion's wingman dodged the first missile but took a direct hit from the second, exploding into a ball of fire.

"Shit," Scorpion grunted under the G-forces created as he threw his aircraft vertically and horizontally to dodge another volley of missiles headed their way.

Scorpion managed to move toward the cliffs for some cover. He popped out with his 30mm chain gun roaring up the eastern river bank while Scooter launched two Hellfire missiles at the radars. The Pakistani 23mm air defense battery was able to hit one Hellfire, but the other struck the FM-80 radar vehicle in a thundering explosion that rocked the ground forces around it. With the pause in the ground missiles, Scorpion had the remaining aircraft move fast up the river, raking the ground troops with rocket and 30mm gunfire. The formation then pulled up and west over the ridgeline on the opposite side of the river, dropping back down in the valley on the other side to cover their withdrawal.

"Lighthouse, Lighthouse, this is Cobalt-1. Be advised a large mechanized ground force moving south along the eastern bank of the Kunar River about one click north of the Naray Bridge. FM-80 mobile battery's escorting them. We got one, but Cobalt-2 went down in the area, no chutes, requesting search and rescue," reported Scorpion pounding his fist on the sun shield of the helicopter.

"Son of a bitch, when did the Taliban get FM-80 SAMs?" yelled Scooter.

"They weren't Taliban, they were Pak regulars! Shit, shit, shit, this just got really complicated," answered Scorpion.

* * *

General McAffey looked at the big projector screen that had various datasets and imagery displayed as allied assets were moving. The report of a downed aircraft stunned the operations center into silence for a brief moment, but McAffey was focused on the growing situation of enemy forces flowing across the border. There was little he could do to stop them. The ops staff had been working tirelessly trying to put together the responses across the entire country and now with a major incursion by Pak regulars, this was looking more like a coordinated operation that McAffey felt unprepared to deal with. The demands for assets in so many locations made prioritizing the need extremely challenging.

The report of 155mm artillery now hitting the force in the valley changed the dynamic of the war unfolding before McAffey. Pakistan had downed a U.S. aircraft on the Afghan side of the border and was engaging a joint patrol of ANA and American troops with direct fire heavy artillery from Pakistani soil. The situation had definitely changed, and McAffey didn't have time to wait for permission to strike directly into Pakistan.

"Time on those A-10's?" asked McAffey.

"Ten minutes sir, but we have to silence those 155's before the A-10's go in. We need them to come in low level. Otherwise, they have to stay above the artillery flight path and do high altitude ordinance drops. That higher altitude will make them extremely vulnerable to Pak SAM systems that are most certainly escorting the Brigade," Holt advised.

McAffey looked at the satellite imagery again, "There's artillery just the other side of the border. Looks like 155's and rocket systems, they must be the ones hitting 2nd Battalion in the valley," he said to Holt.

"Agreed. We'll datalink the coordinates and maps to the Weasels," Holt answered as he turned and gave orders to one of his operations specialists.

"Gerry, how long for the Weasels to get to the target?" asked McAffey.

"40 minutes, we've got a flight of F-16's and Harriers at Bagram ready to go, can have them TOT in 30. We'll datalink the Weasels mission details en route," Holt answered.

"40 minutes! 155mm artillery can do a hell of a lot of damage in 40 minutes," McAffey mumbled a bit louder than he thought.

"Sir, Weasels are airborne we have a tanker up already for Lighthouse, and he's got extra gas so we'll hold him to refuel the strike package on egress. F-16's, Apache's, and Harriers will launch in 15, they'll rendezvous with the Weasels and move in. Weasels punch holes, Apaches will cover the 16's ingress to the bridges, and the Harriers will go after arty. Once arty is silenced the A-10's will come down the valley and hit the leading elements of the enemy force engaging 2nd Battalion. Had to keep it pretty simple, could have done more with more planning but it will do," Holt briefed.

McAffey marveled at how fast the aerial plan came together. Seemed a lot more complicated when Holt described it for a bunch of airplanes moving faster than the speed of sound. But like his days as a Brigade commander, he had to move infantry, armor, and air cavalry on a dime and coordinate their fires perfectly. Ultimately it was all about the hours of mind numbing training that allowed these warriors to create a deadly ballet on the fly and make it look easy.

"Okay, call the Pentagon, let them know we're attacking Pak territory. Give them the situation and get ready to brief SecDef. This is going to get uglier before it gets better people so let's just work the problems, don't make them worse," commanded McAffey.

CHAPTER 19

Strike/Counter-strike

General Al-Zuq set up a mobile field headquarters command center in a warehouse by the river east of Chitral city center. The small mountain city was a regional trading center in the heart of the restive Northwest Territories and close to the disputed Kashmir region. This made it an important strategic city for the XI Corps, despite the perceived danger due to its location. Virtually surrounded by potential enemies it was Al-Zuq's base for influencing events in both regions. Dotted with warehouses that stored everything from food to weapons, it was a bustling place even without the added troops supporting the current operation.

Al-Zuq sat sipping tea as the operations reports flowed in. He was pleased with himself for orchestrating the advance into Afghanistan. The unit that was bombed had deployed to the Northwest Territories from Islamabad for training and provide support for his alleged operations there. They weren't his men, so they became a convenient tool for his plans.

The bombing had the desired effect of enraging the nation and demanding blood for blood. Al-Zuq was more than happy to oblige. With the help of his friend in LeJ, they manufactured the "proof" that Afghan government agents were protecting the people who did the bombing. So there was little resistance from his superiors when he asked to chase the "perpetrators" across the border.

He chuckled to himself. The people he was supposed to be chasing were leading him to the Valley of Stars and the precious resources located there. Once secured, he would control a vast amount of wealth to hand out to his trusted allies to guarantee their continued loyalty. Overnight he had moved a full Brigade with 500 Taliban fighters across the river and had begun moving up the rugged path to his prize.

The force had run into resistance in the valley, but it appeared it was all ANA troops. Al-Zuq was confident that they would dissolve quickly once the full force hit them. His lead elements had reported heavy casualties in the initial engagement due to an enemy ambush, but they were now moving steadily behind the artillery barrage.

Suddenly General Rabbani brought him an urgent message, "General, Third Brigade has engaged a flight of American Apache helicopters. One was shot down, but our troops took nearly two dozen casualties, and one SAM system destroyed."

Al-Zuq's joyful demeanor vanished. "What were the Americans doing there? Our latest intel was that the U.S. President had restricted them to their bases," he said angrily.

"If the Americans get involved it will make things more difficult but not impossible, sir. With the Taliban offensive in the south, it should keep many of their forces tied up," replied Rabbani.

"True but the death of an American aircrew will virtually assure that the American air assets are now involved. Fortunately, they have withdrawn much of their airpower, and we should be able to handle what is left. Still, we need our friends in Islamabad to start making noise about American interference in Pakistan internal matters. Even so, we need to accelerate our timetable to secure the Valley of Stars," Al-Zuq grumbled as he began to work the new political plan through his head.

They needed to be prepared should the Americans use their airpower to try and stop them. After a brief moment of thought, Al-Zuq picked up the phone. "General Sharif, we have an operation to bring to justice the terrorists who hit us in Chitral. The Americans may be helping the Afghans with air support, so I need our own air cover. Activate your air defense assets and get me some fighter cover for my troops."

* * *

The Pentagon brass had been burning the midnight oil ever since the Taliban offensive started. Madeline had gone home for a bit to get a change of clothes and something to eat but had been back in her office for the past 4 hours. The shrill warble of Madeline's secure hotline jolted her out of the deep concentration over the latest intel reports of the Taliban uprising in Afghanistan.

"Madam Secretary, we need you in the NMCC immediately. A large Pak force of at least two Brigades has crossed the border and engaged the joint patrol on the approach to the Valley of Stars. In addition, one of our Helicopters was shot down by Pakistani forces inside Afghanistan, and we've returned fire. We may be at war with Pakistan," stated Admiral Joffrey.

"On my way," Madeline replied, jumping up from her chair and slamming the phone back into its cradle. As she rushed into her outer office, she called to her Executive Officer, "Jerry, NMCC, call the President's Chief of Staff, tell him we have a situation and I'll brief him once I have all the facts."

With that, Secretary Coltrain moved quickly through the ramps and hallways of the Pentagon with her security detail in tow. It was a building in constant motion, especially with a crisis unfolding and American forces suddenly engaged in the heaviest combat since the invasion of Iraq. Despite the fact that 29,000 people worked in the massive office building, no one took much notice of the SecDef moving through the halls except to get out of her way.

In a place full of big fish, there was always a bigger fish roaming the halls. It was best to give them a wide berth and keep your head down so as not to inadvertently provoke them. And because those fish were always rushing here or there, Madeline and her entourage barely registered with all the smaller fish rushing to complete their own tasks.

The security checkpoint into the National Military Command Center is a busy place during a crisis. Staff officers from the joint military staff would move in and out to supply information to the occupants working the crisis inside. As Madeline approached, those in the security line parted and moved up against the walls to let the SecDef pass.

The armed guards at the entry point stopped her and her security detail, scanned their credentials to confirm their identities, took away their electronic devices and put them into an electronically shielded box. Once their identities were confirmed, they were buzzed through the outer secure entry doors, and the process was repeated. It made no difference who you were, even the President went through the same security protocols making the NMCC one of the most secure places in DC.

Madeline strode through the hallway that paralleled the main operations floor and paused for just a second to peer through the large bulletproof panes at the beehive of activity going on. A hundred or more people at workstations below the giant floor to ceiling video screens coordinated the activities military units worldwide. She marveled at the efficiency of disparate agencies who would fight like siblings during peacetime but work so well together when the shooting starts.

And that's what brought Madeline back to the task at hand. The shooting had started, and she was responsible for every man and woman in the line of fire. She entered the conference room and took her position for the briefing.

"Okay, gentlemen, get me up to speed before I call the President," she ordered.

"Madam Secretary, our forces have been engaged by Pakistan regulars on Afghan soil just north of Naray," General McAffey stated as he highlighted the location of the downed Apache and the race for the Naray bridge via satellite.

"We are now moving to engage them directly along the Kunar River south of the invasion point at Arandu. Be advised that we are targeting both the crossing bridges and the artillery inside Pakistan currently hitting the joint patrol in the approach to the Valley of Stars. Madam Secretary, that artillery is on Pakistan soil. Given the fact that they have engaged our forces directly, we immediately put a plan in motion to silence them," McAffey continued.

"I concur General, they've killed American troops inside Afghanistan. You are authorized to take them out regardless of where they are located," ordered Madeline coldly.

McAffey then took her through the timeline and recent allied troop movements. "Currently with the forces we have in the area we can slow them down but no guarantees we can stop them," finished McAffey.

"What's the TOT of our strike force right now?" asked Madeline.

"The time on target is in 10 minutes Madam Secretary," replied McAffey.

Madeline picked up the hotline to the White House, "Get the President to the Situation Room ASAP. American forces inside Afghanistan have been engaged by the Pakistan military. We have casualties and are counter-attacking Pakistan regulars both inside Afghanistan and Pakistan. We are at war."

* * *

The Air Battle Manager on AWACS, call sign Lighthouse, watched a flight of eight Pakistani fighters take off from their home base in northern Pakistan and head toward the border area. He tracked them as they entered a Combat Air Patrol (CAP) formation near Chitral and another about 75 miles south of them. The flight of American F-16s was highlighted on his screen making their way toward the border while the allied CAP of F-22s circled about 75 miles from the border. The northern flight of enemy fighters suddenly turned west and accelerated to Mach 2 toward the flight of F-16s while the southern flight dropped to low level turning west at the same time.

"Shark One-Zero flight, Lighthouse; bogey's Angels 20, Olympus two-three-zero at 43, snap one-one-zero; Shark Two-Four flight, bogey's angels 10 descending, Olympus two-one-five at 60, snap one-five-five," radioed Lighthouse to the airborne U.S. fighters.

"Lighthouse, Shark One-Zero flight heading one-one-zero, angels 20," acknowledged Captain Eleanor 'Kaz' Kazinski, the pilot of Shark One-Zero.

Kaz looked at her map at the coded position of the enemy fighters as she and her wingman turned their F-22's to the heading as directed and accelerated to one and half times the speed of sound. When Lighthouse confirmed they were at about 50 miles from the enemy fighters, she commanded her wingman to "light them up." The F-22 radar flashed on and within seconds had painted the approaching enemy and locked their radar guided anti-aircraft missiles onto them.

"Fox 3," announced Kaz as the first AMRAAM missile left her rails trailing a thin line of white smoke as it accelerated to over six times the speed of sound within moments of separating from the fighter.

"Fox 3," announced her wingman a second later.

The flights of aircraft screamed toward each other at nearly four times the speed of sound as the two missiles raced to their targets in a matter of seconds.

* * *

The Pakistani flight leader ordered the flight to light up their radars. He saw the American F-16 flight 50 miles in front of them, right where their air controllers said they'd be. His radar warning chirped in his helmet that they were being tracked by long range radar. They had a fix on the AWACS position, but that was the other flight's mission.

He was in mid-sentence commanding his flight to alter course and change altitude to intercept the American F-16s when suddenly the radar warning system chirping got louder and faster indicating targeting radars were scanning him. But there was nothing on his radar. He ordered his flight to take evasive action, ejecting chaff, bundles of little strips of metal to try and confuse the radar seekers of the incoming missiles, and flares to counter heat seeking missiles. Seconds later the two fighters on his left wing exploded.

Having no idea where the missiles came from, he ordered an immediate withdrawal. The chirping in his helmet morphed into a steady tone blaring that the unseen enemy had locked their missiles onto his aircraft. Mid-turn the second salvo of AMRAAMs exploded off his wingtip, blowing his left wing off, and sending his F-16 into a wild, uncontrollable spin.

The pilot struggled against the G-forces of his spinning jet to reach his ejection handles. Grasping them and pulling up, he rocketed out of his dead aircraft as it spiraled into the mountains of Afghanistan. He saw his wingman dive to treetop level as another AMRAAM missed, hitting his chaff, while he sped off in full afterburner toward Pakistan. The pilot floated down to earth, landing hard on a small plateau and wrenching his knee. Unfortunately, he landed a short distance from an Afghan village, and the villagers surrounded him with AK-47s.

* * *

The second Pakistani flight hugged the ground trying to blend into the ground clutter to hide from the American airborne radar. Their own long range radar controllers had fixed the position of the American AWACS as they had dropped to low level flight and provided updates every few minutes. They first turned south for 50 miles, then turned back west and accelerated to get behind the AWACS.

Their goal was to pop up behind the big, slow aircraft and shoot it down to blind the Americans. The last position the flight leader had was five minutes old, but AWACS was flying a predictable orbit so he figured they'd be close. Maintaining radio silence, he gave a hand signal to his flight. Ten seconds later they pulled up in a near vertical climb and turned on their radars. Suddenly his two outside wingmen had missiles explode in the tails of their engines.

The American heat seeking missiles caused a secondary explosion in one of the Pak jets, destroying the airplane and killing its pilot instantly. The other stricken aircraft spun out of control as the pilot ejected before it hit the ground in a massive ball of fire. The flight leader and his remaining wingman pulled over the top and banked hard to the right in a tight max-G turn.

Both pilots strained against the force, nine times that of gravity using a series of grunts and muscle contractions to keep blood flowing to their brain and stay conscious. The anti-G suits around their legs filled with air to keep the blood from pooling in their legs, as their radar warning gave a steady tone, indicating they were locked on by enemy fighters. They tried to violently shake the enemy aircraft, but both rolled into a deadly blast from another volley of missiles...

"Lighthouse, Shark Two-Four, splash 4 bogeys, two chutes."

VALLEY OF STARS

* * *

RIVET JOINT, the large electronic reconnaissance aircraft, was like a giant electromagnetic vacuum cleaner. It sucked up radar, radio, and any other electronic emissions analyzed them and fixed the type and positions of the electronic signatures. It quickly found and fixed the positions of the Pakistani air defense radars, and that information was data-linked via satellite to the F-16CJ Wild Weasel anti-air suppression aircraft.

"Hammer 21 flight, time to tickle their bellies. Let's find and fix," ordered the pilot of Hammer 21, the lead Weasel.

"Roger," responded each member of the four-aircraft fighter flight.

The Wild Weasels started running parallel along the ridgelines, popping up and down to tease the targeting radars from the surface-to-air missile batteries guarding the Pakistani forces crossing the river. This was a deadly serious game of cat and mouse. It required the Weasels to expose themselves to the enemy fixed and mobile radar systems just long enough to expose their positions and analyze the enemy firing timing. It was a delicate balancing act to get the enemy to target them then disappear right before the Surface to Air Missile systems could fire their missiles. It required nerves of steel and exquisite timing so they could strike at just the perfect moment.

"Lighthouse, Hammer 21, get everyone ready and good luck. Hammer flight, drop, pop, and roll on my mark...three, two, one, execute," ordered Hammer 21.

The Wild Weasel flight ducked below a ridge flying low level then quickly popped over it to engage the short range SAM batteries. Just before the SAM batteries could get a lock on the Weasels, they blew gaping holes in their targeting radars with anti-radar HARM missiles. With the radars dead, they followed with Hellfire missiles that took out the missile launchers. Hammer 23 and his wingman sped through the air defense hole at Mach 2 hammering the ground troops with their sonic shockwave. Repeating the HARM and Hellfire volleys of their own, they destroyed the medium range anti-air systems forward located in Pakistan.

Right behind the Weasels a formation of Apache attack helicopters popped over the ridge and raked the whole area with Hellfire's, rockets, and 30mm gunfire. Dozens of

Pakistan armored vehicles exploded in brilliant white-orange flashes and thunderous explosions as soldiers were cut to pieces from bullets and flying shrapnel. The screams of men and machines desperately trying to find protection from the devastating attacks added to the confusion of the sudden onslaught of fire coming from the gunships.

The ferocity of the attacks laid waste to the Pakistani units on and around the bridges and covered the approach of the F-16's. As the Apaches withdrew, the F-16C flight released their GBU-38 JDAM bombs against both bridges. The steerable bombs hit the southern bridge about a third of the way in from each end, dropping the center span, along with the men and equipment running across it, into the river. One out of commission. The northern bridge took three hits, two on the eastern end nearest Pakistan and one in the center. Damaged but still usable, though it would significantly slow the movement from Pakistan.

The flight of Marine AV-8B Harriers roared down the Kunar River Valley from the north at low level, popping over the ridge as the F-16s withdrew from the bridge strike and then split into two elements. They dropped their 500 pound MK-82 bombs on the Pakistan artillery and multiple rocket batteries. They pivoted to rake the vehicles and the battery troops with their 25mm cannons before speeding off to the south, leaving the smoking carcasses of men and machines littering the terrain on both sides of the border.

* * *

As the artillery and long range rocket fire stopped, Qadir breathed a momentary sigh of relief, but his situation was still very tenuous. The heavy guns of the Pakistani brigade in front of him were still extremely deadly, and his situation was only a little better than it was five minutes ago. He was still outnumbered and out-gunned, but he had the terrain advantage. With the guns silenced, a flight of A-10 Warthog ground attack aircraft sped down the valley overhead of Qadir's troops from the direction of the Valley of Stars. It surprised him a bit because he didn't hear their approach until he saw their Maverick missiles roar off the rails, the smoke trails streaking toward the enemy.

The forward mobile air defense machine guns of the Pakistani force erupted into plumes of fire and smoke as the missiles found their targets. The 30mm Gatling gun cannon of the A-10's roared like a hundred thousand buzzing bees, churning the ground, trees, and rocks into chards of destruction. The Pak armored vehicles became hulking death traps as the depleted uranium tipped cannon rounds vaporized man and metal into molten gas hot enough to incinerate everything inside them.

Pak ground units were suddenly pinned down with nowhere to run. As the flight continued down the valley, they dropped cluster munitions on the now exposed Pak troops in the valley. Pulling up and looping back around, they again raked the enemy armored vehicles with 30mm cannon fire creating panic and confusion for the Pak soldiers both inside and out of them. Dozens of secondary explosions rocked the valley floor as ordinance inside the vehicles exploded, doubling the carnage of the initial strike.

The walls of the valley reverberated with the sounds of war and the screams of the dying. With the enemy force in disarray from the vicious aerial bombardment, Qadir ordered his troops to push forward against the stunned Taliban and Pakistanis. The wings of the V opened fire on the flanks of the enemy while the center opened fire with mortars and the MRAP .50 caliber machine guns. It forced the enemy to retreat back down the valley as the center moved forward.

Over the next several hours, Qadir and the allied force slowly pushed the enemy back as American reinforcements began arriving from the Valley of Stars. Qadir moved down the valley past the burning hulks of Pakistani vehicles, retaking some of the ground in the valley lost this first day of fighting. In the shadows of the setting sun, the intense heat radiating off the burning armored vehicles made the valley floor feel like the Sahara Desert in the summer. But their advantage was short lived, clouds started rolling in. The cold grey mass enveloped the mountain ridges and glided silently down the slopes to the valley floor like the icy fingers of death.

* * *

Major Andreesen was not only racing against time but against an enemy force of unknown size on the opposite river bank heading to the same bridge. Before the call about the Pakistani incursion, he had moved his patrol deliberately along the river. After leaving Sosha, they had checked out the small villages as well as numerous tributaries that joined the river along the route.

Once the report of the enemy engagement in the mountains came to him, he recalled the blocking force from Sao, but it would take a few hours to reach them. After the news that one of the armed recon helicopters got shot down, it made his task go from important to critical. It also meant the enemy he was about to meet was not Taliban, but Pak regulars and they were close. And the call from HQ meant they needed to move and move fast.

Andreesen sent three platoons from Charlie Company, comprised of Cougar MRAPs and Stryker vehicles, speeding to take the west end of the Naray Bridge. The rest of the force moved as quickly as possible, as he loaded all the infantry he could into the available vehicles. Those who couldn't ride, jogged next to the vehicles. Every couple miles they would switch out to give each squad a chance to rest.

Fifteen minutes after the Apache's had passed overhead, the lead element arrived at the west end of the bridge. The bridge was in a wide semi-flat area anchored on both ends by several village compounds. The west side had little cover with a couple small building compounds and some gullies. This side of the bridge was at the outside apex of a rough U-shape following a looping bend in the river. It had a paved road following the river making movement much easier, but there were over 300 meters of nearly flat terrain to the nearest major ridgeline.

There were a couple gullies that led away from the river about 200 meters to the north that had a perfect angle to cover the northern approach to the bridge. The Charlie Company commander quickly positioned a rifle platoon in the most northern gulley and another platoon with Stryker's and MRAPs in a larger gulley just south of the first. The larger gulley had deep meanders that provided cover for the vehicle's heavy weapons in cut-outs and behind huge boulders. Further south was a grouping of buildings in two compounds straddling the highway just north of the bridge where he positioned his last platoon so that the entire force could hit the northern leg of the U in the bend of the river.

VALLEY OF STARS

The east side of the river sloped up in a sweeping vista along a ridgeline with two large compounds straddling both the northern and southern end of the bridge. This gave the enemy command of higher ground. While it provided the approaching enemy some terrain advantages, the road they were traveling was more gravel than pavement. That would slow their progress and increase their exposure to the American firing position.

The northern legs of the U lined up with the gullies on the western side of the river, making the enemy vulnerable to enfilading fire, hitting their formations from the side. This meant that there were several hundred meters of open terrain the enemy had to cross before getting to the cover of the northern compound. However, if the enemy got to the compound on the southern leg of the U, they could engage Andreesen's remaining force before it could reach the bridge, giving them a clear path across. Charlie Company had to prevent the enemy from getting established in the southern compound.

A demolition squad dashed across the bridge to rig the east end with explosives as the rest of the units prepared their defensive positions. They had placed the charges and just began to string the detonator cables when the lead elements of the enemy column rounded the bend about 300 meters away. The American side of the river bank erupted with the roar of machine gun, rocket, and mortar fire that smashed into the leading vehicles and infantry of the approaching enemy force.

The tracer rounds arced across the river like red-white lasers, ripping apart men and machines everywhere they touched. The ferocity and abruptness of the American volley clearly stunned the Pakistani column as the realization of the start of battle rippled through their ranks. An American mortar team dropped smoke in front of the approaching enemy to provide some cover for the demolition squad on the bridge. Unable to fully complete their task, they raced back to their side of the river with enemy machine gun fire nipping at their heels as the enemy fell back around the bend under the withering attack of Charlie Company.

Moments later the distinct rumble of main battle tanks reached the defenders on the east side of the river. The enemy column had stopped and retreated only briefly before the sound of their heavy armor guns, rockets, and mortars preceded their counter-attack. Mortars began landing near the northern gulley as three Pakistani Al-Khalid main battle tanks came around the bend, their infantry following close behind. The tanks opened fire on the second gulley to try and keep the American armored vehicles at bay while the Pakistani force moved forward. The Al-Khalid smooth bore 125mm rounds hit with thunderous explosions against the rocks near the American defenders sending thousands of shards of white hot rock and steel flying, buffeting the American troops. The small American force was holding its position but taking a pounding as the enemy slowly but deliberately advanced under fire to the northern building compound.

Despite the Pakistani force taking heavy casualties, their numbers far outstripped those of the defenders and allowed them to press forward. After 30 minutes of intense fighting, they had finally consolidated their defenses in the northern compound and started their advance on the southern compound behind the Al-Khalid tanks. They were half way between the two compounds when the lead tank exploded in a spectacular plume of red, white, and orange flames from an American anti-tank missile. The concussion from the blast knocked Pak infantry close by to the ground. A second after the missile impact, secondary explosions from the dead tanks ordinance ripped through the infantry following the smoking inferno that used to be a tank.

Then the whole eastern bank of the river opposite the southern compound exploded with multiple volleys of automatic and rocket fire. Major Andreesen and the rest of 1st Battalion had arrived with a vengeance. The intensifying fires now coming from two directions forced the Pakistanis to retreat to the northern compound.

* * *

Al-Zuq's executive officer brought the latest reports, and the General exploded in anger, throwing them across the room. The complete failure of the Pak Air Force to give them cover put him in a truly foul mood as he cursed his commanders.

"Get me, General Rabbani, now!" Al-Zuq hissed.

Rabanni entered the room and saluted.

VALLEY OF STARS

"Tell me General, how did these inept, backward savages from Afghanistan stop our troops in the valley? And those Taliban dogs, who got cut down like sheaves of wheat, forcing us to do all of the fighting," Al-Zuq thundered. "This failure gave the Americans time to use their airpower, and now we've got vulnerable supply lines and one damaged bridge for this operation. This intel is shit and completely wrong, the Americans were supposed to be restricted to their base more than 100 kilometers away from the battle. What the hell were they doing there?" Al-Zuq demanded.

"Sir, I've already spoken to our ISI contacts about this. They insist that the latest pronouncements from the American President stated they were to be restricted to their bases, so any units operating there were doing so in violation of his orders. We captured an injured ANA soldier and found out that the force in the valley is 2nd Battalion, 1st Brigade, 203rd Corps. This unit is based out of Khost and is the same one that ran their successful operation at Zakar Khel," Rabbani began.

"Their commander is extremely capable, he has the high ground, and he knows how to use it. We were unaware they had moved this battalion north until now which makes our task difficult. We have miniature drones airborne to scout the enemy formations and it turns out there is slightly less than a battalion strength in the valley and about a battalion strength near Naray. But we have the advantage of proximity for more reinforcements and firepower," Rabbani finished.

This wasn't the first time a battle plan went awry, and after his initial anger at the swiftly changing situation, instinct took over for the XI Corps Commander. Instincts born out of his experience in countless battles with the hated, but more advanced Indian Army over his career. Al-Zuq pulled the maps out and looked at the positions of his forces and the enemy. A heavy overcast and fog had settled in the valley, and his force north of Naray was stopped short of the bridge entrance. He stared at the map considering the new intel and a plan began to form.

The ANA forces had been pulled from the Khost area. Why he didn't know, but the nearest reinforcements would be in Kabul and Kunduz in northern Afghanistan. The most likely reinforcements were the Americans in the Kunar

River valley opposite his brigade in Naray. The Americans had an advantage in the air but to make a move to secure the Valley of Stars before hostilities were stopped, he had to make a maximum effort push to overwhelm the limited forces before him and get to his objective.

"Okay, Ahmad look at this," Al-Zuq said as he pointed to the maps. "They've pulled this battalion from Khost with their most capable commander and are in the valley on the approach to the Valley of Stars. We must assume they know about it, otherwise why have both this unit and an American battalion so close by when the Taliban are fighting all over the country to the west of them. That's a lot of manpower pulled away from the Taliban uprising.

"We've already ordered the movement of our forces across the damaged bridge at Arandu as quickly as possible and tripled the mobile air defense units supporting both the bridge and the valley campaign. If the Americans send their air support again, it will truly become a very dangerous and bloody affair for both sides. But we have more men and machines to draw upon than the over-extended Americans. The wide-spread Taliban attacks across Afghanistan make sure of that," Al-Zuq continued.

His engineers had temporary patches on the damaged bridge while Pak armor and mechanized infantry moved across as fast as they could before the Americans could come back to finish the job. Troops were literally running across so that they wouldn't get trapped when the American aircraft returned. They also had started three pontoon bridges as a backup plan in the event the Americans did take out the second bridge.

"While our troops around Naray are stopped, for now, they're still serving a purpose holding the American reinforcements in place. We need to make a full scale assault in the valley using the heavy low clouds and fog as a cover, limiting the American air support. We will lose units to their close air support due to their thermal targeting, but if we maximize our infrared tracking systems, we'll make the air above the valley a nightmare for them."

"At the same time, our force in Naray will push hard against the bridge, further tying up the Americans on the opposite side of the river. It should draw any reinforcements to protect the road to Kabul. Finally, we'll send a brigade across the border to engage the ANA near Khost. This will prevent reinforcements from the south. We force the ANA to decide where to use the meager units they have, and we use 'shock and awe' to secure the Valley of Stars, then call for a halt of hostilities," Al-Zuq finished.

"To keep the American air busy, we need two full squadrons of fighters to overwhelm their air defense capabilities," Rabbani added.

"Agreed, make it happen," answered Al-Zuq.

"I'll make the calls sir," replied Rabbani as he saluted and swiftly left the room.

* * *

The heavy overcast and fog enveloped the mountains and obscured whatever starlight that could help on this moonless night. The only good news was that the night vision equipment was nearly worthless on both sides. With the effective range on the NVGs degraded to less than 25 meters, any effort to recon the enemy would be extremely dangerous.

Qadir knew the Pak commander was furious and would now make a max effort to remove them from the valley. While his unit had performed extremely well, they took casualties they couldn't afford while the enemy had ready reinforcements flowing. He had a report that one of the bridges supplying them had been dropped but the other was still passable. Plus, Andreesen had stopped another force along the Kunar, at least for now.

He pulled his wings back in a slightly inverted V with the center now forward, expecting the enemy to try and roll up their flanks. The enemy's time window was closing fast, and Qadir's only option was to trade territory for time, hoping for more reinforcements tomorrow. Watkins had sent additional manpower from the Valley of Stars as 1st Air Cavalry troops from Mary-4 began to arrive. But when the clouds and fog settled in, the landing zone was closed, and no more air resupply was possible.

So, it wasn't only a battle with the Pakistani force in front of him but against the clock and the weather as well. Qadir had his platoons in the center positioned line abreast across the valley but staggered into two rows about 30 meters apart. He had the Companies on each wing in two rows as well but in a slight echelon angled back away from the center with the forward positions anchored on the ends of his second-row center.

If the enemy attacked the wings in a flanking movement, he would have the lead squads on the wings pivot backward like a swinging door, anchored on the center forming an L. This would draw the enemy into position where he could rake their formation from the side as well as the front. The forward squads in the center would then pivot up the hill, like a swinging door slamming into the enemy from behind, closing like a vice on the attackers. That line would then move back to take the front-line position on the flank. As each swinging maneuver was executed, the whole force would pull back a little at a time while the swinging units replaced each other in the formation, reforming for the next attack.

If they hit the center, Qadir would reverse the maneuver toward the center, and if they attacked across the whole front, they would do a staggered withdrawal with the squads in front withdrawing 60 meters covered by those in back. He assigned each maneuver a code word, Lima for attack on the flanks, X-Ray for an attack on the center, and Whiskey for an attack on the whole front. It was high risk, but one Qadir had to take. The enemy would expect him to continue to withdraw as he had all day. They were partially right.

The night sank into absolute blackness, obscuring the carnage in the valley from the morning's fighting and the devastation of the American air attack. A soldier couldn't even see their own hand an inch from their face without NVGs, and even those weren't much help. Qadir's men waited nervously, engulfed by the cold blackness when gunfire erupted on both wings. The men in the center strained to see any movement as the battle raged to their left and right. Qadir ordered everyone to hold for what seemed like an eternity, then he called on the radio, "Lima, Lima, Lima, execute!"

The leading squads on the flanks melted away as they pivoted back toward the center. The Pak Company commanders, sensing a withdrawal, pushed their soldiers forward. They slammed head-on into the second lines suddenly taking fire from their flanks. The confused commanders tried to maneuver some of their squads to fight the troops on their sides when gunfire erupted from behind them, trapping them in a devastating three-way crossfire with no escape.

As the fighting on the hillsides subsided, the squads continued their pivots taking positions thirty meters behind those in the center while the center platoons that pivoted took their place. Thirty minutes later, the enemy hit the center and Qadir executed their X-Ray maneuver with similar results. In less than two hours, the enemy had nearly two Companies of soldiers cut to pieces in their probing attacks while Qadir had retreated only about 60 meters. The next attack would not go so easily.

CHAPTER 20

Stalemate

The light of the new day made everything look dark grey as the sun struggled to cut through the heavy overcast that still shrouded the mountains. As the sounds of battle got closer, the pace of dead and wounded coming from Qadir's lines increased. Watkins moved his forces from inside the Valley of Stars to the entrance of the narrows. With the weather preventing aerial reinforcement, he was the last line of defense. And there was no word yet on the reinforcements coming from Asadabad.

The Americans had managed to do some air drops of supplies, but the crews of the cargo aircraft had to rely on GPS and radio beacons to mark the drop zone. It wasn't very efficient, and they lost some equipment in the rocks. Watkins did manage to get several good drops of ammunition though, and the Air Cav guys brought more medics before the LZ closed, but they were running low on medical supplies.

Watkins knew Qadir was trading ground for time and had been making a steady retreat for the past several hours. The Pak commander was throwing everything he had at him, pushing him back but at a devastating cost to the attackers. The over-extended close air support was doing what it could, but despite the periodic air attacks, it was clear that Qadir's retreat got faster as his casualties mounted. With each passing hour, both allied commanders hoped they could hold out long enough for reinforcement.

With Qadir now just 500 meters from the narrows, Watkins had his remaining Stryker vehicles open up with their 30mm guns on the approaching enemy. He positioned mortars and heavy weapons along the ridgelines on each side of the narrows to cover the valley approach. Despite the volume of fire pouring into the oncoming enemy, they steadily moved up behind their Al-Khalid tanks and had a definitive advantage in firepower.

To Watkins, it felt like time had stopped, and time was the one thing he desperately needed. As the deadly ballet played out in front of him, the desperation of the situation caused a thought to flash through his mind. This was how his father felt at the La Drang Valley in Vietnam; outnumbered, outgunned, and possibly the last battle he'll ever fight.

But as quickly as it came into his head it was gone. He had work to do, and he'd be damned if he wasn't going to fight with rocks and clubs if he had to. And he was off barking orders and redirecting fires. There was a bulge forming on the left flank, and they had to plug the hole.

* * *

Kirkorian estimated they were facing two full Brigades now, but the enemy had taken severe losses to get here. Qadir was in full retreat, his force down to half the strength he started with. On the left flank, one of the ANA squads got trapped with enemy quickly surrounding them. Without hesitation, she called for covering fire as she and Tasker rushed to provide help to some ANA soldiers wounded and in the open.

As they reached the wounded soldiers, Kirkorian took a kneeling firing position and neutralized four enemy soldiers. Splashes of dirt and rock went flying from the gunfire hitting all around them. While she kept up her covering fire, Tasker grabbed the most seriously wounded pulled the ANA soldiers behind some boulders for cover.

With gunfire and mortars exploding around them, they were greeted by Sergeant Hassam. "You shouldn't have come my friends, we are surrounded."

"I heard you were having a party and I just couldn't pass that up," replied Kirkorian popping up to return fire. "I love a good party!"

"I see you forgot the tea then," replied Hassam laughing as he tossed a grenade toward some enemy troops trying to approach from their right side.

"Ya, she dropped it on the way over. Seems we hit a few bumps in the road to get here," shouted Tasker over the din of battle. "Hey Hassam, what do you call it when a Jew, a Christian, and a Muslim are surrounded by the enemy?" asked Tasker making a joke between bursts of gunfire.

"I don't know, what?" Hassam asked before unleashing a burst of gunfire into the chest of a Pak soldier about to throw a grenade. It exploded at the soldiers' feet, shredding him and another Pak soldier with shrapnel and throwing them both through the air like rag dolls.

"An unfair advantage. When all three branches of the root of Abraham are fighting together, the enemy hasn't got a chance," Tasker replied ducking behind a boulder as stone chips showered him from the high velocity impact of the heavy machine gun rounds hitting above his head.

"Then perhaps we shall all meet father Abraham soon!" Hassam replied, chuckling as they kept up their fire.

The three laughed at the joke despite the dire situation they faced. It's the sort of gallows humor that anyone who's been in combat understands. The way that soldiers deal with the fear and stress of imminent death; laugh in death's face or be paralyzed with fear. And paralysis in battle means certain death.

"Here they come," Hassam yelled as Pak infantry began rushing their position.

Kirkorian saw a group of five Pak soldiers running from their left. She spun around to engage them. It was like a slow motion movie. First, she would hit the one second to the left, he was closest, then the one to his right, then the left. The one on the far right was the slowest but would be the one to get to her, she would be able to shoot three before they were on her. She would have to turn to her right, because the second from the right would likely get her with his bayonet in a glancing blow but that slow guy, she couldn't account for him.

With a burst of gunfire, the first three went down. The fourth managed to barely slice her side with his bayonet as she spun to her right and slammed her rifle butt into the back of his neck, snapping it. Pain buffeted her brain like a bolt of lightning, feeling like a white hot iron pressed into her side. Time seemed to stand still as the force of the attack knocked her off-balance. Images of her son flashed through her mind as she struggled to try to defend herself from the fifth soldier she couldn't account for.

As Kirkorian was falling, she saw the last man's head explode, taking a blast from a squad machine gun as Tasker's squad quickly ran to their rescue. Qadir had orchestrated a counter-attack just as the trapped squad was about to be overrun. He pulled the soldiers from their trap and retreated under heavy covering fire from Watkins' troops in the narrows.

Kirkorian was taken to the medics where Delara saw her and immediately rushed up to her. "Zmarei, Zmarei are you hurt?"

"I'm fine, Delara, just a flesh wound. The medic will close it, and I'll be good," replied Kirkorian.

"Did you kill the man who did this to you?" asked Delara.

"Yes, little sister, I did, but it was a close call," answered Kirkorian. She then saw the blood that covered Delara's clothing. "Are you injured child?"

"No, Zmarei, this is not mine but that of these brave men. I do what I can to help them," replied Delara.

A medic moved over to treat Kirkorian's wound and Delara rushed off to help another wounded coming in.

"I saw you talking with the girl, she and the boy are something else. What's her name?" the medic asked.

"Her name is Delara, and the boy is Ramin," replied Kirkorian grimacing as the medic cleaned her wound, put a clotting agent on it, then closed it with derma-bond and covered it with a field dressing.

"Well, they refuse to leave the troops and insist on helping. Ramin has been a stretcher bearer and literally carried men on his back to us while the girl, Delara you said? She's been helping us medics. I've kept an eye on her as she moved from one wounded to another; giving food, water, checking their IV's and injuries, tearing strips of her own clothing to use as bandages, comforting some who were dying, and praying over the dead.

"She's extremely observant, and though she doesn't understand what we're saying, she learns quickly and even helped triage the wounded. This one ANA guy had a gaping hole in his leg from a mortar blast. As the stretcher was put down, his femoral artery burst. Delara never hesitated. She drove her fingers into the wound, clamped the artery with her fingers until I got there and took over. She saved his life. Pretty fucking impressive for a civilian who's never seen battle," the medic stated.

"Holy shit," Kirkorian said as she marveled at the two Afghan teenagers and looked at Delara with pride and admiration as she worked.

"Okay Sarge, you're good to go. Need anything for the pain?" the medic asked her

Although her side burned like hell, the adrenaline of battle, and her years of training to block pain would have to be enough.

"No, thanks. It'll just slow me down," Kirkorian replied.

"Okay then, good luck," and with that, he ran off to treat another wounded soldier.

Her wound tended to, she grabbed her rifle to rejoin Watkins and coordinate between the Americans and the ANA.

* * *

The courier handed Al-Zuq the latest reports. His forces were finally at the entrance to the Valley of Stars but at a heavy cost. The commander of the ANA forces was exceptional and always seemed to know what his troops were going to do and had a plan to counter it. Plus, these ANA troops fought extremely well, and with extraordinary discipline. These were clearly not the rabble Al-Zuq was led to believe they'd be. They were now reinforced at the entrance by the Americans, but the weather prevented their aircraft from resupplying them or providing anything but sporadic close air support due to the heavy air defense in the valley. Allah be praised for the clouds at least. Now for the final stroke, he was nearly out of time as the Americans had almost certainly called his superiors in Islamabad trying to get them to stop. Al-Zuq issued the order to move.

VALLEY OF STARS

Twenty-four fighter aircraft lifted off from their bases in northern Pakistan and turned west, climbing and accelerating to nearly twice the speed of sound. AWACS sent flash messages to the allied airbases to launch their alert fighters. A flight of two F-16s sped out of Bagram to join the eight fighters already airborne, guarding the skies while another flight of two F-22s climbed out of Mary-4, speeding to the area.

The northern CAP of four F-22s engaged the attack force from 70 miles away, their missiles slamming into their targets a few seconds after launch. As the first attack aircraft were hit, the whole enemy force split into a winding, weaving mass of aircraft. The F-16s launched at about 40 miles, but the element of surprise was over, so they hit with only half of their shots as their targets took evasive action. Seconds later, attackers and defenders were in a deadly dance in the skies over Afghanistan as each side worked to gain an advantage.

* * *

While the furball of airplanes curled around the sky, a flight of enemy F-16s broke away from the pack, headed straight for AWACS. As the Pak flight leader tracked the hulking airplane on his radar, he could feel the excitement growing in him. Kill that, and he would kill their ability to coordinate their close air support, and the ground forces would be free from coordinated attacks. The tone of his targeting missiles chirped as his flight quickly closed the gap to their target. When they were finally in range, the beautiful steady tone of their missile radars locked onto the big aircraft desperately maneuvering to get away.

He confirmed missile lock with his wingman, and as his finger went to the trigger to launch his missiles, his aircraft exploded beneath him.

* * *

"Lighthouse, Shark one-zero, splash two, you can head back to station now, we got your back," announced Captain Kazinski.

"Kaz, let's get into this fight now before it's over," radioed her wingman.

"You bet, Dragon, let's light 'em up," replied Kaz as they rocketed toward the roiling ball of fighters. The enemy had lost almost half their attacking force, and the survivors were bugging out, retreating to Pakistan. Three American F-16s were lost and a couple more damaged, but the skies were clear again as the search and rescue assets responded to pick up surviving friends and enemies alike.

* * *

Lieutenant Colonel Abdullah stood on the ridge scanning the road into Pakistan through his binoculars. The ridgeline was perpendicular to the highway about a mile inside Afghanistan before the road swept west toward Khost. Oriented north/south through a mountain pass, it opened onto a small plain on the Afghan side with several hills overlooking it. While the weather shrouded Qadir's position in the north, Abdullah's was clear. The hot midday sun beat down on his helmet. Combined with the nervous expectation of the deadly engagement he knew was coming, it made sweat drip through his jet black beard.

The radio call from Corps command said that the Pakistanis were on the move along the only paved highway giving access toward Khost from Pakistan that could handle their armor. Intel indicated that Pakistan had at least a Brigade sized force heading toward him, nearly four times his size. This was the highway, and Abdullah's battalion was the only force between Khost and the Pakistani attacking force.

Abdullah had fought under Qadir for nearly five years and worshipped his former commander, absorbing as much knowledge as he could. He figured if he was half the commander Qadir was, then he was better than most anyone. He positioned his troops and prepared for contact in less than an hour. Despite being outnumbered, he had a UAV overhead monitoring the border and would be ready for the enemy force. He knew it was unlikely he could stop them completely, but he had to hold long enough for reinforcements to arrive.

Abdullah set up a platoon of Soviet relic T-62 tanks on the top of the ridge straddling the highway. While most of the tanks in the ANA were rusty and in questionable condition, Qadir had insisted that any tanks supporting his troops be refurbished using scavenged parts, new paint, and even black-market parts. Abdullah followed his lead and demanded the same. These tanks may be old, but they were still deadly.

VALLEY OF STARS

He placed anti-personnel mines 100 meters either side of the road just beyond the point where it emerged from the mountain pass. In several culverts along the road, he had firing positions dug in, giving his men cover to maneuver. With an enemy this size, he would have to trade ground for time. By concentrating his firepower on the lead and trailing units at the start of the engagement, he would briefly trap them in the mountain pass and slow their advance.

His orders were to allow the enemy to move clearly into Afghan territory before engaging. Peering through the binoculars, Abdullah watched as the lead element of the Pakistani brigade crossed the border.

"Sergeant, call Corps and tell them a Brigade size Pakistani force has crossed the border and we are engaging. One mechanized battalion and three infantry battalions. Get the ANA Special Forces and Apaches airborne for reinforcement now," he ordered calmly. His calm exterior hid Abdullah's nerves as he said a silent prayer to Allah to give him and his men the strength and courage to fight well.

The enemy's lead elements were about one-third of a mile inside Afghanistan and still within the mountain pass when Abdullah keyed his radio. "Charlie-Two-Mike, target lead tanks...FIRE!"

The 115mm smooth bore guns of Abdullah's tanks roared to life. Their armor penetrating rounds slammed into the lead tanks of Pak brigade in an eruption of fire and flying shrapnel. Three rounds hit each of the two lead Al-Khalid tanks knocking the track off of one and destroying the other. As Abdullah's T-62's poured fire into the Pak column, the ANA mortar teams launched 81 mm high explosive mortars into the oncoming Pak troops.

Despite the direct hits on their lead elements, the Pak Al-Khalid tanks returned fire as their supporting infantry began spreading out behind them. As they entered the ground beside the road, they ran straight into the minefields, creating chaos in the troops. Taking advantage of this chaos, Abdullah's heavy weapons opened up on the troops in the open from both sides, pushing the breach back. The confusion was short lived as the Pak commander quickly recovered and started directing artillery fire on the culverts and had his tanks target the ridgelines. Abdullah responded by having his D-30 122mm howitzers target the pass, walking their fire back from the Al-Khalids.

The battle raged for about an hour with Abdullah's forces along the road being pushed back to the ridgeline. Two of his tanks were destroyed, but his smaller force was able to stop the Pak brigade for a while before their superior numbers and firepower pushed him from his positions. He ordered his men to fall back to the next ridgeline, forcing the enemy to funnel through the gap in the ridge he just vacated. But behind him now was wide open space for the Pak brigade to maneuver should they break through this line. Without reinforcement, they had a clear path to Khost. Abdullah's artillery pounded the oncoming enemy, but they had taken losses themselves with at least one battery destroyed and a second damaged but still firing.

With two more tanks out of commission and casualties mounting, Abdullah was contemplating his next move when the forward elements of the enemy in front of him were engulfed by huge explosions. The Apaches had announced their arrival with a barrage of rocket and 30mm fire that brought a smile to Abdullah's face. A volley of Hellfire missiles took out three of the Al-Khalid tanks supporting the infantry as the 30mm fire raked the armored personnel carriers, turning them into flaming hulks. Behind the ridge, the Chinook and Blackhawk helicopters landed with the ANA quick reaction force which immediately took up positions beside the embattled 3rd Battalion troops of Abdullah.

About an hour later, the lead elements of the ANA 3rd Battalion, 1st Brigade came crashing into the enemy force from the north, coming from Peer Kalai. They hit the right flank of the enemy so hard that it immediately buckled the Pak line of attack, virtually sheering it in half.

With the advantage now in his favor, Abdullah called on the radio to the entire ANA force, "Attack now! Send these animals to paradise!"

A guttural roar went up from hundreds of voices along the ANA lines, mixing with the thunderous crack from nearly a thousand rifles at once. The ANA slammed into the leading elements of the Pak forces who were now fighting on two fronts. Pockets of Pak infantry would get surrounded as fierce hand-to-hand combat forced them to finally succumb.

As the day's fighting progressed, wave after wave of close air support aircraft swept the plain of Pakistani troops in the open as the allied force pressed their counterattack, pushing the enemy all the way back to Pakistan. While Abdullah's men wanted to pursue the retreating force, the battle in their area was over. They secured the border and collected the dead, wounded, and POWs.

* * *

Major Andreesen had battled the enemy across the river for hours as they probed. While the losses mounted on both sides, the enemy probing attacks got stronger and stronger as their reinforcements arrived from the north. The tension on the faces of the men up and down the dwindling American lines was obvious. With close air support stretched thin Andreesen could count on only sporadic air strikes and had to wait until things were truly desperate before calling for help. But the Pak commander knew he was wearing down the American defenders through sheer volume of attacks he could throw at them. And the Americans still had no reinforcement.

Suddenly the enemy pushed hard out of the northern compound with a large force of tanks and armored vehicles, finally gaining a position in the southern compound while another force made a dash for the bridge. Andreesen had to decide quickly where to concentrate his fire. He chose the bridge and began taking heavy fire from the southern compound. With his force now taking a pounding from two directions, he made the decision to blow whatever charges they had on the bridge to slow the enemy advance.

He was about to give the order to blow the bridge when his radioman interrupted him. "Major, the ANA 1st Battalion, 201st Corps commander is calling."

"This is Whiskey Two Two, go," Andreesen shouted into the radio over the din of the battle going on.

"Whiskey Two Two, we're on the west bank a few hundred meters from the bridge. Sorry for being late but did you leave us any enemy to fight?" the Afghan commander asked jokingly.

"Seven One Juliet, you're right on time. Armor and mechanized in the southern compound, we'll hit the bridge and southern compound to cover your arrival. Come in hot and hard!" Andreesen replied almost laughing.

"Whiskey Six Charlie, concentrate fire on the bridge and northern compound. Everyone else, concentrate on the southern compound, mortar barrage to cover 1st battalion's approach. FIRE!" Andreesen ordered.

The ANA battalion was accompanied by a platoon of American M1A1 Abrams tanks. Andreesen's mortar teams showered the southern compound with 120mm high explosive rounds creating havoc in the Pak force. With the mortar fire covering their advance, 1st Battalion slammed into the southern compound led by the M1A1's. Their depleted uranium armor penetrating sabot rounds hit three of the Al-Khalid tanks in the southern compound in a shower of white hot molten metal. The Pak troops were rocked by thunderous secondary explosions from the superheated gases igniting the Al-Khalid onboard ordinance.

The force of the impact of 1st battalion's attack on the Pak left flank collapsed the enemy line and drove them toward the northern compound. Andreesen ordered his units along the river to hit the tail of the enemy formation from the opposite bank, forcing the Pak force to retreat from the bridge completely. For the rest of the day, the two allied forces pushed the enemy back up the Kunar River valley.

CHAPTER 21

Power Play

From the moment of the first confirmed engagement of Pakistani troops on Afghan soil, Madeline had been on the phone with the Pakistan Defense Minister. At first, he denied that his country's troops crossed the disputed border. Then he said that the Afghans had crossed into their territory first. Then he complained that his forces were simply chasing the Taliban terrorists who had just executed the attack on their military barracks and the ANA was protecting them. Madeline was frustrated. As she sat in the NMCC briefing room listening to the latest update, she wanted to explode. This is exactly what she told the President would happen if he withdrew too fast.

Afghan and U.S. military forces were engaged all across the country with the Taliban uprising and the Pak Army along their border. In the south, Iran put its forces on alert moving troops to the Afghan border to counter yet another brutal and despised Sunni sect trying to gain control of territory on its doorstep. But the most dangerous development was India which put its forces on alert, moving troops to the Pakistan border and preparing its fleet to put to sea. India and Afghanistan already had friendly relations and shared military training and technology. If India came to their aid, it could start a regional war with nuclear implications. But this time Americans had already died in the fighting, and the U.S. was knee deep in this conflict and getting deeper by the minute.

By now the fighting had raged for over two days across Afghanistan. In the south, the Taliban had taken heavy losses as the Marines moved out of their bases and engaged them in maneuver rather than being a stationary target. With the UAVs overhead and the Taliban wantonly putting civilians in harm's way, the populace who normally would be sympathetic were angry.

The ANA troops and Afghan Police had conducted themselves modestly well, but the real damage came from the Marines who chased down the attacking cells less able to melt into the populace. With each Taliban attack came a vicious counter-attack, and the Taliban had lost a lot of fighters. Still, it was a dangerous operation, reminding many of the brutal fighting in the streets of Fallujah and Ramadi.

The Marines had learned hard lessons there which were now being employed in the Helmand province, resulting in much greater success. They hadn't been sitting still during the previous lull in fighting. Their commanders had constant meetings with the ANA and local elders to work on security and assistance while allowing the ANA to be the visible face of the protection force. Similar to the tactic used to quell the Sunni uprisings in Iraq, the Marines had largely worked with the ANA commanders to gain the confidence of the elders. It was easier the further east they got as the influence of Qadir's efforts, with both villagers and ANA troops, was getting more widespread attention.

It was clear that the attacks of the Taliban across such a wide area, corresponding to the incursion by Pakistani troops, was more than a coincidence. And while the U.S. had taken the Pak Air Force out of the fight, the troops engaging with the Pak Army were, at best, in a stalemate. At worst they were forced to conduct a fighting withdrawal against the main attack force in the approach to the Valley of Stars. Not good news, as the biggest thrust was against the Valley, and that area was shrouded in heavy clouds. But it did prove to the Generals that it was Pakistan's main target all along.

General Jameson finished his intel brief, and turned to Madeline, "Questions Madam Secretary?"

"Have we identified a direct link between the Pak Army and the Taliban?" she asked.

"No Ma'am, not yet," Jameson replied.

"Who did the attack on the barracks then?" she asked.

"We don't know yet Madam Secretary," answered Jameson.

Madeline couldn't hold back anymore and slammed her hand on the table, "goddammit General, what the hell do we tell the President about why Pakistan is risking a full scale regional war by attacking Afghanistan? Who's orchestrating this charade, and what's their ultimate goal? We have absolutely no fucking idea except for some messages in an online war game that told us so? Get me some god damn concrete answers before we have World War fucking three break out!"

And with that Madeline pushed back away from the conference table with such force that her chair went flying. She stormed out of the room and went to the ladies' restroom, her hands shaking. She'd been awake for over 24 hours and was exhausted. Adrenaline and caffeine couldn't sustain her much longer. She knew she needed sleep, but she had to brief the President in less than an hour. She splashed some cold water on her face and dried it with a paper towel. As Madeline turned to leave, she ran right into a young female Airman.

"Shit, watch where you're going bitch...," the Airman started in anger when she looked up, and the shock of recognition came over her face. "Ma...Madam Secretary, I'm, I'm so, so sorry," stuttered the surprised Airman.

Madeline laughed. "That's okay Airman, it was my fault, I wasn't looking where I was going. I'm sorry. Better than having to piss in a hole in the field, right?" she joked.

The Airman gave a nervous laugh and a 'Yes Ma'am' before moving on, but it was just the thing Madeline needed to break the tension.

Madeline collected herself and returned to the briefing room. She strode to the head of the conference table and sat down, her chair having been returned to its rightful place. "Ladies and gentlemen, I apologize. I know you're all working very hard and I appreciate everything you've done during this difficult time. General Jameson, are there additional assets you need for us to put the missing pieces of this puzzle together?" she said calmly to the military leaders in the room.

"Madam Secretary we need access to another satellite to get more coverage but it's not ours, it's India's. They have the most comprehensive military coverage," stated Jameson. "They have a K-Band and Infrared bird up there that they secretly put into orbit on Russian launchers when the Russians were short of cash. The Indians bought the birds from the Russians, modified them, and sent them up giving the Russians cash to rebuild their oil production facilities. In return, they got cheap oil for at least the past 10 years. It gives us 24-hour coverage."

"Okay, I'll put a call into the Indian Defense Minister. First, I need to convince him to stay out of the fight and second, ask for access. What are we prepared to share with him?" asked Madeline.

"Madam Secretary, we should share current Pak unit positions and battle results. That will be the minimum they'll expect. But they're going to want our intel about what started this. That's going to be up to the President to decide how much we share," added Admiral Joffrey.

"Admiral, we'll discuss that with the President when we brief him. General Jameson, please pass along my thanks for the hard work your people in the joint intel center have done pulling this thing together. Tell them I'm confident they'll find the link we need to put a stop to this soon." And with that Madeline dismissed the meeting and went to her office to get a change of clothes and freshen up before heading to the White House.

* * *

Mo and Karim had spent all night trying to track the movements of the suspected leaders through their IP access to the game. *Seleucus I* didn't play much, but he was traced to the northern territories with his last location being Chitral just before the bombing of the barracks. *Wolfhunter 12* was mainly around Islamabad but also showed up in other places around Pakistan. The two players intersected once in Peshawar weeks before this whole thing blew up.

The unit that was bombed in Chitral wasn't part of XI Corps, but it was a unit that was reportedly sent to the northern territories for training and operations support. The odd thing was it was the only outside unit there and the only one targeted. With that information, the military analysts started tracking the movements of the commanding General of XI Corps. He was in Peshawar and Chitral at the same times as *Seleucus I* was logged into the game, and both times the IP traced back to ones assigned to the Pakistan military.

Seleucus was not as careful as *Wolfhunter*. *Wolfhunter* used proxies and routed his signal through multiple network nodes, trying to hide his location. With NSA's help, Mo had cracked his protocols and could quickly trace his location in near real time. As the battle in Afghanistan progressed, *Wolfhunter* got continuous updates, and the Intel team quickly tried to correlate details with locations. Some were harder than most but, as the team became more familiar with the players they were tracking, they could pass near real time information to the Marines about possible Taliban movements and intentions.

With the Marines no longer restricted to their base, they became the hunters rather than the hunted and were decimating Taliban cells in the Helmand Province. The more successful the Marines became, the more frustrated the players in the game became as they questioned why they were sacrificing so much for so little progress.

Karim looked at the pieces of information and laid out the picture for the General on duty of the intel center and Gerlacher. Within minutes, Karim was instructed to brief the SecDef and CIA Director on their theory as they were in the White House Situation Room about to brief the President. As members of the Intel team sent the intel reports through the secure email network, Gerlacher and Karim entered the briefing room just as the video conference with the Situation Room flickered to life. Karim was introduced and instructed to brief the current status of the links they found.

"Madam Secretary, Director, as you can see from the information in front of you, we have deciphered the communications link through the game and correlated Taliban movements with actual events on the ground. We've been able to direct Marine counter tactics in near real time. The Taliban cells are becoming increasingly frustrated, and that frustration is mirrored in messages sent between players in the game. Many Taliban attacks were stymied as a result of analysis of targets and movements derived from the game. This proves that the game is a communications conduit for the enemy," Karim began.

"In addition, we have definitively connected *Wolfhunter* to the Taliban network, the Caliphate, and to *Seleucus I* who we are confident directed the attack on the Pakistan Army barracks. *Seleucus* used Pakistan military networks to communicate, and the tracing of IP usage matches the movement of Lieutenant General Muhamad Al-Zuq, Commander of Pakistan's XI Corps. There was no communique from the Pak Defense Ministry or high command that indicated a reason for the XI Corps troop movements before the bombing. The response to the bombing was being driven solely by General Al-Zuq, the regional military commander.

"We are ninety percent sure that *Seleucus* is General Al-Zuq and messages in-game directly implicate him in the bombing of the barracks as a ruse to justify the incursion into Afghanistan to secure the Valley of Stars. Given the location and troop strength of the Pak forces, we are ninety-five percent certain that the Valley of Stars is their primary objective and that it's rich in precious metal resources. It's these resources that the players in Pakistan want.

"Only XI Corps ground forces are currently engaged in operations inside Afghanistan. Though their Air Force was involved, they were units directly responsible for supporting XI Corps and stood down after severe losses to U.S. air assets. While there is currently no direct connection to the Pakistan government, given the high level nature of the moves, and the intransigence of the Pakistani military and intelligence agencies, it cannot be ruled out. Finally, through IP tracking we have identified an intersection between *Seleucus*, believed to be General Al-Zuq, and *Wolfhunter* believed to be the Caliphate leader in Pakistan. This indicates a very dangerous link between Sunni factions in Pakistan, Afghanistan, Iraq, and Syria, likely expanding even further," Karim finished.

"Director Anderson, I believe this is the concrete evidence the President demanded, do you agree?" asked Madeline to the Director of the CIA.

"I fully agree Madam Secretary. This information makes the incursion much more dangerous not only for regional stability but has wide ranging ramifications for the whole Middle East as well," Anderson replied.

"I concur," stated Madeline. "Thank you for your incredible work over these past several days Mr. Rezek. Mr. Gerlacher, tremendously impressive effort by you and your team. Our Nation is in your debt."

And with that, the video feed went black, and the intel analysts went back to work.

* * *

Everyone stood as the President entered the Situation Room, followed by Secretary Massey. CIA Director Anderson took the President through the progression of intelligence from what they had gathered before the invasion. He finished with the latest that he and Madeline were briefed just before the President arrived. Madeline stared at Massey throughout the DCIA's briefing.

As he finished, Madeline looked at the President. "Mr. President, you now have the concrete and verified information you demanded. I remind you that we warned you of this invasion and it has progressed almost exactly how we predicted."

Madeline then continued the briefing with the current military situation. As she detailed the status of forces and the mounting casualties, Massey visibly blanched.

She continued. "Sir, we managed to minimize our casualties by being creative and proactive at implementing your orders. We repositioned combat assets from Afghanistan to Mary-4 and B-2's to Diego Garcia as the intel indicated increasing threat levels. Once U.S. forces were engaged, and Pakistan regulars were confirmed in the attacks, we redeployed our in-country units into the field immediately."

"You disobeyed a direct order from the President?" interrupted Secretary Massey indignantly, trying to regain the upper hand in this war of Cabinet Secretaries.

"No, Jonathan, we moved combat forces out of Afghanistan, as you advised the President in your grand plan, but said nothing about keeping it in theater, which we did," responded Madeline.

"But he specifically said that our forces should remain on their bases to prevent American casualties, yet another order you ignored, which got our people killed in the process," argued Massey defiantly.

"Jonathan, I'll excuse your ignorance about military operations, but we followed the President's orders exactly. Remember that he said, and I quote, 'our forces will remain on their bases and will only support the ANA if things get out of hand.' Well, when your enemy outnumbers you five to one and has more advanced firepower, things are definitely, 'out of hand.' I gave the order to get our people in the field so we could maneuver to respond to the threat and not have another Beirut on our hands.

"The only reason the casualties of both American and ANA forces aren't higher is that we worked in unison with our allies. We provided close air support, we neutralized their air forces so they couldn't be used against the troops on the ground, and we damn well engaged a hostile force who killed Americans first. If you want to put your strategy up against mine in the public forum, who do you think the American people will side with?" Madeline stated calmly and matter-of-factly.

"That's bullshit Madeline, now you're trying to play politics with the lives of American soldiers?" Massey pompously spouted.

"No Jonathan, you played politics with the lives of our soldiers, and now many of them are dead," Madeline responded coldly.

Massey's face went beet red as he sat there stunned. There was silence in the room as everyone just looked at the two combatants, waiting for the next volley. The

President knew that Madeline had taken great leeway in following his orders, but the results she detailed could have been worse. And she had warned him. But Massey insisted that Pakistan would never invade, it wasn't in their strategic interests. He was wrong.

Saldana held up his hand to silence the argument. "Everyone, please excuse us. I'd like to speak with Secretary Coltrain and Secretary Massey alone." Madeline never took her eyes off of Massey as the room cleared.

The political scenarios were racing through the President's head. Nothing had gone as he thought, or was advised. He had stubbornly held onto his belief that the U.S. should not be in Iraq or Afghanistan, and now in both cases, he pulled troops out too fast and left both areas vulnerable. The Caliphate was entrenched in Syria and Iraq. It was only the Kurds who stopped their advance in the north and northern Syria.

Iran was flexing its muscles in the vacuum of military and political leadership in Iraq. The illusion of a unified Iraq had been shattered and his strategy in Afghanistan, where even the Afghan government begged him to keep more troops there to stabilize it, had evaporated with the raging battle with Pakistan. Worst of all, his political legacy was in shambles, and the opposition party smelled blood.

As soon as the room was empty, Massey spoke first. "Sir, she deliberately countermanded your orders, and it was because of her interference that Pakistan sent such a large force in pursuit of the terrorists."

"Jonathan, you're grasping at straws. The intel clearly shows that this Al-Zuq engineered the barracks bombing as a cover for his incursion," responded Madeline.

"But our people should have been on their base. Our casualties should have been minimal, and who the hell authorized moving strategic bombing assets into the theater?" argued Massey.

"So your defense is that we should have let Pakistan kill our allies, take their territory, and act as a piggy bank for the Caliphate? Is this really what your grand plan was intended for? I ordered the B-2s to the theater as well as the USS Ronald Reagan to put together plans to strike directly at Pakistan if ordered by the President. I remind you, Jonathan, you own this. Your spokesperson was all too eager to let everyone know it." Madeline had just delivered the fatal blow, and Massey knew it.

The President finally spoke. "Madeline, Jonathan, we need to have a united front on this. Our political enemies will have a field day, and we need to respond with one voice. Jonathan, you were wrong. You should be thanking Madeline for saving your ass."

Madeline had to smile at that statement. She knew it wasn't Massey's ass she saved, but the President's, and the President just threw him under the bus.

The President turned to Madeline, "Madeline, what do you suggest as the next steps here?"

"Mr. President, you need to phone the Pakistani Prime Minister, Jonathan the Indian Prime Minister and I will contact the Pakistani Defense Minister. We need to drive home the point that we have intelligence implicating General Al-Zuq, XI Corps Commander, behind the barracks bombing and the incursion into Afghanistan and that we know the Pakistan government is not involved. We tell them we don't know his exact motive, but that he was working with a high ranking member of a Taliban group aligned with the Caliphate. We tell them we know India is moving troops to the border, and believe this act of a rogue General should not cause a full scale regional war that they don't want any more than we do. And above all else, we need to get reinforcements in there right now.

"We tell Pakistan they have the power to halt hostilities. American blood has been spilled due to their aggression, and our country is rightfully angry, demanding a strong response. We promise no U.S. retaliation against Pakistan if their forces withdraw from Afghanistan. We want confirmation that Pakistan has brought the conspirators to justice, publicly. Remind them they have a dangerous, nuclear enemy to their east and they have created another enemy to their west aligned with the United States. We will defend our ally to the fullest extent.

"I understand, this will be uncomfortable for you, Mr. President. But make no mistake, this cannot be a false red line. Americans have been killed by forces of a sovereign nation, you must absolutely be prepared to commit the full military might of the United States to this."

As Secretary Massey rose to oppose the rush to war, the President held up his hand and stopped him in his tracks. "Jonathan, sit down," the President ordered, "Madeline, please continue."

"Sir, we already have bombers overflying Pakistan in support of our forces fighting along the border. The Gipper has armed their aircraft in preparation of your authorization to attack Pakistan's naval assets and facilities should it come to that. We have ordered a Marine Amphibious force to the Indian Ocean, and India has sortied its carrier fleet already," she said.

"From Pakistan's perspective, they got a bloody nose against an inferior foe, albeit with several terrain advantages. But bloody it's been, and they can't afford to call us on it and fight a two front war. Better to execute a General than fight two advanced enemies," stated Madeline.

The President thought for a moment. "Madeline, I agree. Let's get everyone in here and hammer out the details."

When everyone returned, defeat was written all over Massey's face. From then on, the meeting was led by Madeline. She spelled out the strategy and suggested actions for the different departments. The President was more engaged in discussions of alternatives and asked several questions regarding coordination should the worst case scenario play out. To everyone in the Situation Room, it was clear, the political balance of power had shifted, permanently.

CHAPTER 22

Judgement Day

Qadir's fighting retreat was better than the textbook, but he was now at the mouth of the narrows surveying the battlefield with Watkins. They were thin on soldiers and ammunition after more than 24 hours of constant fighting. It had been nearly 18 hours since the last reinforcements arrived and only intermittent resupply from the air. An unforeseen updraft or downdraft would throw off an airdrop to where it was virtually impossible to recover. Yet despite all that, enough got through to sustain them for a while. But the enemy was pushing hard, and another powerful thrust just may push them back into the Valley of Stars and cause them to lose the territory to Pakistan.

If the sun were visible through the clouds, it would be quickly setting. The dark gray obscured where the ground ended, and the sky started. There was a slight pause in the enemy offensive, not a halt but less shelling. The two commanders knew that the enemy commander was about to hit them with whatever he had. Pak forces had been reinforced all day and could throw fresh men and equipment at the battered allied lines. Qadir and Watkins repositioned their dwindling force to where they felt the most likely push would come. It didn't take long for the attack.

The distinctive sound of tank treads announced the assault was beginning as their 125mm shells started peppering the allied lines even before they were visible to the defenders. Three Al-Khalids were line abreast on the valley floor with Infantry following close, while Infantry Fighting Vehicles and more infantry advanced on the flanks extending up the valley sides. The allied troops were slowly pushed back into the narrows which was both good and bad news.

The good news was that the terrain narrowed to less than 100 feet, and even less in many places due to large boulders on the valley floor. This would funnel the enemy into a highly confined space and make them vulnerable. The sides were extremely steep, precluding the enemy armored vehicles from maneuvering on the flanks. The bad news was that the narrows extended less than half a mile in length and prevented the allies from maneuvering either. The equivalent of two heavyweight fighters standing in the middle of the boxing ring throwing haymakers at each other and not moving.

When Qadir was fighting further down the valley, Watkins had used the time to prepare the narrows. He planted anti-personnel and anti-armor mines that could be remotely detonated. If they stopped an Al-Khalid in the narrows, it could slow their advance dramatically, like a cork in a bottle. The enemy pressed the attack and within an hour had pushed the allies a quarter mile into the narrows. Soon they'd be fighting in the open ground of the Valley of Stars.

"Cover, cover, cover; fire in the hole," Watkins yelled into the radio.

Watkins detonated the first set of mines. They erupted like volcanos under the leading Al-Khalid battle tank and the trailing Pak soldiers, shredding the infantry moving up behind it. Pressure waves from the multiple blasts shook the floor and walls of the narrows like an earthquake. The stricken tank was trapped between some large boulders and the valley wall, temporarily blocking the enemy advance.

Flames engulfed it making it glow orange and white as its onboard ordinance exploded in huge secondary explosions. Fire shot more than 50 feet into the air like a blow torch and created dancing shadows of death on the grey walls of the narrows. The heat radiated like a blast furnace all along the narrow passage and made approaching it deadly dangerous, stopping the advance in its tracks.

For the next 20 minutes, the combatants traded mortar, rocket, and cannon fire that reverberated in a constant deafening roar in the confined space of the narrows. The enemy brought up another Al-Khalid with a giant bulldozer blade on its front to push the dead tank out of the way. Mortars and 125mm high explosive rounds from the enemy armor rained down on the allied lines, pounding those positions to cover the clearing of the tank. Once the tank was cleared from the passage, a modified tank designed to clear a path of mines moved up. Enormous steel arms reached out with rotating chains that spun at high speed.

The blur of the spinning chains made it look like a giant round brush from the side. The chains ripped up dirt, rocks, and shattered any mines in front of it. Mines would explode when the heavy chains made contact and the energy absorbed by the moving chains. And the flying steel of the chains would detonate any anti-armor missiles the allies shot at it before they hit the tank.

The Pak infantry shot long ropes of explosives, detonating many of the anti-personnel mines along the route along the sides of the narrows that Watkins troops had planted. The restricted confines within the walls of the narrows meant that every yard of enemy movement was met with extremely concentrated fire in both directions. But with many of the mines now cleared, the enemy slowly and deliberately pushed their advantage and forced the fight all the way back to the entrance of the Valley of Stars.

Watkins and Qadir withdrew into the Valley, positioning on both sides of the narrows with as much of a blocking force as they could spare. An enemy tank at the entrance to the Valley of Stars from the narrows took a direct hit from a shoulder launched anti-tank rocket as the infantry started flowing around it. The surviving allied MRAPs opened fire on the enemy troops, but their sheer numbers were overwhelming the defenders. The leading ranks of the allied force were now engaged in vicious hand to hand fighting.

The wounded who were just inside the Valley were told to arm themselves and prepare to defend their positions. Ramin rushed to the side of Delara, who still had the AK-47 she took off the Taliban that attacked her in what seemed like years ago. She swiftly and efficiently moved from man to man tending to the wounded, ignoring the furious battle raging around her. A group of enemy soldiers suddenly burst through the lines, heading straight for them. Several of the injured returned fire, willing to fight to the very end if need be. Ramin positioned himself between the onrushing soldiers and Delara, firing at threats as they came.

Ramin swung around, "Get down," he yelled knocking Delara to the ground as a burst of gunfire erupted around them.

As Ramin spun to return fire, a Pak soldier was already on top of him. He just managed to deflect a bayonet thrust from the enemy soldier with his rifle. The Pak soldier's momentum carried him into Ramin, and the two tumbled to the ground in a deadly wrestling match. Ramin took a hit to the side of his head from the stock of the Pak soldier's rifle, stunning him.

As the Pak soldier raised his rifle to deliver the fatal blow, his chest exploded from burst of automatic rifle fire from behind. As he fell, Ramin saw smoke rise from the barrel of Delara's gun. Then watched as she quickly pivoted on one knee and fired again cutting down three more incoming enemy soldiers. No longer the scared girl from the day before, but a determined woman defending herself, and the soldiers under her care.

Watkins called on the radio, "Lighthouse, Lighthouse, Whiskey One One, Earthquake, Earthquake, Earthquake! Enemy inside the lines. Require immediate air support on our coordinates. Hit everything 100 meters to the east, now!"

Earthquake was the code word for an American position about to be overrun, and the situation was suddenly very dire. Virtually every air asset in country would be diverted as this became the most important mission above all else, and no matter the cost.

"Whiskey One One, Lighthouse, help inbound. Better take cover it's going to get really loud," AWACS responded.

"Dammit, better hurry!" Watkins shouted back on the radio.

"Whiskey One One, Spirit 51. Sorry, we're late, mark your line with a GPS beacon, and then put your heads down," called the pilot of the inbound aircraft.

"Jenkins, GPS beacon now! Mark the enemy line!" Watkins ordered one of his troops with a grenade launcher.

The soldier launched a projectile that had a beacon set to transmit when it hit ground fifty yards away. Squads of enemy troops were now moving against the flanks, and the defenders were engaged all across the front. There was no more line to separate friend from foe, and the best Watkins could do was kill as many approaching troops as possible. The beacon arced through the air and started broadcasting its position on impact.

* * *

The B-2 bomber glided silently through the air, its bat-like frame and black anti-radar coating made it virtually invisible to the enemy radars below. Flying more than seven miles above the savagery happening in the Valley, the flight crew methodically worked through their attack checklist while the automated defensive system scanned for any possible detection. The cockpit was deathly quiet except for the low hum of the giant aircraft's engines and the noise of the air passing over its skin. The tranquility broken only by radio commands from AWACS coordinating air support for the fighting across Afghanistan and the desperate call from the troops in the Valley.

The copilot of Spirit 51, the lead aircraft in the flight of two B-2 bombers, set the offensive system to automatic as their ground mapping radar painted the enemy force on the approaching the Valley of Stars.

"Holy shit, Whiskey One One wasn't kidding about the enemy inside their lines," he said as he looked at the computer display of the thermal infrared sensor system. He set the targeting system to search for the beacon. "Okay, positive beacon, GPS position locked, bomb bay doors open, targeting set to auto," the copilot stated.

"Confirmed GPS lock, doors open, lights green, system set to auto, system green, initiate. Release point in 15 seconds," replied the pilot confirming initiation of the bomb run.

The lead B-2 carried 200 GBU-40 Small Diameter Bombs. They were packed with 285 pounds of high explosives linked to the automatic targeting system and a terminal radar seeker head behind an armor piercing shaped charge. Spirit 51 could lay down a blanket of 200 individual missiles that the enemy couldn't see or hear until all hell broke loose.

"Whiskey One One, ten seconds, get low," the pilot radioed as they approached the release point.

The bomb load released automatically. Each bomb targeted its own armored vehicle on the ground as the big bomber flew down the line of the valley. Spirit 52, the trailing aircraft in their flight of two bombers, dropped his load of CBU-97s. These were cluster bombs with 1,000 pounds of sensor fused projectiles that detonated just above the ground, clearing a wide area of anything nearby.

* * *

The Pakistan commander sensed that he had the objective in his grasp. His lead elements had broken through the defenders' lines. He simply had to make one final hard push, and then the Valley of Stars would be theirs. Once in the open, the defenders would be forced to surrender or die. He needed to be there when they did. He urged his troops to move faster as his command vehicle sped up the valley. Praise be to Allah for the low cloud deck giving him some respite from the American close air support, allowing him to move faster than expected. After the disastrous beginning of the fighting, victory was his.

Two hundred meters from the narrows, he could hear the pitched battle raging in front of him. The smell of gunfire permeating the air made him euphoric as every fiber in his body anticipated the victory that was now in his grasp. Suddenly armored vehicles in front of him started erupting in violent explosions and flames. No warning and no reports of American aircraft. He grabbed the radio, ordering the air defense units to respond, but they reported no targets. He was in mid-sentence when his vehicle evaporated from a direct hit.

* * *

The narrows in front of Watkins and Qadir exploded into flames. The ground shook with the bombs hitting vehicles, causing secondary explosions of their ordinance. The walls of the narrows confined the explosive power of the heavy bombs hitting the ground, amplifying their concussive effects. The two allied commanders not only heard the explosions reverberate off the valley walls, they were buffeted by the heat and pressure waves rushing from the entrance to the narrows.

The air attack annihilated the Pak troops inside the narrows as the enemy momentum evaporated along with the men and machines hit by the American bombardment. The two aircraft had just created over a mile of sheer devastation. Pakistan had lost more men and equipment in less than 5 minutes than in two days of fighting as their attack force crumbled from the shock in front of the allied troops. Qadir and Watkins' organized their surviving units and forced the surviving enemy to retreat back through the narrows.

They pushed the advantage as the stunned Pakistani troops retreated past the burning wreckage that was once their attack force. Men and machines littered the battlefield as the allied forces stopped at the mouth of the narrows. The enemy was in full retreat and Qadir scanned the devastation in the valley that was the broken remains of perhaps two full battalions of men and machines. He quietly said a prayer for the hundreds of dead lying before him.

About 15 minutes later, the lead elements of U.S. 2nd Battalion, from Jalalabad entered the back side of the Valley of Stars using the same route Qadir and Watkins had taken more than two days before. Troops flowed in as darkness began to envelope the Valley. They immediately started tending to the wounded. The clouds began to break, and they were able to reopen the LZ for helicopters to land and evacuate the most serious casualties.

After nearly two days of fighting Qadir and Watkins took a little time to resupply and organize their forces with the new arrivals to make a push down the valley against whatever enemy remained. The stars came out, and UAVs took up a station overhead as the troops moved out down the valley. Qadir ordered that the Pakistani dead be collected and prepared in accordance with Muslim traditions. On this, he wouldn't budge, and then left behind two squads of men to ensure his orders were obeyed.

* * *

Madeline pressed the Pakistan Defense Minister hard, "Minister Khan. Nearly 15,000 combat troops from your XI Corps entered Afghanistan and engaged both Afghan and American forces at a heavy cost. We've verified that at least four Brigades from the 7th and 9th Divisions of the XI Corps, supported by about 500 Taliban fighters and more than two squadrons of fighters are involved in this action. We have proof that Lieutenant General Al-Zuq, Commander of XI Corps, has been working with Taliban and Islamic radicals aligned with the Caliphate in Syria and Iraq. He orchestrated the barracks bombing as a ruse to justify this invasion.

"We believe his objective is to capture land along the disputed Durand Line, based on a recent discovery of a rich deposit of natural resources. We have concrete evidence from imagery, communications, intel sources, and captured Pakistani officers, that link Al-Zuq with a Caliphate aligned leader in Pakistan to coordinate their actions. Their intent is to use the captured resources to fund Caliphate operations worldwide. There is no more denying this involvement, so my question, Minister Khan, is whether he's a rogue general acting on his own, or acting at your direction? Please consider your answer carefully, Sir," Madeline commanded coldly.

There was stunned silence on the other end of the phone as Minister Kahn considered what Madeline had just said, and the very clear threat that accompanied it. "Secretary Coltrain, I assure you I did not give any such orders, nor did the Prime Minister. If this is as you say, then General Al-Zuq is a subversive, and a traitor. We had intelligence that the bombing was done by the Taliban who were supported by Afghanistan. He sent reports of actions against Taliban targets that retreated across the border, and his troops were engaged by Afghan military, so he responded. Given your information, this must have been false. Please, Madam Secretary, allow me some time to consult with our internal security leadership to confirm what you say, and then speak to the Prime Minister."

"Minister Kahn, I'll believe your sincerity if you issue an immediate order to cease all offensive operations and withdraw your troops from Afghanistan. And, I'm sure you are aware of the Indian response to this. We've contacted their Prime Minister to reassure them that we don't believe your government was behind this aggression, but the longer it's allowed to go, the greater the risk for Pakistan being drawn into a two front war. None of us wants that, do we, Minister Kahn?" replied Madeline tersely.

The tension was palpable even through the phone line, as Minister Kahn assessed the danger of Madeline's threat. He was a proud man and seethed at the indignity of being threatened by a woman of all people, but her point was valid. It would be virtual suicide for Pakistan to fight both India and the U.S.

"Secretary Coltrain, I fully understand your position but also understand mine. I must confirm that what you say is, in fact, true, and if so, we shall deal with those responsible swiftly. I will agree to a cease-fire and order our troops to withdraw one kilometer from current lines if you do the same," replied Kahn.

Madeline had him by the throat now. "Minister Kahn, I cannot speak for the Afghan government, but given the ferocity of the aggression, they may not be in a very agreeable mood. If you did not give the orders to cross the current internationally recognized border in-force, as you just stated, then it should be a simple case of recalling your troops and talking. I ask you, what would Afghanistan's purpose be to work with their sworn enemy? The new Prime Minister has made efforts to reverse the rhetoric of his predecessor about reunification of the Pashtun tribes, so there's no strategic purpose."

Kahn was in a box. He had to agree to the withdrawal. All he could do was try and make the best of a bad situation. "Madam Secretary, I promised that we would deal with this swiftly, and we will. Once we do, I hope we can meet with you, and the Afghan Defense Minister, so we can ensure this never happens again. We don't support what the Taliban and Caliphate stand for and, as you have said, it wouldn't be in our strategic interest. If the situation is as you described, please understand it may take us alternative methods to communicate to our forces in the field."

"It would be a pleasure to have that discussion, but time is of the essence, Minister Kahn. I assure you, if not done immediately then Pakistan risks the full force and fury of our military forces and no response is off the table. Trust me, sir, as much as Pakistan was demanding 'blood for blood' after the attack on your barracks, our people are now demanding the same for your aggression. I wouldn't delay too long," responded Madeline as she abruptly ended the call.

Madeline returned to the NMCC situation room to get the latest updates. The first B-2 strike had just departed Pakistani airspace undetected. The second flight was en route, and Madeline was prepared to recall them should the Pak forces retreat back to their own territory.

* * *

Pakistani Brigadier General Patel, Commander of the 123rd Infantry Brigade, was at the mouth of the valley across from Arandu organizing his Brigade's move across the river when his radioman tapped him on the shoulder. "Sir, Major General Bahmani, and Brigadier General Gabol are both dead. A massive American airstrike hit them, and our forces are in full retreat from the Valley of Stars. Brigadier General Katana is alive but badly wounded and is on his way back. Lieutenant Colonel Jappa, commander 3rd Battalion 70th Infantry Brigade has taken command and requesting orders. He reports there was no early warning of the strike and sensor fuzed weapons with cluster munitions were dropped."

Patel cursed under his breath. With the death of his Division commander and the other two Brigade commanders either dead or wounded in the American airstrike he was now the senior ranking officer. But the ranking officer of what was his real question. It fell to him to desperately try to organize the shattered remains of the brigades both in the valley and still coming over the repaired bridge from Pakistan. It was clear they failed to break through to the Valley of Stars, and he needed more air defense units if he was ordered to counter-attack. Certainly, the defenders have been reinforced so any further battle won't be against ANA but against the Americans.

"Tell Jappa to collect as many officers and senior NCO's as possible and gather up survivors and organize a fighting retreat. Position into a blocking formation and use terrain to slow the enemy counter-attack. Double the air defense units supporting the retreating force and tell him we'll move reinforcements to him as fast as possible," Patel ordered.

He was stuck. Al-Zuq insisted there would be no retreat, and the capture of the Valley of Stars was the highest strategic goal for Pakistan. He had to follow orders even if it killed him, which was looking more likely every hour. It wasn't his job to question the orders of his superiors, even though he doubted the reasoning behind it. But he had thousands of men depending on him right now, and worrying about why he was here wasn't going to help him deal with the current situation.

The dead and wounded from the engagement in the valley began flooding back to him. He dedicated an entire company of vehicles to evacuate them to field hospitals he had quickly set up in Arandu. Medevac helicopters already were flying around the clock between Arandu and Peshawar so the casualties from this action couldn't be hidden or ignored. His medical people were overwhelmed. He already asked for additional medical and field hospital units from Corps, but it would take time to arrive. Time the wounded didn't have. It virtually assured that a number of these wounded would die before receiving the care they needed. But there was nothing more he could do.

Patel quickly repositioned the air defense missile and gun systems around the bridge and up into the valley to protect from the American air power. He swung a new battalion north of the bridge to block any flanking attack from that direction and recalled the units in the south to reform into a defensive position to prevent the American force from Naray attacking his southern flank. He had to ensure this bridge survived, if for no other reason than to allow him to retreat into Pakistan and reform a defensive position there.

VALLEY OF STARS

His positioning wasn't ideal, but it would have to do. The American led force from Naray would be pressing hard, so he shifted additional units to the south to reinforce. The Battalion to the north needed to be positioned carefully to maximize their effectiveness, so Patel moved north of the bridge to oversee it personally. He had just positioned two of the Battalion's Companies when the attack from the ANA 2nd Brigade, 209th Corps slammed into them.

Patel's forward line buckled briefly but held. He immediately repositioned his remaining force at a bend in the river where the channel narrowed to give them covering fire. While the ANA force had managed a very good attack, his quick action halted it with minimal losses, and he now had the terrain advantage. 2nd Brigade pressed, but the narrow river valley prevented them from getting a strong flanking maneuver, and the fight stabilized into a virtual stalemate.

With the north flank stable, Patel moved back to the bridge and up the valley to organize the mass of troops retreating from the Valley of Stars. While the Americans hadn't counter-attacked yet, he knew they would, and he had to hurry before the entire force was routed. The additional air defense units he moved into the valley had already hit two American A-10 attack aircraft, damaged but not downed, and shot down another attack helicopter. Damn those A-10s, the Iraqi's called them the "Cross of Death", how right they were. They could take a beating and still fight. Oh, what he could do with a few dozen of those. If he survived this fight, he'd suggest that Pakistan buy all of those planes the Americans wanted to get rid of.

After the air attack on the bridges, they had implemented additional anti-radiation missile precautions and increased their heat tracking and seeking systems. While it didn't prevent the Americans from using their close air support, it did make it more dangerous. With the reports of the carnage in the valley from the American air strike, it could only have come from stealth assets, likely a B-2 given the amount of ordinance dropped. And if so, it had to overfly Pakistan. Patel knew that any full scale action with the Americans would mean their early warning systems would be useless.

He moved up the valley toward the retreating attack force. The valley floor was littered with battle damaged equipment, and many of the units that went in were in shambles. Within an hour Patel met up with Lieutenant Colonel Jappa.

"Sir, we have collected the survivors and reformed into some semblance of platoons and companies. I've filled in the line with the fresh units you sent, but we are being pushed about a kilometer west of here by a reinforced American regiment sized force," Jappa reported.

"Colonel position your forces echelon right and left and make a staggered fighting retreat. Use the terrain and covering fire to slow the enemy advance. We may not be able to completely stop them, but we can make it damn hard for them," Patel ordered.

It was ironic that Patel was using the very same tactics to retreat as Qadir had used against the Pak force heading into the Valley of Stars. He then raced back to the bridge area so that he was central to the three points of defense he had set up. That way he could move units inside the triangle to the most serious threat. When he arrived, Colonel Tariq, Patel's Operations Officer came up to him with the current status report.

"General, our units south of the bridge report heavy attacks from the American and Afghan units from Naray. They have armor and infantry supported by helicopter gunships pressing on our position. Colonel Randa reports being forced back faster than expected and taking heavy losses," stated Tariq.

"Well Tariq, we have attacks from the north and the south. Our valley force is just remnants of our shattered division, our objective is lost," Patel answered his second in command dejectedly. Turning to his radioman, "Sergeant, contact the American commander and request a temporary truce to hold talks," he ordered.

"Sir, are you sure that's our only move?" asked Tariq.

"You and I have fought many battles over the years, what other option is there? Without air support, the enemy pressing on three sides, and the loss of at least a third of our combat power, we have no choice. We must now think of protecting our homeland," Patel answered Tariq. Next, he would have to put a call into General Al-Zuq to inform him of his decision.

* * *

Al-Zuq received the initial communique that the 7th Division Commander was dead, killed in an American airstrike and that General Patel was now acting division commander. It provided the latest disposition of troops, and it was clear the situation was hopeless. There was a knock on the door and the Defense Minister's personal attaché, Lieutenant General Ahmed Ghani, entered with an armed guard. Al-Zuq knew their intent and slumped in his chair, all was lost.

"Lieutenant General Mohammed Al-Zuq, I'm placing you under arrest for treason and assuming command of XI Corps. Stand up and put your hands behind your back," ordered General Ghani.

Al-Zuq complied and asked for mercy for his men, though he knew that they would already be arresting virtually every officer Al-Zuq had personally placed in their positions. As they exited the small warehouse that was his Corps Headquarters, he saw his most trusted ranking officers kneeling in handcuffs. He called to them, "Allahu Akbar," then bowed his head in shame.

In all, Major General Rabbani, two Brigadier Generals, seven Colonels, and nine Lieutenant Colonels would have swift Court Martials, quiet executions, and many would be listed as killed in action. Al-Zuq would be tried for treason for his role in the barracks bombing and conspiring with the enemy. He would suffer the indignity of a public execution. In the global chess match between the rising Islamic movement and the western powers, the movement in Pakistan had just lost its Knight.

General Ghani moved quickly to gain control over the forces in the field when the communications specialist informed him that Brigadier General Patel, acting 7th Division Commander was calling for General Al-Zuq. Ghani grabbed the radio receiver, "General Patel, this is Lieutenant General Ghani, Al-Zuq has been relieved of command, and I am the acting Corps commander. What's your status?"

Patel was stunned for a moment, it was highly unusual to remove a commanding general just days into a fight. "Sir, I request permission to seek a cease fire to discuss cessation of hostilities with the commander of the Afghan and American forces. My intent is to get them to allow withdrawal of our forces with no more casualties. We are surrounded, and they currently have air supremacy over us so it's a matter of time before we would be completely overrun at a massive loss of life and equipment.

"General Al-Zuq told me I would get no more reinforcements from outside the Corps and without them, I cannot hold the ground. We've lost over one third of our division's combat capability, and I believe it best to save what remains pending a decision about how to respond under the current situation. Sir, if you say we must stay and fight, we will obey and do our best to inflict as much damage as possible. But 7th Division will cease to exist," reported Patel.

Ghani smiled, "General, you are one step ahead of me. Do you have a cease fire in place?"

"No, Sir. But we have repositioned our forces to fight a defensive withdrawal so we can inflict heavy casualties should they press. Given the ferocity of the last 36 hours, I believe they will be open to talk," answered Patel.

"General Patel, I've ordered the rest of XI Corps to stand down, and was about to order your withdrawal, so this comes at just the right time. Get the best terms you can. If it's anything but allowing a full withdrawal under a cease-fire, contact me immediately," ordered Ghani.

"Yes, Sir," was the response.

* * *

Brigadier General Ahmadzai, Commander of the ANA 201st Corps, had just arrived in the valley with Qadir and Watkins to take overall command of the operation. The reinforced joint force was pushing the enemy from three sides as General Ahmadzai moved forward to consult with Qadir and Watkins.

Even though they were the junior ranking officers, General Ahmadzai deferred to the two men who clearly had superior combat experience to him. Their actions the past day and a half proved they understood the situation better than anyone, and Ahmadzai was not a stupid man. He survived the recent purge of politically connected commanders from his time in Helmand province. But fighting the Taliban is vastly different than fighting a modern armed adversary.

Qadir spoke first. "General, the enemy has taken heavy casualties and can get reinforcements across that bridge. They've reinforced their air defense making close air support more challenging for us, but we are still pressing forward. While we can flow more troops faster, it's only a matter of time before we overwhelm them, it will be a very high cost. The roles have reversed. They are on the defensive and can fight a battle of attrition as we did, and you see how effective that was on this terrain. Sir, I recommend contacting the Pak field commander and asking for a temporary ceasefire so we can talk about ending hostilities."

"Sir, I agree with Colonel Qadir. The forces south of the bridge have pushed the enemy to within two kilometers of Arandu. Our valley forces have pushed them back to the positions we held at first contact, and the northern Brigade stalled but is slowly pushing forward. The Pak army hasn't sent any other major units across the border since their aborted incursion near Khost, and they got hammered by the B-2 strike in the valley. We have another inbound, so if they don't withdraw, the Pak 7th Division could lose more than half their combat power. Tactically this is a losing position for the Pak commander. Unless he's a fanatic who will fight to the last man, I believe talking with him would be beneficial," added Watkins.

The two commanders understood the General's desire for revenge but were also very pragmatic, making their advice, and agreement on the course of action carry that much more weight. Ahmadzai was well aware of Qadir's reputation for tenacity in battle but also his mercy toward the enemy. He always seemed to know when to push the advantage and when to disengage, not only to save the combat power of his own forces but the optics of his treatment of fellow Muslims. The political clout gained from this was almost immeasurable.

"Agreed, make it so," answered General Ahmadzai.

At that moment the radioman tapped Watkins on the shoulder, "Sir, the Pak commander is requesting to speak with you."

Watkins turned to the two ANA commanders, "Seems he may have the same idea."

Watkins set a meeting between the opposing forces in the valley. Both sides ceased fire and withdrew 250 meters. Qadir led a small squad to set up a tent with a field table, chairs, and a field stove for tea. He knew the details of this meeting were very important and made sure everything was correct. Then the squad provided perimeter security.

Watkins and Qadir met General Patel and his aide and saluted him, catching Patel by surprise. The two escorted him into the tent, and while Qadir offered him tea, Watkins called for General Ahmadzai. Ahmadzai entered the tent with Sergeant Kirkorian. Once again, Patel was taken by surprise as he expected to meet with an American general. Introductions were made, and the two men sat down at the table to talk over tea.

"General Ahmadzai, I commend the skill of your forces. As soldiers, we both have followed the orders from those above us, even as the reasons behind them may not have been revealed. But we must also be practical men. Given the situation, it seems that further bloodshed serves no purpose for either of us," began Patel.

"General, it is Allah's will that guided the actions here, but the decisions of men that will dictate what happens next. Pakistan has invaded our country, for what reason we don't know, but your country started the bloodshed. Your forces are quickly being surrounded. What is the benefit to us for halting this operation?" replied Ahmadzai, pressing to ensure the Pak commander was sincere.

"General, you are correct that your forces are on our flank, but we have stopped all movement by you and have the advantage of the terrain which would allow us to hold for a very long time. Our orders were to chase the terrorists who attacked our country first and were told they fled here. We both know that the border between our countries is in dispute and have taken measures to avoid collisions like this. Therefore, I must assume this fight started as a misunderstanding, but we have the power to stop it," responded Patel.

"General, I can confirm that the unit who first engaged us had approximately 500 Taliban fighters supporting them. They were not chasing them but moving as one force," added Qadir.

The surprise and confusion on Patel's face were obvious. "That's impossible. Like you, we have been fighting the Taliban for some time."

"Yes, General, so it's equally questionable that we would have helped the Taliban bomb your barracks like your Corps Commander claimed," replied Ahmadzai.

"As you said sir, we are soldiers. We only execute the orders of those who may have ulterior motives. Whether or not we've been misled, the fact is that my men engaged a joint force of Taliban and Pak soldiers which has now brought us to this point," answered Qadir.

Patel's mind was racing. Nothing about these claims made sense, but they had no reason to lie about it. They were winning, and it was Pakistan that entered their territory, disputed or not. But it did give some insight as to why General Al-Zuq had been relieved.

"General Patel, perhaps we let the leaders of our countries decide the facts of how we got here. Let us decide how we stop it. We propose that you call an immediate halt to all offensive operations and withdraw back to Pakistan territory as defined by the Durand Line. Once you have withdrawn all combat forces, we will exchange prisoners, wounded, and dead in the village of Arandu. General, let us not make this any more complicated than it needs to be. How many more must be sacrificed for an outcome we both know is coming?" stated Ahmadzai.

Patel got what he wanted. But the discussion caused more questions than answers for him about the reasons why they were here in the first place. He quickly agreed, shaking hands with Ahmadzai, and the two toasted the agreement with tea. Watkins radioed Lighthouse about the agreement and requested that airstrikes be put on hold pending confirmation of the withdrawal.

Patel left the meeting site and issued orders for the immediate and permanent halt in hostilities for all forces of the 7th Infantry Division. He then called General Ghani and began the process of making an orderly withdrawal from

Afghanistan under the watchful eyes of his adversaries. As hostilities ceased, information was passed up the channel to the leaders of both countries. This crisis was over, for now.

Chapter 23

Aftermath

Confirmation of the withdrawal of Pakistani troops came into the NMCC and a collective sigh of relief came over Madeline and the Joint Chiefs. It was still a tense situation on the border between Pakistan and India, but this would give the President more bargaining power with the Indian Prime Minister. Casualty numbers were still coming in as injuries and dispositions were cataloged and verified by the military. The Taliban uprising was winding down after nearly a week of fighting. Their forces were decimated and vanishing into the countryside. The biggest blow was the loss of over 200 fighters in the valley alone.

Pakistani casualties were high, with an estimated 1300 dead and over 3000 wounded. ANA losses were slightly higher as a percentage due to the ferocity of the fighting against Qadir's men and their inferior equipment. Qadir lost just under 200 dead and 300 wounded from his battalion alone though many of the wounded continued to fight. The

Americans in the valley campaign fared a bit better as the largest share of their force was in the Kunar River operation, but they had about 120 dead and 270 wounded, the highest losses of any American unit during the week long fighting across the country. The Marines fared the best even though they were in urban firefights losing just 75 dead and 130 wounded.

Over the whole operation, it was the deadliest week for American military forces since the Battle of La Drang Valley during Vietnam. Politically, President Saldana was absolutely hammered over this. His detractors blamed his premature withdrawal from Afghanistan, just as they did the disaster in Iraq. There was no hiding the fact that despite the ANA performing better than expected, they were overmatched if not for American military power to stop the aggression.

The press still had people embedded with U.S. forces, though only a handful, and the action and mounting casualties from all over Afghanistan captivated the country. Questions about what started the fighting began almost immediately, as apparent coordination between Taliban and Pakistan was highlighted by experienced journalists in the region. Contrary to the bold pronouncements made by the State Department spokeswoman, SecState's strategy had failed. It would have been disastrous if not for the actions Madeline had orchestrated.

Madeline made sure that carefully placed leaks kept the narrative of the failed strategy going. Like dogs with a bone, the press laid the blame at the feet of Secretary Massey, replaying his spokeswoman's words over and over. With every new report of body bags and wounded, the calls for Massey's head grew louder and louder.

President Saldana was taking serious hits of his own. His staff desperately tried to deflect blame toward Massey while the opposition took huge bites out of his political hide for his many foreign policy failures. Members of Congress from the President's party nearly trampled each other on their way to a microphone to scream for Massey's firing. All to protect Saldana; but it was too little, too late.

The political foundations Madeline had so carefully laid for months were bearing fruit. The obvious disagreements with State, the whispers of anger over Presidential decisions, the blurred lines of dissention and soldierly support made Madeline a martyr rather than the object of disdain. Hidden behind the joy of extinguishing a flame that could have ignited a world war, Madeline smiled at her orchestration of the downfall of her political enemy, and the rise of her own political capital within the party.

Madeline picked up the secure phone and called the President. "Sir, the Pakistani withdrawal is complete, and the Valley of Stars is secured. Current intel indicates a series of mass arrests of officers within XI Corps and other places tied to General Al-Zuq, the XI Corps commander who started this whole thing. We have confirmation that Al-Zuq, the suspected mastermind of the bombing of the Pak Army barracks, was arrested for treason. Mr. President, the immediate crisis is over."

Madeline could hear the President's voice tremble just a bit as he replied to her. "Thank you, Madeline, and the Chiefs, for doing everything you could to minimize American losses. This is a proud day for America and Afghanistan."

The President was not just a lame duck, but a severely wounded one at that. To remain relevant, he would have to grab hold of Madeline's coattails and hang on for dear life.

* * *

Qadir and Watkins managed the transfer of prisoners at the bridge. They had the Pakistani and Taliban dead brought forward. As the trucks came to the bridge, the Pak officer managing the transfers from their side recognized immediately that the dead had all been wrapped in linens. He looked at Qadir in stunned silence.

Qadir understood the man's question without his asking. "All of the Muslim dead have been washed, wrapped, and had Yasin recited in accordance with Muslim traditions out of respect for them and their families who will mourn them," he stated calmly.

The Pak officer and the men under his command were surprised, and a bit ashamed as the Afghan dead were simply put into trucks. Qadir had obtained permission from several villagers on the Afghan side of the bridge to use their buildings for proper preparation of Afghan dead. This had a profound impact on the Pakistani soldiers who were working the transfer and watched the care that Qadir and his men took with their Muslim brothers.

The nature of war encouraged hatred for an adversary, but here was a man who showed as much respect for the enemy as his own troops. And the attention the Americans gave to the Pakistani wounded, and the care given them, saved countless more lives. This was not lost on the Pak soldiers who received that care, nor on those who repatriated them as well.

The withdrawal of troops and transfer of prisoners and dead took just over 24 hours without incident. The ANA 2-209 Brigade took up positions in the Afghan village on their side of the bridge for security as Qadir and Watkins collected what remained of their battered battalions. They were finally able to rest and moved out in the morning working their way back down the Kunar River valley.

About 15 miles downriver, they came to Ramin's village. Since the time he was taken by the Taliban, he had a birthday and was now 18. As they entered the village, his father caught his eye and began to weep. Ramin smiled and proudly strode to him. Delara followed.

"My son, Allah be praised, is it really you? They told me you were dead!" cried Ramin's father as he cupped his son's face with his hands.

"Father, yes it's me. They tried to kill me, but it was Allah's will that I survive. I believe I was spared to protect this woman. Father, I want you to meet Delara. With your blessing, I'd like to seek her father's permission to marry," replied Ramin.

Delara blushed just a bit but stood straight and proud as Ramin reached out for her hand to bring her forward to present to his father. "She is strong, brave, and she saved my life during the battles with the Taliban and Pakistan troops. I have vowed to protect her, and through actions not words, she has done the same."

Ramin's father stood dumbfounded for a moment, not sure what to say as his son presented Delara.

Qadir stepped forward, "Sir, your son is every bit as brave as any man I have under my command. He was critical in repelling more than one enemy attack and the young woman you see before you was by his side the whole time. She saved the lives of scores of my men, not only helping to treat their wounds but taking up a gun to fight. Together, these two are remarkable."

Ramin's father was even more stunned as he looked back and forth at the teens. He stepped forward and looked Delara in the eyes, took her face in his hands, looked at his son and took his hand and Delara's hand and cupped them together in his. "Son, I don't know her family or the village she comes from, but it's clear that Allah's will is for you to be together. Let us go speak with her father."

And with that, Ramin's father smiled and gave his son another hug and grabbed the two teenagers' hands. "But first we must celebrate your return!"

The joint patrol set up a defensive perimeter around the village as Qadir and Watkins were introduced to the village elders and the whole village brought food for a feast to celebrate Ramin's safe return. The next morning the troops continued down the river until they came to Delara's village of Sosha. It had been over a week since she left and the news of the battle not far from their village was a heavy burden for her father. She was his last surviving child, and her loss would be devastating.

Once again, the patrol established a secure perimeter as the commanders, and a small contingent of soldiers entered the village with Delara, Ramin, and his father. Delara's father had to steady himself against the doorjamb of his home as Delara entered the village. Seeing him, she ran to him and nearly leapt into his arms, hugging him as the two of them wept.

Kirkorian, Watkins, Qadir, Ramin, and his father walked up. "Father, we promised we'd bring her back safely, and we did," Kirkorian said smiling.

"Sir, your daughter is extremely courageous and saved the lives of countless men. If your sons were half as brave as she, then they must have made you very proud," added Watkins as Kirkorian translated.

That was when Delara's father held her out to look at her and noticed her clothes were torn and still had blood stains on them. "Child, what happened to you?" exclaimed her father.

Qadir answered. "Sir, your daughter tended to our wounded and dying. She was strong and persistent, even in the face of an enemy attack, killing several of the attackers. She saved many men, not only by helping with their medical care but through direct action in fighting off an attack against our wounded. She's tenacious, and will prove to be a handful for any husband." Qadir, Kirkorian, and Watkins all shot a look at Ramin, chuckling.

Delara's father was speechless, alternately looking at the soldiers and his daughter.

"Father, I'd like you to meet someone. This is Ramin," Delara said as she grabbed his hand and pulled the young man forward. "He saved my life and has protected me ever since."

It was Ramin's turn to blush a bit, but he extended his hand to shake with Delara's father. "Sir, I'm honored to speak with you again. We met before these soldiers left to find the Valley of Stars." Ramin introduced his father, then continued, "I have made a vow to protect your daughter as long as I live and ask your permission to marry her."

Delara's father was taken aback. Kirkorian spoke next, "Father, this young man saved my life and Delara's during a surprise attack by the Taliban, with his bare hands. He never left her side, protected her, and fought bravely even when it seemed all was lost. The bond between them has been forged by fire. I can think of no better match for your daughter than this man."

"No disrespect for Ramin's family, but I will match whatever dowry is requested. I am honored to have fought with both of these extraordinary young people," added Qadir.

Delara's father could have been knocked over with a feather as Ramin's father leaned in. "I was just as surprised as you," he said with a chuckle. "Shall we go in to discuss this over some tea?"

"Yes, yes, I believe we should," Delara's father stuttered as she squealed, giving him a giant hug, then grabbed Ramin's hand and pulled him into the house.

Her father's head was spinning as Qadir slapped him on the shoulder laughing and turned him to head into the house as well. As the group settled in, Delara immediately began cooking while Kirkorian helped serve tea. With the match agreed upon and announced to the village, another celebration was held for the two young people.

VALLEY OF STARS

* * *

"And now for the latest on the bitter fighting in Afghanistan over the past few days from Torvath Dean, embedded with the 25th Infantry Division. Tori, what can you tell us about this crisis between Afghanistan and Pakistan?" asked the cable news anchor.

"Megan, this all started with the bombing of the Pakistani barracks in Chitral, Pakistan. It was alleged to be committed by the Taliban in the Northern Territories assisted by members of the Afghan military. But it now appears that it was orchestrated by a rogue Pakistani General in command of the army forces for this area. Sources say that Lieutenant General Mohammed Al-Zuq, commander of the Pakistan Eleventh Corps, was aligned with radical elements in the Pakistan Taliban, who have pledged allegiance to the Islamic Caliphate. The incursion was apparently a land grab, but to what purpose is still not known at this time.

"We know that at least four brigades of the Eleventh Corps were involved, and took extremely heavy losses at the hands of a joint Afghan and U.S. force. The Pakistan 7th Infantry Division crossed into Afghanistan here at Arandu and were engaged by elements from the Afghan National Army 201st, 203rd, and 209th Corps, along with units from the U.S. 25th Infantry Division and combat air forces. My sources have confirmed that the heaviest fighting, and the bulk of the casualties, occurred in a high mountain valley just west of here in Afghanistan. The main thrust of the Pakistani forces was against the allies in this valley and south along the Kunar River. Elements of the Pakistan 9th Infantry Division briefly crossed the border to the south in a push toward Khost, Afghanistan. But they were repelled by Afghan and allied forces.

"I was part of a group of journalists who toured the valley a short time ago. The scars of this intense battle have shattered the serenity of this peaceful place. While the charred remains of fighting equipment are still being cleared, the pockmarks of the bomb craters and burnt scars along the valley will remain for a generation. A true testament to the ferocity of the fighting, and sacrifice by both sides for this largely unknown piece of ground.

"The forces in the valley were commanded by Lieutenant Colonel Abdul Qadir, 2nd Battalion, 1st Brigade, 203rd Corps. They were supported by the U.S. 1st Battalion, 3rd Brigade, commanded by Lieutenant Colonel D.B. Watkins. These are the same two commanders who led the operation in Zakar Khel a couple of months ago. That was the location of the Taliban propaganda film alleging an allied massacre debunked by eyewitness accounts of that battle.

"I had the distinct honor to speak with these two commanders and observe their interactions with each other, and the villagers of Zakar Khel. Especially the growing legend that is the Afghan commander, Colonel Qadir. It's not only his prowess on the battlefield that both friend and foe admire, but his demand that all be treated with the utmost respect; allies, noncombatants, and even the enemy. While the dead were being collected, Colonel Qadir's men prepared them in the Muslim tradition for their final journey home, while prayers are spoken with the wounded and captured. It's this combination of military skill, tenacity, and humility that President Zazai wants to spread throughout the Afghan military.

"I spoke with the Pakistani General who negotiated the cease fire, and his respect for these two warriors was obvious. He was impressed with the tactics and strategy employed by the allied forces, especially these men who bore the brunt of the fighting in the mountains just west of here. But more than the successful tactics employed against him, he commented about the care that the Pakistani prisoners, dead, and wounded were given, clearly surprising this battle-hardened commander. It's rare, Megan, that the enemy who was defeated will speak so highly of their adversary.

"Given the intense fighting here, where a severely outnumbered allied force managed to stop a modern, well equipped adversary, I think it's clear how remarkable this result was. The success of the Afghan Army in this operation may well have changed the course of Afghan national identity forever.

"As for General Al-Zuq, he's been found guilty of treason and was quickly executed along with several of his co-conspirators. The regional tensions from this incursion have subsided as combatants on both sides have pulled their forces back, and so have Iran and India. This crisis is over. But a new day is dawning on this war torn country, and the national pride this action has inspired is sweeping across Afghanistan. I'm Tori Dean reporting from Arandu, Pakistan. Back to you, Megan."

Farooq listened intently to the news of the rogue General executed for treason. Given the fact that the ISI or the Americans hadn't knocked down his door already, put Farooq's mind at ease that the General had taken his secret to the grave. The failed operation was a severe setback for the cause. Not only did they lose a large number of fighters, but access to the Valley of Stars as well. The long term financial loss was steep, but more disconcerting was that the ANA and Americans were so effective in tracking his fighters' movements. They must have a spy somewhere, and he needed to smoke them out.

The recent operation had interrupted the flow of material support to his operatives in the Middle East. It delayed some of the operations he had hoped to execute by now. *Hephaestion* had messaged him in-game to say the op was nearly ready to go against Shush. To be successful, they had to make it look like the Saudis had done it, or at least the Jews with help from the Saudis. Either way, it would be a political win to drag the region into a sectarian war that would ally the Sunnis against a common foe and eradicate the apostates once and for all. But he would have to wait a little longer due to the delays in his supply routes.

Unfortunately, some of his lieutenants didn't hold communications security very well during the recent fight so he'd have to reinforce this for the future. He had made his usual rounds to several dead drops, stopped for tea at the tea house, and wanted to send out some messages before turning in for the night. It was late, around midnight, and his security was making their hourly check around the perimeter of the compound. They had learned a few things since the op against Osama Bin Laden; one of them was not to stay in one place too long.

He had three different compounds and randomly picked where he stayed each night. He logged onto his game computer and initiated the protocol to make him a ghost. A few minutes and nearly a dozen zombie computers later, he got the icon indicating he was a computer located in Switzerland. Logging into the game, his first message was to *Hephaestion* to let him know the replacement resources would be delivered by the end of the month. After a few more messages, both to operatives and game players, he made some moves within the game. It was needed to keep his activity levels up for his cover, but it was also relaxing to kill a couple thousand fantasy troops.

Farooq had been online less than an hour when he heard a dull thud outside his window. He went over to see what the sound was, and looking out the window saw nothing. As he turned back to his computer, there was a loud pop followed by the distinct metallic clack, clack, clack of silenced automatic rifles. Farooq rushed to the door locking it and then turned back to his computers and hit the hotkey sequences to erase the hard drives.

He went to grab his rifle when the door exploded followed by a blinding flash and deafening bang that stunned Farooq, knocking him to the ground, making his ears ring and totally disorienting him. Suddenly he was on his stomach, a bag placed over his head, hands zip tied behind him, and the sharp jab of a needle in his arm when everything went black.

* * *

Karim, Mo, and Jake had spent the past several days pouring over the data from GillNet and tracking several targets through their game communications. They had triangulated *Wolfhunter* and quickly pinpointed his location. Mo had set up an automatic trace using the known network nodes used to try and cover his tracks so that every time he logged on they had a position in virtual real time. Using the traces, they tracked his movements and found the locations he used to access the internet. He was careful, and he was good. Mo was better.

CIA had three compounds under surveillance and had inserted Special Ops assault teams into safe houses within minutes' drive from each. The target was known to stay in one of these randomly, so they had to have separate teams cover each. While the teams were smaller than normal, the target only had a few guards, and their security sweeps were too predictable. Once they received confirmation, the team closest would do a snatch and grab, then all teams would withdraw at the same time. The target would be moved to a safe house across the Afghan border for interrogation, then by helicopter out of the country.

As soon as *Wolfhunter* logged on, Mo's trace program had his exact location within a few minutes. "Got him, Wolf-3," Mo announced.

"Jackhammer, execute," ordered the General on duty in the Intel fusion center.

The tension in the intel center was high as they watched the Navy Seal team move in via satellite feed. Video from helmet cams was fed to another screen.

"Zebra-3, perimeter guards," the team leader ordered.

Two Seals moved in and neutralized the two guards outside the house doing their security sweep, taken down by knives driven into the side of their throats and slicing outward, severing the carotid artery and vocal chords. They were dead in seconds.

"Perimeter secure," replied Zebra-3.

"Zebra-5, breach," ordered the team leader.

The Seals put shaped charges on the door, breaching it instantly and then killed two more guards inside the house. Four Seals raced up the stairs, breached another door at the top, and saw a man at a laptop as the flash-bangs went off, stunning him.

Mo grabbed a mic, "Grab those laptops, unplug them, and remove the batteries now!"

It was done extremely fast, but she wasn't sure if they were fast enough to stop the wipe program their target most assuredly initiated. As two team members carried the now sedated target away, the remaining members pulled everything they could grab, stuffing them into bags to be reviewed by the Intel folks back in Afghanistan. Their assault was virtually silent, and the spotters reported no lights coming on in the houses nearby. The fact that they didn't use an airborne assault made it both more dangerous, but stealthier, though helicopters were on standby with fighter escorts if needed. After an hour of searching the safe house, the team withdrew, and all assets were recalled.

The success caused jubilation in the intel center. Karim hugged Mo and told her they had a lot more work to do now. They needed to get someone in theater to conduct the interrogation. The military insisted they would have first crack at him and the Director caved. He had insisted that CIA be present for the questioning and the condition was agreed to.

Gerlacher turned to Karim. "You want the pleasure?"

Karim sat stunned. "I'm not a field agent, Zack."

"But it was your idea that caught him," Gerlacher replied.

Mo giggled with excitement. "Go ahead, KZ, show him who *The Great Kazam* really is. Plus, we have his logon info so we can keep his account active and roll up his whole network."

"Pack, Son. That's an order," smiled Gerlacher.

CHAPTER 24

Epilogue

About ten miles southeast of DC in the Maryland suburbs, the flight of giant C-17 transports carrying the American dead back to the U.S. landed at Andrews Air Force Base under a bright, sunny, cloudless sky. They taxied to predetermined spots with the precision of a military drill team and parked with their tails angled toward the massive hangar where the dignitaries waited. Secretary of Defense Coltrain led the Joint Chiefs out onto the parking ramp with a large formation of soldiers, sailors, airmen, and Marines to meet the aircraft. As the cargo ramp of the first aircraft opened, the Army Chief of Staff led a contingent of military pallbearers to the bottom of the ramp.

He took a position in front of the ramp as four lines of pallbearers moved solemnly past him and entered the aircraft to retrieve their precious cargo. As the first flag-draped coffins appeared at the top of the ramp, he saluted, turned about face, and led the procession of caskets off the aircraft. The two lines of caskets moved slowly to the hangar where a mass eulogy would be given by the

President. This process was repeated with each successive aircraft, led by another service Chief of Staff as the entire complement of military personnel quietly saluted their fallen comrades.

With the caskets of the dead filling the hanger, Madeline had to choke back tears. She flashed back to a similar ceremony for her friends killed in the Scud strike on the barracks in Dhahran, Saudi Arabia, during Desert Storm, killing twenty-eight. President Saldana was eloquent in his praise for the sacrifice of the fallen, even though most of the military in attendance blamed him for it. His pronouncement that they would not have died in vain was received with skepticism at best, and disdain at worst, though the faces of the military members present were too professional to show it.

Madeline's prediction had come true. She said the dead would be laid at the President's feet, and the optics couldn't have driven that point home better than the live television coverage of the ceremony. She knew this was an attempt at political resurrection, but anyone who tied themselves to this President was tied to an anchor being thrown overboard.

For the remaining year and a half of his term, he would be "dead man walking," a pariah even in his own party. Massey's political career was shattered as well. The final nail in his coffin was the President's pronouncement that Madeline and the Joint Chiefs' actions had ensured victory and that the loss of life would have been larger if not for their creativity.

At the end of the ceremony, Madeline escorted the President to Marine One, the Presidential helicopter, to take him back to the White House. As she shook his hand, she handed him an envelope.

"Mr. President, I have a plane to catch, but this is my resignation. You'll be happy to know I'm preparing to run for Governor of Pennsylvania and I look forward to your support. I expect you will want to make the formal announcement after a few news cycles to allow the solemnity of this event to subside," Madeline said casually.

This stopped the President dead in his tracks, but he had to remain neutral-faced as the cameras were still on him. Squeezing Madeline's hand more tightly, he leaned in. "And you had to do this now?" he said with annoyance trying to hide his anger.

"Yes, Mr. President, I did. Have a safe flight, and I'll call when I return to the Pentagon," replied Madeline.

* * *

President Zazai presided over a similar ceremony in Kabul as the American President had. After his comments, he presented Qadir with his country's highest military honor and asked him to speak. Qadir began with a prayer, for the sacrifice of all who fought on both sides and asked for his countrymen to show restraint and patience. He was honored and humbled to serve the people of Afghanistan and prayed for Allah to show mercy on those who would use the Prophet for their own mortal plans.

It was a short speech but one that was so different from those the Afghan people were used to. Here was a Shia man who had the levers of Sunni power in Afghanistan falling all over themselves to grab hold of his coattails, and he only spoke of serving them. So many Afghan leaders spoke of a unified country but ruled through their tribal affiliations. This man was clearly different.

Zazai wanted to make him a General, but Qadir refused. It would cause dissention among the officer corps to jump over others who were equally deserving in his mind. But he accepted a promotion to Colonel and a position as liaison with the Americans to advance training and integration of the ANA.

Zazai was both impressed and intimidated by Qadir. He was raised to distrust members of other tribes even within his native Pashtun, but especially the Shiite Hazara like Qadir. Yet this man seemed to transcend those differences. Qadir was strong, calm, pious, and charismatic.

It wasn't that he was reluctant to lead; his men of all backgrounds and tribes with their discipline and tenacity in battle testified to that. There was just something about him. He intuitively sensed the long term implications of things. A strongly religious man, he never used his religious beliefs as a sword to justify destroying others, but a salve to heal both literally and spiritually. Zazai had never seen anyone like Qadir before. No one in Afghanistan had...until now.

* * *

General McAffey moved down the line of soldiers as the decoration narratives were read. More than a dozen Bronze Stars were awarded for gallantry. Watkins, Andreesen, Tasker, and four others received Silver Stars, the third highest honor for combat bestowed by the military. Finally, McAffey came to the last one. A medic who saved dozens of lives, not only by treating their wounds but by fighting furiously during the hand-to-hand combat in the Valley, protecting the wounded despite being wounded himself. He received the Distinguished Service Cross, the second highest combat award, just beneath the Congressional Medal of Honor.

When the ceremony was completed, McAffey had Watkins follow him to a nondescript hangar on Bagram Airbase. A white G4 executive jet pulled into the hangar and, as the aircraft door opened, Secretary of Defense Madeline Coltrain and her security detail stepped out. General McAffey and his small contingent of military personnel came to attention and saluted her. He then escorted her to a small conference room with his most senior officers, Colonel Abdul Qadir of the ANA, and Staff Sergeant Shirin Kirkorian.

Lieutenant Colonel Watkins brought the room to attention as Secretary Coltrain stood facing Kirkorian while the military decoration narrative was read. Madeline pinned the Distinguished Service Cross onto Kirkorian's uniform and shook her hand while handing the written award to her with the other. As Madeline took a step back, Kirkorian saluted her, and the two women broke into big smiles.

With the formal ceremony complete, Madeline leaned into Kirkorian. "Sergeant, sorry to have such a clandestine ceremony for what is truly a momentous occasion. You're the first military woman ever awarded the DSC for direct combat, but you're too important of an intelligence asset for us. Rest assured, the President and leaders in Congress are well aware of your accomplishment and, one day, the rest of America will be too."

"Thank you, Madam Secretary, though I didn't do anything anyone else would've done in my position," responded Kirkorian.

"Well, Sergeant, I believe you did. And seems I was justified in agreeing to that request in your letters," winked Madeline.

Kirkorian stood stunned. "Ma'am, I never knew you had seen them."

"Well, when someone is so determined to get into Ranger training as you were, it catches people's attention," chuckled Madeline.

General McAffey came over and introduced Qadir and Watkins. "Colonel Qadir, it is an honor to meet you," said Madeline as she offered her hand to the Afghan commander.

"Thank you, Madam Secretary, for inviting me to this special ceremony. Sergeant Kirkorian is a remarkable soldier and very deserving. My men call her The Lioness. There is no better description, and no one carries more respect among them than she does," replied Qadir.

"That's quite an accomplishment for a woman in your culture, is it not, Colonel?" asked Madeline.

"Yes, Madam Secretary, though it is easier because she is not Afghan. She understands the cultural dynamics and works within them to be effective. I've worked with her for several weeks, and that is the most telling response from soldiers and villagers alike. She honors the village elders by working in the background with them but makes the women comfortable to speak to her. They know she's a soldier but even as a woman, she has this quiet, dangerous confidence that all can see. As I said, a remarkable soldier, man or woman," answered Qadir.

"Colonel Watkins, seems you and Colonel Qadir have quite the working relationship. First Zakar Khel and now this. What do you attribute that to?" asked Madeline.

"Madam Secretary, we think very much alike, not just tactically but strategically as well. As the only representative of our country that most Afghans will ever meet, it's my responsibility to implement our strategy of helping the ANA be effective without alienating their populace. Colonel Qadir has made that easy. His men are the most disciplined and highly trained of any I've worked with in the ANA. It was his men who executed so brilliantly at Zakar Khel, and especially in the valley. And if you'll forgive a little political commentary, if we help them develop more Colonel Qadirs, this country could prosper," answered Watkins.

"Commentary forgiven Colonel, I agree with you. The good news is you get to work with Colonel Qadir to do just that. General McAffey, a word please," ordered Madeline.

The two of them went off into a corner to discuss something as the rest of the officers milled about. When they were finished, Madeline excused herself to speak with several American units who were also involved in the recent action. McAffey walked over to Kirkorian. "Sergeant, pack your gear, we have an assignment for you."

* * *

Farooq's mind was in a constant fog, he had no idea how long he'd been awake. He knew something had to be attached to his head and torso that must be monitoring his vitals. Each time he was about to drift off to sleep there would be slight electrical shocks, not to cause pain but to cause a jolt of adrenaline to wake him up. Then there was the constant changing of temperature, light, colors, and sounds so he could never focus his mind on anything. Finally, the complete darkness and absolute silence. No noise, no voices, no mechanical sounds, just complete nothingness except for the random electrical shocks to keep him awake.

No one had interrogated him since his capture, not one word. He tried praying to keep focused but the numbing silence and fatigue made his mind wander aimlessly as the hours, or days passed. He had no idea. He found himself almost yearning to be tortured, just to feel something besides this suspended animation. His arms were shackled over his head with his hands together like he was praying but he couldn't move them. He wasn't even sure if he was standing or not; his body felt numb. He tried to pull against the shackles just to create some pain in his arms or shoulders, but his muscles wouldn't respond.

Then he thought he heard a woman's voice speaking Urdu, Pakistan's national language. He struggled to hear it, concentrating to see if it was real, or just his mind beginning to play tricks on him. It was so quiet he just couldn't be sure. What was she saying?

Farooq tried to focus all his energy on her voice, and finally, in frustration, he screamed for her to speak louder.

VALLEY OF STARS

This voice went on. She was asking him something, but he couldn't hear it clearly. He tried thrashing around to make a noise. He felt paralyzed. Was this real or just in his head? He had no idea how long this went on until he could hear himself begging the voice to talk more loudly.

Wait, Farooq thought he heard a question. What was that? He struggled even harder. "'Why did you send my brothers to die for nothing?' Was that the question?" pleaded Farooq.

"'Who will speak for them now?' Is that what you want to know? Tell me," screamed Farooq.

"Who will protect us now?" the woman whispered, barely audible to Farooq.

Farooq was crying in his confusion, saying that Al-Zuq had failed to secure the Valley of Stars, that the leader of the Caliphate was angry. He called his second in command by name as the person to take care of them. Farooq had no idea how long this went on or realized just how much information he gave up. Contacts, dead drops, meeting places, safe houses, all came pouring out of him as if pleading with the voice would make her understand that all was well.

Finally, the door opened, and the lights came up. They were so bright they hurt Farooq's eyes. He could only squint to allow them to adjust. Blinking, he saw someone coming toward him. The voice got louder, but it changed.

"You deceived your brothers. Their blood is on your hands. You're a traitor, why did you abandon us?" the woman said menacingly.

She was accusing him of betraying his brothers. Farooq desperately tried to deny it.

"No that's a lie, we have a spy in our midst, they betrayed us not me. Al-Zuq failed us, and Bhargouti is angry," he pleaded in vain.

As his eyes finally came into focus, he saw a woman wearing a uniform leaning over him. She was an American soldier, but she spoke perfect Urdu! The horror of what he had just done flooded over Farooq. Then the anger rose inside of him. He was furious that he allowed himself to be broken by...this woman. He began to curse her as he found the strength to resist.

Farooq tried to struggle but still felt paralyzed. Though he couldn't move, he could talk. He began to shout prayers at the top of his lungs. Suddenly the door slammed open, and a second person entered the room. A man in civilian clothes. He came up to Farooq whose defiance was clear on his face.

The man leaned over, close to Farooq's ear, and in a calm, almost quiet voice he said, "Hello, *Wolfhunter*. I'm *The Great Kazam*."

That was the final blow, Farooq's spirit was crushed. His defiance vanished as he realized that everything he had built, had sacrificed, and lived for, was now gone. He had betrayed his brothers, the failure, and deaths of the thousands of martyrs were his fault and ultimately, achieved nothing. They knew everything, and it would be used to destroy his entire network.

The End

About the Author

Niels Andersen is a retired Air Force Lieutenant Colonel whose career took him to operating theaters around the world. From desert sands to the storied halls of the Pentagon, he taps a deep well of experience working on long range national and military strategy. As an amateur military history and strategy buff he draws on past and current events to shape his stories and blur the lines between fact and fiction. He hopes this is the first of several books in a series that highlights the extraordinary work of ordinary people in the relentless pursuit of our national defense.

Niels lives in Minnesota with his wife and family cat. In addition to writing, he works with recovering and at-risk adults to help them rejoin the competitive workforce. Between work, writing, and helping his wife with her quilting projects, he keeps very busy.

Valley of Stars is Niels Andersen's first book.

Milton Keynes UK
Ingram Content Group UK Ltd.
UKHW010308170224
437973UK00007B/686